RUN

Annie Kaye

REAMSPINNER
PRESS

Published by
DREAMSPINNER PRESS

5032 Capital Circle SW, Suite 2, PMB# 279, Tallahassee, FL 32305-7886 USA
www.dreamspinnerpress.com

Run
© 2016 Annie Kaye.

Cover Art
© 2016 Anne Cain.
annecain.art@gmail.com
Cover content is for illustrative purposes only and any person depicted on the cover is a model.

ISBN: 978-1-63476-924-2
Digital ISBN: 978-1-63476-925-9
Library of Congress Control Number: 2015953575
Published February 2016
v. 1.0

Printed in the United States of America
∞
This paper meets the requirements of
ANSI/NISO Z39.48-1992 (Permanence of Paper).

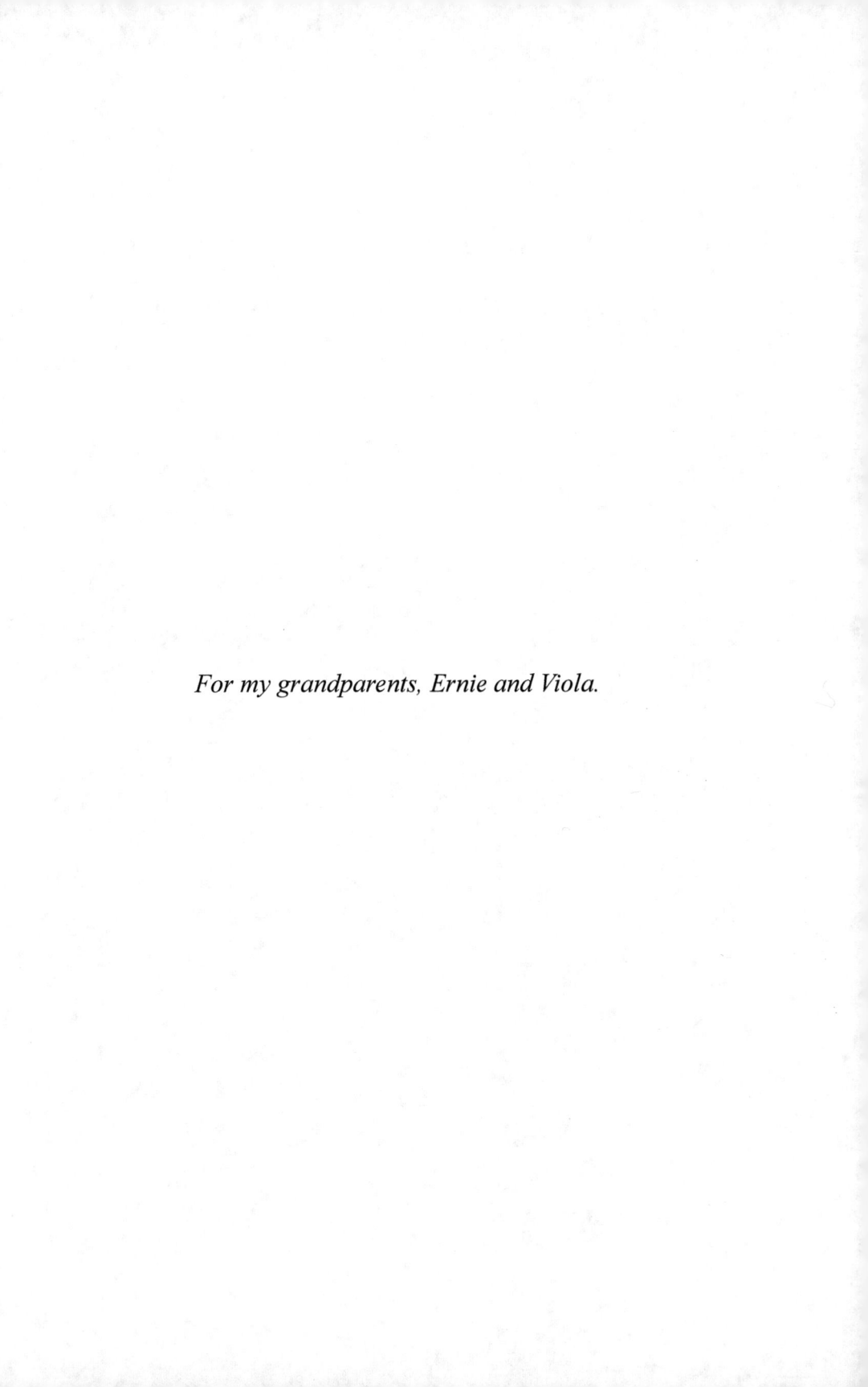

For my grandparents, Ernie and Viola.

ACKNOWLEDGMENTS

First and always, my love and gratitude to my husband Brandon, my best friend.

To our children, Joey and Caroline. We love you when you're wonderful, and we love you when you're driving us batty. We also probably deserve you at both ends of the spectrum.

My little sister is the only person I actually like talking to on the phone. Thanks for your friendship, Julie (and for being my gym buddy. Twenty minutes on the elliptical—are we skinny yet?). I like you so much better as a grownup.

Lisa Achtzehn; in all things, your support, honesty, encouragement, and love are more precious than rubies. You are a sister of my soul.

Once upon a time, two aspiring writers realized each was reading the other's work. For me, Beth Sabatino has tiptoed into shady corners of the Internet where the messy bit of sheep husbandry is whispered about. Thanks for being my lobster (and for getting the reference the first time).

In writing this story, I hit up some good friends for advice and guidance. Suzanne Garwood, thanks so much for your valuable insights. Thank you to Melissa Arizola and Danielle Mutsaers for reading and providing honest feedback.

I'm especially grateful to my editorial team at Dreamspinner Press: Sue Adams, my senior editor who oversaw the process from start to finish, and patiently explained a great deal to a neophyte; and editors Jacky, Alison, and Lauren. I had looked at this manuscript for so long on my own that I couldn't see it anymore. Working with all of you was vastly beneficial to the story and to me as a writer. Thank you for your wisdom and suggestions.

Finally: my grandmother was over ninety when her minister transitioned from male to female. She accepted it with barely the bat of an eyelash, and used the appropriate pronoun thereafter. May I live to the age of ninety; but even if I don't, may I always accept others with as much empathy and compassion. Thanks, Gram. xoxo

JANUARY

THEY MET in a hurricane.

Well, not a literal hurricane, and Tom had always felt proprietary about that word, growing up in South Florida and having far too vivid memories of the destruction hurricane season could bring. He didn't throw around the word, because a hurricane was a weather event and anything else just didn't qualify.

But he'd never witnessed the Iowa caucuses before, and if there was ever a time to reconsider his position on the word, this evening in a Des Moines high school gymnasium certainly suggested it. He'd been to many rallies, fundraisers, even some demonstrations, but this was something else completely: tumultuous, overwhelming and exciting.

As campaign staff, you're allowed to observe only—you're not to speak to the participants, the precinct officer had sternly warned Tom and his colleagues at the beginning of the night... as if senior staff on a presidential campaign needed these instructions. In any case, Tom, a speechwriter, was only there out of curiosity for the process. He was glad he wasn't precisely required tonight, so he was free to watch and listen and attempt to take it all in.

When the caucusgoers had all been counted and the electioneering had begun, Tom left his spot on the bleachers to stroll around the room and listen to the participants: hundreds of people, voices upon voices as the caucusgoers spoke passionately in support of their respective candidates, trying to woo others to their camp.

In a far corner of the gym, he found a feisty elderly woman who was telling three young men, evidently of college age, why they should support Senator Wagner. Tom was impressed, and was so absorbed by her persuasive, impassioned speech that he didn't notice the tall figure approaching him until suddenly a hand pressed into his palm. Startled out of his preoccupation, Tom's fingers reflexively closed around the hand. It was already pulling away, slipping out of his grasp but leaving a folded slip of paper in his hand. He turned, expecting one of his colleagues on Senator Wagner's campaign, but the eyes he met belonged to no one with whom he'd spent long days and nights drafting speeches, arguing over one word or the placement of a comma. Deep and intense, they belonged to someone he recognized but had never met, and they looked deliberately down into his, for a heartbeat. Then the man turned and strode away, leaving Tom with paper in his hand and an unsettled feeling in his stomach.

Tom turned back to the group he'd been watching, but he was no longer listening to the small silver-haired woman. Instead he was wondering why he was being passed a covert note from Nathan Harris, the deputy campaign manager for another candidate. It seemed unlikely that it was any type of official communication between campaigns— surely that would be made to someone with more seniority than Tom— but in spite of his curiosity, Tom hesitated to open it here with so many eyes, knowing the campaigns had aides who were doing nothing but observing, noting every detail in case something could be used in the future.

Presently, the precinct officer asked all participants to return to their designated area of the gymnasium for a count. Tom made his way back to the bleachers where his colleagues on the Wagner campaign were sitting. As the first group was being counted, he leaned in close to Mitchell Enns, the communications director and his direct supervisor, and murmured, "Bathroom."

Mitch merely nodded, his gaze never straying from the events unfolding before him. Mitch always gave Tom the impression of an aging surfer, with a shock of thick blond hair punctuated by a high widow's peak; deep-set hound-dog eyes; a large, bumpy nose that had certainly been broken at least once; and a tall, ungainly body given to careless posture. It gave him an air that could have led one to underestimate his focus, but anyone at all familiar with the inside players of high-level politics knew better than to judge Mitchell Enns by his appearance.

Tom was new to this world, but he wasn't fooled either. He was familiar with his boss's uncanny ability to hear at least three conversations at once and to retain them like a steel trap. Here in the gym tonight, he would pay particular attention to the pitches given on behalf of the candidates, knowing that the points covered in these speeches were an indication of how well the campaign's messages were being relayed to the local volunteers. Later he would recount them in detail to the communications staff, using those examples to illustrate how carefully they had to tread the line between propagating the theme for the campaign versus repeating catchphrases that could see the senator turned quickly into a caricature.

Surrounded by staff who were among the best at what they did, Tom had learned quickly that he could succeed or he could get the hell off the campaign. There was no room for deficiency here, not when one speech could win or lose twenty states. Tom felt a little faint at the thought of Super Tuesday, only three weeks away now…. But the speeches for the Super Tuesday states had been in the works for weeks already, and Tom would continue to develop and shape them as events unfolded between now and then, with input from Mitch, campaign strategists, and about a hundred others. There was nothing to be gained by worrying about it tonight.

Right now all he could do was lock himself into a stall in the deserted men's room and unfold the note, the ink slightly smudged and the paper damp from being clutched in his sweating palm. Were these confident block letters Nathan Harris's writing or was he the courier for someone else's words? A steady hand, no nerves shaking it when it scrawled the message that both surprised and irritated Tom:

> *You're very good, but you'll be unemployed by May.*
> *Pollard's interested.*

Of course he knew who Susan Pollard was: Mitchell's counterpart in Senator Erin Michaels's campaign. Tom knew Pollard by reputation, had studied her career when he was doing his masters in poli-sci at Emory. She'd been working with her Yale classmate Erin Michaels since Michaels was a New York state senator, and stayed with her when she went to Washington as New York's junior senator. It was commonly understood that Susan Pollard's opinion was as important to Michaels as that of her campaign manager. From a professional standpoint, Tom admired her greatly. On a par with Mitch Enns, she was a talented communicator.

Which was more than he could say for Nathan Harris, Tom thought as he crumpled up the slip of paper. *Unemployed by June?* He gritted his teeth and thought of all the things he would love to have said if he'd planned to reply... because of course he'd ignore it. He knew he was good and certainly didn't need a condescending note from Nathan Harris to tell him that. There were exactly two people whose opinions mattered to Tom, and Nathan Harris was neither of them.

Tom was lucky to have Mitch as his supervisor and his mentor. He knew Mitch believed in Bill Wagner. For his part, Tom had voted for him as the senator from Georgia ever since he'd become old enough to vote. Tom had no plans whatsoever to change camps. He was committed for the long term and he truly believed Bill Wagner was the best person for the Democratic nomination and the presidency.

So the only response to Nathan Harris was no response at all. Tom flushed the note down the toilet where it belonged, washed his hands, and straightened his tie in the mirror. He allowed himself a moment to put his game face back on before leaving the quiet of the men's room. His blond hair was straight and tidy, his nearly black eyes inscrutable as they always were when he was at work. The new suit, one of several he'd bought for the campaign, made him feel like a professional, instead of the kid he'd often felt like in the presence of political heavy hitters.

After leaving the bathroom, he crossed the hallway where various staffers were hanging around, thumbs flying over their iPhones. He opened the door to the gym and the roar spilled out, a cacophony of hundreds of voices engulfing him. The counts had finished and several candidates had been declared inviable. Michaels and Wagner were the strongest two of only three viable candidates and the governor of Colorado, Jayne Duffy, was a near third. Tom returned to where his fellow staffers were gathered on the bleachers and sat down beside Sarah Lonstein, an aide to the campaign manager. Sarah had her laptop open, compiling results from staffers at other precincts. Midway through the night, things across the state looked much as they did here: Wagner and Michaels in a near tie, with Duffy close behind.

With nothing to do but watch and wait, Tom repeatedly found his gaze returning to Nathan Harris, who strolled around the floor, stopping to listen to a snippet of conversation before moving on to another part of the room. He was handsome, there was no denying that, and under different circumstances, Tom might have let himself dwell on Nathan's dark features and intense gaze. He was tall, over six feet, with carefully styled black hair, rich brown eyes, and heavy eyebrows that gave him a slightly intimidating look. Nathan was the deputy to campaign manager Jason Eisenberg. Together the two had worked for Senator Michaels since her first US senate run. Tom had seen him several times during the fall at candidates' debates, but before today had never exchanged a word with him.

Well, technically, I still haven't, thought Tom. As he gathered up his things to head to the ballroom where Senator Wagner would give his speech, he decided that if Nathan Harris was the arrogant jerk he seemed to be, he wouldn't mind if things stayed that way.

NATHAN HARRIS was only mildly bothered that Tom McAlindon had completely ignored his note. He certainly hadn't expected Tom to stroll on up to Susan Pollard and ask for a job. He had imagined the thought sitting in Tom's mind for a few days, the idea germinating into curiosity, curiosity flowering into action, and then maybe Tom might get in touch with someone from the campaign... or they'd hear he'd been making quiet inquiries about Susan... something to show he was at least giving it some thought and considering the possibility.

Nate had done his homework on the young speechwriter, even beyond what Susan Pollard had told Jason and Senator Michaels about him. He knew Tom grew up in Miami and moved to Atlanta to do his undergrad in political science at Emory. He'd stayed at Emory to do his master's, though completing the degree had taken him four years—Nate hadn't been able to determine why. Nate was particularly interested in the rumors about the way Tom had been hired as a speechwriter by the campaign of Isaiah Lee when he was running for mayor of Atlanta. The story he'd heard was unusual enough that he wasn't sure he trusted it. It was a fact, though, that after Lee was elected, he'd kept Tom on as the communications and public relations director for the office of the mayor, a post at which Tom had excelled until he was scooped up by the Wagner campaign a couple of years later. It also seemed that he was liked and respected wherever he worked, and his talent was well-known. It would be quite a coup if they could persuade him to join their campaign.

However, nearly two weeks later, when the New Hampshire primary was only a day away, Nate hadn't heard anything, not a whisper that would indicate that Tom was even curious about the opportunity. The

Michaels campaign had kept a full schedule since Iowa, with numerous rallies across the country, concentrating heavily on New Hampshire and on Nevada, whose caucuses would follow New Hampshire. During that time, despite the hectic pace and the sea of faces he passed, the thought of Tom kept nagging at the back of his mind.

Having worked on Capitol Hill for ten years, Nate was no stranger to the world of politics at this level. He knew better than to take the rejection personally, but he was not accustomed to being turned down. Erin Michaels was well-liked, respected and—perhaps most important— influential on Capitol Hill. As such, she was sought out and courted for her support on various issues. Nate was used to having people come to him to ask a favor of Senator Michaels, and if he was the one asking something on her behalf... well, it was very seldom that anyone passed up the chance to align themselves with Erin. Even if she was asking for a favor, those who knew what they were doing saw it as an opportunity for leverage, something that, later, could be judiciously applied to get her support for one of their projects.

In short, Nate wasn't used to being refused.

Except he hadn't been refused, he'd been steadfastly ignored. It was the ignored part that bothered him most, he mused as he stretched out in his hotel room bed the night before the primary. He knew this situation was quite different from one he would encounter on the Hill: no one owed him anything, and Tom McAlindon was very likely not looking to be recruited to a different campaign. And yet it continued to nag at him. It was an odd feeling, difficult to articulate, almost as though it wasn't only a rejection of Erin and her campaign, but of Nate himself.

And why should he feel that? Sure, he was intrigued by Tom—the same interest he'd have in anyone who was talented, who was intelligent, who could be a huge asset to the campaign.

Who was gorgeous, Nate's brain volunteered... or maybe that wasn't his brain talking. He grimaced and dragged himself back to the present. The next day was the primary, and they would have to hit the ground running first thing in the morning. Mentally he reviewed the next day's itinerary before double-checking the alarm on his phone, and then, finally, he drifted off to sleep.

Tuesday was a good day, Nate later reflected. New Hampshire was a state of Libertarians, and Erin Michaels's outspoken support of personal freedoms, and vocal opposition to significant growth within the federal government had always brought her significant support in states like New Hampshire. Nate had privately wondered if Erin Michaels might have been a Libertarian herself, had it been politically feasible.

So yes, it was a very good day, with Erin taking the primary by 3 percent over Wagner. It was also the day that, based on poor results in Iowa and New Hampshire, Jayne Duffy announced she was discontinuing her campaign and placing her support behind Erin Michaels. With his colleagues, Nate watched Duffy's speech on television from the Hanover campaign office, and allowed himself a moment to indulge in a little dream about Erin taking the nomination with Jayne Duffy as her running mate, the first all-female ticket in United States presidential history. The thought brought a smile to his face, and it felt like the first time he'd really smiled in days.

But he was getting ahead of himself. They were only two states in, and yes, Erin had won both, but with very narrow margins. There were no foregone conclusions, and Bill Wagner would continue to be a threat, especially with Tom McAlindon for a speechwriter....

Nate shook his head as he realized his thoughts had gone there again. He hadn't seen Tom since the night of the Iowa caucuses; the campaigns hadn't crossed paths again. He found himself hoping for an opportunity to see him, to make eye contact and watch Tom's reaction; to at least make Tom acknowledge him.

Or rather, acknowledge the offer, right, Nate?

A fair question, to which Nate wasn't sure he had an answer.

Tom GROANED, angling his body toward the weak, early morning sun as he stretched muscles that were stiff from sleeping on the campaign bus. After he'd relaxed out of the stretch, he still stood, eyes closed, facing the sun. He hadn't been warm—truly warm—since the dog days of summer had ended, five long months ago. Granted, Daytona Beach at 7:00 a.m. in January wasn't quite akin to the sweaty heat of a Northeast summer, but in a few hours more they'd be in Miami. Tom was a Florida boy, not bred for Northeast living, and now, after an overnight trip south from DC, he was very close to being home.

He stood for several moments silently worshipping the sun's warmth until, opening his eyes, he found Sarah Lonstein grinning at him. He returned the smile, not even feeling sheepish about his open adoration of the sun.

"Glad to be home, sunshine boy?" Sarah asked affectionately.

Tom sighed. "You don't even know." He rolled up his shirt sleeves and together he and Sarah started across the parking lot toward the restaurant.

"You're right I don't," she agreed. "Not a big fan of the sun, myself."

"How can anyone not love the sun?" Tom asked incredulously.

"Honey, look at me."

Tom obliged, stopping to look her over. A year younger than him, Sarah had flawless pale skin, full russet lips, and a fan of dark lashes. With a smooth, long cascade of dark brown hair, she looked like a porcelain doll. She held out her arms, bare in her sleeveless blouse, and traced the translucent skin with her carefully manicured fingertips.

"I'm almost pigment-free. You're awfully lucky with your pretty blond hair and your golden skin. The sun just makes me blotch."

"Well, you're a delicate flower," Tom replied, and they resumed their walk to the restaurant, where their colleagues had already started to file through the doors. "But you stay out of the sun, and when you're fifty, you'll still have the smooth, unblemished skin of a twenty-year-old."

"You better believe it." The two of them parted long enough to visit the restrooms before joining the group where they had taken over several tables in one corner of the restaurant. Sarah sat in a booth across from Mitchell Enns, Tom sliding in beside her. Mitch was frowning at his iPhone as they joined him, but he soon laid it aside.

As they ate, the entire group chatted noisily, making the most of the chance to relax for an hour or two, and think and talk about something other than strategy and itinerary.

Through the window of the restaurant, the arrival of another bus caught Tom's eye. The bus was brightly colored with an American flag emblazoned on the side and… *shit*.

"What?" Mitch and Sarah asked in unison, and Tom realized he'd sworn out loud.

"Erin Michaels's campaign bus just pulled in," Tom murmured, nodding his head in the direction of the parking lot. Both heads swiveled to look, and a millisecond later, Mitch was out of his seat, leaning over the table at the next booth, where Bill Wagner and his campaign manager Kim Harvey sat with Bill's wife, Rebecca. Tom joined them and they quietly discussed how to react when Senator Michaels and her staff came in.

"It's casual," Mitch was saying. "This is a restaurant off the interstate, not an event. The Senator will certainly come over to say hello, and you'll greet her in a way that's as friendly and relaxed as you would any other colleague you might run into at a restaurant."

Bill nodded. He actually was as relaxed about it as Mitch wanted him to seem. There was no reason not to be, of course, but Tom envied his calm, friendly personality, his ability to relate to almost anyone in a way that put others at ease. Tom, on the other hand, was shy. He could write words for others to say, but abhorred situations that put everyone's eyes on him. In Atlanta he had been the mayor's PR coordinator, but they had a spokesperson who dealt with the press. On the few occasions she wasn't available to run a press conference and Tom had to field questions himself, he'd thrown up beforehand.

Now, he slid back into the booth beside Sarah and watched, waiting for the key players of the Michaels campaign to make their way over to where they sat. Bill stood, smiling broadly at his senate colleague and extending his hand to her.

"Erin, good to see you."

"You too, Bill. This is a nice coincidence."

"Have you met my wife, Rebecca?"

"We haven't been introduced. Lovely to meet you, Rebecca." Erin Michaels had a great smile and a friendly, open demeanor. She'd been elected to the Senate because she had managed to balance a frank style of delivery that was humorous but not sarcastic, forthright but not tactless. She'd been reelected because she did exactly what she promised she would.

Those in the group who knew each other said hello, introducing others who hadn't met. Tom smiled at a couple of people he recognized and shook hands with a few Sarah introduced, all the time distinctly aware of a pair of deep brown eyes whose gaze had fastened itself upon him and wasn't turning away. Tom tried hard to ignore them, tried not to give in to their draw. He tried to focus on listening to Mitch make small talk with Susan Pollard, but those eyes kept burning into him. Finally he reminded himself of the counsel Mitch had given Bill. *This is casual.*

Keep it relaxed. To it he added, *Don't let him intimidate you.* With that in mind, he allowed himself to turn slowly to meet that gaze.

His instincts were good. Nate was watching him intently, holding the gaze even when Tom met it. For several seconds, neither looked away. One of Nathan's eyebrows twitched slightly upward—indicating what? Tom didn't know, but he wasn't backing down. He allowed his own eyebrow to creep up, silently challenging Nathan. *Well?* After another moment, Nathan smirked as though satisfied with the exchange and finally broke eye contact, turning to say something to one of his traveling companions before striding off in the direction of the men's room.

Tom was left feeling bemused by the whole thing, wondering what the point of it had been. He looked around and was glad no one seemed to have noticed their brief staring contest. He was about to excuse himself and head back out to the bus for a few moments of quiet before everyone else started returning, but Mitchell turned to him then, asking him if he'd met Susan Pollard before. He hadn't, and they were introduced. He managed to make small talk with Mitchell and Susan for a few moments before he was able to slip away to the bus. He wanted a chance to think in peace before his colleagues joined him.

The encounter with Nathan had seemed almost hostile… though wasn't hostility rather an extreme reaction to simply ignoring what had been pretty much a vague suggestion? Tom sighed. He'd begun the day feeling so relaxed, so glad to be back in his home state. Now the positive feelings had all but evaporated, replaced by a general disquietude. He'd only met this guy twice—both of which barely qualified as meetings, since Tom had yet to utter a word to the man—and he'd managed to unsettle Tom both times. Nathan Harris might be very good at his job, but his social skills left a lot to be desired.

Soon the rest of the staff were making their way back to the bus, and they were preparing to leave again. They had many miles to cover, with primaries taking place in both Florida and South Carolina two days from today. They would continue on to Miami to attend several events there this afternoon; then overnight the bus would travel to St. Petersburg before continuing to Orlando and back up to South Carolina to cross that state before the end of voting on Tuesday. Tom had work to do between here and Miami, and once they were underway, he put on his headphones and got to work. Whenever he paused in thought his eyes were drawn out the window, glancing over the sun-drenched buildings as they flashed past on the interstate. And palm trees—it'd been so long since he'd seen palm trees. He didn't realize how much he missed them until he was seeing them with his own eyes once more.

He chided himself gently and pulled down the window shade. Today he needed to focus; and then tonight he'd have the night to himself. Tom had asked for the evening off, because there was someone special in Miami. They hadn't seen each other in too long… tonight they would be together.

Tom had left home at eighteen to pursue a degree in poli-sci at Emory, but even then he always thought of Florida as home—it was where his parents and sisters were, where he grew up. Life at Emory had given him a freedom he'd never had when he lived with his parents, a freedom to be himself, to be open with his friends, and to be out as a gay man, at least at school. Being out of his parents' house those four years—maybe time had softened his recollection; perhaps he thought that because he was accepted by his friends and coworkers, he'd be accepted by his parents too; maybe it was subtle pressure from the guy he'd been seeing… for whatever reason, when he was twenty-two and was only a month away from finishing his degree, he decided he was finally going to come out to his parents.

He came home on Easter Weekend to spend the holiday with his family, ready to attend church with them though he wasn't all that religious anymore, and looking forward to seeing everyone. On Saturday of that weekend he asked his parents out for lunch, and over dessert he took a deep breath and gently told them that the reason he'd never brought any girls home from college was because he knew he was gay; that he loved them and hoped they would accept him as he was, and that he hoped they'd meet his boyfriend next time they came up to Atlanta to visit him.

His father's face went red, then purple; his mother cried silently behind her napkin. They didn't say a word until they were out of the restaurant and in the car, and then his father exploded. Epithets of such bigotry, such hatred…. Tom sat, stunned, in the backseat of the car as his father ranted, hoping he would eventually run out of graphic, disgusting ways to describe gay sex, but it went on and on. His father even seemed oblivious to how greatly he was increasing Tom's mother's distress, as she simply bowed her head beside her husband, her shoulders shaking with soundless tears. Tom was truly frightened as they drove home, worried his father would have a heart attack behind the wheel. By the time they were back at his parents' house, he had been condemned by both his parents to a life of sin and disease, followed by an eternity of torment.

It was the worst day of his life. It ended with Tom packing his suitcase and taking a bus to the home of his mother's parents, 185 miles away. Not having time to call his grandparents before he left Miami, he planned to phone them from the bus station in Port Charlotte. As he disembarked the bus, he was brought up short by the sight of his grandfather, apparently already waiting for him, sitting on a bench in the shade outside the station, his straw hat resting on his knees. Tom locked eyes with him for a moment, then slowly made his way over to the round-shouldered old man. Without a word he sat beside his grandfather, drawing his suitcase up in front of his knees. Silently they sat, taking in the sight of people bustling around them, dashing for buses and taxis and hauling suitcases and backpacks. Several moments passed before his grandfather said, "We love you, Tommy. You are always welcome in our home, exactly the way you are. The way God made you."

They were such simple words, but they broke a dam inside Tom. For the first time that day, he burst into tears, dropping his head into his hands and sobbing right there on a bench outside the Port Charlotte bus station. His grandfather gently soothed his hand over Tom's back, and Tom couldn't help turning into him, burying his face in his granddad's shirt as though he was a little boy again. After a few moments, the worst had passed and he was able to gather himself a bit, to follow his grandfather to the car and make the short drive to the house where his mother grew up.

His grandmother met them at the door, dabbing at tears of her own but welcoming him into the little house he knew so well. She wasn't upset by his announcement, she insisted as she made him a sandwich, but by the way his parents had reacted. "Your father," the little woman said ruefully, "your father is such a hard-headed man, so opinionated. He has all of the rules of Christianity and none of the peace. Well, I don't subscribe to his brand of Christianity, and your mother didn't either, until she married him."

"Dear," his grandfather had gently chided, "let the boy eat in peace."

"It's okay, Grandpa," Tom said, weary but smiling for the first time in hours. "I don't mind."

Despite his exhaustion he didn't sleep well that night. He got up and went to church with his grandparents on Easter Sunday, then came home and helped them make Easter dinner. They fielded several calls from his parents, who were furious at his grandparents for taking him in. During one call, his father must have said something particularly offensive, and Tom, who had never heard his grandfather raise his voice except in laughter, was shocked when he caught what sure sounded like a curse word come out of his grandfather's mouth. The call ended soon after, and neither Tom nor his grandmother could get the old gentleman to tell them what exactly had been said, except to admit that it didn't look like there would be any happy family dinners any time soon. "However," his grandfather added, "no matter what, I will never tell my child they're not welcome in my home, and that's more than I can say for—" He broke off, shaking his head in disgust, and refused to elaborate further.

Even with the passage of time, nothing really changed after that. Tom's parents hadn't spoken to him, even on his birthday or holidays, since that day. He had made numerous attempts to reconcile with them, phoning, writing letters, and e-mailing; every effort went unacknowledged. His grandparents continued to be the loving, stable anchors of his life—became his surrogate parents, really, never mind that he was an adult and didn't technically need to be parented any longer. His relationship with them was a saving grace.

With his parents' disapproval came financial insecurity, as they refused to pay for his continued education. He wasn't quite destitute; he had held a part-time job throughout school anyway, to help pay for the additional cost of living off-campus, and had a bit of money saved. His undergrad was nearly finished and fully paid for. He knew, though, he would have to step it up if he was going to pursue a master's as he'd planned. For that reason, it took him nearly five years to obtain his master's degree. His budget was very tight, and he always had to have housemates—though at least grad students were far better to live with than undergrads—but with a little help here and there from his grandparents whenever they were able, he did it. He felt a fierce sense of pride that he hadn't when he was doing his bachelor's degree, and his grandparents were proud of him for doing it.

Tom had two sisters, one older and one younger, both of whom shunned him as their parents did. The youngest, Lizzie, was still living at home when he came out, and even when she got married a couple years later, Tom was not invited. His grandparents were terribly hurt, again; they were so torn about attending when Tom hadn't been invited, but Tom put his foot down and said they had to go. Lizzie was their granddaughter, after all, as much as he was their grandson.

He visited his grandparents whenever he could, which wasn't that often. They traveled to Atlanta to attend his graduations, both his bachelor's and master's degrees. In fact, the last time Tom saw his grandfather was the weekend of his final graduation ceremony. It was two weeks later that he received a phone call from his only cousin on his mother's side, telling him that their granddad had passed away peacefully in his sleep. Tom held it together long enough to get the details of the service from his cousin and thank him for calling, before hanging up and succumbing to his grief. The breath was pulled from his lungs, and pain… pain that brought him to his knees, the loss of the gentle, faithful man, a man for whom family was everything…. Even the pain of his parents severing their relationship didn't compare to the raw anguish he felt knowing his grandfather was gone.

He made it through the next several days by reminding himself that his grandmother needed all the support her family could give. When she whispered to him at one point, "Maybe seeing you again will make your parents realize how wrong they've been," he had to bite his lip to keep from retorting that he'd rather have his grandfather back. At the wake, he stood with his uncle—his mother's brother—and aunt and the cousin who had called him. His own parents and sisters simply ignored him—the intervening years had done nothing to soften them. The service was the same, sitting beside his cousin instead of his sisters. To his surprise he wasn't terribly upset by their snub. He'd come to a place where he knew who he was and was at peace with that. He had accepted that he couldn't control his parents' reaction.

And when it was all over and he'd returned to Atlanta, his closest friends took him out and got him good and drunk, and that helped too.

THERE WAS no city like Miami, in Tom's opinion, or at least no place he'd ever visited, and that wasn't just because he'd grown up there. There was an almost hedonistic quality to the nightlife—things happened there that didn't happen elsewhere. If events skirted the outer edges of propriety, pleasure seekers were more willing to try them. There was beauty everywhere, even among the poorer neighborhoods. Unlike LA, which was grimy and gritty, Miami was lush. The art deco architecture and pastel tones were synonymous with home. Tom himself had spent the most debauched weekend of his life—the only truly "lost" weekend he'd ever had, in fact—in Miami, experimenting with drugs and sleeping around indiscriminately, at the White Party when he was twenty-four.

But Tom was no longer twenty-four, and one experience with poppers and E had been enough for him. Now he was returning to Miami with the campaign and with a very different purpose. He still had some personal plans for Saturday evening, but they weren't quite what he would call a party.

Since the last time he'd seen his grandmother, a year earlier, she'd sold her little house and moved to an assisted living facility in Miami, where she didn't have to cook her own meals, do the vacuuming or clean by herself anymore, and where she was closer to both her children. She had a friend who'd already moved to the same facility, and she'd made many more new acquaintances since taking up residency there herself. She'd been so happy to hear Tom would be in the city for a day, and that Saturday evening, the two of them had a wonderful visit. She couldn't stop smiling as she introduced him to her friends, telling them all what he did for a living and why he was currently visiting his hometown. Bill Wagner was well-respected among seniors and they were all impressed that Tom worked for his campaign.

After they had dinner together in the facility's large dining room, the two of them returned to her room for a quieter visit. Tom sat at her feet, looking at a photo album of his grandparents in their younger days. Grandma stroked his hair, as she'd always done. Even when he was a teenager, he'd never asked her to stop doing it, sensing how difficult it would be for her to stifle that natural action and how hurt she'd be to be asked to stop; now, as an adult, he was glad he never had. Especially now, when he wasn't in a relationship, lived in DC where he knew so few people, and didn't see his Atlanta friends often, he craved human contact. This—Grandma's trembling fingers combing through his fine blonde hair—was like manna for the touch-starved. In the midst of his very busy, demanding life, being with her was so uncomplicated. He sat with her for as long as he could, and it was only when she started to yawn that he could bring himself to say good-bye to the frail little woman and return to real life.

SATURDAY, SUNDAY, and Monday brought a steady stream of events, photo ops, speeches, and rallies, keeping campaign staff busy from the time they awoke in the early morning until they collapsed into bed late at night. It could have been—and maybe should have been—exhausting, but Nathan found it exhilarating. Even with his experience working on Erin Michaels's two senate campaigns, nothing compared to this schedule. He loved being a half step behind Jason Eisenberg. He loved handling situations, putting out potential fires. Sometimes he helped find everyday individuals, real people whose experiences were indicative of problems in the political system, whom Erin would mention by name in a speech, putting a face on changes that needed to be made for the good of all Americans.

Nate knew how pundits viewed moments like those, often writing them off as opportunistic and insincere. It didn't matter to him; he had met these individuals personally, had spoken to them, had empathized and given quiet assurances that Erin would personally look into what she could do to help their situation. Constituents were the people who humanized Washington life for Nate, who kept him grounded. He saw so many faces on a daily basis, even more so now during the campaign, that it would be easy to simply gloss over them. But these people—they were the reminder that Nate and his colleagues were here to serve the public. He wasn't completely altruistic, of course, because he wanted his candidate elected. But he knew that, as alone as some constituents might feel, there were many others across the country in similar circumstances. Hearing Erin address their own situations would show that she was in touch with their issues and planned to do something about them. Anyway, the pundits could scoff all they wanted. This was what it was all about.

Tuesday was another busy day. By early evening senior staff had fallen back to their hotel in Charleston to relax a bit, have dinner, and wait for the polls to close. It was a welcome reprieve, a brief moment to breathe before results would start coming in from poll watchers throughout Florida and South Carolina. Later there would be a speech in the hotel conference room downstairs; volunteers, staff, press, and other interested parties would gather, and, Nate hoped, hear Erin thank them for delivering Florida and South Carolina to her campaign.

For now, though, he had an hour during which no one needed him. He did what he so seldom had time for these days: absolutely nothing. After telling Jason where he'd be, he went up to his room, closed the blackout blinds, and turned on the HVAC unit fan to give him some white noise. When that was done, he stretched out on his bed and chilled. He took some deep breaths and allowed his mind to relax out of its usual state of intense focus, letting it wander to any inconsequential place it chose to go. He had learned the technique from a friend when he was studying for the bar exam, and on days like today he found it more refreshing than a nap, which always left him groggy and out of sorts.

After wondering how many episodes of *The Big Bang Theory* had now accumulated on his DVR and considering what to buy for his brother's upcoming birthday, he felt his mind slip into a place that was becoming a well-worn groove: Tom McAlindon. Nate had accepted that Tom wasn't going to respond to his note, but seeing him in the restaurant several days earlier was exactly the opportunity he'd hoped for: a chance to gauge how Tom would react to him. It had taken several minutes for Tom to return his gaze, but when he finally looked at Nate and gave him a raised eyebrow… it was small, but it was something. An acknowledgment, with an ounce of challenge attached to it. Nate liked that. He'd also heard Tom's voice for the first time, if only briefly. It was quiet and clear, exactly what Nate had expected.

His eyes still closed, Nate grinned into the darkness of his room and shook his head at himself. Every time he saw Tom McAlindon he found him more attractive, with his soft-looking blond hair and those eyes that were so dark brown they were almost black. Nate didn't even know if Tom was gay, but it didn't matter anyway. They were working for opposing teams, and that had to be the last word on the subject, at least where reality was concerned. Fantasy, however….

The rest of the night, once he rejoined his colleagues, went by in a blur. Erin didn't win Florida and she didn't win South Carolina. It wasn't a surprise, really. With Georgia being adjacent to both states, Wagner was practically a local and he'd been consistently polling ahead of Erin in both. These were the first states Wagner had actually taken, and Nate wasn't worried at all. A week from today would be Super Tuesday, which in Nate's mind was better than Christmas. But before the team could begin the marathon campaign leading up to the big day, they were headed to California, where a televised debate would take place Thursday night at Stanford University. It would be the first time Erin took on Senator Wagner one to one since Governor Duffy had dropped out, and Nate knew she was ready.

It was time for Senator Erin Michaels to shine.

FEBRUARY

CALIFORNIA WAS one of Nate's favorite places to visit, and the Bay Area in particular. Visiting with Jason Eisenberg was even better, because this was Jason's alma mater. He'd obtained both his poli-sci degree and his JD from Stanford. Being here to see Jason's expression gradually warm as they walked the beautiful campus with its hacienda-like buildings and uniform red roofs, to witness his enthusiastic love of the school and the city of Palo Alto was a huge source of amusement for Nate. Jason was typically pretty dry, focused on his work and quite solemn. It was only on occasions like this that Nate saw a spark of Jason's sense of humor and got to hear stories from Jason's college days. Several times when he and Jason crossed the quad on the way to Memorial Auditorium, Nate found himself throwing his head back to laugh out loud as Jason wryly recounted some of his college antics.

Once they arrived at the auditorium, though, the moment passed, and of necessity, Jason's demeanor returned to his usual serious and straightforward manner. Nate, too, refocused his attention on the matters at hand—preparing for the debate, ensuring that the set was laid out as agreed upon, and other last-minute tasks.

When only fifteen minutes remained before the debate was to begin, Nate excused himself to visit the men's room. He was wearing a new dress shirt for the first time, and something terribly uncomfortable was scratching at his skin under the arm. Inside a stall, he pulled the shirt off to examine the seam, where he found a bit of plastic from a tag still caught in the stitching. Once he'd pried the offending item out of the thread, he pulled his shirt back on and started rebuttoning.

As he was slipping his tie back over his neck and working the half-Windsor back to where it should be, the door to the restroom opened to admit several others. The men were talking as they entered, and Nate thought he recognized the voice of Mitchell Enns, Bill Wagner's communications chief. His attention was piqued.

"Hey, I've been meaning to ask you—did you call your folks when we were in Miami?" *Definitely Mitchell*, Nate thought.

"Nah," replied a quiet voice and Nate's stomach fluttered. "There's no point. My mother won't talk to me at all. My father will shout a bunch of gay slurs and call down AIDS and hellfire on me."

"Charming fellow," Mitch muttered.

"But I spent Saturday night with my grandma," the man softly continued, "and that was great."

Nate missed what was said next, lost in the sound of the urinals flushing. He leaned closer to the door, hoping he could see through the gap to catch a glimpse of the sinks and confirm his suspicions on the identity of Mitch's companion. As the two men came into view, he had his answer. Tom McAlindon threw his tie over his shoulder before bending to wash his hands. Nate stepped back then, waiting quietly until the two men had left the restroom. He unlocked the stall and finished straightening himself in the mirror. As he did, he had to give himself a stern talking to. He'd been given the answer to a question just now, but he had to clamp down on the desire to enjoy his new knowledge. Now wasn't the time for silly fantasies. Now was game time.

Satisfied with his apparel and demeanor, he strode confidently from the men's room and into the auditorium where his colleagues and his candidate awaited the game.

WHEN THE evening of the debate arrived, Tom was still high on Wagner's double win in Florida and South Carolina. An hour before the debate began, the auditorium was still mostly empty, aside from the campaign staff from both teams, and the television network's technical staff who were doing final tests on the audio and video equipment, preparing to sound check the candidates. With Mitch, Kim and Sarah, Tom walked the stage, their steps and voices echoing throughout the cavernous auditorium. Soon this space would fill with people, everyone feeling the nervous excitement of seeing Wagner and Michaels square off against only each other for the first time.

As their group left the stage to make way for the Michaels team, Tom's nerves threatened to overwhelm him. He felt helpless in this situation: Bill would speak off the cuff, and there was nothing Tom could do about it. Of course, Tom and Mitch had taken the time for extensive review with Bill, discussing how to ideally state his position on various issues; and Tom trusted in Bill's abilities, he really did. Still… it was going to be hard to watch the debate and feel the redundancy of his job for the night.

Up on the stage, Erin Michaels, fresh from the makeup chair, had taken her place at the podium and was being walked through a sound check. Several feet to her left, Nathan Harris stood in close conference with Jason Eisenberg, gesturing toward the stage backdrop as he spoke. Nathan was too focused on their conversation to notice Tom, who watched him discreetly from several rows away. He was the archetypal tall, dark, and handsome man, no doubt about it; and he must have a keen political mind to be Jason's deputy. Again Tom wondered if Nathan had been the originator of the note he'd passed to Tom at the Iowa caucus; and if so, was he actually as boorish as the note made him seem?

The debate was intense, or at least it felt that way to Tom, who sat beside Mitch in the auditorium with a notepad and pen, furiously scribbling notes throughout the entire thing. Tom had seen Michaels in debates before—there'd been several held in the fall before the primaries began—but never in a one-on-one situation. He couldn't help appreciating her style. When she smiled, it was a real smile, not a smirk. She spoke confidently but without being condescending. She wasn't afraid to crack a joke when it was appropriate—or to laugh heartily when Bill did the same—nor did she shy away from approaching difficult issues head-on. Tom decided, as the evening continued, that he liked Erin Michaels.

Nevertheless, Bill Wagner was his candidate, and Tom was very pleased with how Bill represented himself. When all was said and done it had been an interesting and well-fought debate. Many pundits commented afterward that it was quite cordial, no elbows thrown or serious snark dropped, and they had trouble coming to an agreement as to who had fought the better fight. Neither had dominated, neither had faltered under the pressure. When Tom and Mitch joined Kim and Sarah backstage to look at the numbers, it seemed both candidates had polled well. They had both laid out their platforms, and now it would be up to voters to determine with which candidate their own ideology was most closely aligned.

For Tom, with only four days remaining before the big day—Super Tuesday—his schedule would be absolutely punishing until the polls closed Tuesday night. After two events in Southern California, the campaign would work its way back across the country, visiting Albuquerque, Denver, and Kansas City. From Missouri they would fly to Connecticut and work their way through New York and New Jersey on their way to Atlanta. Tom would essentially eat, sleep and write. As excited as he'd been for the approach of Super Tuesday, now all he really wanted was for it to be over.

THE MICHAELS campaign had quite a different campaign route, since Erin needed to be in New York on Tuesday to vote in her home state. They worked their way east, staying south of the Mason-Dixon line all the way to Georgia, before heading north through Delaware and New Jersey to New York.

Nate, however, wouldn't be continuing all the way to New York with Erin, Jason and the others. He would be left in Atlanta to liaise with local campaign staff. The situation made him a bit cross, as he didn't see much point in him being in Atlanta or anywhere else in Georgia. It was Bill Wagner's home state—he was a well-liked senator and he'd been polling far ahead of Erin in the state. However, Erin and Jason insisted on campaigning in Atlanta and then making sure Nate stayed to keep an eye on things. It was one of the few times he'd really disagreed with Jason on where he was being sent, but the decision was made. Nate stayed.

The campaign was in Atlanta on Sunday afternoon. Erin spoke at a rally, which was surprisingly well-attended, all things considered. The day was sunny and reasonably mild, and the crowd were generous with their applause. By that evening, when the campaign moved on and Nate settled into his hotel room, he had begun to harbor new optimism about Georgia.

It was optimism that, unfortunately, did not serve him well. Late Tuesday evening, he stood in the Atlanta office of the Michaels campaign with several dozen other volunteers, watching the results as they came in from the eighteen states of Super Tuesday. New York was theirs—no surprise—and so were Connecticut, New Jersey and Delaware. Georgia was a dismal failure, with support for Wagner outnumbering Michaels two to one. It was much as Nate had anticipated in the first place, and he had to acknowledge—with no little chagrin—that the only reason he was disappointed now was because he'd allowed his expectations to become unrealistic. The volunteers around him were utterly dejected. They'd worked hard for Erin Michaels, after all. Nate rallied his own spirits enough to give a short speech acknowledging their support and hard work, conveying Erin's gratitude.

He didn't stay long after Georgia was decided—he could continue to get results on his phone while in transit. He grabbed his suitcase from where he'd stashed it in the back of the campaign office, and after a few final handshakes, grabbed a taxi to Hartsfield Airport. While on route, he tried repeatedly to book a flight to Washington, but over and over, the app kept timing out. Once he'd actually arrived at Hartsfield, he found the situation was no better.

"I'm sorry, sir," the young man at the ticket counter told him. "All flights to Washington tonight are delayed indefinitely, as the capital has a heavy blanket of fog. I can book you on a flight that's currently scheduled to leave at 5:30 a.m., but I can't guarantee it'll actually leave at that time." The ticket agent smiled apologetically.

Nate thought for a moment before agreeing. At least if he had a boarding pass, he could get through security and then get something to eat in the terminal before trying to sleep for a bit. He bought his ticket and, with no line at security, was inside the terminal in under ten minutes. He bought a light dinner at a small cafeteria, one of the few places in the airport still open at the late hour, and settled into the waiting area adjacent to his gate. He chose to occupy a section of the floor in a corner against a large window, instead of the uncomfortable, molded chairs.

After he'd scarfed down his food, Nate stretched out on the floor, padding his head with a thick sweatshirt from his bag. The conditions weren't exactly conducive to restful sleep, but he was exhausted, and it wasn't long before he slipped into a dreamless slumber.

WHEN HE woke with a start some time later, it took him a moment to remember where he was. He sat up, trying to blink the sleep out of his eyes. His throat was parched. Not until after he'd drained the rest of the water from his bottle did he look around at the three or four other people sitting in the waiting area.

Two rows away from where he sat, an unmistakable head of messy golden-blond hair rested on a duffel bag. Tom McAlindon was slumped sideways in one of the seats, apparently sound asleep. Nate wondered when Tom had arrived. Obviously he, too, was flying back to DC and had encountered the same problem Nate had. Had he seen Nate asleep on the floor? Had he recognized him?

Tom's jaw was slack and his lips parted slightly, giving him a look of relaxation that belied the less-than-ideal setting. Nate wondered if Tom was one of those people who could sleep pretty much anywhere, or if he had simply been unable to fight off his exhaustion after the day's events. Before long, Nate's brain began to fuzz again, and he stretched out his legs and let himself drift back to sleep.

The next time he woke, he knew exactly where he was. It was nearly 5:00 a.m.—close to when he usually began his day anyway—and his circadian rhythm told him it was time to get up and seek coffee. Slowly, stiffly, he picked himself up from the floor and stretched, stifling a groan. He wandered over to where the screens were displaying flight information. The flight he was booked on, scheduled to leave at five thirty, was showing as "Delayed." He wouldn't be going anywhere soon, that much was obvious. He headed back to his place on the floor. As he began folding his sweatshirt back into his duffel bag, movement from the seating area caught his eye. Nate looked up in time to see Tom McAlindon's eyes turn away. Nate wondered how long Tom had been awake and watching him. Would they really sit so near each other, perhaps for hours, without acknowledging each other's presence?

Nate made a quick decision. He zipped up his duffel, pocketed his iPhone, and made his way to stand in front of Tom. Tom looked up, and Nate didn't give Tom a chance to ask the questions that filled his eyes.

"We could sit here and pretend we don't know each other," Nate said quietly, "or we could have a coffee and maybe chat for a while. We might have a long wait yet. Having someone to talk to would probably make the time pass more quickly."

Tom's silence and raised eyebrow expressed skepticism, not that Nate could blame him. "No ulterior motives, I promise," he added, but he could see Tom still wasn't convinced. Finally Nate realized there was something he'd skipped. He held out his hand, and with a tired but genuine smile, he said, "We haven't been introduced. I'm Nathan Harris."

Tom held Nate's gaze for a long moment, clearly debating his options. Finally he capitulated, clasping Nate's outstretched hand. "Tom McAlindon," he replied, adding, "Nice to meet you, Nathan. Let's have breakfast."

Nate waited as Tom zipped up his Kindle in a leather case and slipped it into his carry-on bag. "Au Bon Pain?" he suggested.

Tom nodded. "They have the best coffee."

They made their way to the coffee shop, not really talking much until after they'd sat down with their coffee and breakfast. Nate blew on his coffee—since he drank it black, it stayed hot forever—and nibbled at a bagel. He was curious about why Tom had ordered two identical coffees—large, non-fat vanilla latte—until he watched him drain the first in under two minutes. He didn't mean to stare, but he'd never seen anyone drink a piping hot latte so fast. Tom caught Nate's wide eyes and grinned sheepishly, and somehow it was what broke the ice between them. "A jump start," Tom offered by way of explanation, picking up his bacon and egg sandwich. "My first coffee of the day goes down pretty fast."

"Holy shit," Nate replied. "Wouldn't it be faster to mainline it?"

Tom chuckled. "Probably, but I love the taste too."

Nate grinned back at him, and they both chewed in silence for a few minutes. After another bite, Nate said, "Congratulations on your wins yesterday, by the way."

Tom stared at Nate warily. "Thanks," he replied after a moment. "You too. Senator Michaels's numbers in New York and Connecticut were fantastic."

"Home state advantage. Well, in New York at least—they love her. Same with Wagner in Georgia. He beat Erin two to one."

"You had a good turnout at the rally Sunday," Tom offered politely.

The conversation was impeccably polite, Nate thought, one carefully diplomatic sentence after another. It was a little stilted but better than an argument—and definitely preferable to no conversation at all. Gradually the underlying frost thawed. Little by little, each relaxed as they realized the other wasn't going to verbally ambush them.

"How did you get involved with Senator Michaels's campaign?" Tom asked.

"I actually started working for her when she ran for the Senate, ten years ago. I was hired for that campaign, which is when I met Jason

Eisenberg. When Erin was elected, Jason and I were both offered jobs in her senate office."

"I guess if you could all work together well and still stand each other after a campaign, anything after that would be easy."

Nate grinned. "I'm lucky that they're both pretty great to work for. What about you? Did you know Senator Wagner when you were in Atlanta?"

"Not really. I'd met him a few times through my job for Mayor Lee, because they were friends. They both served in the state senate at the same time, and then Wagner went on to Washington. And after Isaiah was elected mayor, they had some joint initiatives in the city. So I suppose the senator heard some of my speeches at those events, and eventually, when he had put together his exploratory committee, he brought Mitchell Enns to one of the events. And now we both work for him."

"They must have liked what they heard."

Tom's cheeks tinged pink. "Mayor Lee is an excellent orator."

Nate didn't miss how Tom deflected the compliment. "They didn't hire Mayor Lee, though, did they?"

"True enough." Tom grinned at Nate. "They did warn him, though."

"Warned him of that?"

"That they were going to offer me a job."

"Wow—what did he say?"

"Depends on who you ask. According to Mitchell, he told them that if they were going to poach his staff, they couldn't do better. According to Mayor Lee"—here Tom dropped his voice discreetly—"he told them to fuck off and find their own damn speechwriter."

Nate joined Tom's laughter. "So who do you believe?"

"Well, I worked for him for three years, and in that time he told me on several occasions that he knew the city of Atlanta wouldn't be able to hold on to me forever. So I don't believe for a second that I left without his blessing. However," Tom added wryly, "I am equally sure that when Senator Wagner shared his plan to hire me, there *were* four letter words involved, at least on the mayor's side." He looked affectionately amused.

As they chatted, Nate thought about how nice Tom's voice was— quiet, gentle and discreet. The time passed more quickly than he realized, and he was surprised when Tom looked at his watch and said, "Well, it's nearly eight. We should probably get back out there and watch for the flight information."

"Yeah," Nate agreed. "Let's hope for bright sun in DC to burn off the fog."

As they approached the waiting area, the airline employee at the gate announced that the flight was beginning preboarding. They were nowhere near each other on the flight, and Nate saw Tom again only briefly as they each stood in line for a cab at National. Tom saw him as well, and gave him a little smile before he disappeared into a taxi. Despite his exhaustion, Nate felt triumphant at having had the chance for a civil conversation with Tom. He'd kept his promise not to try to recruit Tom to the Michaels campaign during their chat, but he couldn't help thinking that after Erin Michaels got the nomination, maybe Tom would consider joining them. Every opportunity he had now to make nice with the sought-after young speechwriter could only improve the odds of that happening.

He couldn't wait to tell Susan Pollard.

THE REST of Tom's week was quiet compared to the frenetic pace of the preceding week. Though there would be a couple of caucuses and one primary over the weekend, he was to stay put in DC until the Michigan primary at the end of the month. He worked Thursday and Friday on the Hill, and Saturday from home, spending all his waking hours drafting speeches for the next several days. By the time Sunday arrived, he was completely exhausted. He allowed himself to sleep in until noon, then made himself go out for a run.

He couldn't remember the last time he'd been outside during daylight hours for anything other than dashing from a car to a building and vice versa. For the first time in his life, his skin was pale instead of warm golden. It was cold out—slightly below freezing, which to Tom might as well be subzero—but the sun was brilliant, sparkling blindingly off a fresh skiff of snow on the ground. The cold air prickled icy in his lungs, and he was a little hesitant when he first set out, afraid to slip on a patch of ice, but soon he found a comfortable rhythm. He did two miles easily, and arrived back at his apartment building feeling sharper, more energetic than he had in weeks.

As he showered off the sweat, Tom chastised himself for letting his workouts slip over the past few weeks. Exercise always helped improve his concentration—he knew it well, and yet when he was having trouble with a speech, that knowledge somehow escaped him. He would settle into a sort of tunnel vision, with the only objective being *finish this speech* and the only path to that objective being *stay right here till it's done*. He decided he would mention it to Mitch and perhaps Sarah, so that the next time they saw him struggling, they could remind him to get out of the office, even if it was only to walk for half an hour.

He spent the rest of the day writing for Tuesday's primaries in DC, Maryland, and Virginia—the local crowd who'd seen it all, and the not-so-locals, such as the southern Virginia residents who somehow seemed entirely different from those who lived in the northern part of the same state. Monday he was at the campaign office before the sun came up. His office door remained closed all day, except for when Mitch evicted him around 1:30 p.m., insisting that Tom get some lunch and spend at least fifteen minutes outdoors. Throughout the day he got updates on how the campaigning was going—Wagner was in Maryland that day—and adjusted his writing accordingly to respond to one issue or another. By the time he got home, it was nearly nine o'clock. He was grateful he only had a studio apartment, as he honestly didn't know if he'd have made it as far as a bedroom. He didn't even undress; he kicked off his shoes and stripped his tie and belt before passing out on top of the covers.

The next morning when his alarm went off, it was the first time since joining the campaign that he honestly wished he could take a personal day. Nevertheless, he dragged himself out of bed. He would be going to Capitol Hill today, spending the day at Bill's suite in the Senate office buildings rather than going to the campaign office. Mitch had promised that Tom wouldn't want to be anywhere else today *but* on the Hill—today was going to be special. Almost everyone who worked there—staffers, journalists, politicians, even Capitol Security—were residents of DC, Virginia, or Maryland, which meant they'd be voting in the primaries. On days like this, no one could help being caught up in the excitement of being active participants in the democratic process. No matter the eventual outcome, while the polls were open and history was being made, the enthusiasm was infectious—even the most cynical pundit wasn't immune.

It was the promise of that buzz, that excitement, that drew Tom out of bed. He'd slept well, at least, barely moving for seven hours; by the time he'd showered and downed his first cup of coffee and was savoring his second, he felt like a new man. It wasn't until he thumbed his iPhone that he realized what day it was: February 14. He blinked at his phone in dismay, wondering if the date setting had been messed up somehow. Could it actually be the fourteenth already? It felt like the last time he'd looked at a calendar it was still January. His life over the past few weeks had been a daily marathon, working from morning till night and collapsing into bed for a few hours. He'd barely even needed to know what day it was—only how many days he had left until a particular primary or event. There were always several dates to which he was counting down.

Realizing it was Valentine's Day wasn't especially pleasant. He'd never really cared before about the holiday—never worried about having a boyfriend or a hookup just because the calendar said he should—but this year, somehow, the holiday brought with it the consciousness of how slim his prospects were of having any sexual contact in the near future, or even having the time for it. The only people he saw these days were campaign and Hill staff, and really, it was all but limited to Sarah and Mitch when he was in serious writing mode. His friends Maxwell and Colin, who'd been his best friends in Atlanta for a decade, had visited him over New Year's, coming up to DC to see his new apartment. The Iowa caucuses followed a few days later, and he'd lived the whirlwind of the campaign since then. How long had it been since he'd done more than texted either of them? Too long. As he drained the last of his coffee, he resolved to call them tomorrow when he had time to take a breath.

The day was another maelstrom of activity. He cast his ballot midway through the day, refusing to miss the chance to make his mark on the outcome. Capitol Hill was strung with nervous undercurrents of expectation and promise, the atmosphere vibrating with it until the polls closed and results started to come in.

When enough of the numbers had come in to give them a decent idea of the overall outcome, it seemed that Michaels had taken Maryland and DC, Wagner had Virginia, and all three races had very narrow margins. When Bill thanked his volunteers at the end of the night, it was obvious that their confidence was undiminished in spite of not taking the capitol or Maryland.

Tom wished he could feel the same hopeful optimism of the volunteers; but the truth was he was beginning to wonder when the margin between the two candidates would start to widen, when one or the other would have a decisive victory anywhere other than their home state. He supposed there were worse things—for instance, if instead of having two likeable, well-qualified candidates, there were no decent options available. That had certainly been a problem before. Still, both campaigns were expending a lot of energy—and money—and he couldn't see a clear victor between the two, not anytime soon. He almost wished he didn't feel quite so strongly about supporting Bill Wagner, that he was just doing a job instead of being so personally invested in the outcome....

Almost.

Realizing that his current line of thinking was incredibly negative under the circumstances, Tom decided he'd be best to head home.

"Hey," he whispered to Mitchell, "I'm hitting the wall. I think I'd better go before I forget how to get home."

"Yeah. I'm going to head off soon too."

"Do you want a ride?"

"Nah, my car's parked on the Hill. I'll get a ride with Kim—she lives two blocks from me."

"Oh, right. Okay, I'll see you tomorrow."

Mitch nodded. "I don't want to see you before noon, though. Sleep in and enjoy a morning off. You sure as hell deserve it, kid."

Tom almost wished he could hug Mitch for that small validation. Instead he found Sarah and gave her a hug and a kiss on the cheek before he headed outside to his car. He was glad he'd thought to drive his own vehicle here—he'd have had to pass his apartment to get back to Capitol Hill if he'd ridden with someone else. He got into his freezing cold car and started it. As he watched his breath crystallize in the air before his face, his stomach grumbled. He suddenly realized he was starving.

It was ten o'clock, and his favorite Thai restaurant would close at ten thirty. Knowing he could get there before they closed, he called in an order of green curry chicken and spring rolls. This particular restaurant was close to his apartment and was on his way home from the Hill. He ordered so often that the late evening staff knew him by name now.

Tom made it to the restaurant in under fifteen minutes, parking on the street in front of the tidy white building. Inside, he thanked the owner's son, Pham, who was packaging up Tom's order. Tom apologized for yet another under-the-wire order, but Pham waved off the apology.

"Always a few last-minute calls—had another one right after yours," he smiled. "We're glad to see you're still around. Haven't seen you in a few weeks, and we started to wonder."

"I've been on the road with the campaign, but it's nice to know someone's thinking of me." Tom smiled at Pham. For the first time since he'd moved to DC a few months earlier, he felt a glimmer of community, like he wasn't completely alone and anonymous in the city. The thought warmed him.

The bell on the door behind him jingled, and he pocketed his wallet and thanked Pham again. He turned to make room for the patron who'd come in, and almost ran right into Nathan Harris.

"N-Nathan?" he stammered.

Nathan's brown eyes were teary from the cold night outside but shone warmly at Tom. "Hey, there! I suppose I shouldn't be surprised to run into you here." He spoke over Tom's shoulder to Pham. "It's an order for Harris, please."

"It's not up yet," Pham replied. "Couple of minutes." He headed to the kitchen, leaving Tom and Nate alone for the moment.

"What do you mean, you shouldn't be surprised?" Tom asked.

Nate grinned. "You told me about this place, remember?"

"Oh, that's right."

"I was on my way home from the campaign office in Arlington, totally famished, and I thought, 'What was the name of that place Tom mentioned?' So I decided to check it out."

Tom returned Nate's smile. "So I guess this means you're on your own tonight too, huh?"

Nate chuckled. "Yeah. Another romantic evening with takeout and a *Law & Order* DVD, until I fall asleep alone."

Tom grimaced. "Sounds way too familiar."

Nate paused a moment, then carefully asked, "Do you have… anyone? A partner, or whatever?"

Tom mirrored Nate's hesitation before replying. "Um, no. It's been a while. I'm married to my job. Even when I was working for Isaiah Lee, I was a workaholic. I would have made a terrible boyfriend." Tom knew he didn't imagine the slight upward twitch in Nate's right eyebrow, as though he was considering Tom's candidacy where boyfriends were concerned. He chose to ignore it as he turned the tables on Nate. "You either?"

Nate shook his head. "I'm in a monogamous relationship with my iPhone. I haven't had a boyfriend since I moved to Washington. I don't think I've been on a date in at least a year. Same as you: married to my job."

I haven't had a boyfriend. Tom nodded while mentally high-fiving himself for his instincts.

Pham returned to the counter then, with Nate's order. Tom waited as Nate paid and thanked Pham, and then they both headed back out into the freezing cold night.

The stars glittered above them as they walked slowly in the direction of their cars. "Fucking freezing," Nate muttered under his breath, clouds of frosted steam billowing as he did.

"This is my first winter in a cold climate, and I hate it," Tom admitted. "If it got cold like this in Miami, everyone would die."

"It's hard to believe when it's bitter cold like this, but in six weeks, the cherry trees will be in full bloom," Nate remarked.

"I'm looking forward to it."

"Which—the trees or the warm weather?" Nate grinned.

"Both," Tom replied without hesitation.

Nate stopped beside a black Audi. "So, this is me."

"Right. Well, then, have a good night."

"Thanks, you too. It was nice to run into you again."

"Yeah." But Tom didn't continue on to his car. Instead he stood where he was for several seconds, looking up into Nate's face, pale in the bloodless glow of the streetlights. Maybe it was because he was lonely; maybe it was the empathy he felt knowing that Nate had a very solitary life like his own. For whatever reason, he found himself stepping toward Nate, lifting his chin, and gently pressing a kiss to Nate's mouth.

Nate didn't return the kiss immediately, but as Tom pulled away he felt Nate's lips press back against his. Nathan's eyes were wide, his lips parted slightly; he exhaled a shallow breath, huffing ice vapor into the shared space between them. Into the still of a city going to sleep, Tom whispered, "Happy Valentine's Day." Then without another word, he turned and continued to his Jetta.

In his car, Tom fought the urge to curse his impulsive action. Tomorrow would be soon enough for regrets; tonight, he wanted to enjoy his food and watch something mindless on TV before collapsing for ten hours or so. As he sat idling at a red light, he saw the black Audi pull up behind him. He smirked into the rearview mirror until the light turned green, then continued on toward his apartment, only a few minutes away. When he got to New Jersey Avenue, he expected the Audi to turn north, heading toward the Capitol, as he knew Nate's place was near Dupont Circle. Instead it turned south with him, following him all the way to his apartment building.

Wondering why Nate was following him, Tom decided to pull over beside his building instead of into the parking garage. Nate pulled up behind Tom and got out of his vehicle. Tom got out too, becoming nervous now. *Stupid, impulsive move*, he chided himself, and as Nate walked toward him, he found himself trembling.

"Nate, I'm sorry, that was—" he began, but Nate was already close enough for Tom to see the look in his eyes.

"Maybe I shouldn't have followed you," Nate murmured. "I'll leave if you want." His eyes flickered to Tom's mouth, leaving no doubt what was on his mind.

Tom should have asked Nate to leave. He should have parked his car, gone upstairs and eaten his Thai food and watched TV and slept hard all night long. He knew what he should do. Instead he found himself breathlessly replying, "Bring your food. I'll park in the garage and meet you at that door to let you in." He gestured to the side door that led into the building's stairwell.

Nate nodded, turning on his heel and striding quickly back to his vehicle. Not giving himself time to reconsider, Tom pulled into the garage and into his space, grabbed his dinner and sprinted up the stairwell to the ground floor. His heart pounding, he pushed open the door, terrified that Nate would have changed his mind; but there Nate stood, cheeks rosy from the cold. Tom beckoned him in. Silently they took the stairs to the second floor and rode the elevator the rest of the way up to the eighth.

Inside his apartment, Tom suddenly felt self-conscious. He welcomed Nate in, taking his coat and hanging it in the closet. Nate set his food on the counter that separated the kitchen from the living room; Tom did the same. They stared at each other for a long moment before Nate stepped in close, one arm curling around Tom's waist and the other cupping his cheek. He kissed Tom, gently at first, but with increasing urgency.

Tom moaned softly. Nate's lips were soft and warm, and soon they were parting, letting his tongue tease Tom's mouth. Tom shivered at the feel of Nate licking kisses into his mouth. His hands stroked down Nate's back before slowly inching lower, crossing Nate's belt, and finding his slim backside. Tentatively Tom squeezed. Nate's breath caught in his throat, and his entire body tensed beneath Tom's touch. "Please don't stop," Nate whispered into Tom's mouth.

Tom did stop, but only long enough to undo Nate's belt and release the clasp of his pants. He slid the zipper down, letting Nathan's pants fall to the floor, and then his hands were slipping into Nate's briefs and back to that muscular ass. Nate hummed his approval, his mouth moving to place warm, sucking kisses down Tom's neck. It was Tom's turn to gasp. He sharply pulled Nate's hips closer, feeling the hardening length press against his own.

Surprised, Nate groaned at the sudden pressure and jumped back a bit. Urgently he began to strip off his remaining clothes, revealing a lean, sinewy body beneath. Across his chest was a generous patch of black hair, tapering down toward his waist; his legs were slim but defined, and they too had a liberal covering of hair. It was exactly the body type Tom found most appealing, and he hurried to remove his own clothes so he could get his hands all over it.

When he was down to his briefs, though, Tom found himself hesitating. He wasn't ashamed of his body, but he was still shy, and he was modest. Casual sex had never been part of his life, and it'd been a while since he'd been with anyone, let alone someone new. Nate too had removed all but his own underpants, placing his clothes on an armchair opposite the bed, and turned to Tom.

"Wow," murmured Nate. "You're gorgeous."

Tom felt his cheeks flush. "Thanks," he whispered. He didn't think gorgeous was the right word, but it was rude to turn down a compliment. He wanted to return it, to tell Nate that his slim body was the sexiest Tom had ever seen, that the dark hair covering his long legs was beautiful and masculine; but he couldn't force the words from his throat. Nate stepped closer, his fingers reaching out to skim across Tom's chest and down his abs. Tom closed his eyes, focusing on the sensation. He felt Nate's lips against his in another searing kiss, and he wrapped his arms around Nate's neck, their bodies pressing together again.

Tom let himself be guided to the bed, where he lay on his back. Nathan stood beside the bed and hooked his thumbs under the waist of his briefs before sliding them down over his ass and off completely. Tom couldn't help staring at Nate's cock, flushed dark and hard as it stood out from a thatch of dark hair. Nathan knelt on the bed beside Tom and slid his fingers under the elastic of Tom's briefs, looking at Tom questioningly. In answer Tom lifted his hips off the bed, and Nate divested him of that last remaining garment.

It was Nate's turn to stare, taking in Tom's nude form. Nate's fingers followed his eyes over every plane and every angle. It had been so long since Tom had been touched; those warm hands across his skin were incredible.

"Are you cold?" Nate whispered.

"Why?"

"You have goose bumps." Nathan leaned down to kiss Tom's arm where, indeed, goose bumps were raised across the surface.

"Not because I'm cold," Tom murmured. Nathan's body sank to cover his, and the not-cold goose bumps proliferated across his skin.

AFTER, WHEN they had both showered off the sweat and the smell of sex, they reheated their Thai food and ate at the breakfast bar in Tom's little kitchen. Having both a couch and a bed in the studio apartment, he didn't have room for a dining table, even a small one.

"This is a nice little place," Nate remarked.

"Little being the operative word. My place in Atlanta is three times this size."

"You still have your apartment there?"

"I'm subletting it. I'll let it go after the election."

"If Wagner wins," Nate supplied.

"Yeah." Tom tensed. He didn't want to talk about the primaries. It was dangerous to discuss anything election-related with a staffer of another campaign—far too easy to let something slip, even something that seemed innocuous.

But Nate had another question for him. "So, hey, can you verify a rumor for me?"

Tom's eyebrows crept up. "About what?"

"I heard that when Isaiah Lee was running for mayor of Atlanta, you wrote a speech for him, completely unsolicited, and sent it to his campaign."

"I did do that."

"And then he called you up and offered you a job?"

"It wasn't quite as easy as that. He asked me to write another speech for him, and I did." Tom dipped his spring roll in fish sauce before adding cheekily, "*Then* he offered me a job."

"Right out of grad school?"

"A few months out, yeah."

Nate looked impressed. Tom was feeling pretty good until Nate asked, "Why did it take you so long to finish grad school?"

"Well…." Tom weighed how to respond. He was having a great time with Nate, and his coming out story was a serious downer. He didn't want to go into the whole story. "I paid for grad school myself, so I worked my way through."

Nate nodded. "I guess that's better than graduating with thousands of dollars in student loans."

"For me, it was. I would have spent so much time worrying about the debt that I wouldn't have been able to focus on school. What about you? Where did you go to school?"

"Undergrad at NYU, law degree at Cornell."

"You're a JD? Have you ever thought about practicing?"

"Noooo." Nate drew out the word, shaking his head as he did. It was such a definite negative that it made Tom laugh. "I never wanted to practice. I wanted to work here in Washington, and I needed the knowledge."

"You knew exactly what you wanted."

"Always." Nate looked intensely at Tom, and Tom felt his arms prickle with goose bumps again. He hoped it didn't show.

Their dinner was long gone when Nate looked around for a clock. "Jesus," he muttered, "it's after one. I've got to get to bed."

"If you're too tired to drive home, you could stay," Tom offered.

"I'd still have to go home for a change of clothes in the morning." Nate pulled on his suit pants. "And… not like we're running black ops or something, but in daylight…. Well, it's probably best that no one sees me leaving your building. There are eyes everywhere here."

"I see your point." Yes, the sex had been good—great, in fact—but obviously it had been an impulsive thing, and it could never happen again. There was no way he could have a long-term relationship with a member of an opposing campaign. If there was ever any suggestion that one of them had shared information about the inner workings of the campaign or upcoming strategies… hell, for the sake of appearances, they shouldn't even have been together tonight.

Tom got Nate's black wool topcoat out of the closet and held it for him. Nate shrugged into it and turned to face Tom as he buttoned it up. "This was nice. Unexpected, but nice." When Tom agreed with him, he continued, "But, um… it probably shouldn't have happened."

"I know. It can't happen again."

"No. Exactly." Nate looked relieved that Tom understood. "So… I'll probably see you here and there."

"Probably."

"Okay." Though he was ready to leave, Nate stood gazing at Tom for a long moment. "But before I go…." He stepped in close, giving Tom a deep kiss. Tom warmed again to the feel of Nate's tongue against his own one last time. Finally Nate pulled away, whispered, "Bye," and slipped out the door.

NATE WAS not spontaneous. He could count on one hand the number of times in his adult life he'd leapt without looking, and the other hand would probably cover similar events from his childhood. He had always analyzed, calculated, examined a situation before proceeding thoughtfully and deliberately with his plan of action. His mother had often remarked that he was his father's son in that regard. It was one of the things that made him an excellent political advisor.

But it did nothing to explain how he found himself making his way home in the wee hours of a cold, dark February morning, feeling more relaxed than he had in several months. The odd thing, he realized as he drove past Capitol Hill, was how very okay he was with it. The sex had been great, the food was good even reheated, and he was content with how they'd left things. It happened, and he had no regrets. It wouldn't happen again, and he was fine with that too.

The rest of Nate's work week consisted of the usual postmortems, the breakdowns of how Erin had polled among various demographics and strategizing on how the campaign could capitalize on the gains they'd made. At night, though, when Nate had left the buzz and distraction of the office, when he had returned to the quiet and solitude of his condo, his thoughts wandered from spin and tactics. His mind insisted on whispering to him about sweat-darkened blond hair, damply soft at his fingertips… a slim body, taut, wrapping around him… wordless murmurs that built into one long, low moan as Tom went to pieces beneath him.

It gave him a swooping feeling in his stomach, remembering Tom and some of the more intense moments of their night. There was no doubt the experience would rate the top spot in his spank bank for a long time, and Nate saw no harm in letting it stay there. It wasn't going to happen again, but there was no reason he couldn't get a little fantasy mileage out of it in his downtime.

Late that week a cold snap descended upon the Eastern Seaboard, sending the temperatures down into single digits. The Michaels team was headed to Wisconsin for the following week's primary, scheduled for the same day as the Hawaii caucuses. No matter how many hints Nate dropped about the temperature in Kauai, Jason and Erin's plans were set—though at least Erin acknowledged Nate's wry comments with a broad smile. The team spent several days in Wisconsin, ending up in Milwaukee on the day Erin took that state's primary; with Hawaii going to Wagner. While the rest of the Michaels campaign was headed to Arizona, Nate had to fly back to Washington for a Wednesday afternoon meeting. With the last flight to DC leaving at 7:00 p.m., he'd been forced to say farewell to his colleagues before the polls had even closed, and found himself at Mitchell Airport early Tuesday evening, waiting for his flight.

He was sitting with his iPad on his lap and his iPhone clutched in his hand, obsessively checking e-mails and news websites, trying to stay as in the loop as he could before he had to board and lose contact for several hours. He was too distracted to pay attention to anyone around him, and so he was startled when he felt a hand on his shoulder. He looked up to find a kind, familiar face grinning down at him.

"I thought that was you," said Tom McAlindon, straightening up and slinging his carry-on back over his shoulder. "I was on my way to my gate, but I thought it was you."

Nate returned Tom's smile. "Yup, here to catch a ridiculously early flight back to DC."

"Jesus, no shit." Tom rolled his eyes. "No flights out after seven thirty? Do they roll up the runways or something?"

"Exactly. What about you—going back to Washington?"

"No. I'm on my way to Phoenix."

"Alone?"

Tom looked a little sheepish. "It's nice to travel alone sometimes. If we're all on the bus, that's one thing—I don't really have a choice. But when I can fly, sometimes it's nice to go on ahead, have some solitude for a few hours or half a day. I'll get some work done at the hotel tomorrow before everyone else gets in."

Nate understood. It wasn't easy to spend twenty-four hours a day with anyone, let alone a colleague you had to work with regardless of whether you really liked them. "Well, it's nice to see you," he smiled at Tom before lowering his voice. "If it wasn't for airports and takeout food...." He let the sentence hang in the air.

"Yeah." Tom's cheeks flushed slightly. He checked his watch self-consciously and cleared his throat. "I should get to my gate."

"Of course," Nate agreed. "Enjoy Arizona."

"Thanks, I will. Safe travels." Tom flashed Nate one more shy grin before turning and continuing down the terminal. Nate watched him go until he'd disappeared down the corridor. He returned to his electronic devices, but if his focus wasn't quite as intense as before and if a hint of a smile continued to lurk on his face until well after his flight was in the air, well, no one he knew was around to see it.

NATE'S INTEREST in politics had begun at a fairly young age, and he attributed that partly to his parents' influence, and partly to the abundance of liberality in his hometown of Ann Arbor, Michigan. The city had a small but vocal conservative base as well, which made life interesting for politicians and their supporters. Nate's liberal influence came heavily from his parents, both of whom closely followed politics at all levels of government.

His parents had taken Nate and his brother to political rallies and candidates' debates for as far back as Nate could remember. As a child he had seen Jimmy Carter; in high school, it was Bill Clinton. Now, with the Wagner campaign planning a stop in Ann Arbor in the lead-up to the Michigan primary, Nate's father Ron would once again attend a political rally for a potential presidential candidate. This time, though, Nate would be one of the people standing behind that candidate as a trusted member of her staff.

That day hundreds showed up to support Erin, standing out in the bright, cold winter sun, hanging on to every word, sharing her brilliant smiles and cheering at the end of almost every sentence. It was a great day for the campaign, but a bittersweet one for Nathan. While he was proud to be beside the stage, standing shoulder to shoulder with his father, who was himself so proud he could scarcely contain it, Nate couldn't help thinking about someone else who should have been there with him.

Nate turned to meet his dad's gaze, doing his best to smile through the glistening moisture welling in his eyes. Ron, who had always been affectionate with his boys, had no hesitation about throwing an arm over his son's shoulder. "I know," he said quietly. "I wish she was here too. She was proud of you." He gave Nate's shoulder a squeeze. "So am I."

"Thanks, Dad." They both focused their attention back on Erin, and the excitement of the crowd and fond memories warmed them where the winter sun could not.

Ann Arbor was only the first stop. The team crossed the lower half of the "mitten" portion of the state over the next couple of days, visiting Detroit, Flint, Saginaw, and back down to Lansing, before finally landing in Grand Rapids on Monday night before the primary. Erin's campaign had a suite of rooms booked in a hotel; downstairs in the conference room of the hotel, the local volunteers would gather to watch the results come in and Erin would greet them later in the evening.

As it turned out, the hotel was directly across the street from the only other high-end hotel in Grand Rapids—the same hotel that was housing the Wagner campaign and their own planned victory party. It was unfortunate, Nate thought to himself, that both campaigns would end up in the same small city that night, where they would be in such close proximity. Michigan was already such a damn close state. He and Jason were concerned about trouble arising between supporters of the two camps at the end of the day, after the results were in and volunteers either imbibed in celebration or in disappointment, depending on how they viewed the results. One word snarled at the wrong time to the wrong person could be a match in a powder keg. Their concerns were shared by the Wagner team, and Jason had been contacted by Kim Harvey, Wagner's campaign manager, about it. Together the two groups had approached the Grand Rapids police force to increase the police presence on the street that night. It didn't guarantee a trouble-free night, but it was better than crossing their fingers and hoping for the best.

The close proximity of Senator Wagner's campaign meant that Tom was right across the street too. Several times throughout the day Nate spared a thought for how close Tom was; how if circumstances were different, maybe they could have had dinner together.

But the emotional climate of the day demanded most of his attention. Nate usually fed off the energy of primary day. He often found it invigorated him and reminded him of the ultimate goal. Every primary night when he listened to Erin's speech, mentally he would recommit to the campaign and to seeing Erin elected.

The energy of that primary day in Michigan was certainly nothing on which Nathan wanted to draw. The volunteers were exhausted, for one thing; every poll that had been unfavorable to Erin had made them redouble their efforts, getting out and pounding the pavement hard in the weeks before the primary. By all reports, the Wagner volunteers had done the same thing. Neither side had made significant gains over the other. Everyone was tired and frustrated, hoping for the best but spending the evening watching the news reports that kept telling them the numbers were too close to call. Neither side was willing to concede; but at different times through the evening, the news anchors were reporting that one side or another had claimed victory.

At a certain point shortly before 11:00 p.m., Nate hit a mental wall where, for one brief moment, he actually wished for a loss in Michigan so they could get the damn day over with. He'd never been so wound up or felt like his hands were tied as he did now. Erin, who had been scheduled to talk to her supporters at around 10:00 p.m., didn't take the stage till nearly eleven thirty; and when she did, the victory speech, the clear ringing triumph was subdued into something flat, Nate thought. The team had scrambled before she went on, trying to strike a balance in a hastily written speech, since neither of the prepared speeches were written to deal with the possibility of a dead heat.

When Erin's speech was over, Nate said good-bye to Erin, Jason and his fellow staffers, all of whom were leaving tonight on the campaign bus back to Washington. Nate, on the other hand, had rented a car in Ann Arbor. He'd be driving back there tomorrow to spend a few days with his dad before returning to Washington. He bid everyone farewell and headed upstairs to his room.

As tired as he should have been, Nate was still wound up by the tension of the day. He took a shower and then tried watching TV, but neither helped him relax. He was starting to consider the idea of packing up, checking out, and driving through the night to his dad's, when his cell phone rang, startling him.

Nate grabbed the phone and peered at it, but he didn't recognize the number. It was after one o'clock in the morning. He couldn't imagine who would be calling him, unless something dramatic had taken place. He grabbed the phone, his heart pounding. "Hello?"

"Nathan?"

Nate didn't recognize the male voice on the line. "Yes, it is."

"I'm sorry if I woke you. It's Tom."

"Tom?" Nate repeated, surprised. "How did you get my number?"

"You gave it to the campaign, in case of problems."

"Right, of course. Is something wrong?"

"Are you alone?" Tom sounded tense.

"Yes."

"I know you and I said we wouldn't… you know… again, but I really… I just need…." Nate, in his surprise, didn't answer, and after a pause, Tom said, "This was a bad idea. I'm sorry I bothered you, I—"

"Tom," Nate interrupted. "I'm in room 1015."

At the other end of the line, Nate heard a soft exhale. "I'll be there in two minutes."

It was more like five. Nate paced as he waited. He considered putting on more than his briefs, but really, what would be the point? Soon enough there was a soft knock on the door. He checked the peephole first to make sure, then he pulled the door open to usher Tom into his room, quickly closing it behind him. Tom was dressed as Nate had never seen him before, in a hooded sweatshirt and tennis shoes, his hands shoved in the pockets of faded jeans.

"Nathan," Tom said, his voice a shade above a whisper. He looked like he wanted to say more but didn't know how to start.

"C'mere," Nate mumbled, drawing Tom close and kissing him, eliminating the need for those words. He knew what Tom needed and why, because he felt the same way.

Tom responded immediately, wrapping his arms around Nate's neck and moaning into the kiss. Nate insinuated his hands between them to unzip Tom's hoodie, finding him bare-chested beneath it. The shirt hit the floor as Tom kicked off his shoes, his lips still sealed to Nate's. In seconds his jeans were on the floor. Nate grabbed Tom's hips, pushing him to lean against the wall as he dropped to his knees, but Tom stopped him.

"No, please. I need...." Again he seemed desperate to find the words, yet at a loss. He gripped Nate's upper arms, pulling him up.

"Shhh," Nate soothed, taking Tom's hand and leading him to the bed. "Okay, I know." Tom shucked his briefs and immediately climbed onto the bed, crossing to the middle to wait on his hands and knees. Nate took a few seconds to look at him. Tom's head was down, his body rigid with tension as he waited for Nate to join him.

Nate pulled off his own briefs and grabbed the lube he'd pulled out of his suitcase after Tom's call. Tom squirmed as Nate's fingers painted the lube around his sensitive opening.

"Come on," Tom grunted when Nate's fingers slipped inside.

"Be patient. I'm not going to tear you open."

"I know what I can handle. Please, just do it."

Nate hesitated, but God, it was hard to resist Tom's pleas urging him on. He ripped open the condom packet and quickly rolled it on; Tom dropped his chest lower to the bed and Nate took hold of his hips. "You have to tell me if I'm going too fast," he told Tom who responded with one quick, tense nod. Nate started to push inside, slow but steady. As he did, a moan began to rise from Tom, increasing in volume as Nate slid deeper inside, ending in a near-shout when Nate was all the way in. Nate stilled for a few seconds. "Still okay?" Another nod from Tom, and Nate pulled out a bit, then sank deep again.

To Nate's surprise it took only a few deep strokes before Tom was moaning loudly, coming hard without having touched himself at all. The spasms that rocked Tom's body were gently milking Nate's cock, still deep inside Tom.

Tom collapsed on the bed, panting heavily through the aftershocks of his orgasm. Nate, nowhere near completion and hard as steel, moved with him, following his hips down so he could stay inside him.

"Fuck," Tom gasped. "Sorry I came so fast."

Nate rubbed a hand over Tom's shoulders, trying to smooth away the tension. "You needed it."

"Yeah, such a fucking stressful day." He took a deep breath. "I can go again. Give me a minute...."

"Of course." Nate lowered himself onto one elbow, pulling Tom over onto his side so he could spoon him without pulling out, wrapping his arms around Tom and holding him close. The urgency of a few moments earlier had passed; Tom's shoulders had relaxed out of their bowstring tautness. After a moment he pressed back and Nate started to rock slowly into him, luxuriating in the exquisite heat of Tom's body. Tom sighed, reaching back to cup Nate's ass and pull him deeper, whispering filthy things about how Nate was making him feel. When Nate came he pushed as deep as he could, holding Tom close and still, pulsing inside him before reaching for Tom's cock and slowly bringing him off again.

Tom's body was now slack, fully satiated, and it was Nate who got up to find something to clean Tom and the bed. Tom's eyes were already half closed and Nate didn't have the heart to suggest he go back to his own hotel, despite it only being across the street. Instead he got back into bed beside Tom, who turned over, slipping into Nate's arms, resting his head on Nate's chest. Tom mumbled, "I know I shouldn't have called. So stressed, I couldn't relax...." After a huge yawn, he added, "Glad you didn't say no."

Nate didn't acknowledge Tom's admission, instead replying, "Sleep well." Tom mumbled something unintelligible, and within moments his upper body was rising and falling with deep, regular breaths.

The activity and the stress relief should have had a similar effect on Nate. They didn't. Rather, he found himself wide awake, unable to settle. For nearly two hours, he lay staring into the dark, feeling less and less comfortable as the minutes passed. In his arms was a man with whom he shouldn't even have contact, except through sanctioned channels. He was risking the appearance of collusion, for the sake of sex? It was an incredibly foolish thing to do.

Nate was racked with guilt, and thought ahead to an awkward exchange with Tom in the morning. As he turned it over in his mind, a solution presented itself to him. He'd already planned to check out the next morning and drive to his dad's for a few days' visit. He would simply get up now and go before Tom awoke. His suitcase didn't need much attention—only a matter of packing up his toiletries in the bathroom and getting dressed.

But first he needed to extricate himself from the warm, sleeping body that was still draped over him.

It took him several minutes, and it was a careful, protracted process to do it without waking Tom, but he managed. Stealthily he slipped the few remaining items into his suitcase and quickly dressed. Then he stood at the end of the bed and watched Tom. He had rolled to his other side, and the back of one hand was pressed against his face as though he was leaning on his elbow. His mouth was slightly open, and his face, which always looked young, now seemed almost child-like.

Nate debated waking Tom before he left. He didn't *have* to wake him; the hotel would process an automatic checkout, which meant Nate could simply leave. In the end, though it felt vaguely sneaky, he wrote Tom a note on the hotel stationery.

Checkout's at 11 am

He put the note on the night table on top of Tom's iPhone where he couldn't possibly miss it. Then, after a long final look at the figure in the bed, he slipped out the door.

TOM WAS used to waking early. In the months since he'd joined the campaign, the alarm on his iPhone had become the one constant when he was waking up in hotels and airports, planes and the campaign bus. No matter where he was the alarm was always the same, and it was enough to keep him from feeling entirely disoriented as he returned to consciousness.

But waking at 4:00 a.m. to the soft, insistent chime and finding himself alone in someone else's hotel room was something else entirely. He'd fallen asleep next to a warm body, feeling like he was with a friend. But that "friend" had left as he slept, without a word—unless you counted an unsigned, hastily scribbled note telling you to be out by 11:00 a.m.

You got it, Tom thought crossly as he pulled on the jeans and sweatshirt he'd hastily thrown on after calling Nate. He trudged back across the frozen street, slipping as he hopped snowbanks, his sneakers ill-suited for the icy patches. Back in his own hotel room, he flopped on the unused bed, not bothering to undress or pull back the covers. He lay for several hours without returning to sleep, thinking.

He felt abandoned; worse, he was angry at himself that it had him so miffed. After the conversations he and Nate had shared, Tom believed they could consider themselves friends—new friends, of course, but at least warranting more than a stealthy getaway in the dead of night. But perhaps he was wrong. Maybe Nate regretted his spur-of-the-moment decision to let Tom come over, or maybe it was because Tom stayed.

There was no way to know without actually talking to Nate, and *that* wasn't going to happen. Nate hadn't cared to stay long enough to explain, so he supposed it would have to remain a mystery. All Tom could do was promise himself that in future he would hold Nate at the same distance as he would anyone else on the Michaels campaign… and never, ever ask anything of him again.

MARCH

PRIMARIES ARE an odd sort of creature, administered through a patchwork quilt of rules held by the party committees for each state. Some states allow every registered voter to cast a ballot in the primaries, regardless of political affiliation or lack thereof. Some states only allow registered party members to vote in the primaries. Some states hold caucuses in advance of their official primary date, an old way of doing things, and to some, a process that steps beyond the bounds of democracy and has far exceeded its useful lifespan.

With the Massachusetts and Ohio primaries falling on the same day, the Wagner campaign had to decide where they would invest the majority of their time. The finance coordinator had voiced her opinion that they would see greater eventual returns if they spent more time and money in Ohio now. A swing state, Ohio could always go either way in November and was never a sure thing for any party or candidate. Massachusetts, on the other hand, had supported the Democratic Party for as long as anyone in the campaign had been old enough to vote.

However, every other senior staffer, including Kim and her strategy consultants as well as Tom's boss, Mitch, disagreed with the beleaguered finance coordinator. The campaign would only benefit from investments in Ohio later if Bill Wagner actually won the nomination, and neglecting the very blue state of Massachusetts was not the way to accomplish that. Mitch also suggested that Erin Michaels's views might be too libertarian to truly win over Massachusetts Democrats, and Senator Wagner could make significant gains on that basis. The itinerary Kim proposed had the senator in Massachusetts on Friday and Saturday, and Ohio on Sunday, Monday, and Tuesday. It was decided, and the scheduling coordinator breathed a sigh of relief and went off to start making arrangements.

At issue were two states who, based on their political experiences at both the state and federal levels, would examine the same candidate from two rather different viewpoints. For weeks Tom had been hard at work on speeches for various events in both states. After Michigan it appeared his anger with Nate hadn't affected his writing mojo at all. If anything, it seemed to work in his favor when he had had to draft Wagner's speeches to contain a hint of an offensive against Erin Michaels.

Tom refused to stoop to slander or smear tactics. It didn't matter who he worked for or how much they paid him. It was dirty, lowest common denominator stuff, and he wouldn't do it. But he could rationalize. Erin Michaels *wasn't* the same kind of Democrat as Bill Wagner. Wagner's brand of liberalism probably *was* more in line with Massachusetts voters than Senator Michaels's… and that was the key.

Tom wove his words back and forth across the page like a shuttle guiding thread through a loom, working together layers of *accountability* and *ideals* and *future*, all the while spinning the finest thread of scorn between the lines, very subtly, a turn of phrase that discerning voters would understand as the verbal equivalent of a sly wink that whispered, *She's not the same kind of Democrat as you and me*. If there was another thread in that tapestry, one that expressed a hint of animosity or sharpness, it was visible only to Tom.

When his speeches for the Massachusetts rallies had been given to Mitch for review, it was on to the Ohio speeches. Ohio had to be treated completely differently, of course, and here Tom ran into some trouble. It was time to let go of the anger he'd allowed to fuel some of his Massachusetts work, and it wasn't easy to do. He was still stinging over the feeling that Nate had abandoned him in the middle of the night. He had to find a way to get past it so he could focus on what needed to be done.

By Friday night, when the first day in Massachusetts was behind them, he had met with limited success. Mitch, no doubt recognizing Tom's struggle, suggested that Tom needed a break. "The more you try to force it, the more you'll get yourself worked up about it," he counseled as they walked back to their hotel after dinner. "Take the night off and relax, and then come back to it tomorrow morning. You'll get it back."

"I suppose. But I'm worried that when I come back to it, nothing will have changed, and then I'll have lost that time…."

Mitch shook his head, holding his hand up to hush Tom. "I have faith in you. Anyway, don't borrow trouble from tomorrow. Take care of yourself tonight."

Tom thanked Mitch and wished him good night, heading to his hotel room. As he showered he contemplated how glad he was to have Mitch as his supervisor and mentor… and his friend. Mitch was a voice of reason when other staff members got a little too worked up. He had a talent for remaining calm and circumspect amid distractions. He was also an excellent boss who was interested not only in seeing his candidate win but also in mentoring his staff to success. Mitch was the stabilizing force on the campaign and in Tom's professional life. Tom was aware of his own talent as a speechwriter and was proud of it, but he recognized that, compared to Mitch, he was still a relative political neophyte. Tom's aspiration was that eventually he would be as well-respected and highly thought of as his boss was.

After his shower Tom visited the gift shop in the hotel lobby to invest in some junk food. On his way back to his room he knocked on Sarah's door and asked her to join him for an evening of mindless comedy on television. Her own boss having been a bit high-strung the last few days, Sarah was all too happy to come along, and when she offered to spring for a couple overpriced mini bottles of vodka from the hotel fridge, the night got even better.

NATHAN'S USUAL quiet intensity might have led those unfamiliar with him to believe that he was naturally irritable. In truth, he wasn't at all, and the difference was marked to those who knew him well. When he was at work, he had a singular focus. He rarely smiled, and seldom frowned. He used an economy of words, keeping his contributions succinct and to the point. He even moved differently, with a quiet, lithe grace and barely heard footsteps. Very seldom was he truly cross. But when he was, he was a different creature, one who petulantly banged cupboards, scowled, and muttered things under his breath as he slouched around.

Today he really was in a foul mood. After the disastrous night in Grand Rapids, he'd returned to Ann Arbor to stay with his father for a couple of days. The visit, however, had lacked its usual warmth, marred by the nagging feeling that leaving Tom without waking him was the wrong thing to do. The reception Erin had received in Massachusetts had been lukewarm at best—not even close to what they'd hoped for. The campaign had fared better in Ohio, but Nate's mood hadn't improved. The longer his conscience nagged the grumpier he became.

Now, on the Friday after the primary, he was back in DC, and things were going from bad to worse.

"Are you actually illiterate, or can you just not follow instructions?" The source of his ire, a volunteer at the campaign headquarters in Arlington, blanched. "Did you attend the same training session all the other volunteers did?"

"Y-yes." The man's stammer was clearly audible throughout the office, where everyone else had gone silent.

"Do you remember being told not to answer questions from reporters?"

Before the man could answer, the volunteer coordinator stepped in. "Nate, I think you've said enough. Anyway, volunteers fall under my jurisdiction."

Nathan glared at the man a moment longer and, after a final parting shot at his intelligence, retreated to his office, banging the door behind him.

Less than an hour later, Jason Eisenberg knocked on his office door. By that time, Nate had calmed a bit and had already phoned the volunteer to apologize for losing his temper, if not for the necessity of setting the man straight. He'd gotten the man's voice mail—the poor man probably thought he was going to get yelled at some more—but left a conciliatory message. Answering the knock on his door and finding Jason there shouldn't have been surprising, under the circumstances.

"Nate. Can we chat for a few minutes?" Jason's statement sounded like a request, but they both knew it really wasn't.

"Of course." Nate set aside his iPhone and put his office extension on Do Not Disturb. "I thought you were on the Hill today?"

Jason closed the door and sat in one of Nate's chairs. "Sheri called and asked me to come. She said there was a bit of an issue here earlier. Want to tell me what happened?"

"I came in to return some calls and get some papers before we go to Mississippi. I'm out on the floor talking to Sheri, and I overhear this guy answering questions on the phone. And it's not, like, what the office hours are and the numbers from Ohio and Massachusetts. It's, like, foreign policy and late-term abortion—big issues. How many times do we have to tell volunteers that they're never to answer questions from the press, to tell reporters they have to talk to Susan Pollard? How many ways can we say it to make it clear? And I….." Here Nate stopped because Jason clearly already knew how he'd reacted.

"You lost it."

"Yes."

"Yelled?"

"Yes."

"Told him if he couldn't follow simple instructions he might be too stupid to vote?" Nate winced, then nodded. Jason continued, "Well, maybe you were correct in your assessment. But now we've lost a volunteer, and Erin has almost certainly lost a voter. And that voter is going to tell his friends, and they'll tell their friends, and maybe along the way somebody tells the press, yeah?" Another nod from Nate, and this time Jason was silent until Nate met his eyes. "You apologize?"

"Yes. Well, I called, but I got voice mail. I did leave an apology for losing my temper."

"It's not like you to yell, Nate. I've seen you deal with volunteers and press and staff, and even if you roll your eyes after they're out of sight, you still manage to keep your temper when you're face to face with them. Normally you're better than any of us when it comes to that." He peered at Nathan critically. "You look exhausted. I know what the pace is like here, but we have to be responsible enough for ourselves that we speak up when we're worn out and need a day to rest. From now on you need to keep better tabs on that, is that clear?"

"Yes, sir."

"And I want you to start by taking this weekend off."

"But…. Mississippi—" Nathan started, but Jason interrupted.

"Don't argue with me, please. I think I can manage Mississippi on my own," Jason retorted dryly. "I'll be back Wednesday morning, and you know what comes then."

"Illinois," Nate replied. There would be a debate Saturday night at Loyola University before Tuesday's Illinois primary.

"Exactly. I need you at one hundred percent for Illinois, so you have to take care of yourself in the meantime. Stay home and relax, rest up, watch a season of something on Netflix." Jason got up from his chair and started toward the door, turning back to Nate to caution, "Not *The West Wing*, though, right?" Nate managed to crack a smile at that, and Jason seemed to find it mildly encouraging. "See if you can get rid of those dark circles under your eyes. I'll see you here, Wednesday morning."

"I'll be here," Nate replied, lifting his coffee cup in salute before Jason nodded and continued on his way.

Nate spent the weekend at home as instructed, sleeping in and catching up on non-work-related things. He watched an entire season of his favorite comedy and puttered around his apartment. He called his best college friend who was now married with three children and living in Cleveland, and they talked for over an hour. He called his brother and his dad. For five whole days he lived slowly—or at least it felt slow in comparison to his usual pace—and for the first time, he thoroughly enjoyed it. It was a far cry from his usual vacation-induced battle with himself, where he had to force himself not to compulsively check his e-mail and news websites. He set his iPhone to ring only when he had an incoming call but not to notify him of e-mails and text messages, opting to check those once a day. Instead of itching to get back to work and back in the loop, he found himself letting that stuff drift away from him for a while. He enjoyed his downtime tremendously.

The only moments of discomfort came when he thought about Tom. He would remember Tom at random times, and it was always accompanied by a brief pang of angst in the pit of his stomach. He tried to reason it away, kept reminding himself that after the first time he and Tom slept together he'd run into him again at the airport in Atlanta and it was fine—they'd greeted each other and chatted pleasantly.

Nate wanted that to happen again. He needed to know his rash decision hadn't damaged their fledgling friendship. The CBS network debate was a week away. He and Tom would both be at the debate. He would see Tom and catch his eye and see him return a smile, and then he'd know they were okay....

... he hoped.

NATE'S RUN-IN with the volunteer didn't make the papers, but there were whispers in Mississippi that weekend that Nathan Harris had been told by Jason Eisenberg not to accompany the Michaels campaign to the state... and those whispers made their way to Tom McAlindon's ears. As is usually the case with gossip, no one had a clear picture on why Nate had been benched for the weekend. Tom hadn't seen or spoken to Nate since Michigan and had no inside information—not that he'd have shared it if he did. Though there was little chance he'd have run into Nate in Mississippi, their short history illustrated that it wasn't impossible. In the almost two weeks since they'd seen each other, Tom had come to the conclusion that Nate didn't want to see him again, so knowing he would avoid an awkward encounter should have brought him some relief, and it did... mostly.

But in addition to still harboring some hurt, he was also a bit concerned. He couldn't imagine what would keep Nathan from Jason Eisenberg's side, short of illness—or punishment for an indiscretion? As much as Tom didn't want Nate to be sick, he was almost hoping for it rather than the alternative. Regardless, the weekend passed with no further word and no whisper of inappropriate behavior, and by Tuesday night when Bill Wagner was being declared the winner in Mississippi, Tom was getting good at putting it out of his mind.

That night the campaign staff stayed overnight in Jackson. There were no events scheduled until Thursday, giving them the small luxury of sleeping in Wednesday before hitting the road for Illinois. Their route took them directly through Memphis, where they stayed for the night. With the exception of Bill and his wife Rebecca, who opted for a quiet evening in, the group went out for dinner at a barbecue joint. It was a relaxed, and at times raucous, evening with lots of laughter. Everyone had been working hard for weeks, and it was great to think and talk about something else. Especially for those who didn't know the others well, like Tom, they enjoyed the opportunity to get to know their colleagues a bit better.

After dinner Sarah talked Tom into going dancing at a club. It was the first time in Memphis for both of them, and Sarah wanted to experience the nightlife. They drank a little and danced a lot, and laughed almost continuously. Tom had clicked with Sarah almost as soon as they met last fall when he joined the campaign, but it wasn't until they'd begun to spend these days and weeks on the road that their friendship was really cemented. Sarah employed sarcasm liberally and had a biting wit that Tom loved, especially when he was getting all serious and focused on his work. They returned to their hotel after midnight, slightly tipsy, better for having had the night off.

The next day they were back to work, Tom writing away and Sarah doing what she did to make Kim's job easier. The campaign made its way across the southern part of Illinois, stopping in several smaller towns. With the exception of Chicago, Illinois tended to support the Republican

Party, and the rallies weren't exceptionally well attended. Friday night in Chicago there was a fundraiser for Wagner; the team got to get dressed up in the fancy clothes they'd brought especially for this night. It had been a stretch for Tom, who loved his jeans and T-shirt, to get used to wearing a suit every day to work; wearing a tuxedo was something else altogether.

Saturday evening both teams were scheduled to attend Northwestern's Pick-Staiger Hall for the network debate. Tom had always enjoyed watching debates, though he was much too shy to ever participate in one, preferring to let someone else voice his political beliefs in the form of the speeches he wrote.

Tom had a few hours off during the afternoon before the debate. He was filled with nervous energy in anticipation of the evening's events—not only the debate itself but knowing Nate would be there and he'd see him for the first time since Michigan. He couldn't sit still, definitely couldn't sit in his hotel room and do nothing while he had what felt like pure adrenaline coursing through his veins. He needed to get outside. He needed to run.

He dressed in layers—it was still cold in Chicago though spring was only a few days away—and headed out. From his downtown hotel, he jogged by the Art Institute of Chicago, past Millennium Park and the Cloud Gate sculpture, which distracted him from his run for a bit; he had to take a few minutes to approach the sculpture, walk around and under and appreciate its flawless mirrored beauty. Back on the pavement and he was heading down Randolph Street before circling back around toward the hotel. It took a while but he finally started to feel the adrenaline burning off and pleasant endorphins taking its place. When he arrived back at his hotel he felt much more relaxed, able to collapse on his bed and chill for an hour before he had to get up to shower and prepare for the evening.

He ate a light dinner and was putting on the jacket of his best suit when there was a knock on his door. It was Mitch, there to tell him they'd be leaving in ten minutes. The campaign bus was waiting for them on the street in front of the hotel, and they all boarded it for the ride up to Evanston where Northwestern's main campus was located.

Tom had never been to the Northwestern campus. Sarah, a Chicago native, had attended Loyola but had visited the Northwestern campus many times in her life. The concert hall where the debate was to be held was an impressive building; Tom was fascinated with the plastic hexagons suspended from the ceiling, which served to amplify the sound from the stage. He had little time, though, to focus on details that weren't directly related to the debate. When members of the public started to fill the auditorium, the campaign staff gathered in one of the rooms backstage. Their team had arrived first, but it wasn't long until someone mentioned that the Michaels team was there, too, inhabiting another part of the backstage area. A few minutes before the debate was to begin, they wished Bill good luck and headed out to the auditorium to take their seats.

Sarah had spent her afternoon off with her parents at their home in Lakeview. Sarah was an only child and as such, was the sole subject of their parenting focus. She'd kept Tom entertained at the fundraiser the evening before with stories of their overinvolvement in her life. "I love my mom and dad and I know I'm lucky to have parents who care about what happens to me," she admitted, "but sometimes I wish they'd diversified. Maybe if they had another kid it would take some of the focus off me."

Now that she'd spent the afternoon with them, she was full of new anecdotes. Chief among their concerns was that, working so hard, she would be lonely. "And by lonely, they mean 'unmarried,'" she whispered as Tom escorted her to their seats. "My mother doesn't understand how my career can be so fulfilling. I mean, yes, I do want to get married someday, but I'm only twenty-eight. I have lots of time. Years. Decades. Ah, there they are." As she spoke she waved at her parents in their seats, about halfway back in the auditorium. As they returned her wave Tom looked at Sarah. Despite all her complaints, she was obviously pleased that they were there to watch the debate and be part of her career world for a little while.

Tom and Sarah took their seats in the front row. Tom couldn't help leaning over to whisper to Sarah, "I'm guessing you didn't use the word 'decades' when you were talking to them this afternoon."

Sarah nearly burst out laughing. "Holy shit," she whispered when she'd successfully fought back the giggles. "And give my mother a stroke? No."

Any reply Tom may have had was prevented by the debate's moderator asking for quiet from the audience as the network's television coverage was about to begin. A hush fell in the auditorium, and the television producer gave instructions to the audience. Upon the producer's cue, the audience began to applaud, the moderator welcomed everyone in attendance at the hall and watching on television, and the candidates were introduced and took their place on the stage amid thunderous applause from the thousand-or-so audience members. From then on, Tom had no thought to spare except for what was taking place onstage. He and Mitch both had their spiral notebooks to jot down their thoughts and observations as the debate proceeded.

The theme of the debate was foreign policy, and the repartee between Erin and Bill was thrilling. Bill countered Erin's points with ease; Erin responded with grace. Each argued their points intelligently and earnestly. Those who truly enjoyed the art of debate were treated to an excellent contest of words, and those who were simply trying to decide who to support got to compare and contrast their different platforms.

In the wrap-up coverage of the evening's events, the people who made their money commenting on politics would gleefully dissect each answer, every look, every grimace. They would try to determine a "winner," because there had to be a winner in these things; but tonight they would have difficulty coming to a consensus on that point. The commentators who weren't already in the tank for a particular candidate would answer honestly, when all was said and done, that there was no clear victor.

In the slowly emptying auditorium, Sarah took Tom over to her parents to introduce them. Sarah was a carbon copy of her mother. Both Mr. and Mrs. Lonstein were very friendly and made pleasant small talk with Tom for a few minutes. As Mr. Lonstein was asking Sarah something about the day of the primary, Tom looked back down the aisle toward the stage and was caught in the gaze of Nathan Harris, standing slightly apart from his own colleagues, looking across the empty seats directly at Tom.

Tom had managed, from the time he'd reentered the auditorium before the debate began, not to try to find Nathan in the crowd or even look in the direction of the Michaels team. Now Nathan's eyes were locked with his, and a second later, Nathan gave him a tentative smile. Tom managed to hide his surprise and, without returning a smile of his own, he turned and refocused his attention on the Lonsteins. It was nearly impossible to keep from sneaking glances toward the front, but by herculean effort he managed it. At least twenty minutes passed before

Sarah told her parents she and Tom both needed to rejoin their colleagues backstage. When Tom finally turned back to head to the backstage area, the Michaels team were nowhere to be seen.

Erin Michaels took the Illinois primary by a 4 percent margin. It was the widest margin of victory so far, aside from the candidates' home states. Commentators gave credit to the more moderate areas of the state that lay outside Chicago, as well as an industry bill Michaels had cosponsored three years before, one that had resulted in some tax cuts for the manufacturers in the state, prompting an increase in production and subsequently in hiring. The bill had even made the unions happy—not to the point that they came out and endorsed Michaels, but they didn't endorse Bill Wagner either, and that hurt.

Tom was discouraged by the results in Illinois. Yes, he'd grown tired of the constant dead heat between the two candidates, but this wasn't how he'd hoped the tie would be broken. As always, Bill spoke to his supporters in Chicago after the results had come in, his speech intended as a balm for disappointed hopes, gratitude for their support and hard work, and encouragement to go on. Maybe it was because Tom had written the words himself, but he didn't find them comforting in the least.

Shortly after midnight the Wagner campaign bus left Chicago, heading southeast toward DC. Tom had been on the road for eleven days and he was so ready to get back to his own place, his own bed, and stop living out of a suitcase for a while. The next primary was over a month away. There was another network debate in a couple of weeks but it would actually be held in DC, and the pace would be nowhere near what it had been for the last few months. Mitch had already suggested to Tom that he take a few days off to bookend the weekend when they got back to DC, and Tom had gratefully accepted. He was exhausted, and a four-day weekend sounded like paradise.

NATE WAS accustomed to a clear conscience.

Not that he was a rigidly moral person, but he had a pretty conservative set of standards regarding honesty and ethics. He knew what he could live with, and he found it worthwhile to remain within those limits.

It was decidedly uncomfortable then, when Nate smiled at Tom McAlindon at the Northwestern debate and Tom looked right through him, turned his back, and didn't look at Nathan again. That small voice, the one that had nagged at Nathan for a few days after Michigan, had eventually faded away. Now it was back, and its return was both immediate and vociferous.

Nate barely slept that night. He tossed and turned for hours, and was forced to admit that his conscience was making him miserable. He couldn't leave things as they were, not for his own sake and not for Tom's. He *had* to talk to Tom—somehow, he had to talk to him.

He'd have to be careful about how and where he broached it. Calling him was out of the question—telephone records were far too easy to obtain. Sunday morning after the debate, he asked one of the campaign aides to get him a copy of Bill Wagner's schedule while he was in Chicago; fortunately it wasn't an unusual request for a senior staff member to make. He hoped his path would cross Tom's again, that maybe he could talk to him sooner than later, but no such luck. There was no overlap in the two campaigns' itineraries. It had been a long shot anyway. Nate resolved that he'd seek Tom out at the end of the week when they were both back in Washington.

It wasn't easy to wait for the end of the week to arrive. He was busy enough up until the primary was over, and the results were certainly cause for celebration among everyone involved with the campaign. Back in DC, though, when he had free time, he spent much of it thinking about Tom, and not just about how he desired Tom's forgiveness. His thoughts wandered to dangerous, impossible things… kissing Tom… the press of his body… spending time with him… having a relationship with him.

Always he was engaged in an internal battle between what he knew he should do and what he wanted so much. Contemplating his options didn't help—the more he thought about it, the less power he had to resist the pull toward Tom. Friday night when he'd finished work for the weekend and left the campaign office, he knew where he was going… and it wasn't home.

He waited nervously at the front desk of Tom's building as the doorman called up to announce his visit. What if Tom said no? What if he told the doorman he didn't want to see Nate and to ask him to leave? Nate's palms were damp with sweat. He'd run over so many possibilities in his mind, and now that he was hanging by a thread, he was trembling.

"You can go up, Mr.… Nathan," the doorman told him, using the only name Nate had been willing to give him.

"Thank you," Nate replied, already on his way to the elevator bank. He rode the elevator, his heart pounding in his ears. Out of the elevator and down the hall to Tom's apartment, and his hand was trembling as he raised it to knock. The knock seemed thunderous, echoing throughout the hall. He heard Tom's footsteps approaching, and took a deep breath.

Before him stood Tom, wearing only a pair of black flannel sleep pants. His hair was damp-dark and messy from where he'd rubbed it with the towel in his hand. Droplets of water still clung to his bare shoulders and chest.

Nate noticed that Tom deliberately opened the door only as wide as his shoulders, then leaned casually against the doorframe. Wordlessly he cocked an eyebrow at Nate.

Okay, thought Nate, *you're going to make me go first*. "Hi."

"Hello." Tom's voice was flat.

"How are you?"

"Fine." There was an awkward pause before Tom, looking like he was forcing himself, asked, "You?"

"I'm okay."

Tom nodded. "Why are you here?"

Nate winced a little at Tom's bluntness. "I wanted to see you, see how you're doing."

"Well, here I am and I'm fine, so if that's all…." He stepped back as though preparing to close the door.

Nate reached out. "Tom, wait. Please?"

Tom sighed. "What do you want, Nathan?"

This was going even worse than Nate had expected. If he would only have a few seconds before Tom closed the door in his face, he'd have to go for the direct approach. "I saw you at the debate Saturday. I know you saw me, too, but you acted like you didn't."

Tom gave him a scornful look. "I was with my colleagues, and in front of about a thousand citizens and members of the press. What did you expect me to do?"

"You can't return a smile?" Nate asked.

"Oh, are we allowed to smile at each other? I'm going to have to get you to write down all your rules for me. I can't keep them straight."

Nate ignored the barb, and tried to keep his voice calm and level, though his stomach felt like ice. "I know you're angry that I left you in the hotel in Michigan. You have every right to be."

"Well, that's generous, thanks." Tom's voice dripped with sarcasm. "But I don't need you to give me permission to be pissed off about it."

"Tom, I want to tell you that I'm sorry."

"For what? Fucking off in the middle of the night without a word?"

"Yes. I should have woken you. I'm sorry." Tom regarded Nate for a long moment, one eyebrow cocked appraisingly. Eventually Nate asked, "Would it be okay if I come in?"

"Why?"

"I'd like to talk about it. Preferably not in your hallway."

"Afraid my neighbors will hear us and turn you in?" Tom's tone was sneering, but he stepped back, opening the door wider so Nate could enter the apartment. Once he had closed the door, he turned to face Nate, his feet braced and his arms folded across his chest. "You're inside. Say what you have to say."

Nate's hands were shaking, and he clasped them behind his back to steady them. "I shouldn't have left without waking you. I felt... well, I felt guilty about being with you."

"Charming. Just what everyone hopes to hear."

"I'm not trying to hurt you, Tom. I'm trying to be honest and explain what happened. I'm human, and I made a mistake. You don't know how sorry I am that I hurt you."

Tom exhaled a deep sigh, and turned away, walking to the breakfast bar at the end of the kitchen. For a long moment Nate couldn't tell if he was going to accept his apology, or tell him to get out. When at last he spoke, the ugly harshness was gone.

"It did hurt. I know I was the one who called you, and it was only supposed to be a hookup. But I thought maybe we were becoming friends, and then... you were gone." Tom spoke to his feet, his voice barely audible. "It felt like shit. Because someone who thinks of me as a friend wouldn't do that."

Nate stepped closer to where Tom stood. He had to clench his hands to keep himself from reaching out for Tom. "I panicked." His voice was pleading. "I'm sorry."

"Okay." Tom finally turned to meet Nate's gaze, his near-black eyes fathomless. "It's okay. Thank you for apologizing."

Nate hardly knew what he was doing. He moved toward Tom automatically, gathering him into his arms. "Thank you." The words were whispered into Tom's damp hair. It took Tom a moment to reciprocate, his arms sliding around Nate's waist. They stood for a moment, holding each other.

It was obvious that they had physical chemistry—Nate had many times remembered Tom's lithe body, the way he smelled, the way he looked when he came. Now, with Tom in his arms, he realized how often he had also thought of Tom's other qualities: his intelligence, his kindness, his sense of humor. He wanted more of those things in his life, if only Tom was willing to let him.

Nate pulled back enough that he could look down into Tom's eyes. He didn't want to presume, and he was wary of hurting Tom again. Carefully he placed a soft, tender kiss on Tom's cheek, close enough to the corner of his mouth that Tom would know it was not simply a friendly kiss. Tom inhaled sharply.

"What do you want from me?" Tom's voice was husky.

"I want to be with you."

"For the night? Because I don't want it that way. Not if you're going to leave again."

Nathan took Tom's face gently in his hands. "I won't leave unless you tell me to."

Tom peered at Nate for a long moment, as though searching his face for the sincerity of his promise. Suddenly something shifted, sliding back into place, and Tom was kissing him. His lips, warm and soft against Nate's, parted with a moan. Nate felt Tom yield, and a fire spread through him. His hands slid up and over Tom's bare shoulders to rest against his neck, thumbs stroking Tom's cheeks. Tom pushed Nate's wool topcoat off his shoulders and tossed it to the side. Together they slowly removed the rest of Nathan's clothes and the one article of clothing Tom was wearing, letting their hands explore as they gradually made their way to Tom's bed.

Nate gently pushed Tom down to lie on the bed and knelt beside him, his hands stroking over the unmarked expanse of bare skin. Tom was so beautiful… dark eyes nearly swallowed up by pupils blown black with desire… his skin pale golden in the low light of his night table lamp. Nate wanted to look and touch and kiss and *savor*.

After, Nate bid Tom stay put while he went to the bathroom to retrieve a warm washcloth. When he'd cleaned them both and thrown the cloth into the hamper, he returned to sit on the bed beside Tom. For long moments Nate was the subject of Tom's steady gaze, and couldn't help feeling like Tom was waiting for him to get up and leave. Nate met his scrutiny unflinchingly. "Would it be okay if I stayed?"

"You said you weren't going anywhere, so I guess you better." Tom's tone was teasing.

Nate exhaled a long breath and nuzzled a kiss into Tom's soft blonde hair. He slid under the covers beside Tom and gathered him into his arms. Tom murmured a little sigh, and they both drifted off to sleep.

TOM WOKE the next morning as pale sunshine was making its way across his living room wall. He yawned and stretched deeply, feeling sore, almost bruised inside. For a groggy moment, he couldn't understand why—then he remembered. With a start he was fully awake. He turned quickly in bed, and there was Nate lying beside him, watching him. "Hey. Morning," Nate greeted, his voice sleep-roughened. He leaned close to kiss Tom. Then, one hand gently stroking Tom's cheek, he murmured, "I honestly didn't come here expecting this to happen. I only wanted to apologize."

Tom reached out and ran his thumb across Nate's brow, smoothing out the creases there. "It's okay, Nate. We're good." He smiled at Nate, and was rewarded with a matching smile and another kiss. Tom licked at the seam of Nate's mouth until Nate opened to him with an appreciative hum, stretching his legs out to cover the length of Tom's body.

Tom flexed his hips upward, pressing his hardening length into Nate's. Nate gasped, breaking their kiss to work his way across Tom's neck and shoulders, down his chest and over his stomach, finally going down on Tom… and neither of them came back up for an hour.

Eventually sated, they lay tangled up in each other. "So… I'm off all weekend."

"Mm-hmm," Tom murmured noncommittally as he carded his fingers through Nate's thick black hair. "Me too. Till Tuesday."

"Anything planned?"

"Yep, I plan to stay home and do absolutely nothing."

Nate chuckled. "Good plan." He hesitated before adding, "Want someone to do nothing with?"

With a grin Tom replied, "Are you asking if you can stay longer?"

A faint flush crept across Nate's cheeks. "Maybe. Till tomorrow, anyway. I have to work Monday. But if you want to have the weekend to yourself, I totally understand—"

"I'd love it if you stayed."

Nate's cheeks flexed against Tom's skin as they pulled up into a smile. After a moment he replied, "Cool."

Tom knew Nate would hate being called *adorable*, but in his mind there was no other word for it. Tom was completely charmed by this sweet and careful Nate, who had finally apologized for Michigan and angled for an invitation to spend the weekend. It was obvious that he really wanted to stay, but didn't want to impose or rush things.

Adorable Nate remained the rest of the weekend, helping make breakfast, watching *Friends* reruns with Tom, and talking. It was hard for Tom to remember that they'd only had a couple of actual get-to-know-you conversations before. Eventually the television was forgotten as their exchanges grew more personal, covering deeper topics. Tom had briefly alluded to not having a relationship with his parents; now Nate asked Tom to tell him about them. Tom described his coming out experience. He could see that Nate was affected by it, a look of deep sympathy darkening his handsome face along with no small amount of anger. "That is *bullshit*. I will never understand people who can do that. Aren't parents supposed to love their children unconditionally?" He took Tom's hand in his. "I'm sorry, Tom."

"Thank you. It's sweet that you're so pissed off on my behalf. You know what, though? I'm sort of okay with it." Nate looked skeptical. "No, it's true. I mean, at first, of course I was devastated, and I was really angry for a long time. Maybe I still am, a little. Mostly, though… well, it's not that I don't care. But time does heal, and it helps you get perspective. This is who I am; I didn't do anything wrong choosing to live my life honestly. They've made their decision, and if that's how they feel, it's better that they're not in my life. I wouldn't do anything differently."

"Good. They're the ones who are missing out."

Tom squeezed Nate's hand. "Thank you for saying so. And at least I was already an adult. Plus, I had my grandparents, and they became like my surrogate parents. When you think of kids that are kicked out when they're still in high school… or the ones who go through even worse… there are a lot of people who have much worse things to deal with." He cast around for something that might lighten the conversation a bit. "Anyway, what about your parents? Do they still live in Michigan?"

Nate looked stricken. Slowly he replied, "My dad still lives in Michigan. My mom… passed away. A year ago in January."

"Oh… Nate." Tom felt as though a rock had dropped into his stomach. "I'm sorry." Nate looked down at their joined hands, saying nothing for a long time. "I'm sorry," Tom said again in a whisper, stroking Nate's hand with his own.

Nate nodded, swallowing. "She had cancer," he said in a strangled voice. "Breast cancer, first, three years ago. She had treatment and a double mastectomy. A year later, her liver. More treatment. And then they found mets on her lungs, and that was enough." He looked up at Tom, his eyes swimming. A lump grew in Tom's throat. "She was a nurse, she knew what was coming. And she was exhausted. She told us she was done with treatment, done feeling like shit all the time. She decided she wanted to go home. We tried to talk her out of it—" Here, again, he paused, and tears slid down to his jaw. Tom released Nate's hands to reach for a box of tissues. "My brother was the last to give in. She spent some time at our cottage and at the house, and eventually she went to hospice. She died on New Year's Day."

"What was her name?"

"Mary." Nate wiped his tears, and Tom was struck by how different this Nate was to the man he'd first run into at the Iowa caucuses, only a couple of months ago when Nate had seemed intent on portraying himself as a jerk. In the meantime Tom had gotten small glimpses of the man inside, but any positive opinions he might have been forming had been abruptly ended by what happened in Michigan. It was only now that he felt like he was seeing the real Nate. Not the campaign staffer, not the senator's aide, not the man driven by strategy and polls. This was a man who loved his parents and brother, who wished he could have a dog but knew his busy schedule made it impossible, who loved the ocean and had never really liked snow despite growing up in Michigan.

Nate was learning things about Tom, too, such as when they were making sandwiches for lunch and Nate opened the refrigerator. "Oh my God," Tom heard him say from inside the fridge door.

"What?"

Nate's head reappeared, his eyes wide. "You have, like, fourteen jars of mustard here." He rummaged through the assorted bottles that took up one entire shelf on the door. "They're all different."

Tom joined him. "Uh… yeah. Well, different mustards go with different foods. Like this one…." He pulled out a small, squat jar, its contents brownish-yellow. "This is deli mustard. It's pretty bold—goes well with cured meats. This one is called Sweet with Heat—you can only get it in Canada. A friend from college sends it to me. It's perfect on honey garlic sausages. This is a classic Dijon…." Tom continued, giving Nate a brief overview of each of the jars on the shelf, finishing with, "And the old stand-by, plain prepared yellow mustard."

Nate grinned. "Really? That isn't too common for you?"

Tom laughed out loud, replying, "Oh, shut up." He took the yellow mustard out of the fridge, grabbing the deli mustard for himself. "What else am I going to put on hot dogs?"

Nate put a generous slathering on his sandwiches. "You should have a blog. A gourmet mustard blog."

"It's been done," Tom answered, smirking, to which Nate shook his head.

As they ate, their conversation returned to more sensible topics, but as the day went on Tom found himself thinking about the silliness and the teasing. It was the first time they'd really engaged in that sort of dialogue, and it been very natural and easy between them. It gave him a warm feeling and did nothing to dismiss the word *adorable* from his head.

Over the rest of the weekend, Tom and Nate spent a lot of time talking and a lot of time doing things that required very few words. Tom was completely enthralled with Nate's long, lanky body. He found he could spend hours obsessing over it, running his hands through the dark hair on his legs and the patches on his chest and stomach. Tom voiced his appreciation of it Sunday morning as Nate lay stretched out naked on Tom's bed, his eyes closed, enjoying the feel of Tom's hands roaming up and down his legs. "You can thank my Greek ancestry," Nate murmured.

"Harris doesn't sound very Greek," Tom remarked, to which Nate chuckled.

"No, the Harrises are Welsh. My mother was Greek."

"What was her maiden name?"

"Papastathopoulos." Tom stared. Nate continued, "I know, right? When she was in school, the kids called her Mary Alphabet. Imagine learning to spell that as a little kid?"

"No shit. McAlindon was bad enough. Bet you're glad your name is Harris."

"Exactly. What about you? McAlindon is, what, Scottish?"

"Irish. My great-grandfather, who was also named Tom McAlindon, emigrated from Londonderry in 1925. He came to Boston completely alone at the age of sixteen, with two pounds in his pocket. His mother had died and his father remarried, and when he was sixteen his step-mother told him and his brother that they had to leave."

"She made them leave the country?"

"She gave them a choice between the United States and Australia. He'd heard there were a lot of Irish people going to Boston, so that's where he went. Married my great-grandmother, who had also come from Ireland, and they lived in Boston for the rest of their lives. Anyway, I seem to have gotten the full Irish blast in my genes, which is why I'm short, blonde and relatively hairless," he finished, shrugging self-consciously.

Nate took hold of Tom's arms and rolled them together. Tom ended on his back with Nate kneeling over him. "Except for here," Nate murmured huskily, nosing into Tom's armpit, "here…," kissing the very few hairs on Tom's chest, "mmm, here…," against the fuzz of his lower belly, "and here." He dragged his tongue around the base of Tom's cock. He paused long enough to whisper, "This is my favorite," before continuing his oral tour of that area. He was very good at it, and as Tom threaded his fingers through Nate's thick black hair, he decided that Nate could spend as much time there as he wanted.

DESPITE NATE'S promise to stay, Tom knew he and Nate needed to talk about the nature of their relationship. He didn't want the weekend to end without coming to some understanding they could both live with, because he didn't want to get hurt again. Sunday afternoon they sat down and hashed it out.

"If anyone found out about us, you know it would be… well, bad. Like, career-ending bad." Nate looked at his lap, where Tom's feet were resting on his legs.

"I know."

"There would be questions about our loyalties and whether we shared information about the candidates, about our jobs."

"I know this should go without saying, but I'm going to say it anyway." Tom's near-black eyes were serious. "We can't talk about it—any of it. Not about our jobs, or our schedules, where the campaigns will be, what we'll be doing, who we'll be seeing."

"I agree. Some detail might seem so small and insignificant, but you never know what insight that thing could provide."

"Exactly. So no shop talk."

"Campaigns only? Or political talk in general?"

Tom frowned slightly as he thought. "Well… it's kind of a slippery slope. Our jobs are so closely intertwined with the political world. How do you have a political discussion without your job coming into it at some point? I think it's safer to have a total embargo. And then if some information does leak, your conscience and mine can be clear, because we'll both know it wasn't us."

"Which is good for the campaigns, but it's also good for us. Because let's say you tell me something that could be beneficial to Erin Michaels. Do I share that information with my campaign, knowing I'll be hurting you? Or do I keep my mouth shut and let my candidate slip behind, knowing I could have done something about it? We're both going to do whatever we can to get our candidate elected. I don't want to have to choose between you and my job. Obviously, if I could make that choice, we wouldn't be having this conversation. But, Tom?" Nate looked like he was steeling himself for something unpleasant, and Tom felt a flutter of anxiety in his stomach. "I'm committed to my candidate. If something comes up that could jeopardize her chances, my job is going to have to take precedence over my personal life."

It wasn't a happy thought, but Tom was grateful to Nate for his honesty. "I would never expect anything less of you."

They made plans to spend the next weekend together at Tom's apartment; Nate's was much closer to Capitol Hill and in a highly visible area. They knew they wouldn't be talking on the phone, texting or e-mailing before then. All forms of electronic communication jeopardized the secrecy of what they were embarking upon. As he prepared to leave, Nate kissed Tom deeply, inhaling his scent and soaking up the warmth of his body once more, before stroking his cheek gently and murmuring, "Have a good week."

Tom whispered, "You too," and opened the door. Nate gave him one last grin, and was gone.

Outside, the late afternoon sun was painting the city pink-orange. Nate emerged from Tom's building, inhaling the cool, fresh spring air that gradually chilled as the sun waned. He and Tom had spent nearly forty-eight hours living a fantasy, cut off from e-mails and phone calls, only having watched the news once... it was like having his eyes closed for two days. Now they were open once more, and the world had gone on. It was time to reengage in reality.

Reality brought with it the consciousness that this arrangement, the understanding he and Tom had, was far from perfect. Nate was a very private person, and that would have been the case regardless of who he was seeing, but it was one thing to choose privacy, and something else to enforce absolute concealment.

Nate especially hated the thought of deceiving Jason Eisenberg, his mentor and the closest friend he'd made in his professional life. He wanted Jason to know about his... boyfriend? Nate's eyes widened at the thought of that word, and he decided he wasn't ready to use it yet. He wanted Jason to know about this part that made him happy, made him feel hopeful and excited. He knew that, under any other circumstances, Jason would be glad for him. He might be skeptical; Jason didn't think a political life was conducive to successful relationships, citing the divorces and separations of so many of their colleagues, Erin included. He would still hope for the best for Nate.

No, it wasn't perfect, but the alternative was not seeing Tom at all... and to Nate, that seemed impossible.

NOW THAT there was a significant break before the next primary, nearly a month away at the end of April, Tom's work schedule became much more reasonable. The campaign wouldn't even have to travel for Thursday night's debate because it was here in the city, at Georgetown University. For the first time in almost three months, Tom didn't feel like he was running a never-ending marathon. Every morning he got up early and went for a run before work; every evening he was home well before dark. He felt well-rested and happy. The days were getting longer, the temperature was getting warmer, and the city was awash in soft pink waves of cherry blossoms. Tom walked around all week with a smile on his face, always on the verge of humming a tune.

But he knew the spring in his step didn't arise solely from his easier work schedule. He was buzzing on the weekend spent with Nate, still not quite able to believe how different he'd felt not even a week before. Until he and Nate had given in and admitted they wanted more, Tom hadn't realized how much of a toll the stress had taken on him. He was a lot less tense now. Of course he knew that forty-eight hours and a hell of a lot of sex had contributed significantly to the release of that tension, but it was more than that. He could get back to loving his job and thriving on the excitement of it, without a return of the negative stress he'd felt when he was fretting over Nate's confusing behavior.

Thursday brought with it a buzz of anticipation for the debate. Being local provided candidates the rare benefit of sleeping in their own beds the night before and spending a relatively quiet day leading up to the big night. Tom and his colleagues joined Bill Wagner at his Georgetown home partway through the morning. Everyone in their casual clothes, they had a quiet day of doing not very much. They watched a bit of television, snacked on the trays Bill's wife Rebecca had brought in for them, and otherwise relaxed. It was very different from any of the other predebate days, in Tom's experience. He wished they could all be so low-key. By late afternoon, though, the excitement had begun to build to something they could no longer ignore. One by one, people excused themselves to change into the dress clothes they'd brought along, and nerves began to manifest themselves in Tom's stomach.

Senator Wagner and the staff left his house at five to head to the Georgetown campus, which meant they still had quite a bit of time to sit and wait once they were there. In the staff lounge that was acting as a makeshift green room for the Wagner campaign, they chatted with the woman who was producing the debate for television and with the network anchors who would moderate the evening. It might have seemed to an outside observer that the staffers were relaxed and comfortable, but as the hour drew nearer, the laughter was a little too high-pitched, the voices a bit strained. Watches were checked almost compulsively until finally a production assistant came to fetch Bill and his staff. Kim and Sarah remained behind, as usual, in the green room with other members of the team who would monitor real-time polling and social media buzz as the debate progressed. Tom and Mitch took their seats in the auditorium and Bill waited in the wings for instructions to take the stage.

As always, Tom felt that sense of helplessness at knowing Senator Wagner would be speaking off the cuff tonight. He chided himself a little, because he knew Bill was very good at this. Still, the control freak in him couldn't help tensing at each new question posed, then relaxing slightly as Bill provided a clear, cogent answer, staying on topic and managing to avoid any awkward phrases that would become unfortunate Internet memes within hours.

It was a good debate, and Tom was almost annoyed to admit that, yes, Erin Michaels did well again. Not for the first time, he struggled with being irritated at how Michaels and Wagner continued to be neck and neck in the polls and the primaries, versus being grateful for giving voters a choice between two individuals who were both truly worthwhile candidates. When all was said and done, though, on this night Tom couldn't help thinking that Bill had edged out Erin a bit, and he didn't even think that was solely his own bias talking. Bill somehow seemed to be more "on his game." Erin Michaels was well-spoken as always, but she appeared somewhat subdued compared to her usual self, as though a spark had been dampened this evening. Her normally great smiles were less frequent, less bright.

But if the audience noticed, they gave no indication of it. Their reaction to her answers was no less enthusiastic than normal. The debate was based on social media, using questions submitted via Facebook and Twitter. Tom found the questions thoughtful and insightful. With voter turnout rates as low as they were, sometimes Tom forgot that there were still private citizens in the country who had strong interest and good intentions when it came to the future of their country. An event like this was an excellent reminder of that.

Throughout the debate he was keenly aware of Nate's presence in the auditorium. He was sitting in the same row as Tom, but still far away, almost to the other end of the row. Tom knew exactly where he was, and by the way the row curved, he could occasionally look at Nate without being obvious about it. Once he swore Nate gave him a half smile. A warm feeling burned pleasantly in Tom's chest and he held back a grin before returning his attention to the stage. When the debate was over and the television cameras had pulled back to show the candidates greeting supporters in the crowd, Tom figured it was safe, and he found Nate's gaze and flashed a real smile at him. He was rewarded with a warm grin, and the warmth stayed with him the rest of the night and then some.

The general consensus among political commentators was that Bill Wagner had won the debate, and as it happened, they also noticed what Tom had: that Erin Michaels had seemed subdued. There was speculation as to what might have caused this, but Tom was inclined to believe that she was having an off-day—maybe she was fighting a virus or something. Everyone had a bad day from time to time, and sometimes they fell on days that were really inconvenient.

If circumstances were different, he would have asked Nate if Erin was okay. With things the way they were, though, he didn't want to seem like he was being nosy or angling for information that would give Wagner an edge. He'd best not mention it.

NATE ARRIVED at Tom's Friday night around six o'clock. The sight of Tom, beaming as he threw open his apartment door, gave Nate a leaping feeling in his chest that he hadn't felt since he was a teenager with a crush. He'd missed that face this week.

As soon as the door closed behind him, Nate was pulling Tom into his arms. There was no awkwardness, no reticence; it felt natural and easy to be together again. They had a little reunion in bed and followed it with dinner made by Tom. When they had finished eating and the kitchen had been returned to a pristine state, Nate produced a shopping bag that bore the logo of a wireless company. From it he took two small, basic cell phones. He handed one to Tom.

Tom, bemused, looked at the little flip phone in his hand and said, "Um... thanks? I already have an iPhone, though...."

"Which is registered to you," Nate replied as he opened the other. "These are both pay as you go and both untraceable. I wanted to talk to you this week, but with the hacking scandals that have gone on in the last ten years...."

"Anyone who looked up your phone records would see that you'd been calling me." Tom nodded. "I understand."

"Right. So with these we can call or text each other without worrying."

Tom grinned. He too had wished he could call Nate during the week. This little evidence of Nate's wishes matching his own made him unbelievably happy.

"There's no voice mail on them," Nate added. "And if you need to ask why…."

Tom laughed out loud. "I'll ask Tiger Woods."

"Exactly." Nate beamed. "The phone numbers are already programmed in."

Tom peered at the screen for a moment till he figured out how to navigate to the address book. There he saw the lone entry: "Bobcat." He crooked a quizzical eyebrow at Nate, who held up his own to show Tom: "Dooley."

"Dooley and Bobcat?"

Nate gave a sheepish grin. "Our undergrad mascots." He shrugged.

Tom looked down at the name again. "Code names…."

Nate suddenly looked embarrassed. "Maybe it was stupid."

"No, I understand and I think it's a good idea, but…. Yours is a big, scary cat. Mine's a skeleton who wears a cape and a top hat." He grinned wryly at Nate.

Nate returned the grin. "Yeah, but a big scary skeleton." Tom laughed out loud, and Nate pulled him into his arms. "You don't know how hard it was to stay away from you last night at the debate, especially when you kept sneaking looks at me all night long."

"Shit, was it that noticeable?"

"Well…." Nate hesitated. "Maybe only to me because I kept looking at you too." Tom laughed again and Nate joined him, their happiness at being together again carrying them almost into giddiness. Nate threw Tom over his shoulder and carried him to the bed where he tickled him, Tom's legs flailing and his arms clamped tight to his sides as he shrieked with laughter.

When Nate had at last relented to Tom's desperate gasping pleas to stop, they lay tangled up in each other, talking quietly about their respective weeks until Nate's yawns punctuated every sentence. "Maybe you should sleep," Tom murmured as he moved a strand of hair that had fallen forward onto Nate's forehead.

"I think you're right," Nate said with another enormous yawn.

"We have the whole weekend," Tom added, placing a kiss on each of Nate's closed eyes.

"Mm-hmm." Nate nuzzled deeper under Tom's chin. With a last kiss on Tom's neck he mumbled, "Night."

Tom watched him indulgently a while longer until his eyelids became too heavy and he succumbed to warm, peaceful sleep.

THE NEXT morning when Nate woke up he didn't have to wonder where he was. He knew before he opened his eyes, could smell the musky, masculine scent of the golden skin that was pressed against him. Tom's chest was still rising and falling in a regular rhythm, his breath tickling the hair on Nate's neck. He gently drew Tom's sleeping form closer.

The previous week hadn't been easy for Nate, either in his professional life or personally. Erin had been withdrawn and distracted, her usual easy smile seeming to lack much of its warmth. Between Jason, Claudia and himself they'd tried to determine what was wrong, if there was something they could do to help, but Erin only said she wasn't feeling well. She hadn't shown any specific symptoms of illness, and Nate suspected there was more to it than a simple virus. He did express his opinion to Jason, but there was little Jason could do about it either.

As the debate drew closer and concern about Erin wore on Nate, his thoughts had been on Tom more and more. He'd wished he could talk to him—craved it, in fact. He could close his eyes and feel how Tom's body had felt in his arms. He was already in deep for Tom and he knew it. He'd left Tom's apartment Sunday night knowing they wouldn't talk during the week, but hadn't made it past Wednesday before going out to buy the cell phones. He was relieved that Tom had been so receptive to the idea and didn't seem to have found it to be too much too soon. It had solved at least one of the problems that had troubled Nate this week. As for Erin, whatever was going on with her, he couldn't really control it. He would continue to keep an eye on her and hope for improvement, and deal with things as they came.

Tom stirred in Nate's arms a couple of times before he cracked one bleary eye at Nate. "Time's it?"

"Little after seven," Nate replied softly.

"Too early." Tom rolled away, settling onto his stomach. It wasn't too early for Nate, who was used to waking up at five every day. He knew Tom could adjust his internal clock more easily and had no trouble sleeping till 9:00 a.m. on weekends and getting up at five o'clock on weekdays. Nate usually tried not to sleep in too late on his days off—he had a very stubborn circadian rhythm that made it much harder to go back to his usual early mornings during the week. Trips where he ended up several time zones away were a real killer.

He got up to put on a pot of coffee. After he'd fixed himself a cup he wandered over to the small bookshelf beside a deep armchair. Sticking out from between two books was something in a slip cover. He pulled it out to find a decades-old copy of the *Mattachine Review*.

Nate was impressed that Tom had at least one piece of homophile memorabilia, something to remind him of how much was risked by the men and women of the latter half of the twentieth century who fought for gay rights when they were oppressed by virtually everyone—government, corporations, and private citizens alike—and received little or no protection under the law. It was with their blood and tears that they'd finally won the right to laws protecting citizens against discrimination on the basis of sexual orientation.

As a gay civil servant, Nate felt a particular connection to Frank Kameny, who'd been fired from the US government in the 1950s. Nate owned a framed print of one of Mr. Kameny's letters—it had a place of honor on the wall of his office on Capitol Hill. Now, holding this piece of history, Nate itched to slip it from its protective cover and leaf through the pages for a view into the lives of those gay vanguards. He hesitated, though, thinking he'd better ask Tom before handling something that could be valuable. Instead, he pulled out an older novel he'd never read, and settled into the armchair. He read for nearly an hour before Tom stirred again.

This time Tom awoke for good, rolling out of bed wearing nothing and sleepily making his way to the armchair where Nate sat. He slid onto Nate, who gladly set the book aside to wrap his arms around a warm lapful of naked Tom. "Morning," mumbled Tom, closing his eyes again and resting his head against Nate's shoulder.

"Good morning." Nate pulled at the knitted afghan blanket that lay over the corner of the armchair, opening it up to cover Tom. Tom nuzzled a little closer. "Sleep well?"

"Mmm" was Tom's answer, which Nate supposed indicated the affirmative. "You?"

"Very well." Nate placed a kiss on Tom's head. "There's coffee if you want it…."

The words were barely out of Nate's mouth before Tom was pulling away. Afghan wrapped around his shoulders, he went to the kitchen and returned a moment later with a cup of coffee, held well away from his body. Seeing Nate's grin Tom said, "Don't want to spill on my nakedness." He set the cup on the side table beside the armchair and picked up Nate's cold, empty mug. "Want another?"

"Love one," Nate replied. Tom took the mug and was back in seconds with a refill, which he set beside his own. Then he reclaimed the place on Nate's lap, the afghan was rearranged, and he carefully picked up his cup. "All set?" Nate asked, and Tom replied with a long exhale of satisfaction.

"Yeahhh," he returned. "Every Saturday morning should start this way." Nate's stomach gave a surprising flutter of excitement at the prospect of having every Saturday morning with Tom like this. Even if Tom's comment was an expression of contentment, not actually stating a desire for something permanent and long term… even if it was really premature to be making plans along those lines… it was still an exceedingly pleasant thought.

It also led nicely into something Nate wanted to ask Tom. "So, next weekend is Easter," he began nervously. "I'm off Friday till Monday."

"Me too," said Tom, his eyes fixed on something outside far beyond the large glass balcony door.

"Do you go anywhere for Easter?"

Tom grimaced. "Nah," he said resignedly. "After everything happened with my parents—and that was on Easter weekend—it was sort of ruined. I mostly skip it. A few times I've gone away with friends for the weekend, but I've been so busy this year I haven't even thought about it. What about you? Will you go back to… Detroit, is it?"

"Ann Arbor," Nate corrected. "No, my dad has gone golfing in South Carolina, and my brother and his girlfriend are visiting her family. I think we're all still in the frame of mind where we're just not ready for the things that have so many memories of Mom bound up in them." Tom stroked Nate's cheek. Nate caught his hand and kissed it, before continuing, "My family's not religious at all so when we were little,

Easter was mainly about hunting for eggs. And the chocolate. Chocolate's not as big a deal now that I'm an adult and can buy it whenever I want."

"So what are you going to do, hang around the city?"

"Actually, I had a thought about that. I was hoping we could spend the weekend together."

"Definitely!"

"The only thing is if we stay in DC, we're sort of stuck in the apartment all weekend. I mean, I really like being here with you, of course. But I was thinking maybe, since we have four days off...."

"Yeah?"

"When I was in my teens, my family and I would travel to the Outer Banks of North Carolina for a week every summer for probably five or six years. This was before we built our cottage in Michigan. I loved it there and I haven't been in probably eighteen years. I know we haven't been seeing each other very long, so please tell me if you're not ready or I'm rushing you or whatever. But I was thinking that maybe, if you're interested... we could go there for the weekend?"

Tom's eyes widened, but he didn't reply. To fill the silence Nate went on. "The temperature's not bad there this time of year, not exactly swimming weather, but we'd still be pretty comfortable in shorts. There are some interesting local restaurants and maybe we could get a hotel on the beach. Or a little vacation house... something quiet. I thought, if we went there, we'd be able to go out in public together and not worry about running into someone we know." Still Tom didn't respond, and Nate started to backpedal. "You're right. It's too soon for weekends away together. It was just a thought, I—"

"I think it sounds great."

"Really?" Nate said cautiously.

"Yes." Amusement played around Tom's dark eyes. "I love the idea."

"So... is that a yes?"

"That's a yes," Tom replied. "I've never been there, and I'd love to go with you."

All the tension that had built up in Nate during his rambling speech now bled from him at once, replaced by sheer relief and gladness. "Thank you!" he blurted before his face went scarlet with embarrassment. "I mean... something else less pathetic."

But if Tom thought it was a lame thing to say, he certainly didn't look like it. With a smile so wide it threatened to take over his entire face, he kissed Nate quite soundly. He remained on Nate's lap for a long time, only relinquishing his place there when their need for breakfast could no longer be ignored.

MIDWAY THROUGH the afternoon Nate got a call on his iPhone. He glanced at the screen and said to Tom, "I'll take this outside." Tom nodded, and Nate stepped out onto the balcony and closed the door securely behind him, deadening the sound from his conversation.

While Nate was outside, Tom took the opportunity to figure out what to do for dinner. He had pretty well decided to make pasta when the balcony door slid open. Nate came back in and brought with him an air of tension. Tom stayed in the kitchen and though he was wildly curious what had caused the change in Nate's demeanor, he resolutely did not ask. He didn't expect Nate would tell him, either, and so it came as a bit of a surprise when he turned around, intending to ask Nate if he preferred cream sauce or tomato sauce, and found Nate watching him from the other side of the breakfast bar, his eyes wide and excited.

Nate's fingers were drumming the counter top and he was obviously trying to contain a grin. Tom still didn't ask. Did he *ever* not ask. He stood there, meeting Nate's gaze evenly, warring with himself between amusement and a little bit of irritation. Finally Nate burst, "I'm going to be on *Face the Nation* tomorrow!" His secret spilled, Nate didn't bother trying to hide his smile anymore—in fact, Tom was pretty sure he could see all thirty-two of Nate's teeth now.

"You're going on *Face the Nation*?" Tom repeated, both excited and horrified. He was thrilled for Nate, and at the same time, if he had the option of going on a program like that or walking across a bed of hot coals, he would cheerfully choose the coals.

"Claudia was supposed to be on, but she has laryngitis, and Jason's in California this weekend, and he called me, and I'm going to be on *Face the Nation*!" Nate's pitch rose with each word until, by the end of the sentence, he was almost shouting.

"Oh my God!" Tom clapped his hands and shot around the breakfast bar to give Nate a hug. "That's so great! You're going to kick ass!"

"Whose ass?" Nate asked, laughing as he grabbed Tom around his waist. "Do you even know who's on tomorrow?"

"Doesn't matter! Asses will be kicked," Tom grinned.

"Well, thanks for your faith in me!" Nate replied. "I've been dying to do it, but it's usually Claudia or Jason. Finally it's my turn!"

"Yeah, it is!" Tom laughed as Nate tossed him onto the bed and flopped beside him, lying on his back with his arms resting above his head. Tom rolled onto his side and propped his head on one hand to watch Nate, who was staring at the ceiling, absentmindedly running a hand through his hair as though his thoughts were a million miles away. "Look at you," Tom eventually remarked.

"What?" Nate asked, startled by the sudden interruption to the silence.

"You're already there in your head, impressing the hell out of America."

A bit of color rose in Nate's cheeks. "Yeah, a little bit. Sorry."

"Don't apologize," Tom replied. "You have to go with it."

"Thanks for understanding," Nate said, rolling onto his side and mirroring Tom's pose. "I mean, I won't be able to stay the weekend like we'd planned…."

"I know. It's fine. This is a big deal, Nate. I'll get to watch your first time on one of the Sunday morning shows! Just think, if this had happened two months ago, I'd have been sitting there thinking, *Cute, intelligent, asshole*."

Nate's eyes widened. "Oh—ow!" he said, clutching his chest with dramatic flair. "That hurts! I wasn't *that* bad, was I?"

"'You'll be unemployed by May.' Does that ring a bell?"

"Ohhh, right." Nate winced a bit. "Yeah, that wasn't nice, was it?"

"Especially as a first impression. Fortunately, times have changed and now I can watch you and think, *Cute, intelligent, gives great head*."

At this Nate threw back his head and laughed long and loud, Tom joining in. When their laughter had subsided Nate said, "So I guess we'd better make it an early night tonight. I want to be well-rested and I'll have to go home tomorrow morning to pick up a suit and then be at the studio for nine thirty."

Tom knew Nate wanted to stay overnight, and of course Tom wanted the same thing. For Nate's sake, though, for him to be in the best possible state of mind, they would have to make a sacrifice. Since Nate wasn't suggesting it, Tom would have to be the one to do so.

"Do you think it would be better," he began, choosing his words carefully, "if you were to sleep at your own place tonight? Then you wouldn't have to rush tomorrow morning. Your place is a stone's throw from the studio, right?"

Nate's brow furrowed slightly for a moment, then he sighed. "You know, you're probably right. My thoughts are going to be on this all night too, and I'd feel guilty about being with you but my head being somewhere else."

"Stay for dinner," Tom suggested, "and then you can head home whenever and be alone with your thoughts." He smiled what he hoped was a reassuring smile.

It seemed to work. Nate pulled Tom into a full-body hug and murmured, "Thank you for understanding."

He held Tom for a long while, till Tom finally said, "Do you like cream sauce or marinara?"

APRIL

WATCHING NATE on *Face the Nation* was a double-edged sword for Tom. On one hand, he was so proud of Nate and completely excited to see him on TV. The show began with John Dickerson introducing the guests, and as always, the camera focused on each one as they were introduced. Nate looked directly into the camera, smiling confidently and looking devastatingly handsome in his navy blue suit. Tom, being alone and free to act as he wished without any witnesses, squealed out loud and clapped his hands, both out of excitement and in response to Nate's pure sex appeal.

The first topic the host introduced was a follow-up to the debate, a question about Senator Michaels's stance on the Israel-Palestine conflict, and how it differed from Senator Wagner's. Nate's response amounted to a line-by-line evisceration of Bill Wagner's understanding of foreign policy in general. He implied that Wagner had no true concept of America's place on the international stage, and that Wagner's voting record on foreign policy had him siding with the right more often than most Democratic senators.

With a sick feeling in his stomach, Tom muted the television before the next panelist, a liberal radio talk show host, could even begin to rebut Nate's comments. He couldn't stand to hear Nate tear his boss apart, to question Bill's intelligence, and assign right-wing politics to Bill's voting record. He couldn't bring himself to turn it off, though, and so he watched the rest of the show with no sound, sitting numbly and feeling stung.

He'd been so caught up in Nate's excitement over his appearance on the show that the other details—for instance, that Nate would be tearing Bill apart—had slipped his mind. Nate wasn't only campaigning for Erin Michaels, he was campaigning *against Bill Wagner*. Tom felt the same way about his work for Senator Wagner. It wasn't just a matter of winning. It was about defeating the enemy.

Tom was embarrassed at his own naïveté. He couldn't possibly be angry with Nate for answering a valid question with a well-thought-out and well-spoken argument on behalf of his candidate. It hadn't occurred to either of them that, when it came right down to it, there wasn't a great deal of difference between watching Nate on TV or the two of them arguing their candidates' platforms. There was still as much potential for anger and hurt feelings. They had both agreed not to cross the line that separated politics and personal time; but perhaps neither of them had realized what gray areas made up that line.

With the television muted and Tom's attention wandering during his epiphanies, the show had been over for several minutes before he came out of his reverie. He turned the TV off and got up, wandering restlessly around his apartment. He felt trapped and realized he hadn't been outside since Friday evening. He decided to get changed and go for a run. The cherry trees were in full blossom—this would be a great day to drive to the Hill and jog the Mall to get a good look at them.

He was in the middle of changing when an unexpected, unfamiliar sound erupted from his kitchen counter. He stared for a few seconds before remembering: he had a new cell phone. He peered at the screen to find that the incoming caller was, of course, "Bobcat."

He was doing his job. I'm not angry at him, he reminded himself as he took a deep breath and exhaled, hoping it would steady his voice. "Hello?"

"Hey!" came an excited voice from the other end.

"Oh my God, it's Nathan Harris who was on *Face the Nation* this morning!" Tom fake-squealed, to laughs from Nate.

"Did you watch?"

"I had to see your television debut!" Tom replied. "Great choice on your suit—the camera loves you."

"Jason loves me too. He called me from California and he said Erin was totally impressed. Even Claudia—who, it turns out, did *not* want me to be on the show because she thinks I'm tactless, and eventually Erin overruled her and said she was making the decision and overruling Claudia—anyway, Claud sent me a text to congratulate me on managing not to offend everyone on two continents."

It was very unlike Nate to babble. Tom knew he must still be running on adrenaline. "You looked great."

"I felt totally *on*," Nate continued. "And what did you think of the discussion on states' rights?"

"Uh...." Tom faltered, because with the television muted he'd heard neither the question nor the discussion.

Nate mistook his hesitation for a reminder that they shouldn't discuss politics. "Oh—yeah, you're right. We shouldn't be talking about this stuff. Sorry. I'm all...."

"High?" Tom supplied, unable to stop the smile that came to his face.

"God, yes. I feel like I'm flying."

"Well... I hope this doesn't bring you down, but I think I should be honest about something...."

"Uh... okay." Nate sounded dubious.

"I couldn't listen. I really wanted to, but hearing you felt like...."

He heard a sharp inhale at the other end of the line. "It felt like you and I were talking about politics," Nate finished.

Grateful that Nate understood what he was getting at, Tom replied, "Exactly. Like it was intruding on *us*—on our time together. It wasn't a good idea for me to hear it."

"No, of course. I was so excited about being on the show that I never even thought of it that way. I feel like an ass for being so self-absorbed."

"You shouldn't, because it didn't occur to me either. I was totally excited for you and couldn't wait to see you on the show. I'm sorry I couldn't get the full experience of your big debut."

"It's fine. Of course I understand. No worries."

"At least I got to see you for the half hour, anyway."

"I thought you turned it off," Nate said, confused.

"No, just the sound."

There was a few seconds' silence at the other end before Nate replied, "You watched the whole show on mute?"

"After the first question you answered, yes."

"Why?"

"Well, for one thing, you looked seriously hot. Like, sex-in-a-suit hot. For another thing, with no sound I could watch your lips move and pretend you were repeating all those filthy things you said to me last night when you were lying on your back, and I was riding your cock."

"Oh my God." Nate sounded awed and, to Tom's tremendous amusement, a little scandalized. "Fuck, you're going to make me crash my car."

"Anyhow," Tom said, deliberately casual, "I was about to go out for a run. Work off some energy. So I guess I'll talk to you...."

"No, wait!" Nate tried to interject, but Tom was already saying good-bye. With a flourish, he clicked the phone shut and tossed it onto the armchair, feeling completely wicked. Let Nate stew about *that* all week. Tom couldn't wait to see what state he'd be in by the time they headed for North Carolina on Friday. He half expected Nate to call back, but when the phone hadn't rung again after a few minutes, he figured it was safe to head out for his run.

He thoroughly enjoyed the time outside, running in the fresh air, with billowing clouds of cherry blossoms as far as the eye could see. He resolved to come back here to run again soon. He hadn't had a particularly stressful weekend, and yet with each deep breath, he felt like he was expelling weeks-old tension from his body. He could only attribute the change to having spent part of his weekend with Nate, feeling settled-for-now about that situation... and of course, there was the sex.

Tom had never been what he considered hypersexual, but he was a guy, after all—a young, healthy, quite normal guy. When he wasn't in a relationship—most of the time, in other words—he jerked off pretty well once a day, usually in the shower, before bed, to relax him and help him settle in to sleep. With campaign travels his tension level was higher than it had ever been before, and he'd have thought he needed the release even more, but the reality was that when he collapsed into bed, most nights he was so mentally and physically exhausted that he usually fell asleep before he could think of a decent fantasy.

And that was to say nothing of real sex. The night he spent with Nate in Michigan, it had been so long and he'd been so keyed up that he couldn't help coming almost immediately. It had taken him by surprise—nothing like that had ever happened to him before—but he couldn't control it at all. It was as though it had been ripped from him.

Now, having had a very satisfying twenty-four hours with Nate, the difference was profound. He felt settled and centered. Even driving home after his run, he felt like he had a ton of energy. He showered and wandered around his apartment for a while, trying to decide what to do with the rest of the day. Finally he decided to pick up the phone and see what Sarah was up to.

"Hi, Golden Boy!" Sarah greeted him on the first ring. "How's your weekend going?"

Leaving out a few details, Tom told her about having spent much of Saturday relaxing, and then going out for a run earlier. "It was my first time seeing the cherry blossoms in person."

"They're gorgeous. They almost make me wish I had a boyfriend so I could have that romantic scene, you know, walking under the trees with the blossoms falling all around."

Tom hadn't pictured it before, but yes, he could definitely see the appeal, and immediately pictured himself and Nate strolling hand in hand under the frothy pink trees. His reply, though, was limited to, "Definitely romantic." Sarah giggled, and Tom continued, "So I was wondering if you have plans for the rest of the day."

"No, nothing," Sarah replied. "Why?"

"Well, it's a gorgeous day out, and I thought maybe we could go out and do something, you and I, and then maybe get some dinner afterward."

"Yeah, I'd love to go out! Did you have somewhere in mind?"

"Not really. Something outside, that was pretty much my criteria."

"Well, we could go to Eastern Market," Sarah suggested. "They have outside stuff on weekends, and if you don't have a particular restaurant in mind, there's a place I love right around the corner from there."

"Sounds great. That's pretty close to where you live, right? So we could probably walk there?"

"Definitely."

"In that case, I'll drive over to your place and we'll go from there. Say in forty-five minutes?"

The market was relaxing and quaint. Tom bought a package of rich, buttery homemade shortbread cookies to share with his coworkers the following day. Sarah scooped up a bundle of pale pink and white tulips that complimented her fair skin perfectly. They didn't buy anything else as they wandered the lanes between the stalls—chatting, pausing occasionally to pick something up, examine it and put it down, moving off again to the next thing. The conversation flowed freely and didn't stop until after they'd eaten at the bistro Sarah suggested.

"Something's different about you." Sarah had slipped her arm through Tom's as they sauntered up North Carolina Avenue on the way back to her apartment. She looked at him with a critical eye.

"New shirt," Tom suggested dryly.

"Uh, no. Not what I mean. You seem very relaxed."

"Oh. Well, my schedule has lightened a bit, and it's definitely nice to have weekends off for a while. Other than that…" He shrugged in what he hoped was a casual manner. "Must be the good company."

Sarah laughed, her smooth cheeks flushing a delicate shade of pink. "Oh, I have no doubt you've been in good company this weekend, but I don't think you're talking about *me*."

It was Tom's turn to blush, but fortunately, Sarah was content to leave it at that, and by the time they wished each other good night, she hadn't brought it up again. It would have been nice, Tom reflected as he drove home, to tell Sarah the truth. Her comment about wishing she had a boyfriend would have been a perfect time, in fact. But this was the way it had to be. It wasn't perfect, but it was enough.

For now.

NATE WAS flying.

Not literally, but repeatedly throughout the week, he'd had the sensation that he was above the clouds. He'd had a great day Saturday with Tom. The weekend with him had been abbreviated, but what better reason to have to cut it short: to finally get the chance to prove his mettle on a nationally televised political panel show. Jason and Erin were both thrilled, Claudia was impressed, and there was buzz. He'd created *buzz*. He didn't care about buzz for himself, but everything he did publicly had to reflect well on Erin, and he'd rocked it. People were talking about Erin all week.

So, yeah: flying. And now, after an awesome week, it was Friday morning, and he was riding in a taxi on the way to Tom's apartment. Since Nate had made the arrangements for their accommodations in Nags Head, Tom had offered to drive. They wouldn't be back in DC until late Monday afternoon. Jason knew Nate was heading out of town. He probably assumed Nate would be going home to Michigan, and Nate didn't correct him.

All the way to Tom's, Nate kept fighting a grin. He was so looking forward to this little vacation and spending the time with Tom, uninterrupted unless some catastrophe hit over the weekend. The taxi pulled up in front of the apartment and Nate spotted Tom, who had already pulled his car out of the parking garage and onto the street to wait for him. It was only a moment before Nate had thrown his duffel bag into the back of the Jetta and slid into the back seat.

Tom had suggested earlier in the week that Nate ride in the back of the car, at least until they were out of DC. The back windows were quite heavily tinted, and he'd rather people think he was talking to himself, he told Nate, than for someone to recognize the two of them. Nate had agreed with Tom's suggestion and the reasoning behind it. It felt a little silly, like they were bordering on paranoia to resort to this sort of subterfuge, but after all, it was for the sake of the candidates.

After Tom had turned to give Nate a huge smile and a quick kiss hello, they headed off toward the Fourteenth Street Bridge. Nate figured once they were out of the Greater Washington area they'd be fine, so once they'd passed through Woodbridge, Tom pulled over and Nate quickly hopped into the front.

The drive took a little over five hours in total, but the time passed quickly. Nate and Tom still had so much to learn about each other that they never lacked for conversation. Tom told Nate about driving across the country with his parents and two sisters when he was nine, from Miami to Abilene, Texas where his father was from, for a family reunion.

"It was a long damn drive. Eight hours a day for three days, and that was only one way. It was mid-July, the middle of summer vacation, it was hot, and by the time we got to Abilene, the five of us were completely sick of each other."

"Was it at least worth the drive?"

"Actually, it was. My sisters and I met our cousins, all six of them. My dad's family all still live in Texas and his brothers never visited us in Florida, so we didn't know our cousins at all. They were all close to our ages, and we got along like we'd known each other all our lives. For the whole week we were there, the nine of us ran in a pack, outside almost all day long, coming back only for meals and to collapse at the end of the day. At bedtime, all us kids camped out in sleeping bags on the floor of our grandparents' family room, and we'd be up talking and laughing half the night. Every once in a while one of our parents would stomp down the basement stairs and threaten to spank us if we didn't settle down and go to sleep."

"Were there any spankings?"

Tom laughed. "Nope. Just threats."

"Sounds like a great vacation."

"Probably the best one I ever had. And you know, it wasn't just my cousins. It was the only time I ever saw my father with his brothers. He was the youngest of three boys, and with his parents and his two older brothers around, I saw him so differently. I mean, he was still opinionated, but now there were people around who didn't hesitate to talk back to him or even to tell him he was wrong. I'd never heard anyone talk back to my father in my entire life—I didn't know anyone could do that. I certainly had never dared, and if my mother ever disagreed with him, she must have done it privately, never did it in front of anyone, including us. As far as I was concerned, my father's final word was... well, final."

Nate was struck by the difference in their upbringings. His parents had been a team with equal decision-making ability. Though Nate knew there must have been many times they made important decisions in private conversations, they certainly didn't refrain from having those types of discussions in the presence of their sons. Nate felt now, as an adult, that it had been beneficial for him to witness those conversations. He'd learned from his parents how it was possible to have a respectful discussion even if the participants had different views on a subject. He'd learned how to compromise, and witnessed that in his parents' relationship there was never one person who ended up capitulating time after time. He voiced this to Tom, wondering aloud whether it was simply Tom's dad's personality that made him the authoritarian in their family.

Tom was silent for a few moments, and Nate didn't know whether he was considering it or had chosen not to answer. Finally Tom spoke. "There's a verse in the Bible my dad used to use about Christ being the head of the church and the man being the head of the woman. I know that's part of it. But sometimes...." He paused, collecting his thoughts. "Sometimes I think he would have been that way anyway, and that verse was something he used to justify it to us. If the verse hadn't existed, I don't know if it would have changed anything."

Nate considered this solemnly as he thought about what it would have been like to grow up in that authoritarian household. "It seems so arbitrary," he remarked at last.

"What does?"

"That one gender has authority over the other."

Tom shrugged. "Yeah. I didn't think about it much when I was younger. I guess I figured life was like that in everyone's home, that everyone was afraid of their dad."

"Afraid? Did he… I mean, he didn't…." He didn't know how to ask.

Fortunately Tom knew what he was trying to ask. "Did he hit me?" Nate nodded, his throat tight. Tom shrugged. "Spankings. I got the belt a few times, but he wasn't abusive. He never spanked us when he was angry, but that wasn't much comfort when you knew it was coming eventually."

"So that's what you meant by being afraid?"

"Not exactly. Mostly, it was the way he spoke to us. He was sarcastic, and I hated that. It wasn't teasing or playful. It felt… condescending. Like he was trying to make me feel stupid."

Silence fell between them as Nate mulled over Tom's words. He already knew Tom didn't have a relationship with his dad now, but he hadn't realized the issues had started long before Tom even knew he was gay. He wondered if Tom had ever gone to counseling to talk about this stuff. He seemed self-aware enough to have understood the impact his father's words had had on him. In the face of this new knowledge, Nate was more impressed than ever with Tom's professional accomplishments. Not only had he realized the power that words can have, but he had harnessed it to make his livelihood.

Finally Tom broke the silence. "So, what about you?" he asked, sounding falsely cheerful. "Where did you guys go for vacation when you were growing up?"

Nate pulled his head away from soberly contemplating Tom's childhood and thought of his own instead. "Hmm. Well, like I said, North Carolina a few times when I was in high school. We went to Florida once for two weeks. My brother and I were pretty young still. I remember that was the first time I saw palm trees. Then, right before I started college, my grandfather passed away. He was pretty well-off and my mother inherited money from him. That's how they built our cottage. They found some land on a lake a few hours west of Ann Arbor and built there, and the cottage became our second home. We spent as much time there as possible. I love it."

"Do you go back a lot?" Tom asked.

"Not nearly as often as I used to and not as often as I'd like, that's for sure," Nate replied. "But every year since I went to Washington, I've taken two weeks of vacation at the beginning of July, and I go straight to the cottage and I don't budge. Unless it's to go to the liquor store or for groceries. I totally unplug from the world during that time. I take a stack of novels with me, some music and maybe some movies. My parents come…." Nate stopped, and after a painful pause he began again. "My parents *used* to be there for part of the time. Last year my dad was with me the whole two weeks."

He looked out the window, watching the scenery pass, and felt Tom's hand close over his. He didn't turn to look at Tom, but he squeezed the warm fingers, grateful for the comfort. There were still times, though less often now, that he caught himself starting to use *my parents* in the present tense. It was always followed by an unpleasant jolt of memory and a momentary wave of nausea as he remembered that it was just his dad now. "Actually, he spent all of last summer there. He took a leave of absence after my mom passed away. I was concerned about him being so far away from everyone, but I think he needed to get away from the house for a while. That was where she'd spent most of her time when she was sick. He needed a break from it, a chance to rest and grieve. He went fishing, he walked in the woods, he read."

"Sounds like it's really peaceful," Tom murmured.

"It's very rural," Nate replied. "The nearest town is two miles away, and it's a town of about four hundred people. It was good for him in the long run, and when the summer was over he was ready to go back to Ann Arbor and go back to work."

Nate could see Tom nod out of the corner of his eye. He hadn't intended the conversation to take this turn—first talking about Tom's domineering, authoritarian father, then talking about his own dad and their family's grief. Not only was it very heavy for vacation conversation, but it wasn't something he talked about to anyone, really, with the occasional exception of Jason or Erin. Somehow, though, he had no problem telling Tom any of it. He had a feeling Tom, too, was usually reticent to show his emotional scars. Nate was amazed at how easy it was to share these private thoughts and feelings with Tom.

Fortunately, after that they switched to lighter topics. It was a sunny day and the temperature was in the high sixties, warm enough to put the windows down a few inches. Tom's blonde hair was tousled by the wind blowing in. The dishevelment, the vintage Foster Grant sunglasses he wore, and a Beach Boys concert tee made him look like he was ready to hop on a surf board. Crossing the bridge from Hampton into Norfolk, Nate gazed across at Tom's profile, framed against a backdrop of the ocean, and it brought a wide smile to his face.

Nate could see the change in Tom the farther they drew away from DC and the closer to their destination. He always had a bright smile for Nate, but now his entire demeanor was more open. His jaw was slack; his neck and shoulders were soft and relaxed. As Nate saw the difference in Tom, he felt his own tension slipping away. He'd been worried, he admitted to himself, that something would go wrong, and Tom would have to back out; or maybe that Tom wouldn't have fun and would regret coming. So far, so good.

Finally they were crossing the causeway from Point Harbor on the mainland to the long, narrow strip of land that comprised the Outer Banks of North Carolina. From the time they turned and started heading south along the ocean, it was only a few moments until they reached Nags Head, and a couple minutes more before they were pulling into the driveway of the little rental house.

It was small, for sure, but it was perfect for a getaway for two. It appeared to be immaculately maintained and quite private, with a tall wooden fence and palm trees surrounding the yard. The back stone patio had a newly built stone fireplace—"That wasn't even on the website," Nate told Tom—and placed near it was a double-width outdoor chaise. Inside, the house had a bedroom with a king bed, and a bathroom with a soaker tub and a shower big enough for two. The bedroom and bathroom took up more space than the living room and kitchen. Everything was spotlessly clean.

Tom salivated a little at the sight of the huge king bed. Nate was debating whether he'd seem awfully demanding to suggest they test it out right away, but Tom saved him the trouble of deciding.

He shucked his top and kicked off his runners and socks, and climbed on top of the pristine white duvet cover. He patted the bed beside him, and with a naughty smirk, he raised an eyebrow at Nate. In bare seconds Nate had stripped out of everything he was wearing and was beside Tom, insistently tugging at the waistband of Tom's board shorts. Between laughter and breathless kisses Tom finally managed to undo the shorts and get them off, and then… bliss.

There was no sensation in the world, Nate felt, to compare with that first touch of a lover's naked body sliding against him. Every time it happened was as sexy, as sweet as if it was the first time ever. The scent of Tom's hair, the way his skin started dry and cool, knowing that soon it would be flushed hot and glistening with sweat as Tom panted and gasped his name. Nate had never admitted it to a soul, but he was a very tactile person. His mom had been too, and was always touching his cheek or running her fingers through his hair, even long after she'd begun having to reach up to do it. Whenever he'd been in a relationship he was always big on cuddling, but that hadn't happened since he'd moved to Washington.

Now that he had Tom in his life, he had the means to avail himself of it on a regular basis. He greedily touched Tom every chance he got—pulling him in for a hug, resting his hand on Tom's knee, even if they were sitting beside each other reading. Somehow it was different, though, with Tom than it had been with any of his previous lovers. He hadn't felt before that his lovers had been as receptive to it or that they needed the physical contact when they weren't actually having sex. Tom, on the other hand, seemed to rise to meet each touch with one of his own. Sometimes it was a simple matter of moving a little closer; other times he would turn his head into Nate's hand and close his eyes, clearly enjoying it. Tom was also the one to initiate contact almost as often as Nate did, and Nate made sure to reciprocate those, because he didn't want Tom to stop.

Tom arched up into him, pressing his hardness into Nate and moaning softly. Nate's hands roamed all over Tom, over his arms and shoulders, across his chest, down his thighs. Tom threaded his hands through Nate's hair and tugged gently, pulling Nate's face to his nipple and hissing when Nate latched onto it. Nate knew how sensitive Tom's nipples were, and he loved to see and hear Tom's reaction when he teased them.

Too soon Tom pushed him away. "Lie on your back," he told Nate, and when Nate had resettled, Tom went down on him. It was Nate's turn to gasp and clutch at the blankets as Tom's lips and tongue and fingers did incredible things to him, laving over his balls and his cock, fingers pressing and massaging his perineum. He heard the cap of a plastic bottle, and a moment later, a slick finger was tentatively circling his hole. His entire body twitched when he felt it swipe gently over the opening, and Tom released his cock. "Hey," he murmured. "Is this okay?"

Nate nodded tightly. Tom continued, "Say if you want me to stop, okay?" Nate nodded again, and a moment later Tom's mouth was back on his cock, his tongue gently massaging the hard length, and his fingertip easing carefully inside. It had been a while since Nate had done this, and as always there was that odd pressure, the weird feeling of intrusion, but it soon eased, leaving a feeling of pleasure that no other action provided. After a few moments, Tom's finger left him and returned with a friend, and when both were fully inside him they curved slightly and found his prostate. It was the gentlest of touches, but Nate couldn't stop himself from crying out at the shock of pleasure that went through his body.

Again Tom released him and asked, his face concerned, "Still good?"

"Fuck. Do that again."

Tom grinned and complied, but he didn't return to sucking Nate's cock. Instead he got himself into a comfortable position on his side, and as he carefully stimulated that sensitive gland, he watched Nate's face. It wasn't long before Nate was shamelessly pleading for more. He felt Tom's fingers pull out of him, and Tom shifted up onto his hands and knees over Nate. "Can I fuck you?" he whispered.

It had been a long time since Nate had bottomed. He'd only ever done it when he was in a relationship, and his last real boyfriend had been right after he finished law school, almost ten years ago. Tom noticed his hesitation and added quickly, "It's totally okay if you don't want to."

Nate's heart swelled, and he pulled Tom in for a deep kiss. "I do," he murmured. "Fuck, I want to."

Tom smiled broadly and kissed Nate again before getting up to grab a condom out of his bag. Nate got up as well and pulled back the duvet and the sheet. When Tom turned back to him, Nate was lying on the bed once more with a pillow under his hips. Tom climbed onto the high bed and smiled at Nate, taking in his naked form again. "It might be easier for you if you're face down," he suggested. "At least to start with."

Nate turned over onto his stomach, keeping the pillow in place. "Mmm, this ass," he heard Tom say from behind him, two hands taking hold of his ass cheeks and squeezing firmly. Nate flexed lightly and heard Tom chuckle. A moment later Tom was sucking hard on one spot on his right ass cheek. Nate could imagine the dark red bruise that would be left behind, a mark that he would wear for days. The thought made him squirm impatiently.

The squirming broke Tom's suction, and Nate expected Tom would reattach himself. Instead he felt two warm hands grip his cheeks and spread him apart, and then a second later Tom's warm, wet tongue was swiping across his hole. Nate gasped and bucked, pushing his ass back into Tom's face and swearing. He hadn't been rimmed in… God, forever—he couldn't even remember when. It felt amazing. Everything Tom did was getting him worked up, more and more, until he felt like he was going to explode.

Finally Tom moved away, and Nate heard the foil packet being torn open. A few seconds later, the snap of a plastic lid again, and then Tom's cock was resting against his opening. "Are you ready?"

"It's been, like, almost a decade. Go slow, okay?"

"Of course. If you need me to stop, or wait, or whatever, tell me right away." Nate nodded his agreement and ever so slowly, Tom started to press in.

"Ohhh," Nate breathed, trying to stay relaxed and not fight it.

"Mmm." Tom pulled out a little and then pressed forward again, a bit deeper.

"Ohhh, fuck, that's intense. Oh fuck. Jesus. Fuck."

"Okay?" Tom asked without stopping, his voice roughened by need and restraint.

"Yeah. Fuck."

Bit by bit Tom moved deeper inside. He pulled out once, and Nate whined until he felt a drizzle of more cool lube, then Tom was sliding smoothly back in, farther than ever. Finally he took hold of Nate's shoulders and pushed as deep as he could reach, his groin pressing against Nate's skin, and Nate took a deep breath and relaxed his body. It didn't hurt—Tom had used a lot of lube and a lot of patience—but the pressure and the stretch were unbelievable.

Once Tom started to move, Nate was pretty well gone. His only awareness was how amazing it felt to have Tom inside him. Unable to see Tom's face he had to imagine what he must look like, his blond hair darkened by sweat and sticking to his skin around his forehead. His biceps would be flexed as he held himself up over Nate's back. His nearly black eyes would be closed in concentration, and his lips would move as he murmured reassurances between pressing kisses over Nate's back and shoulders. All at once, seeing it in his mind's eye wasn't enough for Nate.

"I want to see you," he gasped, and Tom's movements stuttered to a halt before he pulled out. With shaking legs, Nate flipped onto his back and Tom wasted no time plunging back in, both of them groaning as he sank deep again. Now Nate could look at Tom's gorgeous face, lit golden and glowing by the afternoon sun that streamed in the bedroom window. "You're so beautiful," he whispered. Tom moaned and captured Nate's lips, his tongue sweeping Nate's mouth in rhythm with the thrust of his body.

A moment later Nate felt Tom's hand close around him, and it was like someone had routed an electrical current through his body. Every nerve tingled, every muscle tightened and he could feel himself approaching the edge of oblivion. "Ohhh… I'm close."

"Yeah," Tom said hoarsely. "Wanna fuck it out of you, wanna watch you come hard, wanna feel you clench around me."

The intensity with which Tom spoke surprised Nate, and the unexpected obscenity threw him headlong into the most intense orgasm he'd had in recent memory. He was wailing, digging his heels into Tom's ass, trying to pull him deeper, as though he could swallow him up. It took Nate a few seconds to realize that Tom was coming too, shuddering and cursing, his sweaty body sliding against Nate's until he finally collapsed on top of him.

For long moments they lay, catching their breath, their sweaty skin sticking together. Eventually Tom stirred, rising to his knees and pulling out slowly and carefully, Nate wincing as he did. Tom got up and disappeared into the bathroom, returning a moment later with a warm, wet washcloth. Nate, feeling like his legs had turned to jelly, lay motionless as Tom cleaned him up, gave him a tired, satiated smile, and a kiss on the forehead. He still didn't move when Tom came back, pulled the sheet up over them both, and snuggled in beside him. The last thing he heard before he drifted off to sleep was Tom murmuring into his hair, "Thank you."

WHEN TOM awoke a few hours later, he felt parched and disoriented. The bed was unfamiliar, and even with his eyes closed he could tell the sun was coming from the wrong direction. It took him a few sluggish moments before he realized why. Then he remembered, and he opened his eyes to find Nate lying on his side, watching him with a smile.

"Hey," Tom said sleepily.

"Hey, yourself."

"How long have you been awake?"

Nate shrugged. "Few minutes."

"What time is it?" Tom looked around for a clock.

"Six thirty."

"Holy shit, we slept all afternoon." Tom flopped onto his back and squinted into the sunlight that was now streaming through the window directly into his face.

Nate moved close to rest his head on Tom's shoulder, and Tom wrapped his arms around him. "So, I don't know if you noticed that I was a little incoherent after you fucked me through the mattress," Nate said with a smile in his voice.

Tom chuckled. "Incoherent, immobile…. I noticed, yeah."

"So I didn't get a chance to tell you then, but I wanted to tell you now: thank you."

"For fucking you through the mattress?"

Nate grinned. "Yes. It was amazing. *You* are really good. It's been a very long time since I did that, and even with the lapse of time, I don't think it's ever been that good."

Tom felt like he was blushing to the roots of his hair. It had been a long time for him too, and he hadn't been at all certain he'd last long enough for Nate to get off. It had certainly appeared in the midst of it that Nate was enjoying it, but having Nate confirm it was a huge relief and no small ego boost. "Well… um… I'm glad you enjoyed it. It was really good for me too. No bogarting the bottom, though."

Nate laughed out loud at this and shook his head. "Don't worry, you're safe."

"So," Tom said by way of changing the subject, "I'm starving."

"God, me too. I think we should shower and then find someplace to eat."

"Sounds great."

"Do you want to go first?"

"We could shower together," Tom suggested. "The shower is huge and there are two shower heads."

"Um…."

Nate hesitated long enough that Tom quickly backtracked. "We don't have to. It was—you know—we don't have to."

Nate's face colored scarlet. "It's just… I'm really, um… sore? And I sort of… need some privacy."

Suddenly Tom realized what Nate was trying to say. He felt stupid for not considering how Nate's body would be feeling after what they'd done earlier. "Of course. I'll go ahead." He kissed Nate's flaming red cheek, then got up and took his toiletries kit to the bathroom. Inside he showered quickly and dried off with one of the huge, fluffy white bath sheets. Under the circumstances he probably would have offered the shower to Nate first, who could probably use some hot water to ease his soreness; but Tom had brought something with him that he knew would help Nate's troubles. He didn't want to give it to him outright as Nate already seemed terribly embarrassed by it. For Tom, it was one of those things that happened sometimes, and as he was expecting a lot of sex this weekend, he'd come prepared. So before he left the bathroom, he placed the small tube on the counter of the bathroom vanity where Nate couldn't help but see it and, Tom hoped, use it liberally.

By the time they were both ready to go out for dinner, Nate's embarrassment seemed to have waned somewhat. He didn't mention the tube of ointment Tom had left, but when they were both dressed and almost ready to leave, he took Tom's face gently in his hands and looked deep into his eyes before kissing him sweetly. Tom took that as thanks enough.

Since their rental was so close to the main street, they decided to take a walk and find a place to eat. They'd dressed fairly casually, and after passing a few places decided on a place that looked somewhat like a pub, though the signs outside indicated that they had a full menu. Loud music spilled through the open door. Inside, most of the tables were occupied and servers carefully threaded their way around the packed tables.

"Is this place okay with you?" Nate asked Tom, and Tom grinned. It looked like a lot of the people here were locals, and in his opinion that was a good indication.

"Looks like we seat ourselves," Tom remarked. "Let's see if we can find a booth." He'd noticed that the booths had padded seats; the tables had hard wooden chairs. Nate nodded and they made their way to the far corner of the room where a booth was available.

The rest of the evening was great. The atmosphere of the restaurant was very informal. Their server was very friendly, and when she found out they were tourists, she also gave them recommendations on good places for breakfast and coffee. The food was good and the beer was cold. Tom and Nate laughed a lot, especially when Tom pointed out to Nate that he had dripped melted butter on his chin from the clams he was scarfing down. "Look at you—you're all shiny," Tom grinned as he reached out with his napkin to dab at Nate's chin. "Can't take you anywhere."

"Hmm, thanks. Not sure you got it all, though. Maybe you'll have to have another go at it later." Discreetly he wagged his tongue at Tom, whose grin grew even wider.

After they'd paid their bill and left the server a generous tip, they strolled down the main street of Nags Head. The sun was down now and the sky was almost black, except for the full moon that had risen over the ocean.

They decided to cut over a couple of blocks to walk along the beach. The beach was mostly deserted, the white sand lit by the full moon in a cloudless sky. That, combined with the repetitive crash of the surf, made for a setting that was romantic almost to a cliché. For the first time, Tom reached out and threaded his fingers through Nate's, his heart stuttering in his chest when he felt the answering press of Nate's hand against his. Sex was sex, but this was… intimate. In silence they walked, ever so slowly, as though to rush would ruin the moment. Eventually Nate stopped, turning toward Tom and pulling him close, and there they stood in the moonlight. They kissed, again moving almost in slow motion, the world pausing around them as their lips and tongues sought and found.

Finally, when Tom's mouth felt kiss-swollen, Nate whispered against his lips, "Let's go back." Tom nodded, and instead of holding hands again, Nate kept his arm around Tom's shoulders, holding him tucked close to his body. Soon they were back at the rental, and Nate was laying Tom out on the bed, pulling his clothes off him and removing his own, and then slowly, methodically, tenderly kissing over every single inch of Tom's body. His feet, his ankles, and knees; his thighs, stomach, chest; his arms and shoulders; each eye in turn and the tip of his nose; the hollow at the base of his throat. Every spot was lovingly covered with Nate's lips, until finally he moved to place his face level with Tom's hips.

And then his mouth was on Tom's cock—not taking it into his mouth but kissing it, licking it as though he was making out with it. Tom had never been subjected to this brand of exquisite torture, had never been with anyone who had the patience to take so much time to *worship* his body. Finally, after what seemed like forever, Nate went down in earnest, taking Tom deep, sucking, mouthing, humming around him, never stopping until Tom was clutching desperately at Nate's hair, moaning, coming hard as he sent hot spates of jizz down Nate's throat.

This time it was Tom who was boneless and totally satisfied, as though Nate had literally sucked every bit of energy out of him. He felt Nate release him and slide up to lie beside him. Tom mumbled, "Fuck, that was amazing. Thank you." He started to roll toward Nate. With every intention to reciprocate, he reached for Nate's cock, but Nate stopped him.

"Don't worry about me tonight." Tom tried to protest but Nate shook his head and gave him a tender smile. "No, really. We've got the rest of the weekend. Relax and enjoy the endorphins." He gathered Tom up into his arms and held him close, kissing him on the forehead. "Thank you for the ointment you left on the bathroom counter earlier. It was… you really…." He didn't seem to know what he wanted to say and ended up finishing with, "Thanks."

"You're welcome." Even in his drowsy haze, Tom wanted to ask if the pain-relieving ointment had helped, but Nate already seemed mortified enough by the necessity of it. He decided not to ask. Instead he gave Nate one last deep kiss, wished him sweet dreams and floated away on the sound of the waves.

THE NEXT day seemed to be the day when everyone in the town was out getting groceries and making whatever preparations were necessary for the weekend's Easter celebrations. As Tom and Nate had no such obligations, they were free to escape the busy streets. At Nate's suggestion they drove down the coast a little way to Cape Hatteras National Seashore, a little way south of Nags Head. There they walked the beach, collected shells, and watched the creatures that were stranded in the warm tidal pools. Nate watched with wide eyes as Tom took off his shirt and balled it behind his head, before stretching out on the sand, letting the sun soak into him.

As they drove back toward Nags Head, Tom pointed out a sign that advertised kayak rentals. After lunch, and after applying, at Nate's insistence, copious amounts of sunblock, they found the store that rented the kayaks. They spent the afternoon paddling around Kitty Hawk Bay. Neither had kayaked before. Nate had often canoed around the lake where his family's cottage resided, but it was different to be so much lower, feeling closer to the water. He enjoyed the lighter, double-ended paddle compared to a canoe paddle, and found it exhilarating to slip rapidly and noiselessly through the water. Tom, who said he'd never canoed or kayaked, seemed to have a great time too. After a couple of hours, they had to return the kayaks to the outfitter. By then Nate was feeling protest from muscles in his shoulders and upper arms that had lain forgotten for a long time.

Dinner that night was relaxing. They chose a smaller, quieter establishment and again they feasted on the local specialties. After dinner, they walked slowly back to the little house, and it felt so natural when Nate's hand found Tom's, their fingers lacing together.

"The wind has died down," Nate commented as they separated to pass through the gate of the patio. "It would be a good night to have a fire out here."

"Do you know how to make one?"

"A fire? Of course."

"That's good, because I have no idea."

"Really? Didn't you go to Boy Scouts?"

Tom shook his head. "Too shy for Boy Scouts. I always wanted to try camping, but my family wasn't into it."

Thanks to instructions that had been thoughtfully left on their kitchen counter, Nate opened the small storage shed and found a supply of paper, kindling and firewood, provided by the property owner.

"Want me to teach you how to build a fire?" Nate asked. Tom looked dubious, but nodded. "First you take a bunch of the newspaper, and you crumple it up, like this."

Together they placed the newspaper in the grate and added the smallest pieces of kindling to the top. Nate lit the paper in several places, and as it blazed up hot and bright, the kindling caught. They added more pieces, and within twenty minutes they had a good, established fire, with several split logs crackling merrily.

"That was easy." Tom sat at the end of the extra-wide patio chaise, staring into the flames. "I thought making a fire was supposed to be hard."

Reclining on the chaise, Nate grinned at him. "That kindling is dry as a bone, and the wood is well seasoned. If your wood is green, or you don't have enough kindling, or you're trying to light a fire in the rain... that takes some skill." Nate stretched out his arms to Tom, adding, "You can see it better from here."

Tom laughed and crawled up beside Nate, turning to press his back against Nate's chest. Together they lay, the stars winking high above them. The fire danced in its place, its music the snaps and pops of the burning logs and the unrelenting crash of the surf nearby. Nate drew in a long breath and let it out in a slow sigh of contentment. Holding Tom in his arms in this idyllic place, Nate felt the tranquility of a perfect moment, and he closed his eyes to let it wash over him.

It seemed only seconds later that he heard Tom's soft voice saying his name. He opened his eyes to find that the fire was mere embers now, and a damp chill had sunk over them. "Hey, you. Wake up, Nate. We fell asleep out here."

Nate struggled to sit upright. "Crap. What time is it?"

"After midnight." Tom held out a hand to Nate. "Come on, let's go get in bed and warm up."

Nate nodded and took Tom's hand, allowing himself to be pulled up. "I'm sorry," he said as they went up the long steps to the front porch. "I wasn't very interesting company tonight."

"No complaints here." A few moments later, they cuddled together under the duvet, trying to warm up the chilly Nate, who had neither been closer to the fire, nor had a personal space heater spooning him for several hours. He felt Tom wiggling under the covers and realized Tom had removed his underwear. "Skin-to-skin contact," Tom explained before adding, "To warm you up more efficiently."

Never one to disagree with such sound logic, Nate slipped his underwear off as well and soon his cock was nestled against the soft roundness of Tom's ass. "Hmm," Nate muttered. "I don't think you wanted to warm me up. I think you wanted to torture me."

"Torture you?" Though the room was too dark for Nate to see Tom's face, there was a note of exaggerated innocence in his voice.

"Yeah. Getting me naked and rubbing up on me, and expecting me to go to sleep."

Tom reached back, all the way around to Nate's ass, and pulled Nate's hips forward, shoving his own back at the same time. "Who said anything about sleep?" he replied. "I said get in bed and warm up." Slow and deliberate, he swiveled his hips. Nate's cock responded to the softness of that round ass with an answering hardness, which he pressed against Tom. Tom didn't waste time, reaching to the bedside table to grab a condom and the lube. It was the work of only seconds before Nate was sliding into Tom, feeling the hot depth embrace him. Nate fucked Tom slowly, languidly, wrapping around his body and feeling Tom's muscles bunch and release as they twisted together. When they both came, it wasn't a rushing, screaming climax. Instead it was like the surf on the ocean beyond their window, a rhythm pressing them along, rocking their bodies in waves until it released them onto the shore of that vast sea, at last to rest together.

IN THE early hours of Sunday morning, Tom woke to the sound of an approaching thunderstorm. He slid out of bed and went to the window. Lightning flashed almost constantly, and the rumbles grew louder; soon the rain began and the thunderstorm hit in earnest. Tom looked over at Nate in one of the flashes to see if the storm had disturbed him, but he was still slumbering peacefully. Tom turned his attention back outside, where great bolts of lightning split the sky above them, and crashes of thunder shook the floor. The rain was hitting the window, turning the world outside into a deformed, abstract mass, the streetlights shining through the water drops to form ever-changing patterns onto the wall.

After a few moments Tom returned to bed, sliding in beside Nate, who still hadn't moved. Tom closed his eyes and listened to the storm for a while longer before dropping back to sleep himself.

WHEN THEY both awoke several hours later, the storm had passed. The rain remained, though, coming straight down in an unrelenting patter, looking prepared to stay a while. Tom and Nate decided to stay in for breakfast, having picked up a few things the day before for exactly that reason. Indeed, they remained in bed most of the day, leaving the room only for the absolute necessities. They didn't even get dressed until nearly six o'clock when, after a nap and a shower, they decided to venture out with the hope that one of the finer dining establishments would have a table available without a reservation, or at least with a reasonable wait time.

The restaurant they ended up at was right on the ocean. The rain had finished around midday, and the sun that shone all afternoon meant that the outdoor dining area had opened for the evening's dinner service. Nate and Tom were seated at a table that was only yards from the shore; a few steps would have carried them through a sparse growth of sea grass and to the ocean's edge. Their dinner was perfect and the setting was incredible. After dinner they decided they would, after all, cross the dune and take a walk along the beach. Tom, for one, could never get enough of the ocean, and to walk along the sand barefoot, hand in hand with Nate, was a double shot of happiness.

"Want to take a drive down the coast?" Nate suggested when they returned to Tom's car.

"I'd love to, if you wouldn't mind driving."

"Sure. Feeling okay?"

"I feel fine; just want to be a passenger for a while." Tom tossed Nate the keys, and they drove south, heading along the coast to enjoy the view for as long as they could, until the sky had changed from light blue to golden pinks and oranges, to violet and finally to deepest indigo. In the distance they could see a lighthouse standing guard at the shore, as it had done for several centuries, a beacon protecting ocean craft.

Still they drove, the windows down and the salt breeze blowing their hair into utter disarray. It was a significant change from Nate's usual careful style, but Tom believed he could very easily get used to that look on Nate. It made him look like an absentminded genius—an academic or a scientist, maybe. They drew closer and closer to the lighthouse, eventually reaching a visitor's center where they could pull off to see it. It wasn't open at this time of day but Nate suggested to Tom that they could stop, anyway, and have a look.

A few minutes later, they'd parked in the deserted lot, a couple hundred yards from the base of the great black and white spiral-striped structure. It was impressive in its size and its age, and for the thick swath of light that cut a path through dark, fog and rain, and all manner of storms. Nate and Tom leaned against the car's hood, sitting and watching it in silence for a while as the light rotated faithfully. Tom laid his head on Nate's shoulder and put his arms around Nate's waist, clasping his hands together. They remained that way until Nate turned in his grasp, lifting his face and kissing him slowly, tenderly. It was a beautiful and peaceful last night of a perfect weekend.

The next morning, they had to be checked out of the rental house by eleven o'clock, and so they decided to have lunch at a restaurant in Nags Head before getting on the road for the five-hour drive back to DC. The day was sunny and warm, nice enough to eat on the patio of the restaurant. They lingered over lunch, delaying until after one thirty, until Nate finally looked regretfully at his watch and said, "Well… I hate to say it, but…."

Tom sighed. He knew, and once they were on their way, he tried to fight the gloom that threatened. It had been a gorgeous weekend here with Nate—completely relaxing, and yeah, some pretty amazing sex. Things had gone so well between them; any concerns Tom might have had about whether it was too soon for a weekend away, or whether so much face time with Nate would be a problem, had been completely allayed. Before they even crossed back to the mainland he'd had a stern conversation with himself, insisting that if there was melancholy to be had, it wasn't allowed to make its presence known till after he'd said good-bye to Nate and was alone in his own apartment. He wasn't going to dampen the warmth between him and Nate with thoughts of saying good-bye after they got home.

It wasn't easy, and it seemed that Nate was fighting a similar battle. They would lapse into long periods of silence. It was comfortable silence, but while it persisted, the air between them seemed full of deep contemplation. Tom would come out of his thoughts to the realization that neither had spoken in half an hour, and he'd be about to say something when Nate would reach over and take his hand. It seemed to be a wordless reassurance: it was okay not to talk. It was okay to be a little sad that it was over, because it had been such a great weekend.

Eventually they reached same spot in Woodbridge, the place where Tom had stopped to let Nate switch seats. Now he wordlessly pulled over again and turned a regretful look to Nate. Nate sat, not meeting Tom's gaze, looking out the window at the car dealership they were parked in front of. Tom said quietly, "Probably time for you to get in the back seat."

Nate finally turned to look at him, a look of defiance in his eyes; Tom was almost certain he was about to refuse. Then Nate's shoulders slumped noticeably. "Yeah." Without another word he hopped out the door and slid into the back. Tom waited until he heard the seat belt click before returning to the road.

The silence that followed was less comfortable than before. Somehow when they'd been on their way south and had the potential of the weekend spreading before them, this subterfuge had seemed something to laugh at, a little joke they were playing on the city in general. Now, knowing how great the weekend had been and not wanting it to end, the separation felt oppressive, offensive even. Tom could sense Nate's resentment—not at him, but at the necessity of this charade. He felt it too; the humor was gone.

Their silence persisted until after Tom had parked in his garage and Nate had accompanied him up to his apartment. Nate used the bathroom, and then when he came out, he pulled out his phone, the one he only used for Tom, to call a taxi. After he hung up, he turned to where Tom stood in the front hall of his apartment, his hands in his pockets, feeling glum. Nate came to him, gathering Tom into his arms and holding him close, both burying their faces in each other's necks.

"This weekend was amazing," Tom mumbled against Nate's chin, feeling the scruff of several days' beard growth scrub his cheek. "I loved being there with you. And the house was perfect—thank you for looking after it all. Thanks for inviting me."

"It was great." Nate's breath tickled Tom's ear. "Sort of wish it wasn't ending."

"I know. Back to reality."

"But we'll talk on the phone this week."

"Of course. Will I see you this weekend?"

Nate released his hold on Tom to pull out his iPhone, one of the few times he'd looked at it all weekend. "I'm leaving town on Wednesday morning. I'll be back Friday, but it'll be late when I get home."

"Want to come Saturday and stay over?"

Nate smiled. "Try and stop me." Tom smiled in spite of himself. Nate added, "I'll bring food to make us dinner Saturday night."

"I'll look forward to it."

Nate pulled him into his arms again, saying, "Well, I guess I should get downstairs and wait for the taxi." He gave Tom a look of such intense longing that Tom almost asked him to call and cancel the cab, to stay with him another minute, another hour, another night... but he couldn't. It was time they both returned to real life now. They would each need an evening alone to ease their way back to reality.

So Tom didn't ask Nate to stay. He didn't express the moroseness he felt. Instead he looked up into Nate's chocolate eyes and gave him the best smile he could summon. "I had the best time with you. Thank you again."

"My pleasure," whispered Nate. They shared a slow, deep kiss, one that Tom felt everywhere in his body. Then without another word, Nate released him, turned and picked up his duffel bag, and slipped out the door.

The rest of the night, Tom felt as though he was in a cloud. He varied between gloominess that the weekend was over, and near disbelief that it had happened at all. His life was profoundly different from what it had looked like even a year before, and he still had days where he didn't quite believe this was his reality. When he was living in Atlanta and working as the public relations person for Mayor Lee, he'd counted himself extremely lucky to have reached that point on his career trajectory so early. He knew he'd skipped a few steps, knew he'd been given an opportunity that others spent years working toward. It was part of the reason why he'd devoted so much of his time and effort to the job—he never wanted to give Isaiah any reason to regret taking a chance on him.

It hadn't been in his plan to remain at that level of politics forever, of course. He expected that he would gradually work his way onto broader stages—writing for a state senatorial candidate, perhaps, and then working in communications for that individual after they won office; maybe working for a gubernatorial candidate, and then some day, moving on to work for someone who would run for the House of Representatives or the Senate. Of course a presidential campaign was the dream—it would be for anyone who was in Tom's line of work—but it was the ultimate, far off, "pay your dues for a few decades, and then we'll talk" sort of dream. Being plucked from virtual obscurity and skipping about five steps and several pay grades should have been completely outside the realm of possibility.

He could say this for life in political circles: it wasn't boring.

These days he laughed when he thought of what his schedule used to be like, how busy he'd thought he was back then. So busy that he'd barely had time for a boyfriend or even a date in the three years he'd worked for Mayor Lee. And now look at him—far busier than he'd ever been in Atlanta, and he had a… he'd been avoiding using the word boyfriend, but after the weekend they'd spent together, it seemed silly to try to deny it now: yes, he'd found a boyfriend.

And what a person to find. Nathan Harris, whom he'd once thought to be aggressive, driven, rude, and arrogant—but he couldn't have been more mistaken. The real Nate was warm, considerate and kind, passionate, and yet solicitously tender. When they were together his attention was focused solely upon Tom, making Tom feel like he was the only thing of importance in the world at that moment. In his professional life, Nate was dedicated, incisive, and highly intelligent, and it was his boss, his candidate, who benefited from his single-minded, laser-sharp focus. All this, Tom thought, and he was ridiculously hot too.

Tom never stood a chance.

NATE'S MIDWEEK trip took him to Pennsylvania. The Pennsylvania primary was still two weeks away, but it was the first time since the Iowa caucuses that they'd had longer than a week between major events— primaries or caucuses, or a debate. For once they weren't scrambling from one event to the next. Jason wanted them to take a few days to visit some smaller towns, to give Erin a chance to really connect with individuals face to face before the preprimary rush began, and their focus switched to maximum positive exposure.

With the slower pace of both the trip itself and the towns they saw, Nate found himself enjoying the trip very much. They crisscrossed the state, starting in Lancaster and York, then across to Altoona, Clarion and all the way up to Erie. Somehow he'd assumed Pennsylvania would be a difficult sell for Erin. Democrats in general weren't polling all that well in the state, which had a Republican governor and happened to be the home state of President Karl Yoder, who was in the fourth year of his first term. Between the Democratic candidates, Bill Wagner was leading Erin by a few points.

Despite Nate's expectations, the people who came out to see Erin were very receptive and represented a broad spectrum of voters. Some were Democrats who had already decided to support Erin; some hadn't decided yet who they favored for the primary. Some were completely undecided and others were curious to see Erin in person. What they all had in common, though, was that they were so *kind*—friendly, welcoming, and down to earth. He had conversations with people about their lives and the things they were struggling with, the types of conversations that he loved, that made him feel like what they were doing here could really help. If the long primary season had drained him of some of his enthusiasm and fire, this was the sort of trip that rekindled both.

Erin, too, seemed to have improved in spirits over the Easter weekend. Perhaps Jason had been right; maybe she'd been fighting a virus or needed a weekend off. Whatever the reason, her megawatt smile was back in full force at every event. She seemed to draw energy from the people she met; like Nate, the opportunity to talk to people, to learn what they needed from their politicians, was what she lived for. Nate hoped her return to full capacity was permanent, because something fundamental was missing from his workday when he didn't see one of Erin's beautiful smiles.

After they'd left Erie and were heading back across the state toward Allentown, Nate received a call from their scheduling manager, Laurie, who was back in DC. She'd heard from the campaign manager for a Democratic congressman from Philly who was holding a town hall type meeting for his constituents on Friday evening. Would Erin make a surprise appearance to support her fellow Democrat and meet some local voters? Nate posed the question to Jason, Susan, and Erin who all agreed to stop for a short time. It would delay their return to DC by a couple of hours, but that was perfectly acceptable to all of them.

The response from the attendees at the event was overwhelming enthusiasm. The event was in progress already when they arrived, and her presence was introduced quite casually by the congressman right before she walked onto the stage, to thunderous applause. She spoke very briefly, then sat down beside her fellow politician and listened as he answered questions from his constituents. Several times he would turn to her in the midst of answering a question and ask for her to weigh in, which she did with aplomb before returning the floor to her colleague. In the end it was well worth the time they spent there, two hours in total by the time Erin had shaken hands with many of the attendees. More than once, Nate heard people tell their friends, "We'll be calling her President Michaels this time next year." *President Michaels.* He couldn't say it or even think it without a broad smile.

Not that he had a lack of reasons to smile. Thoughts of Tom and memories of their weekend in North Carolina weren't far off at any given time. Nate had called Tom after he got home Monday night, belatedly concerned that Tom might have misinterpreted his silence in the car after he'd switched to the back seat on the way home. The last thing he wanted was for Tom to think Nate was angry at *him*. But no, Tom had, of course, understood, had shared the same feeling of frustration and resentment with the situation. "Maybe we got spoiled by the freedom we had in North Carolina," he'd suggested after reassuring Nate.

"That's… quite possible," Nate had admitted.

"If we didn't have the freedom, we wouldn't have felt its loss. Given the choice, I'd rather have had those days with you than to not know what I was missing."

Nate's heart had swelled a bit at that admission, and yeah, there was a reason Tom was a speechwriter. He had a way with words.

During Nate's trip, he'd also managed to talk to Tom twice during the week, and before Friday evening's change of plans, he'd hoped he might even get back to DC soon enough that he could go over to Tom's early. After they'd decided to stop in Philly, though, he sent Tom a quick text on his "special" phone letting him know he'd be arriving back in DC even later than originally planned.

Almost immediately he got a very short text in acknowledgment, without any identifiers or specifics of any kind. It simply said, *Tomorrow a.m.* Tom would be waiting for him, he knew, whenever he got there. When they were back together, the wait and the separation would be worth the reunion—much as their trip to Nags Head had been worth the cramp in their style after their return.

Thanks to an accident on I-295 that snarled traffic for at least an hour, he ended up getting back to DC so late that it was nearly one thirty before he collapsed into his bed. He slept hard, barely stirring before nine o'clock and not getting to Tom's till after ten, thanks to the dinner ingredients he'd promised to pick up.

However, when he'd let himself in, set the grocery bags on the kitchen counter, and turned to find Tom lounging on top of the bed covers wearing nothing but a seductive smile, all thoughts of the time and the dinner he'd planned and, yeah, pretty much everything else that *wasn't* Tom's naked body, vanished completely.

"Oh my God," Nate breathed, stopping dead in his tracks.

"Hi there. I was hoping you'd be here soon. I've been trying to keep myself amused to pass the time." Tom lay on his side, his head propped up on his arm and one leg drawn up under him. His cock was full and heavy against his groin. His free hand lightly stroked over the length of it and his eyelids involuntarily fluttered in reaction.

Nate couldn't help the strangled moan that escaped him. "I'm sorry, I slept in." He removed his coat and shoes without his gaze straying once from Tom's lithe body. He drew nearer the bed, mechanically removing clothing as he did. "Late night."

"It's okay—don't apologize." Tom got up to a kneeling position on the bed. "I'm glad you got your sleep, because I've got plans for us today that are going to require you to have lots of energy."

Finally completely naked, Nate climbed onto the bed before Tom, mirroring his position. "Really? And what plans are those?"

Tom grinned. "I could tell you, but I'd rather show you." He moved toward Nate, close enough that their dicks touched, close enough that they were pressing against each other from knees to shoulders.

Nate's breathing was growing louder; his heart felt like it would pound out of his chest. "I think I'm going to like these plans of yours," he murmured, his lips brushing against Tom's neck as he spoke.

Tom shivered beneath Nate's touch, and in a hoarse voice he whispered, "There's only one way to know for sure."

BOTH TOM and Nate traveled the next week—it was Tom's turn to visit Pennsylvania with the Wagner campaign while Nate went to Indiana with Michaels—but both candidates were back in DC on Friday. The Pennsylvania primary was the following Tuesday and if not for an important vote that was taking place in the Senate Friday afternoon, Tom might not have seen Nate that weekend at all. It was a quick visit, to be sure. They both had to leave again Saturday to return to Pennsylvania but they managed to steal Friday night together, at Tom's apartment as always, and their time together was no less significant for the short duration.

Tom was in Pittsburgh when Bill Wagner took the Pennsylvania primary by a 4 percent margin. It was by far the largest margin of victory he had earned so far, which made for a very rewarding evening for everyone on the campaign. As Senator Wagner delivered the speech Tom had prepared for him, Tom felt a warm, solid hand rest on his shoulder. He turned to find Mitch beaming at him, pride and approval evident in his face. As Tom nodded his thanks, he realized how fortunate he was to have a boss like Mitch who was as generous with praise as he was with constructive criticism. Even Tom considered the speech he'd prepared for that night to be one of the best he'd ever written. It was hopeful and empowering and positive, all the things Tom felt about his candidate and things that happened to be mirrored in his personal life. Of course, he was a professional, and even if his personal life had been shit, or nonexistent, his work for Bill would still have been absolutely the best he was capable of producing. Being happy in his own life made it that much easier.

However, what was not particularly easy was hiding how he felt. Tom had always worn his heart on his sleeve. To anyone who spent time with him, his "tells" were easily discernible, though it had taken him quite a while to realize that about himself. He hadn't noticed, for instance, how often he hummed a tune in the course of a day, until the mayor's spokesperson mentioned it when he was working for the city of Atlanta. "Tom, why so quiet?" she'd asked one day. When he replied that he didn't think he was any quieter than usual, she'd gone on to remark, "I haven't heard you hum once today." Her comment had come two days after Tom's boyfriend of eighteen months had broken up with him. He hadn't mentioned it to anyone at the office—he was sort of hoping it wouldn't stick—but when Dana asked him, he broke down and told her the whole story.

Now that he knew this about himself, he found himself very conscious of it when he was experiencing extremes in his moods, either on the positive or the negative end of the spectrum. Whether or not it fooled anyone, he didn't know, but no one asked him about it.

No one, that is, except Sarah.

Without a doubt, Sarah was the person in Washington and on the campaign with whom Tom had the closest friendship. She was both keenly observant and very outspoken. Hiding something like this from her was next to impossible when he worked with her every day. She'd asked him within the first two days of their acquaintance whether he was seeing anyone, and when he'd answered with a simple no, she persisted, "And if I was going to introduce you to a special someone, would that be with a man or a woman?" At the time, he'd been surprised; now, knowing her as he did, his only surprise was that she'd waited two days to ask.

So having this awesome change in his life wasn't exactly something he could hide from Sarah.

"Something's wrong with you," she'd told him when he'd returned from his Easter weekend with Nate in North Carolina, sporting fresh color in his cheeks and a look of blissful relaxation. "You look great." Far from being complimentary, her tone was accusatory.

Tom raised an eyebrow sardonically. "Stop it, I can't handle all the flattery."

"No, I mean it. Why isn't *your* jaw line covered in stress breakouts like everyone else's? You look way too calm for someone who's working on a presidential campaign."

"Um… I'm sorry?"

"Oh, shut up. You couldn't look less sorry if you tried. You're seeing somebody. You are, aren't you?"

Tom took a deep breath before conceding. "Okay. Yes, I am seeing someone." Sarah's eyes went wide and she looked about to squeal when he quickly added, "But it's still very new, and there are a number of good reasons to keep it strictly private. *Strictly* private," he repeated pointedly, "which means not a word to anybody."

She put up her hand as if to ask a question. "May I say something?"

"Is there any possible way for me to stop you?"

She swatted him playfully on the shoulder. "I just want to say that I'm happy for you."

"I can tell."

"Also, totally jealous that all your stress isn't erupting on your face. Because it's erupting in your pants."

Tom choked on his coffee.

True to her word, though, Sarah told not a soul, and never pushed Tom for details. He supposed that was one of the reasons she had become such a good friend. She might seem like nothing was off-limits, but in fact, once Tom set a boundary, she respected it completely.

With that conversation behind him, Tom hoped other colleagues wouldn't notice—totally conceivable since he spent a lot of time either working alone or in conference with Mitch, Kim, and Bill or some combination thereof. The only other person who might see a difference would be Mitch, and Tom hoped that if Mitch did notice a change, he would simply be glad that it was for the better and accept it without asking about it.

Coming back to DC the day after the primary felt like a victory lap for everyone in the Wagner campaign. They'd stayed overnight in Pittsburgh and the lapse of time had done nothing to dampen their spirits. The bus felt like a party atmosphere. Tom was excited to get back to the city. He would use Thursday and Friday to start fleshing out some outlines he'd been working on for Indiana, West Virginia and North Carolina. Then, after having spent less than twenty-four hours with Nate in the last ten days, Tom would get him all to himself for an entire weekend.

Friday night Nate was at his door as promised, and their weekend was what he hoped it would be: relaxing and light, with the stimulating conversation they always enjoyed, and lots of sex. Nate actually congratulated him on the win, and though it took Tom slightly off guard—they were supposed to have a zero tolerance policy on discussing anything political or campaign-related, after all—he chose not to mention that. He accepted it as congratulations on a job well done, as a sign that his boyfriend respected his work and was proud of him.

The issue of the B-word—boyfriend—came up that weekend, too, and in fact it was Tom who brought it up. In his head he'd been referring to Nate as his boyfriend since they got home from North Carolina. Saturday night he and Nate were fucking on the couch, Tom straddling Nate's lap, his arms wrapped around Nate's neck. As Tom rode Nate, he casually slipped it into some dirty talk, and Nate's reaction was reasonably positive: he came. Instantly. And it wasn't like he'd been balancing on a knife's edge, either. It was as if he'd been picked up and tossed across the room, smack into an orgasm.

After the climax passed, Nate looked completely bewildered, as though he had no idea where it had come from. It was so comical and endearing that Tom laughed out loud.

"So… that happened," Tom said when he'd stopped laughing.

"Jesus," Nate looked completely taken aback. "I mean…. Jesus."

"Think it could happen again?" Tom squeezed around Nate who seemed to still be as hard as he'd been before. "Because I, um, didn't."

Nate shifted experimentally under Tom. "Oh yeah. I think it could happen again."

"Excellent," said Tom with a satisfied smile.

Afterward they sat together on the couch, covered up in the colorful afghan. Tom was all but sitting in Nate's lap; Nate's arms were wrapped around him, holding him close. "You called me your boyfriend," he murmured into Tom's hair between the kisses he was pressing there.

"I did."

"That's the first time we've used that word."

"Yeah."

"Can I tell you something?"

Tom's stomach fluttered a bit. Had he made a mistake in saying it? Was it too soon? Trying not to show his nerves, he replied, "Of course."

"I've been thinking of you that way since we were in North Carolina."

Tom shifted to look up into Nate's warm brown eyes. "You have?"

Nate's cheeks colored slightly. "The first day, when you topped. I've only ever done that with a boyfriend, and when you asked if you could and I said yes... for me, that was the moment."

Tom grinned. "I've been someone's boyfriend for three weeks, and I didn't even know."

"If it helps, you've been doing a kickass job." Nate smiled warmly and hugged Tom tighter. "Too bad your boyfriend had a bit of a problem tonight with holding his wad."

"Ah, yeah. About that...."

Nate looked apprehensive. "Yeah?"

"That might have been the sexiest fucking thing you've ever done," Tom admitted. "At least it was to me."

"It was?"

"Totally."

"That I came almost immediately, like a teenager—*that* was sexy?"

"That *I* made you come like that. It made me feel amazing." Nate still looked dubious, but by the end of the weekend Tom had been able to convince him that he was telling the truth.

They parted Sunday night knowing they wouldn't see each other again for nearly two weeks. They would both be leaving midweek to start traveling in advance of the following week's primaries in Indiana, North Carolina and West Virginia and wouldn't be back in town until the day after the primaries. When it was time for Nate to leave he stood holding Tom for a long time. It was obvious neither of them wanted to say good-bye; they kept putting off the moment with promises to talk on the phone and admonitions for safe travel.

Finally the moment could no longer be avoided. "Okay," said Tom, gently extricating himself from Nate's arms. "Can't put it off forever."

Nate sighed resignedly. "You're right." He gave Tom a final kiss on the lips and said, "I'll miss you," and with that he was gone.

Tom spent the rest of the night listlessly preparing for his trip, figuring out what to take, what needed to be dry-cleaned before he went, and what he'd have to wash. It occupied his time but not his mind. Nate was at the forefront of his thoughts all evening; but then, there was no reason why this evening should be different from any other.

MAY

IT HAD been weeks since a primary day that involved more than one state. During the month of April, Nate had been spoiled with a fairly easy schedule—a bit of travel, but nothing like what he'd endured the first three months of the year. Now, with three states holding their primary in one day, he and the campaign were back on the road.

Even this, though, was more a sprint instead of a marathon. The campaign traveled to Indiana first, a state that was almost a second home to Nate since his mother had been born and raised in Gary. The state had a proud history of having consistently produced a presidential candidate in almost every election in the late nineteenth and early twentieth centuries. It was also a firmly Republican stronghold.

Senior staff members in the campaign were divided on whether or not it was worth their time to even visit the state. Susan and Nate didn't think they should bother; they wanted Erin to focus on West Virginia and North Carolina, where she was polling behind Wagner. It was Erin and Jason who insisted Indiana was worth a visit, at least for a day. There was some strong Democratic support in the areas close to Lake Michigan, with two House Democrats elected in Gary. Jason had heard that Bill Wagner wasn't planning to go to Indiana at all, and he suggested to Erin that a rally held with those two representatives would be beneficial to everyone. On Tuesday afternoon the bus hit the road for the Hoosier state.

They slept on the road and arrived the next morning at a downtown Gary diner where they were to have breakfast with the mayor. It was covered by the press, as was the rally later that day in front of City Hall where the mayor, Erin, and Representatives Achtzehn and Sabatino spoke.

That night, after they'd stopped to have dinner at a local restaurant and were back on the bus headed toward West Virginia, Nate was catching up on some e-mail when he felt eyes upon him. He looked up to find Erin watching him. She was sitting on a banquette closer to the back of the bus, showered and changed into comfortable clothes for the overnight drive, her feet tucked up under her and her iPad on her lap. Even with no makeup and her hair up in a ponytail, the deeply dimpled smile she gave Nate could still warm the hardest of hearts. "Reading anything good?" she asked.

Nate returned her smile with a grin of his own. "Nothing that can't wait." Erin set down her iPad and patted the couch beside her. Nate gladly put the iPhone aside and moved to join her, asking, "How about you?"

"Isaacson's thing." Rep. Isaacson was going to table an education bill late the next week if she thought she had the support. Her aide had come to talk to Nate about it the week after the Easter break. It would probably pass in the House, but the Republican-held Senate could be another issue. Erin rubbed her eyes wearily as she continued, "I'm trying to focus, but it's just not happening."

"It's been a long day," Nate said. "Maybe you should get some sleep."

"You know, I've never quite gotten the knack of sleeping on a bus. I doze, I guess, but I don't really rest unless I'm in a bed." She looked down at the couch she was sitting on. "A non-moving bed." She turned sideways to face Nate, propping her arm against the back of the couch and resting her head on it. "So what did you think of Indiana?"

"It was a good day. You did well. I think going there was the right decision."

She smiled. "Well, don't worry, I won't tell Jason you said so." Nate laughed quietly and looked up the aisle of the bus where Jason lay with his eyes closed, lounging on a banquette similar to the one they were on. "I suppose you've probably visited the state before, being so close to Michigan?"

"I used to go to Gary to visit my grandparents—it's where my mom grew up."

"Really? I didn't know that. I guess I assumed she was from Michigan." After a pause Erin asked, "How is your dad doing since she passed away?"

Nate looked down at his hands. "Better now. The first six months were pretty tough. He spent a lot of time looking after her, you know? So when she was gone, he had to figure out how to be a person who didn't have to be a caregiver anymore."

"He took some time off afterward, right?"

"Yeah. Lived at the cottage until the end of the summer."

"Oh, that's right. I remember you spending your holidays with him last summer."

"I didn't know if it'd be good for him to be alone so much, but it turned out to be the right thing."

After a respectful pause Erin asked, "And how about you?"

Nate looked up. "Me?"

"How are you doing? God, I feel like it's been ages since we sat and talked about normal stuff," she said, looking mildly abashed.

"Well, you *have* had some stuff going on."

"Still. You and I were friends once, before all this started. We had conversations and everything, I'm sure we did." They shared a smile before she asked again, "So how are you?"

Nate nodded slowly. "I'm good."

"Yeah?" she asked with interest. "What have you been up to, outside of work?"

"Hmm. Well, I've been trying to get out and enjoy the weather now that it's so nice—you know, running outside instead of at the gym. Oh, and I started watching *Modern Family*!"

"Oh, great show!"

"Yeah, I remember you saying you like it so I watched the first season on Netflix. It's awesome. I laugh my ass off at every episode and it's a great stress reliever."

"It is. And, um, speaking of stress relievers… is there any point in me asking if you're seeing anyone? Or will I get the same answer you've been giving me for ten years? 'I'm married to my career, I'm too busy to date,' blah-blah-blah."

"Wow, that does sound like me." Nate laughed and tried to sound casual.

But Erin wasn't fooled. "Well… that wasn't a no," she remarked, hooking a critical eyebrow at him.

Nate gave his answer careful consideration. "Well, there is sort of… someone. Someone I like."

Erin's face lit up. "Really! And does he like you?"

"I think so," Nate hedged, a tendril of guilt working its way through him. "But with this job, it makes it really challenging to find time to get together, to get to know someone." He didn't elaborate, but fortunately Erin took his words at face value.

"I know it is. Even when you already know someone…." She didn't finish the thought, and Nate saw a sad expression flicker across her face.

"Can I ask *you* something?" he said.

"Of course."

"You and Richard…?"

"Ah." She looked down. "That. Well, we're still separated. As of last week, it's been six months. Two weeks before Easter, he called and asked if I could come to New York for Easter weekend, if maybe we could spend the weekend together and try to figure things out. I told him I would, and I spent the time leading up to Easter trying to figure out what to tell him. I mean, this whole time, it's been an impasse. He can't leave New York, and I'm obviously not trying to extricate myself from Washington."

"Right."

"We're getting a divorce, Nate. It's time for us to move on. It hurts us both too much to try to keep this going."

"Aww, Erin," Nate said sadly. "I'm so sorry." He leaned close and gave her a long, warm hug, patting her on the back as he did. "I always thought you two were a perfect couple."

"Oh, not even close." Erin laughed a little through her tears as she pulled away. "But it was pretty great… until it wasn't anymore."

"What can I do to help you?" His hand rested on her shoulder.

"Nothing, really," she replied, "except keep it to yourself. Jason and Susan are the only ones who know. We'll have to figure out when to announce it. What happens in the next few weeks will determine that, I guess."

Nate squeezed her shoulder. "If there's anything you need, Erin, please don't hesitate to ask."

"Thanks, Nate. You're a good friend." She yawned hugely.

Nate stood, picking up a fleece blanket that was folded over the far end of the couch. "As your friend *and* your staffer, I think you'd better at least try to get some sleep." He opened up the blanket and held it up, waiting for her to scoot down on the banquette until she was lying down. He covered her up and switched off the light over her head. "Good night, Senator."

"Good night, Nathan," she replied, her eyes already closed. Nate made his way back to his seat, and settled in with his own blanket.

The conversation with Erin kept troubling him. He hadn't been honest with her about Tom. He was in far deeper than he'd admitted, and he felt guilty about that. Under any other circumstances, he knew she would have been happy for him.

He kept thinking about Richard and Erin too. At the time of their separation, they'd been married for five years. He'd been a guest at their wedding, watching Erin stroll through her parents' apple orchard flanked by her mom and dad, beaming at Richard where he stood beside the rabbi and the minister who had performed the interfaith ceremony. It had been the most beautiful wedding he'd ever attended. He hadn't been kidding when he said he thought of Erin and Richard as the perfect couple. They were his ideal—completely in love and an exceptional compliment to each other. He'd seen how hard they'd tried to make their marriage work in spite of the distance between them. If their marriage couldn't survive the life of a politician, what chance did anyone else have?

WEST VIRGINIA held no surprises for the campaign. The state overall supported the Democratic Party, and between the two candidates, Erin had been polling several points behind Wagner. They spent two days in the state, attending rallies and supporting local candidates, and meeting countless people. Some came because they already supported Erin; some were undecided and were there to learn more about her.

North Carolina was less predictable. For the latter half of the twentieth century it had been a far less friendly state when it came to Democrats at the federal level. It was only in the last decade that they'd started to see an upswing in support there, mostly in the growing urban areas. Small towns were still heavily Republican. Along with their vote in the presidential primary, North Carolinians would also vote on a proposed constitutional amendment that, if approved, would limit legal domestic unions to heterosexual unions only. It was a state where you really couldn't say for sure what would happen, and again Erin was behind Wagner in the polls. They would spend four full days in the state—the most time they'd spent anywhere and twice as long as Bill Wagner was planning to spend.

Nate knew there was a small group of pundits asking if the Michaels campaign was starting to get nervous about their numbers, if maybe the duration of the campaign's visit to the state was a sign of desperation. He tried to ignore them, but as Tuesday drew nearer and their poll numbers didn't change, his outlook was growing dimmer.

Tuesday morning found them on the coast of North Carolina near Topsail Beach—quite a bit farther south than where he'd visited on Easter weekend. The backdrop for the morning's rally was the ocean, the surf pounding behind Erin as she addressed the crowd who had turned out to see her. Nate should have been watching the crowd. He should have been paying attention to Erin's speech. He should have been focused on his job and therefore mentally present when Jason asked him for a statistic as they stood and talked to a voter. He should *not* have been staring out at the ocean, thinking about walking hand in hand along the beach with Tom. He shouldn't have been thinking about how he missed Tom so much he could hardly breathe. And he should not have made Jason say his name twice to get his attention and have to apologize for him to the voter.

Nate was mortified that he'd let his concentration wander to that degree, especially with what was at stake now. For the rest of the day, he was ruthless with himself, berating himself for the lapse and refusing to allow it to happen again. Jason didn't say anything about the incident, not that day, at least. Everyone was too focused, too busy to deliver a dressing down. Nate knew it would come, knew he deserved every word of it.

Nate knew that Jason was approached at least several times a year by a candidate who was trying to poach him away from Erin. Who wouldn't want him on their team? He was the best. He was also the person in Nate's professional life whose opinion mattered most, even more than Erin's. Nate knew Jason wouldn't get angry, wouldn't yell at him or give him a dressing down in the traditional sense. What he would do was express his disappointment, and that would be far worse than being yelled at.

It happened Wednesday morning after they'd learned the results from the three states—Erin took Indiana by a narrow margin, but in spite of all the time she'd spent in West Virginia and North Carolina, she lost them to Wagner. Nate was sitting on the bus, reading a news article online about the campaign's efforts in North Carolina, when Jason slid into the seat beside him. Steeling himself, Nate turned off his iPhone, placed it face down on the table before him, and turned to Jason, ready to accept whatever was coming his way.

Jason looked him searchingly for a few moments, as if hoping the answer would be written on Nate's face. Finally Nate couldn't take the silence any longer. "I let my concentration slip. I got distracted and I embarrassed you in front of a voter. It reflected poorly on Erin and the campaign. I'm sorry."

Jason nodded slowly. "That tells me what happened, but my real question is why. I won't insult your intelligence by telling you what you already know—how important this is and how much was at stake yesterday. It should go without saying, Nate, but here I am feeling like I have to say it. It's not only North Carolina. We're at the point where it's the entire campaign. We lost yesterday. Next week is Oregon and the week after that is Kentucky and Arkansas…. Everything is riding on these next three states, Nathan. If Erin doesn't do well…."

Nate gaped. "She'll pull out?"

"It's been a long fight. Yoder is just sitting and watching this go on, watching these two candidates deplete their war chests while his piles up. The divide in the party is getting more acrimonious…." Jason shook his head. "The longer it goes on, the harder it'll be for the eventual winner. It's already difficult enough to unseat a sitting president as it is."

Nate felt nauseated. Never before had he considered the possibility that Erin wouldn't win the nomination—not for one second.

"That's why we need a hundred percent, Nate—Jesus, at this point we need a hundred and ten, if you've got it. I *know* something like what happened yesterday is completely out of character for you. I've seen you pursue this with the same single-minded dedication you bring to everything else you do for Erin. No one is perfect, and if this was a blip, well, it wasn't great timing, but it happens. We'll forget it and move on. But Nathan." The intensity of Jason's gaze grew to a blaze. "If it was more than that, if you're flagging now…."

Nate was vehement. "I'm not flagging. I'm here. A hundred and ten. It won't happen again, Jason, I promise you that."

Jason nodded, seeming to accept that. "Okay. I believe you." After a moment he added, "And Nate, I know I'm your boss, but I think I'm also your friend, yeah?"

"Of course."

"I know if you have concerns about the campaign you won't hesitate to tell me. That's what you get paid for. But if there's anything else, maybe outside the campaign, or outside of work completely—you know you can talk to me, right?" Nate hesitated and Jason continued, "You've gotta take care of yourself, Nate. You *have* to have someone to talk to. I know how hard it is to have friends outside work, especially when you're going through something as intense as a campaign like this one. Not everyone has someone on their team who really becomes a friend, but I want you to know you can tell me anything. You and I have been through enough together that I think we're at that level. No judgment—just a listening ear. Okay?"

Nate truly didn't know what to say. He was humbled and grateful for Jason's offer; he knew it was a standing offer, too, not a one-time thing. Under any other circumstances, he would gladly have unburdened his mind to Jason, and he knew Jason really did believe that he wouldn't have judgment to pass on whatever Nate would tell him. But about this singular situation, it wasn't true.

So Nate shoved down the guilt he felt—again—and let his gratitude speak when he thanked Jason wholeheartedly for his offer. "I'll definitely keep it in mind," he added noncommittally. Jason seemed only partially satisfied with Nate's answer, but there wasn't much more he could say. He did instruct Nate to keep their conversation to himself, that only the two of them, Erin and Susan knew at this point. It would be premature to mention it to anyone else and create anxiety where it wasn't yet warranted. That said, he gave Nate's shoulder a squeeze and excused himself to go make a phone call, leaving Nate free to steep in a strong brew of self-reproach.

TOM RACED around his apartment excitedly, checking on dinner, wishing for the hundredth time that he had a table where he could have a romantic setting. Candles and a small bouquet of flowers in a vase weren't quite the same at a breakfast bar. He had them anyway, of course, but they didn't have quite the same effect.

But they were only things, he knew, and things weren't really important. What was important was that soon—any minute now—Nate would be here and in his arms again. When that happened, none of the rest of it would matter at all. Tom was aching to see Nate. It had been two weeks since they'd been together, and though they'd managed to catch each other on the phone a couple of times, it wasn't at all the same as when they were together. Being on the road meant they were immersed in work mode, and since they didn't talk about work, conversations consisted mainly of, "God, I miss you."

Tom had put fresh sheets on the bed and given the apartment a final look when his phone rang. It was his doorman; Nate was on the way up. Tom checked himself out in the mirror. He was wearing Nate's favorite shirt—a simple green T-shirt, but Nate loved it on him—and a pair of soft, worn jeans. Unable to contain his anticipation, he tapped his bare toes on the tile of the foyer. Down the hall outside the door he heard the electronic "ding" of the elevator as it arrived on his floor. Finally, after what seemed like an interminable pause, the door opened and there was his boyfriend.

Usually Tom and Nate waited for the door to close before embracing each other—not today. Nate was in the door and wrapping himself around Tom the instant he spotted him standing waiting for him, nuzzling his head into Tom's neck. Grinning at Nate's eagerness, Tom stretched out with one foot to push the door closed.

"Hi."

"Hi." Nate's reply was muffled as his face was still buried in Tom's neck. Tom waited, but Nate didn't seem anxious to move from that spot any time soon.

Dying for a kiss, Tom finally said, "Hey, what's a guy gotta do to get a kiss from his boyfriend?"

Immediately Nate's lips were against his, their mouths opening and tongues finding each other again for the first time in too long. It was as if Tom suddenly couldn't be enough inside, enough around Nate, wanting to be enmeshed with him. It wasn't even a sexual thing; it was more basic, the most powerful longing he'd ever felt. Too soon he felt Nate break their kiss, resting his forehead against Tom's.

"Fuck, I missed you," Nate said, his voice hoarse. "Every second."

Tom kissed him softly, a chaste brush against his lips. "I missed you too. So glad you're here." They stood a long time holding each other, the desperation of a moment earlier having evaporated.

Eventually Nate said, "Dinner smells great."

Tom took his hand and led him to the breakfast bar, where the candles glowed softly. "I managed to get away a little early this afternoon, so I figured since I actually had the time, I'd make dinner." A pan of lasagna was sitting on the stove and a salad waited on the counter.

"You cooked?" Nate's eyes widened. "Thank you. I haven't eaten anything but takeout since...." He stopped and thought. "Probably since I was here with you two weeks ago."

Tom grinned. "Wine?" he asked, holding up a bottle of red.

Nate nodded. "Please."

Nate was usually very chatty when they were reunited after a week's separation, but not tonight. Throughout dinner he seemed quiet and pensive. After dinner he led Tom to the couch, where Tom expected they would start making out. Instead, Nate turned sideways so he could snuggle into Tom's chest. Of course, Tom had no complaints about holding his boyfriend, but he was a little surprised. This was very different from the passionate Nate he knew.

"Hey," he finally murmured. "You okay?"

He heard Nate sigh. "I'm sorry. I'm terrible company tonight."

"You don't have to apologize. You're not terrible company. I am a little concerned, though; you're not yourself at all." As Tom stroked one hand over Nate's shoulders he found them knotted and tense. "God, your shoulders feel like they're tied in knots."

"Stressed" was all Nate replied, and what could Tom do? He couldn't ask about the source of Nate's stress. If it was anything other than the primary results, he was certain Nate would already have told him. They couldn't talk about it; he couldn't tell Nate he hoped things worked out. He couldn't do anything to help.

Or could he?

"Hey," he said, displacing Nate enough that Nate looked up at him. "I have an idea. Stay right there, I'll be back in two minutes." He went to the bathroom where he had a large jetted tub. Practically speaking, it was wasted space, especially in an apartment that didn't even have a bedroom, but he'd been glad to have it more than once, especially after he got back into running and soaked his sore muscles in it. It wasn't large enough for two people, but Nate could fit very comfortably in it.

Tom started the water running at the warmest comfortable temperature. He poured some Epsom Salts into the water, figuring it would help with stiff muscles, and then returned to Nate. "Are you taking a bath?" Nate asked.

"You are," Tom replied, holding out his hand. Nate allowed himself to be pulled up and followed Tom into the bathroom. In the overhead lights, Tom could see what he hadn't been able to before in the candlelight: Nate's eyes were heavy and tired looking, with dark circles under them. He looked completely exhausted. Tom undressed Nate, who stood passively and allowed him to do it, like a child. Tom tested the water, deemed it comfortable, and Nate slipped in, sliding down low enough that the water came up to his collarbone. "Jets?" he asked.

"Okay," said Nate, meekly. As the water gurgled around the soaking Nate, Tom popped in and out of the bathroom, bringing a towel and a few candles. He turned off the overhead light and went back out to the main room to close the windows, not wanting Nate to get chilled when he got out. He put some quiet music on his iPod, similar to the sort of music played by the massage therapist he occasionally visited. He placed a large soft towel on his bed and got a spare sheet, and he found his lone bottle of massage oil. It was labeled as "calming," and Tom hoped that was the case.

Back in the bathroom, he offered to wash Nate's hair, but Nate shook his head listlessly. Tom remained sitting beside him until the jet timer ran out, then he said, "Time to get out."

Nate actually quirked a grin at that, one corner of his mouth coming up as he said, "Yes, mother."

Tom hoped it was a good sign that Nate could joke a bit. After he dried Nate, he led him back out to the bed, instructing him, "Lie on the towel on your front." Tom covered Nate with the sheet and then pulled the duvet up as far as his waist to keep him warm. He folded back the sheet enough to give him access to Nate's back, shoulders, and neck. After warming some oil between his hands, he began to massage. He tried his best to remember and emulate what his therapist did, working out knots in Nate's shoulder blades and neck, down his spine and up under the edge of his skull. Nate hummed appreciatively for the first ten minutes or so, especially when Tom hit a particularly tight spot. Eventually his responses subsided, finally going silent altogether.

Focused on his task, it took Tom a while to realize that Nate hadn't made a sound. Leaning over Nate's body, Tom felt the rise and fall, the unmistakable rhythm of deep, regular breaths. Nate was asleep.

Tom smiled indulgently, pulling the sheet and duvet up to cover Nate's shoulders, glad that Nate had been able to relax. It was only eight o'clock, but he'd certainly looked like he could use an extra-long sleep.

After putting away the things he'd gathered for his task, Tom climbed back into bed with Nate. He wasn't even disappointed that they hadn't made love. He hoped they would tomorrow, but tonight Nate had clearly needed something else and Tom had been happy to give him what he needed. As he lay on his side watching Nate sleep, it occurred to him why that was.

"It's because I love you," he whispered out loud to Nate's near-motionless form. He placed the lightest of kisses on Nate's cheek, and settled back onto his own pillow, where he continued to watch Nate's back rise and fall until sleep carried him away.

THE FEEL of a hot mouth on his cock stirred Tom the next morning. By the time he realized he wasn't dreaming, he was already fully hard and his hands were moving down toward his groin. He sought and found Nate's hair, burying his hands in it and tugging lightly as he slowly thrust up toward that warm mouth. It felt amazing—Nate was so good at it— and Tom was shooting down Nate's throat in no time, gentle spasms rocking him.

Nate slid up, covering Tom's body fully with his own and kissing him deeply. "Want you so much," he whispered against Tom's mouth. "Tom… please…."

Tom was already reaching for the night table drawer. Nate rolled on the condom, and Tom gave himself a quick, cursory preparation, and then Nate was against him, and he was pressing in… so slow. He was being careful and Tom wanted to be taken. "Fuck, just do it," he said hoarsely.

"You sure?" Nate panted.

"Please, fuck me… Jesus… I need you, Nate."

With those words of permission, Nate pushed steadily in, not stopping until he was as deep inside Tom as he could be. Tom cried out, unable to hold back in that exquisite mix of pain and pleasure and the surge of emotion he felt at finally being joined with Nate again in this manner. All of Nate's intensity and fire were focused solely on his lover, sweat glistening on his skin as he sought the farthest reaches inside Tom's body with a fervor approaching desperation. "You're so beautiful… so beautiful…," Nate moaned. Tom sensed the claim, the possession that Nate was seeking, could feel it as surely as he felt his body being taken.

Another orgasm neared—for Nate too, he knew. Twisting, pressing, gasps escaping them, kisses on damp skin, and murmured endearments, a plea… and then it was happening… and Tom couldn't look away from Nate, gorgeous as he came, his head thrown back exposing his long, lean neck, sinewy limbs trembling through his climax and then, when it was over, wrapping around Tom's body, holding him as close as possible.

For a long time—more than an hour—they lay on Tom's bed, Nate having moved far enough to toss the condom into the trash beside the bed and then burying his face in Tom's neck and refusing to let go. In the postcoital endorphin haze Tom didn't fully register how clingy Nate was being. Within half an hour, though, he had tried a few times to talk to Nate—asking him a question, trying to get him to talk about one thing or another, with little success. Nate would answer with a word or two, but nothing beyond that.

Tom fretted about what to do. Last night Nate had seemed tired and stressed out, and though he didn't expect a bath and a back rub to provide an instant cure, he was becoming worried. This didn't seem like his Nate at all. When they were together Nate was warm, chatty, and engaged with him; and above all, he was self-confident—sometimes almost to a fault, as Tom knew from personal experience. This morning he seemed almost debilitated by… something. Anxiety, perhaps, but why? Tom didn't want to break their rule about the topics that were off-limits, but he didn't see how else he could get to the bottom of what was wrong.

"Hey," he murmured, kissing the top of Nate's head.

"Hmm?"

"Is everything okay?" he asked gently.

"Why?" Nate finally lifted his head to look at Tom. "Did you not enjoy it?"

"Oh—no, the sex was amazing. I didn't mean that at all. You were so intense… it was great." Nate dropped his head back on Tom's chest. Tom tried again. "What I meant was, is something bothering you?"

When Nate didn't answer he continued, "You're definitely not yourself, and you weren't last night either. I'm a little worried."

"You don't have to be worried," Nate finally answered, though he still didn't meet Tom's eyes. "I'm tired."

"Last night you said you were stressed."

"That too."

"I know we're not supposed to ask…." Tom began, but Nate stopped him, finally showing something beyond listlessness.

"Don't," he said earnestly, his warm brown eyes looking pleadingly into Tom's. "We can't, Tom, and I don't want to have to say no to you. Please don't ask me about it."

Tom knew Nate was right, but it didn't assuage his worries in the least. "All right. But you're worrying me, Nate. I need to know you're okay, that you're taking care of yourself."

"You took great care of me last night," Nate murmured tenderly.

"I can't do it nearly as often as I'd like to." Tom tried not to sound petulant, and didn't quite succeed.

"I know." Nate sighed deeply and rested his head again.

"It's hard to be away from you," Tom added and felt Nate nod against his chest. "I guess we're back to being together occasionally and having to part versus never being together at all, right?"

"Still willing to choose the one that has us saying good-bye every week?" This time Nate was the one to sound resentful.

"I'm still willing to choose the one that lets me be with you every weekend. I'm grateful that I can at least have that much."

Another deep sigh came from Nate before he said, "Yeah. I am too. I want this."

They remained where they were for some time longer, only getting up when Tom reminded Nate for the third time that they each had to travel later that day and that being late was not the way to keep their bosses happy. They both still needed to pack, and Nate had to go home to do it. They took a long, hot shower together, taking extra time to kiss softly between washing, and by the time Nate was dressed, he really couldn't put it off any longer. Nevertheless they stood at the door for long moments, hugging, kissing each other, promising to talk.

Tom took Nate's face gently between his hands. "Please take care of yourself this week," he said seriously. "Make sure you get enough sleep, and eat properly, okay? And you'll be here Saturday?"

Nate nodded, looking dismal.

"Alright, then I'll see you sometime Saturday, and in the meantime we'll try to talk if we can. I hope you have a good week. I'll miss you."

"I'll miss you too. Fuck, so much, Tom." Nate gave Tom another long hug, holding him until Tom again had to gently remind him of the time. "Okay, okay," Nate said, sad resignation in his voice, finally releasing Tom and backing away. "See you in a week."

"I'll be here." Tom tried to sound reassuring and upbeat.

Nate started to leave, but for a moment he turned back, his hand still on the door knob. "Tom, I…." He hesitated a moment and a rush of anticipation filled Tom's stomach, but Nate simply finished, "Have a good week." Tom gave a final wave, and Nate was gone.

Tom had no time to stand around feeling sorry for himself or worrying about Nate. He had exactly half an hour to pack everything he needed and be downstairs, where Sarah would pick him up on the way to the airport. Not being late to catch the charter to Portland was his sole focus until he was actually sitting on the plane. Only once he was in the sky could he slow his thoughts down and think about what the hell was going on with Nate.

Tom had assumed last night that Nate was just tired and stressed. This morning he'd seemed clingy and insecure in a way that was so out of character for him, and that was what worried Tom. They'd had such a short time to spend together this weekend, really not long enough to talk to Nate, to get him to open up about what was bothering him, and so he was left guessing. It could have been the poll numbers that were being reported lately—maybe Nate worried that Michaels would pull out. Or was something else going on with him?

Tom didn't know for sure, and he didn't imagine there was any way he'd uncover it before he saw Nate again in a week. His brain told him there was nothing he could do, and that in the meantime, he had to go back to doing his job. His heart, though, was not nearly so pragmatic, and it told him that if something was bothering his boyfriend, he had to find out what it was and what he could do to help. He wondered what Nate had almost said right before he left Tom's apartment. He'd been sure he was about to tell Tom he loved him….

So much he wouldn't know, so much he'd have to wait on for a week. Until then he would have to find a way to put it out of his mind, or he'd go nuts.

FOR MANY months after the primary, the word that would come to mind when Nate thought of Oregon would be *dismal*.

His visit that week was the first time he'd been to the state. Under other circumstances he likely would have enjoyed it. Even the rain that settled in for the entire four days probably wouldn't have put him off, had he visited at another time. As it was, the hectic schedule of events had them dashing from one place to another, always running through the rain to get from the bus to the hotel or the restaurant or the campaign office where Erin was appearing. Nate felt like he was in a perpetual state of cold and damp. Finally, when all was said and done and the polls had closed, Wagner came out four points ahead of Erin. It was the final nail in the coffin of how Nate felt about the state in general.

He was self-aware enough, of course, to realize that his state of mind these days wasn't exactly giving him a glowing overall perspective on life. Since his conversations with Erin and Jason on the Indiana-West Virginia-North Carolina trip, he'd been in a growing state of anxiety and restlessness. He couldn't shake his guilt over hiding his relationship with Tom. He knew he hadn't shared any inside information, but the mere fact that they had to hide their relationship spoke volumes. They were both being duplicitous in continuing to see each other secretly. They were so good for each other in so many other ways—their blossoming relationship should have been something that brought them uncomplicated happiness.

Being with Tom at his apartment the weekend before Oregon was difficult. He usually took so much pleasure in their trysts—not only the sex, but being with Tom, laughing with him, having conversations about so many things. It had become his sanctuary in the midst of an otherwise chaotic life. That weekend he'd been so weighed down by guilt and anxiety, and Tom had completely taken care of him, fussing over him and showing such love and concern... and Nate knew. He had fallen in love with Tom. He'd been on the verge of saying it before he left, but there wasn't time to say it properly, to fall back into Tom's arms and *show* him how much he meant it. So he'd clammed up and left before he could blurt it out.

Adding to his stress was the state of the Michaels campaign. The fact was, things on that front were going to come to a head very soon. With the results in Oregon as disappointing as they were, the future of the campaign really rested with what happened next week in Arkansas and Kentucky—two southern states where they were already polling behind Wagner. The talking heads who had been subtly questioning the length of time Erin spent in North Carolina were now openly criticizing the campaign for continuing. Nate knew Susan Pollard and her writers had been instructed to draft a potential speech for next Tuesday night in which Erin would talk about her intention to take a few days to consider the future of her campaign for the presidency. Nate saw his hopes for Erin dying slowly.

So if and when Erin pulled out, she would return to her job of representing the people of New York as their junior senator. Nate would go back to working for her, alongside Jason every day. It was a job he had once loved, but now he didn't know how to feel about the prospect. He felt himself quickly approaching a crossroads and very soon he would have to make a decision. Somehow it had become something he both wanted back, and feared returning to.

He was exhausted. They'd been fighting an uphill battle for months, and now that it seemed inevitable that they would lose the battle, he wanted the end to be past them already, so he could get back to a normal life. On the other hand, he was not used to losing. He had invested so much of himself in this campaign, had believed so fiercely in Erin and her platform. He still believed; in his heart he knew Erin to be the ideal person to lead the country, and that would never change. But going back to business as usual, a life of political posturing and backroom deals and being lobbied…. For ten years he'd thrived on the pace of that life. He'd always known he was choosing his career over a more active social life or the possibility of fostering a relationship. And then Tom came into his life and changed everything. Before, love was a formless, faceless concept; now, love was Tom. Nate was poignantly aware of the life he could have—a life with Tom, one where their friends knew they were together, where they could go out together and explore their city, and then come back to a home they shared. It wouldn't be an easy balance against the hours he kept as an aide to Erin Michaels on Capitol Hill.

Unless by some miracle Erin won Kentucky and Arkansas, he would have a decision to make.

Nate realized, though, that he should never make a major life decision when he was suffering from exhaustion and disappointed hopes. After they were back in Washington for good, he would take a few weeks to get rested up and see how he felt about being back in his old job, and then go from there. In the meantime, the campaign was going to pull out all the stops, give one last massive effort. Nate was going to have to get his head out of his navel and get invested, 100 percent, in the campaign.

The team spent Thursday and Friday strategizing, making calls, setting up as many appearances and events as they thought they could reasonably attend in the two states. They ended up spending Friday evening at Erin's place, eating takeout and arguing about whether they should leave for Kentucky sooner than they'd planned. They'd been invited by the Kentucky governor to be in Frankfort on Sunday to attend church with him. If they left DC early enough Saturday morning, they could join a late afternoon rally in Lexington they'd been invited to attend, and still be in Frankfort at a decent hour that night.

By the time all was decided and the advance team had been notified of the revised schedule, it was nearly one o'clock in the morning. Their drivers would be preparing the tour bus; staff had headed to their respective homes to get a few hours' sleep and pack their bags before getting on the road. Nate gave Jason a ride home, promising to pick him up again in a few hours, and continued on to his own place.

At home Nate set about the task of packing for the trip. He had been traveling so much this year that he kept his shaving kit packed with all the usual things and replenished it when necessary. It saved time, and he didn't have to worry about forgetting to pack something, especially when he was tired or in a rush. After he had everything ready to go and his garment bag and duffel were hanging by the front door, he flopped onto his sofa—seldom used these days—to try to figure out what to tell Tom.

It was far too late at night—or too early, depending on how he looked at it—to call Tom's cell. If it was an emergency, he would have, but it wasn't. Tom would be expecting him sometime Saturday, but by that time, Nate would be on the road. Who knew when he'd have a chance to call during the day? He didn't want Tom to be sitting waiting for him to show up and wondering what had happened to him. There was also the matter of telling Tom why he couldn't come over. If he spoke to him directly, Tom would ask. Nate wouldn't lie and didn't want to have to decline to answer, but telling Tom that the campaign was leaving earlier than planned would be feeding inside information directly to the opposing camp. No one should know they were on their way until they actually arrived at that event in Lexington.

He decided the best way to get the message to Tom was to text him. He agonized over the wording, eventually settling on:

Can't keep the appointment. Disappointed :(but no way to help it. So sorry for short notice.

It was a little dry, but if it was intercepted by the wrong person it would read as someone cancelling some sort of professional appointment— maybe a haircut or something—at the last minute. There was nothing that would identify either of them or the location the "appointment" was to have taken place. He hoped it would convey to Tom how much he regretted that he had to break their date.

Shortly after eight o'clock, he received a reply: *These things happen. :(Please call to reschedule.* As Nate tucked the little silver phone back into the inside pocket of his jacket, he wished desperately that he could tell Tom how much he missed him. He hoped Tom had been able to read between the very few lines of his text and know how greatly he regretted having to cancel.

He eventually managed to talk to Tom from a restaurant after the rally in Lexington, before they continued on to Frankfort. He had excused himself to return to the bus while many of the other staff were finishing their dinner, knowing it might be his only opportunity to call. It was a humid evening in Lexington, and Nate stood in the shade provided by the bus as he scrolled to Tom's last message to call him back.

Tom answered almost immediately. "Hello?"

"Hey, you," Nate said warmly, his heart stuttering at the sound of Tom's voice.

"Hi! Oh my god, I'm so glad to hear your voice."

Nate grinned. "You too. Listen, I'm so sorry."

"It's okay. I understand."

"You do?"

"I know where you are. I mean—I've heard. Today. I heard about…
you know, what I mean. We're not supposed to talk about it, but anyway,
yeah. I understand and it's fine, really."

Nate sighed. "If I had any choice in the matter… if there was any
way I could have been with you…."

"I know." Tom's voice was soothing. "Thank you for saying it, it's
nice to hear. I was disappointed too. But I know how it is."

Nate glanced around the end of the bus toward the restaurant. A
couple of staff members were on their way through the door, slowly
making their way across the parking lot to where the bus sat. "Look, I
wish I could talk longer…."

"I know," Tom said again.

"Thank you for understanding." It helped, he supposed, that Tom
lived this life as well and knew exactly what sort of schedule it entailed.

"I don't know when I'll have another chance to call," he said
honestly. "Perhaps not until I'm back in Washington. But I wanted to tell
you to travel safely and that I miss you, and I'll see you soon."

"I'll be counting the days."

Nate heard his colleagues approaching the bus, and he quickly
finished. "I'm sorry. I have to go. Talk to you soon."

"Bye, Nate," he heard Tom say before he clicked the phone shut
and strode around the end of the bus, grinning at his fellow staff members
as he passed them.

The next four days were an absolute whirlwind of activity. They'd
been quite successful in scheduling a full roster of events, designed for
maximum exposure for Erin. Each night they collapsed—whether on the
bus or in a hotel didn't seem to matter to any of them. They were utterly
exhausted, but there was consensus among the staff: they were glad
they were doing this. They had met so many people in both states who
intended to support Erin on Tuesday. Maybe the miracle they'd thought
was such a long shot was actually a possibility. Polls were wrong all the
time, after all. In spite of himself, Nate actually found a faint glimmer of
hope returning.

On Tuesday night he was in a suite in a hotel in Little Rock, sitting
with Erin on one side of him and Susan on the other, watching the news
and waiting for the polls to close. Various staffers were streaming different
networks' coverage on their laptops, listening with an earbud in one ear;
others were following hashtags on Twitter and other sites. Occasionally

one or another would call out, repeating something of interest that had been said on the station they were watching. Nate was flipping back and forth between iPhone and iPad, watching his twitter account on one and his e-mail on the other.

The polls closed. And then the precincts started to report in. Two percent had reported; five percent had reported. The more precincts that had reported their results, the more frequently the staff members were piping up with bits of information gleaned across the two states. Nine percent reporting. With 10 percent in Kentucky, the race was too close to call. In Arkansas it wasn't as close. Wagner was ahead slightly, but not enough to call it for him. Fifteen percent now. Twenty. Each time the voices piped up, they became a little less enthusiastic, a bit more subdued. The gap was widening between Wagner and Michaels, and not in Erin's favor.

By the time Wagner's lead had widened to 6 percent in Kentucky, the staffers following the social media had been asked to discontinue their verbal updates. In fact, the only ones with the unenviable task of continuing to report on their findings were the ones watching the major cable news networks. MSNBC was the first to call Kentucky for Wagner. Within fifteen minutes they had also called Arkansas for Wagner, where he was seven points ahead and expected to maintain that lead. The staffers didn't have to be asked to stop; they had pulled out their earbuds, standing watching the main television screen in the room and looking completely dejected.

Nate knew exactly how they felt. They had worked so fucking hard. Not just this weekend, although they'd probably gone harder this weekend than any other time in the campaign, including the lead-up to Super Tuesday. They had all sacrificed so much because they believed in Erin. It was almost too horrible to consider that she would pull out of the race before the end of the week.

Susan Pollard came into the living room from where she and her speech writer had been working on the finishing touches for the two possibilities for her speeches. Susan hadn't yet heard the predictions from MSNBC, but when she realized what was plastered on the television screen, she turned to Erin.

"Oh, Erin" was all she said, but her face crumpled and tears filled her eyes. She sat down beside Erin on the couch and put her arm around her shoulder. Erin leaned into her, and they hugged each other for a long time, drawing comfort and strength from a friendship that had spanned more than two decades. Together they had been through a great deal over the years—college, jobs, campaigns, loves, marriages, deaths, Erin's separation and soon divorce. Nate wondered if either of them had ever imagined this when they met as freshmen in college.

Eventually they pulled away and Erin, trying to bring a little levity, said, "Well. Hands behind your back, and I'll try to guess which hand the right speech is in."

Susan grimaced, then held the iPad out to Jason, saying, "It's ready for you." Jason took it and sat at the dining table in the suite, Nate at his side, and together they read. Though it didn't say explicitly that Erin was discontinuing her campaign, one didn't have to read very much between the lines to know that "going to take a few days, consult with my staff, and consider our future course" meant that a concession by Erin would follow shortly.

When they'd both finished reading, Jason stood, buttoned his suit jacket, and cleared his throat to address the room. "We'll be going downstairs shortly, and Erin will deliver her speech. I suggest you all go to your rooms, freshen up, and be downstairs in ten minutes."

Aside from the senior staff, everyone made to follow Jason's instructions, but Erin stood, saying, "Wait." They stopped and the room fell silent as they gave her their full attention. "I want to tell you all how much I have appreciated your dedication over these last months. You are the most committed, intelligent, and hard-working group of individuals I've had the privilege to be associated with. I know this feels like a bitter final leg of our journey, but none of us ever knows for sure what the future holds. In the days and weeks ahead, I'll speak to each of you personally, but I can't let this moment go by without telling you...." Her voice broke and she took a moment to steady it before concluding, "Without telling you how grateful I am. Thank you."

Every person in the room burst into applause, some smiling through their tears, everyone with genuine affection and respect for Erin. When the applause died down, they turned and made their way to their hotel rooms, leaving Erin, Susan, Jason and Nate in the suite.

Jason strode over to the television and turned it off, muttering, "I think we've had enough of that." The four stood and looked at each other for a moment, until Nate realized he was the junior person in the room.

If anyone was going to leave first, it should be him. He would let Erin's two most senior staff have a moment alone with her.

But first he approached Erin and took both of her hands in his, looking down seriously into her kind blue eyes. "Madame Senator," he addressed her formally, "it has been my honor to serve on your campaign, and I thank you for the privilege. I can't foresee anything that could convince me that you were not and are not the right person to lead our country."

"Thank you, Nathan." Erin squeezed his hands for a moment, and then he excused himself and left the three alone.

Already having read the text of Erin's speech, Nate thought he could steel himself against the emotion of hearing it. He was wrong. Being in the ballroom full of people who'd had such high hopes for Erin was utterly demoralizing. The attendees who weren't privy to the inside campaign information were disappointed by the night's results, but they were still hopeful, still prepared to press on if Erin did. When she delivered the line about taking a few days to make a decision about the future of the campaign, the reality was finally clear to all. Their reaction was swift and profound, gasps and protests audible throughout the room. It was the first moment Nate found himself with a lump in his throat, swallowing and blinking furiously to keep the tears from spilling over.

It was well after one in the morning when he finally got to bed. A group of staff had gone for a drink—or three—in the hotel bar. He'd asked Jason to join them, but Jason declined, saying he wasn't up for it. Even after Nate was in bed, it took him a long time to fall asleep, in spite of how tired he was. His brain kept mulling over everything that had happened in the last few days—all the events, so many people and places, and it hadn't worked. They couldn't beat the delegate count Wagner would have. Nate was disoriented, as though he *couldn't* feel. He had clamped down so tightly on his emotions over the last week and a half, willing himself not to feel, not to allow anything to distract him from the task at hand. It was hard to convince himself that it was finally okay to let go.

He slept fitfully, waking often, and was the first person in the restaurant the next morning for breakfast. One by one his colleagues joined him, looking to be in varying states of blurry disbelief. Eventually, Jason sat down across from Nate and nodded a good morning. Once he'd ordered his breakfast and started on his second cup of coffee, he said to Nate, "I spent an hour or so with Erin last night, talking about where and when."

Nate didn't need to ask where or when *what*. He knew Jason was referring to Erin's announcement that she was conceding the race to Bill Wagner. He looked seriously at Jason. "Has she decided?"

Jason nodded. "This weekend, Yorktown."

"At her parents' place?" Nate replied with surprise.

"Near it. She said there's a state park with a lake... I don't know. It's what she wants, and it's up to her, now. She wants her parents with her, and I understand that. It's also a good idea to go back to New York for the announcement. The state gave her the first chance in elected office and now she'll be returning her full focus to her duties in the Senate." Nate couldn't help noticing that Jason wasn't looking at him as he spoke. It was unusual for him—he was usually a direct, "look you in the eye" kind of man. Nate chalked it up to the events of the night before and just plain exhaustion. There wasn't a single one of them who wasn't showing the signs of strain.

"So Sully tells me the drive back to Washington will be about seventeen hours, not including stops," Jason said, referring to one of the bus drivers as he abruptly changed the subject. "If we get on the road within an hour... stop for dinner tonight somewhere around Knoxville, maybe, that's about nine hours, and then continue on overnight. Should be back in DC by 5:00 a.m., maybe? Six? Depending on traffic. I'll tell you one thing I won't miss is that goddamned bus. Sleeping on one of the couches is bad enough—I don't know how the others manage to sleep in those bunks. It's like being in a coffin." Nate saw him shudder and repressed a grin, knowing Jason's fear of small spaces was very real.

Jason's estimates were pretty close. They were back in DC shortly before 6:00 a.m. the next morning and Nate was in his own bed by seven. Everyone had been instructed to stay home that day, though he told Jason to call him if he needed him. Jason waved a hand dismissively at him. "I won't be calling. Turn your phone off until tomorrow morning and rest."

It was exactly what Nate did. He knew Tom wasn't in the city. Tom had texted him that the Wagner campaign were headed to Atlanta and that he wouldn't be home before Sunday, at the earliest. Nate figured they had decamped there to wait out the announcement that Erin was withdrawing. It would put Wagner at home to celebrate with his nearest and dearest, which Nate understood. So with Tom away, Nate had a full day to himself to do nothing but sleep, putter around his apartment, sleep some more, watch television and follow that up with a nap. Having quite a bit of time alone with his thoughts, he found that they continually returned to Tom. As disappointed as Nate was at Erin's concession, he knew Tom was flying high on Wagner's impending nomination. Somehow it made Nate smile to think about how happy Tom must be. More than his own disappointment, more than anything, what Nate wanted most was to see Tom again, to hold him, to kiss him, and to simply talk to him. He couldn't wait until Tom returned from Atlanta.

Nate had no trouble sleeping that night, and woke early the next morning with the best outlook he'd had all week. He was ready to accompany Erin to New York this weekend, to be by her side and support her when she withdrew her candidacy.

However, things didn't turn out quite as he anticipated.

He tried to call Jason Friday morning, knowing he'd be up with the sun, but got no answer. He didn't wait, heading to his office on the Hill where he hadn't been in several weeks. He intended to have a look through whatever nonessential correspondence had been left in his inbox during his absence—anything time-sensitive would have been scanned to his e-mail by the office aide—and then be ready to leave with Erin when she did.

Upon arriving, he found Jason had gotten there even earlier than he had. "Hey—good morning," Nate greeted.

Jason looked up at him from something he was reading on his iPad. "You're in early," he remarked, returning to his reading.

"You too." Nate chose one of the chairs opposite Jason's desk and sitting. "What time did you get here?"

Jason didn't answer right away, eventually muttering absentmindedly, "Uh... five, I guess."

"Wow, right back at it, huh? Good man," Nate tried to inject a bit of levity into the room. The attempt fell pretty flat. In the silence that followed, Nate became aware of an oddly tense air in the room. He couldn't say why exactly it felt that way—there wasn't anything he could put his finger on—but it was... uncomfortable.

Finally Jason looked up. "Sorry, Nate, I can't chat. I've got some reading to do, and then I've got to get to a meeting for nine o'clock."

"Of course," Nate replied, feeling sheepish. If he was distracting Jason from something important, of course Jason wouldn't be rolling out a welcome mat. "Do you need me there?" Jason shook his head. "Okay. Hey, I'm on my way to grab a coffee, can I bring you back one?"

Jason replied by holding up his own paper cup. "I'm all set, thanks." Nate turned to leave when Jason added, "By the way, I was having a look through some of the stuff in your inbox." It wasn't unusual for Jason and Nate to refer to each other's electronic inboxes. All correspondence that came into the office for either of them was filed electronically, regardless of the format in which it arrived; once it was digitized it would be placed in an electronic queue for their review according to priority. "You've got quite a list of stuff in there. I know Iris was sending you all the highest priority stuff, but if you could, I'd like you to at least get eyes on everything in the inbox and prioritize it. Delegate whatever you can."

"Yeah, I figured I would. I planned to work on it this morning and clear up as much as possible before we head up to New York State. When are we going, by the way? There's nothing on my iCal. Is she doing it tomorrow?"

Jason looked at his watch. "I'll keep you posted when everything's finalized."

"The details aren't finalized?" Nate said incredulously, his eyebrows climbing halfway up his forehead.

"Look, Nate, I really do need to get back to this." Jason was abrupt.

"Oh… uh, yeah. Of course, sorry, I'll leave you alone." Nate turned and left, feeling thoroughly confused by the entire interaction with Jason. It had an oddly impersonal tone. And something else… something odd in Jason's manner that he couldn't put his finger on. He was definitely unsettled by the whole thing.

Soon enough he was in his own office and wading through the not-insignificant stack of correspondence. He delegated a great deal of it, forwarding it to the inboxes of other staff members with his comments and copying to Jason when appropriate. With his iPhone on silent, he worked steadily, his only distraction coming around ten thirty, when his little silver phone vibrated in his pocket. He slid it open to see a text from Tom.

(((hugs)))

Nate stared at the phone for a moment before sighing deeply. It was such a simple thing, not even a complete sentence, but it reminded him that he was in Tom's thoughts—as Tom was always in his. He thought about texting back his congratulations or that he was proud of Tom, but as he considered it, it occurred to him that without the benefit of tone of voice or facial expression, it might seem sarcastic or bitter. So instead he sent a reply that was as simple and heartfelt as Tom's had been.

Miss you xo

That was the last time he looked at the clock until his desk phone rang. With a start he realized it was almost one o'clock, and this was the first time it had rung all day.

"Nathan Harris," he said, checking his wall clock confirm the time.

"Nate" came Jason's voice. "Need you in my office. Now, please."

"I'm on my way," Nate replied, already rising from his chair before the phone was back in the cradle. As Nate entered Jason's office a few doors down the hall, he began, "I just realized we haven't seen the text of Erin's announcement yet. In fact, I haven't heard a word from Susan all day—"

"I've seen it," said Jason.

The reply brought Nate up short. "You have?"

"I saw a draft yesterday and the final a couple of hours ago."

Nate didn't know what to say. For Jason to approve a speech without asking Nate to read it was unprecedented. "You… didn't want me to read it?"

"It's no longer in your list of duties," Jason said.

Nate sat in one of Jason's office chairs, feeling disoriented. Yes, the campaign was over and maybe he should have considered that there might be a change of organizational structure within Erin's staff, but changes had apparently been made without his input, changes that affected his job. "May I ask why not?"

"We'll talk about that in a bit," Jason replied coolly.

"Okay." The feeling of disorientation grew, and with it crept in anxiety. "By the way, do you know yet when we're leaving?"

"Leaving?"

"For New York. For Erin to make the announcement?"

Jason looked at his watch. "I'm guessing Erin landed at Westchester County about forty-five minutes ago."

With those words Nate went from disoriented to dumbfounded. He didn't understand, couldn't *fathom* what was happening or why. "Forgive me, Jason, what the hell is going on?"

"I decided you and I would stay here. No point in a campaign manager and his deputy going when there's no longer a campaign to manage."

Nate replied slowly. "When did you decide that?"

"This morning."

Whether or not Jason saw a "point" to being there, Nate didn't really care. He'd been with Erin all along, and to him, that included when she ended her campaign. He was so surprised by this turn of events that he didn't even know what to say.

"I'd like to watch it with you, though," Jason continued, picking up a remote on his desk and turning on the television. They sat in silence, listening and watching as the commentators onscreen discussed Erin's upcoming press conference. The content of the announcement was a foregone conclusion, as it always seemed to be. There was so much talk before the press conference that the actual announcement was almost anticlimactic.

It was difficult for Nate to concentrate on anything but the stiff silence between them. Jason wasn't even making his usual comments on what the onscreen panel was discussing, and that was entirely out of character for him. Painfully slow minutes ticked by, second by excruciating second, until at long last, Erin took the stage. It was, as Jason had said, set at a small state park very near her parents' house in New York State. The weather and the setting looked idyllic, a far cry from the turmoil thrashing around in Nate's brain.

The speech was about fifteen minutes long, lengthy enough considering the subject. Erin didn't only announce her withdrawal; she took time to thank her staff, naming some individually, Nate and Jason included. She thanked her parents as well as Richard, and Nate realized with some surprise that Richard was standing alongside Mr. and Mrs. Michaels. He was glad that, even though they'd decided to end their marriage, Erin still had Richard's support as a friend.

Over the course of the speech, Erin also endorsed Bill Wagner, and that was perhaps the bitterest pill for Nate to swallow. Bill Wagner was a decent enough guy and a good senator, but president? Nate couldn't fathom it, not when the alternative was Erin. Nate would never be convinced that Erin wasn't the absolute best person to win the nomination and the presidency. As Erin asked all those assembled and all who had supported her to give Wagner their cooperation and backing, Nate couldn't help a small snort. Jason looked over at him and grimaced, and it was the first time since Nate had joined Jason in his office that Nate felt a small break in the tension—a very small break.

When Erin was finished, the cameras pulled back to show the assembled crowd. Nate spotted Susan and Laurie, and several other staff members there. The supporters who had joined her were emotional, shaking her hand, some offering hugs, and from the looks on their faces, obviously telling her how very sorry they were. Again Nate felt a little surge of emotion that it was ending and that he hadn't been there with her. Something was very wrong about this, about him and Jason being here, and the fact that Jason was acting so unusually... he didn't know how to interpret that.

The commentators onscreen went into their usual recap of the speech as they did after every debate and press conference. Nate had always found the almost line-by-line analysis horribly boring, and now it seemed particularly pointless. It was over—no voters to convince, no spin to doctor.

On the television, the inset video changed, showing a stage in front of a large old building. Nate didn't recognize it immediately, but the anchor leading the panel soon identified the building as belonging to Emory College in Atlanta, where Senator Wagner would soon take the stage. *Of course*, Nate thought. Erin would have called Bill Wagner ahead of time. She would have told him of her decision so they could be prepared, so that Bill Wagner could deliver his own speech in response to her announcement.

Nate listened to the speech with his hands clasped in his lap—well, maybe clenched was more like it. He could see Wagner's mouth move, could hear his voice, and yet Nate knew those were Tom's words. Tom had written about a love of public service. He'd written about reconciliation, about bringing together a party hurt by months of comparisons and contrasts, debate and division. He'd written about priorities, about knowing what his primary commitments were, and his responsibility to Americans.

The camera panned along the front row of listeners, and Nate saw individuals he recognized—Kim Harvey, her assistant Sarah, Mitchell

Enns… and of course, beside Mitchell, was Tom. Nate's heart clenched and his stomach churned to see Tom standing there, looking so pleased as he watched and listened to his candidate. With warmth in his heart, Nate realized that he didn't resent Tom for that happiness or the sense of accomplishment and pride he must feel. Tom had worked as hard for Wagner's success as Nate had worked for Erin. He deserved to be delighted by the outcome.

The speech ended and Wagner's supporters went wild with applause. The television went back to a split screen, and the panel was about to jump back in, but before they could start Jason turned off the television. He looked at Nate levelly. "Looks like your boyfriend's going to be busy for a while."

Nate stared at Jason dumbly for a long minute, and then…. *Fuck.* Understanding exploded like a bomb; he felt sickened.

"You know," he whispered.

"Of course I know."

"How? We were…." Nate stopped short of saying, *We were so careful.* He leaned forward, resting his elbows on his knees, breathing, looking at the floor, and trying to ignore the ringing in his ears. Finally he asked, "How long have you known?"

"I've suspected something for a while, with you vanishing every weekend. You never used to do that—you had no life, like the rest of us. I was sure you were seeing someone. I don't know when it started, but at least since April. Your Easter weekend in North Carolina wasn't the best way to stay below the radar." Nate winced and Jason went on, "Oh yeah, I know about that too."

"Fuck," muttered Nate. "Why didn't you say anything?"

"Why didn't *you*?" Jason countered, his voice rising in chagrin. "Jesus, Nate! You knew exactly what you were doing. Until this week, all I knew was that you were most likely sleeping with someone. I didn't have any details, I didn't know who. I hoped it would be good for you. Everyone needs to blow off steam. I had faith that you wouldn't let it affect your performance or the campaign." He shook his head. "My mistake."

There was no point in protesting that it hadn't interfered, because Nate's gaffe in North Carolina was proof of that. The guilt he'd already felt about disappointing Jason revisited him with interest. There was a long silence until finally Nate quietly asked, "How did you find out it was Tom?"

Jason exhaled and sat back in his chair, looking levelly across the desk at Nate. "Last Saturday night when we were in Kentucky. It was right after dinner and almost everyone was still in the restaurant. I was on the bus enjoying a few moments of quiet. I saw you come out to the bus, and I thought you were going to get on, but then you pulled out a cell phone and made a call. You use an iPhone but this wasn't it—it was one I'd never seen you use or even carry with you. I couldn't hear what you said, but you kept looking around the end of the bus toward the restaurant, like you were checking to see if anyone was around. When someone was coming, you ended the call." Jason spoke each word deliberately. "You know what that looks like, Nate? Know what it looks like when a senior staff member in a presidential primary, with access to inside information, is sneaking around to make calls on a secret phone?"

Nate stared in horror, his mouth open. "You thought I was spying?"

"I didn't know what the hell to think. But my loyalty—*my* loyalty— is to this campaign and to Erin Michaels, and I have to consider every possibility, Nate—even the possibility that my deputy is selling the campaign up the river. So the next day when you were at church with Erin, I looked through your bag. I found that phone, and I got the number from it. I gave it to Duncan"—here he referred to the secret service agent who was the head of Erin's security detail—"with instructions to get me the incoming and outgoing phone records, texts, voice mail, everything. I asked for everything he could find out on who you'd been speaking to from that phone. And I asked him for a report on you—all your activity for the past two months."

Jason picked up a manila folder, handing it to Nate. "This is what he gave me last night, but let me give you the highlights. Duncan was a little surprised to find you'd only ever made calls to two numbers with that phone. You called a taxi company once, and the rest of the time you called a 202 number—a number that, along with the phone you were using, was registered to you. Well, that didn't make sense to Duncan, so he went ahead and gathered the surveillance report and put that all together too. Because—as you are well aware, Nate—the secret service has files on each of us, and surveillance on senior staff is pretty standard even though we're not under protection. He discovered that over the last few months you've spend a lot of your weekend time at a high-rise apartment building on New Jersey Avenue. It didn't take Duncan long to recognize one of the building residents as a staff member for Wagner. Of course, just because he lived there didn't mean that's who you were going to see, but it did make Duncan wonder about the 202 number you'd been calling. So he got the report for that one too, and you know what the real kicker is? When I look at where and when that phone was used, and compare it to the whereabouts of the Wagner campaign at any given time, they're identical. If the phone was used to send a text from Lancaster, Pennsylvania, Wagner was there that day. If it received an incoming call while it was in Chattanooga, Tennessee, well, the Wagner campaign was there at that time. When the campaign wasn't on the road, the phone's use was here in DC."

His forehead in his hands, Nate stared at the carpet between his feet for a long, silent time. His thoughts swirled in his head. He and Tom had thought themselves so clever, playing an ongoing game of cloak-and-dagger and believing they were the ones who would succeed in living outside the rules. It was so obvious, now, that they had been disgracefully naive. Those weeks of planning and clandestine meetings had been for nothing, the truth discovered so easily that Jason could now recount it in a few sentences.

Nate breathed slowly in through his nose, out through his mouth, trying to calm the nausea. Who had he become? Someone who rationalized away his poor decisions, lying outright or by omission about his life, and now he'd been discovered by his mentor, one of his best friends. He never would have believed it of himself.

How his life had changed since that day five months ago when he first laid eyes on Tom McAlindon.

Finally, speaking as though to himself, Nate murmured, "I'm sorry."

"Come again?"

Slowly Nate lifted his head to look Jason in the eye. "I'm sorry. I jeopardized Erin's chance at the nomination. I got distracted by my personal life at a time when you needed me most, and then I lied to you about the reasons." He took a deep breath. "I disappointed you and Erin...." His voice broke, and he paused a moment before finishing simply, "I'm sorry."

Jason exhaled a long breath through his nose. "I'm sorry too," he said, and his voice took on a tone of deep regret. "Because unfortunately, you're finished."

"Finished… fired?" Bile was rising in his throat.

"This wasn't one isolated screw-up, Nate. It was deliberate, and it was ongoing. You made repeated decisions to mislead us."

Nate had to fight to keep his voice steady. "I need you to know that I never shared any information with Tom about the campaign—nothing. We had a zero tolerance policy on discussing anything work related, and I would *never*—"

"Nate," Jason interrupted, "relax. If I'd turned up anything that even hinted you might have shared information with the Wagner campaign, I wouldn't fire you. I'd *destroy* you." Jason spoke with such conviction that Nate believed him. Even as his body shook with adrenaline, he felt relief knowing Jason didn't suspect him of sabotaging the campaign. "But you knew we wouldn't be happy about this, at least not during the primaries. It must have occurred to you that what you were doing could have looked like collusion—to the candidates, to the press, not to mention the voters. If someone else had found this out instead of me, it could have shaken our campaign—hell, *both* campaigns. Where would the party have been if the undecided voters ran screaming from the only two viable Democratic candidates? All the money that was invested in these campaigns, all the time people have given trying to get to the point where we have a candidate who can win the election over a sitting president… and you were willing to jeopardize that to be with Tom. I wouldn't have believed it of you, Nate." Jason shook his head as though still trying to grasp what had taken place. "I wish you'd made a different choice. But this is where we stand now. You don't come back from this."

But… "I've been here for ten years."

"Ten years during which you had a single-minded focus and commitment to your job; and you were great. You're still good, but you're not great, not anymore. You've lost the edge you had. It's possible that you might have gotten it back eventually. But Nate?" Jason's gaze softened, a gentleness creeping into his voice. "Maybe losing the sharp edge isn't the worst thing in the world."

Nate was mystified. "What do you mean?"

Jason rubbed his hand wearily over his face. "Look, if you'd only been out for sex, you could have gotten that pretty well anywhere. You risked a lot, and you knew full well the possible detriment to yourself, to Tom, and to the campaigns. You don't do that for sex."

"People do."

"*People* might. *You* don't."

Nate thought for a moment before conceding. "No, I don't."

"So I assume that means deeper feelings. Maybe even love. You don't have to answer that, but I want you to consider it seriously, Nate. Because if it *is* love, that means you have a chance at a life, at actual happiness and a relationship. It's hard to keep a relationship going when you work here. Not impossible, of course, a lot of people do it, but it's not the ideal situation. Definitely not one I'd choose for my friends. I know it would have been nice to make the decision to leave on your terms, but… well, maybe in a way, you did. Maybe you were making the decision when you chose to get involved with him."

The room fell silent as Nate considered that. For weeks he'd been struggling not to think too far ahead, not to picture a life with Tom. If he let himself go there, he could envision it very easily, and it looked so good. And yet….

"This is all I know how to do."

Jason scoffed. "Bullshit. Keep doing it if it's what you truly love, but if you want my advice, I think you should grab this opportunity with both hands. You're a lawyer, for Christ's sake. You can practice law. You can teach. You can consult."

"Who's going to hire me with this in my background?"

"It won't be in your background. No one knows, and there's no reason why they have to. Officially, you're resigning to explore new horizons. People will probably assume you had a disagreement with me about ending the campaign, because they know you would never give up. As long as no one else finds out about you and Tom, your secret and your reputation are safe."

For the first time, Nate felt tears threaten, but through force of will he pushed them down. "Thanks."

"Well, it's not only the goodness of my heart. We have to think about the nominee too. No one knows outside of me, Duncan, and Erin, and she was very clear that this would be dealt with privately."

"Oh, shit, Erin." Nate been so focused on Jason's reproach that he'd managed not to think about Erin. Now another wave of nausea hit him as he thought about how he'd betrayed her trust.

Jason's face hardened slightly. "I told her last night."

Nate struggled a moment before asking awkwardly, "How did... I mean, what.... How was she?"

"She was...." Jason paused thoughtfully a moment before continuing. "She was sad. She said she talked to you about your love life not long ago and that you must have straight up lied to her. And she's not happy to have to fire you. If it was only up to her, I think she might not have done."

"I wish I could talk to her," Nate murmured.

Jason nodded slowly. "You should. Eventually, although I don't think she's ready yet. At the very least, you should thank her. She wasn't only thinking of the nominee. She didn't want to spoil your career chances." Jason paused, looking slightly uncomfortable before adding, "Neither do I, now that I know the worst you did was find someone to love. You're my friend, Nate. The best friend I've made in DC."

As they lapsed into silence, each with their own thoughts. Nate felt a wave of gratitude for Erin. She could have reacted with spite for his dishonesty, and his future would have lain in tatters. Instead, she was showing compassion, perhaps more than he deserved. He owed her so much. He would take Jason's advice and contact her later, when a bit of time had passed.

Eventually Nate voiced something he'd been wondering about for days. "Think Wagner will offer running mate to Erin?"

Jason pursed his lips, contemplating. "Tough call. Nothing's impossible, but.... Maybe she'll get offered a cabinet post."

"*President* Wagner," Nate said with a grimace. "God, that sucks."

"Better than President Yoder." Nate's curled lip betrayed how unconvinced he was, and for the first time in their conversation, Jason smiled. "Yeah, okay, it's not *that* much better. But you and I will keep that to ourselves and be good, party-line Democrats, yeah?"

"Yeah." Nate leaned back in the chair, letting his body relax a bit. "I'm really fired?"

"You're really fired." Jason sighed. "But I'm going to miss you, kid. You've been my right hand for a long time. It'll suck to have to get used to someone new." Jason opened a deep drawer in his desk and pulled out a bottle of scotch and two glasses. He poured a couple fingers in each and slid a glass across the desk to Nate.

"What are we drinking to?"

Jason considered a moment before answering. "To the first decade of our friendship. And to new directions."

If it meant he hadn't destroyed his friendship with Jason? "I'll drink to that." Nate lifted his glass in Jason's direction.

The two men sipped their Scotch, silently pondering where those new directions might lead, until Jason lifted the bottle again. "Another?"

"No," Nate decided, setting his glass on the desk. "Thanks, but I've got stuff to look after. Like cleaning out my office. Oh, God," he added as an embarrassing thought occurred to him. "I don't have to do it under the watch of some brawny Capitol cop, do I?"

"Nah. No one knows yet anyway, and most are gone for the long weekend. I'll tell them later, but for now I'll instruct them to give you the weekend off. Do it now and you won't have to see anyone."

"Thanks."

"Night, kid."

"You too, old man. Get some sleep tonight, and no more of that sauce."

Jason grinned, shaking his head. "Nah, I'm done. I'm on my way in a few minutes."

Nate left, closing the door behind him. In his own office—not for much longer—he found a new banker's box sitting on his desk. Jason must have asked one of the aides to leave it there for him. He slowly took down the frames from his wall—his bachelor's degree, his JD, mementos from the time he'd spent in this building, his Frank Kameny letter—and the few photos he had on his shelf. He gathered his suit jacket and briefcase, pulled the door shut, and slowly made his way out of the building, the last time he would leave this building under the employ of the Government of the United States of America.

Despite the lighter note on which his conversation with Jason had ended, a positive mood was impossible right now. He got into his car, put down the windows, and sat for long minutes, staring at nothing. He was unemployed, ignominiously fired from the career he loved, because he'd pursued a relationship with Tom.

Tom, who would continue on with the Wagner campaign, crisscrossing America over the coming months; who would have the privilege and pleasure of writing his candidate's nomination acceptance speech; who seemed so serious and reserved when he was working but showed an entirely different side—warm, open, passionate—when they were together in private. Tom… whom Nate loved.

And Jason had suggested Nate pursue a life with Tom. If only it were that simple, if leaving the Hill could be a magic bullet that made all their obstacles vanish… but it wasn't, and thinking about the reality made a heavy ache settle in Nate's chest. Tom was remarkably talented, his career still very young. He would be busier than ever now that Wagner's campaign was switching gears to focus on a race against Karl Yoder. He'd be on the road constantly in the months between now and the election. There was no way he could openly be in an intimate relationship with the former deputy campaign manager to Erin Michaels, and today showed what folly lay in trying to keep it secret. Eventually someone would find out. Questions would be raised, perhaps even improprieties implied, bringing unflattering scrutiny to both campaign teams. Certainly it would jeopardize Erin's chances of being Wagner's running mate, or at the very least, being offered a cabinet post.

And what about Tom's career when he discovered why Nate was fired? No way would Tom's conscience allow him to leave well enough alone, to let Nate take the fall when they shared equal accountability. No, he would insist on being *noble*, do something stupid like admit everything to his bosses. But Nate couldn't imagine lying about something so important if they wanted to have any chance of building a solid relationship.

Nate shook his head and came back to himself. Lost in thought for so long, his collar was damp with sweat from the warm evening. He started his car and headed home. A breeze blew in the open car windows, fresh and cool across his face, and it seemed to blow away the what ifs and maybes whirling in his mind, leaving a stillness and clarity. He wasn't worried about himself now. He would do whatever it took to protect Tom's career from their indiscretion.

Even if it broke his heart.

OF COURSE it wasn't nearly the first time Tom had heard his own words spoken by someone else, but he was certain it was the sweetest. Bill Wagner's voice was melodic as he acknowledged that he'd received a call from Erin Michaels, a call wherein she advised him she was discontinuing her campaign. Tom stood shoulder to shoulder with Mitch,

Kim, Sarah and other senior staff, a vibrantly proud group to the side of the platform where Wagner spoke, and thought of all the miles he'd logged with these people and all that still lay ahead. He was grateful for their shared vision and for the support he felt among the group.

However, he admitted to himself, what he was most grateful for was that, from this point on, the speeches he wrote would be used in battle against a Republican candidate, not against a member of his own party, particularly one as intelligent and dedicated as Erin Michaels. He knew there would be many within the Democratic Party who would be bitterly disappointed at the events of today—one in particular came to mind. From now on the comparisons he drew would highlight the difference between Bill's platform and that of President Yoder, instead of pointing out to listeners that another Democrat's political philosophy was a little too Libertarian, not quite socialist enough; that she wasn't "our kind of Democrat." He'd overheard someone use that expression early on at one of the caucuses, and he hated it passionately.

But no, now he was here on a glorious Friday afternoon in Atlanta, the town where his career in politics had been conceived and gestated and taken its first fledgling steps. He felt hugely powerful in this group of friends and colleagues, ready to help Bill slay the figurative dragon of Karl Yoder and take the White House.

The last time Tom had spoken to Nate was the weekend before the primary, when Nate had called him to apologize for having to break their plans. They had texted a few times since then; Tom had let Nate know he'd be in Atlanta for a few days and that he hoped they would see each other before Memorial Day weekend was over. Nate had replied that he would have to see what his schedule was like.

But all that had happened before the concession call came from Erin.

The call was by no means unexpected. Erin Michaels's speech Tuesday night had all but admitted she would be announcing her concession within a few days. When she spoke to Bill, she congratulated him on an excellent campaign and told him she would be endorsing him and asking her supporters to back him as well. She wished him luck and told him that if there was anything she could do to help him win the presidency, he need only ask. Tom understood why people respected her so much—she was as gracious and genuine as she was intelligent. His best hope for her was that she could be tapped to be Bill's running mate.

He had no say in such things, of course. There were strategists and advisors and a hundred other people with opinions about it who would have more input into the decision than him. For a day or two, though, he let himself dream about it. Partly he wished it for Erin's sake, but mostly... mostly he was hoping against hope for some way that he and Nate could still be near each other during the campaign. Wagner and his running mate wouldn't be at all the same events all the time, but enough that he could see his boyfriend once in a while, at least. And then when the running mates weren't on the road they'd be back in Washington— both still senators, of course, with obligations there—and he could see Nate then too. Finally, Bill would win the election, Tom and Nate would both be in Washington for the next eight years, and while they wouldn't see each other a great deal at work, their free time—such as it was— would be with each other.

It was a best case scenario, and that was a lot to hope for. It didn't mean Tom wouldn't hope for it, but there were other possibilities. If Bill didn't choose Erin as a running mate, she could still keep her seat in the Senate and he and Nate would both be in Washington for the long term. No matter what happened, they would have to figure out a way to make it work. Tom refused to entertain any possibility that precluded the continuation of their relationship. He was in love. He was not willing to let it go.

That night, after Bill's press conference, the team had a huge party in Atlanta. Bill's wife, Rebecca, with the help of their close friends and family, pulled together a fantastic bash in the back yard of their Brookhaven home. There was a huge barbecue that was being manned by a good friend of Bill's; various kinds of beer and soda were chilling in tubs of ice. Several of Bill's friends were in an oldies band, and they had been all too happy to play a last-minute show for the party. They were belting out the tunes now, and people were dancing on the grass in their bare feet in front of the makeshift stage. Tom had partied the night away, eating and drinking, dancing with Sarah, laughing till his sides and his face ached. They had all worked so hard, and still had a long road ahead of them to win Bill the presidency. It felt great to have a night with no responsibilities, nothing to do but have fun and relax.

By midnight, the band had stopped playing in order to keep the Wagners on good terms with their neighbors. Tom was stretched out on his back on a blanket, looking up at the stars. Sarah was beside him.

For a while they'd been talking quietly, but her voice had become more and more drowsy, and eventually she had drifted off. Tom was a little drunk and very tired, and he was ready to go back to the hotel and sleep. Rebecca had hired a bus to drive everyone back to wherever they were staying, and he heard her across the lawn, telling people it would be leaving shortly. He sat up and turned to Sarah, who was indeed asleep. He carefully stroked her face, bringing her gently back to consciousness and smiling when she blinked up at him, looking bewildered.

On the bus, Sarah settled against his side, her head on his shoulder and his arm around her. As she dozed his memory drifted back six weeks to the last time he had lain looking up at the stars... and he felt a pang of longing for Nate. He missed him so much. He wanted to talk to Nate, to hold him and tell him he loved him. He wanted to comfort his boyfriend, who had suffered a profound disappointment in his professional life this week. He had to call him as soon as he could.

It was far too late now, of course; he would call him tomorrow. He had the rest of the weekend off, and he planned to stay in the city and see some of his friends, but maybe if Nate's schedule allowed they could see each other Monday night after Tom got back to DC.

He slept late the next day, and when he awoke at noon, he felt hung over and cotton-mouthed. A few cups of coffee and a decently greasy breakfast helped quite a bit. So did a couple of ibuprofen and about a gallon of water. Sarah joined him in the hotel restaurant an hour or so after he got up. Looking far worse off than him, she quietly ordered a cup of coffee. He grinned at her indulgently, not used to seeing her in such bad shape. Shortly thereafter, Mitch and a few others slid into the chairs around them. Everyone's voices were unusually quiet, as it seemed they were all suffering from a similar malady.

As they all got coffee and food into them, though, they perked up, looking and sounding more like themselves. Mitch had just asked for a refill on his coffee when his Blackberry, lying on the table, vibrated. As he looked at it, Tom heard him click his tongue. "What's up?" asked Tom.

"Ah, the demise of the Michaels campaign takes its first victim," Mitch said casually. "This one's sort of a surprise—he's been with her since she became a senator. He and Jason both have such strong personalities, though, and everyone knew Nathan didn't want her to end her campaign."

"Wait, do you mean Nathan Harris?" Sarah asked, intrigued. "He left Erin Michaels?"

Mitch read aloud from the news article that had been forwarded him. "Susan Pollard, Communications Director for Erin Michaels's former presidential run, quoted Senator Michaels as saying, 'Nathan Harris has been a valued member of my staff since my first Senate campaign in 2002, and I consider him a close friend. His intelligence and drive, as well as his dedication to public service, have earned him a great deal of respect on Capitol Hill. I'll miss him, but I have no doubt of his success in the next phase of his career, and I wish him all the best.'"

"Well, that was diplomatic." Sarah smirked at Tom but he couldn't return the smile. He was too busy trying to breathe, trying to keep down the breakfast he'd just eaten. He held his hands in his lap so no one could see them shaking. Sarah's smile faded as she realized that he wasn't well. "Tom?"

But Tom was already rising from his seat, muttering an apology and excusing himself from the group… he was leaving the restaurant, ignoring Sarah's voice calling after him… bypassing the elevator, striding for the stairwell, and dashing up to the fifth floor… fumbling in his suitcase for the little phone he seldom used and peering at the screen. *Zero new calls.*

It couldn't be true. The article Mitch had quoted must have been one of those parody articles, like in the *Onion*; or perhaps it was drafted by someone who didn't like Nate. Surely Nate would have called him if it was the truth, wouldn't he?

Dimly, Tom was aware of Sarah knocking on his hotel room door, her voice becoming more insistent. "Tom, are you in there? Tom?" In a haze he crossed the room and opened the door, then turned wordlessly back into the room. "Tom, are you okay? I thought you looked better off than any of us. Is your breakfast not sitting well?" He sat on his bed, staring out the window. Sarah sat carefully beside him. "Are you going to be sick?"

He might, he thought, but not for the reason she believed. "Not sure," he whispered.

"Wow, baby, I thought you were doing okay," Sarah said. "Maybe you should lie down and see if it helps." Tom obliged while Sarah got a bottle of cold water from the fridge and set it within reach on the night table. She pulled the drapes and crossed back to sit on the bed beside him. "Do you want me to hang around?" she whispered, stroking a soft hand across his forehead.

Tom caught her hand and kissed it. "No," he told her, gratefully adding, "Thanks, but I'll rest. I think I'll be okay." *As soon as I find out what the hell is going on.*

"Alright," she replied, unconvinced. "I was planning to go do some shopping this afternoon with Kim. Text me if you want me to bring you anything back, okay?"

"Thanks," he said again, pulling the covers up to his chin. After kissing his forehead, Sarah left.

As soon as she was gone, Tom pulled the little silver cell phone out of his pocket and dialed Nate's number. It rang eight times before he heard the cell phone carrier's message telling him the user was currently unavailable and to call back later. He gave it a few minutes, thinking maybe Nate had missed picking up and would call right back. After five minutes he tried the number again, slapping the phone closed in frustration when the same recorded message began. He cursed the lack of voice mail, though if Nate couldn't hear the phone ringing, leaving a voice mail wouldn't expedite the process at all.

Tom pulled his iPad out of his briefcase and quickly looked up a video of Erin Michaels's speech from the day before—having been at Emory waiting for Bill to deliver his own speech, he hadn't had the chance to see hers yet. He watched the entire thing, waiting to catch a glimpse of Nate, certain he would see his dark head above those of her other campaign staff. But although the camera panned the crowd several times, and Tom recognized more than one staff member among the faces, Nate was nowhere to be seen.

Tom lay in the darkened room debating what to do. He was seriously considering something that he knew he shouldn't do—*knew* he shouldn't. And yet… yeah, he was going to do it anyway.

He dialed another cell phone number, one he had called just once before, from a hotel room in Michigan: Nate's iPhone.

Tom listened as the call went directly to voice mail. Either Nate had his phone turned off or he was someplace without service. For the first time in a week, he heard Nate's deep, confident voice. It gave him a pang of longing. He wanted to talk to him so much. He was going to hang up, but then the voice mail beeped and before he could stop himself….

"Nate… it's me. I just heard a rumor that you resigned, that you're not working for Michaels anymore, and I…. It's gotta be wrong, right? You wouldn't leave Erin, after everything…. Anyway, I'm concerned and hoping you'll give me a call as soon as you can. We haven't talked in a while, and I've been thinking about you. A lot. Even before this rumor, I mean. It's been…." Here Tom dropped his voice as though to do so would ensure their privacy. "It's been too long, Nate. I miss you. Call me, okay? You know the number." How he wished he could end with *I love you*, but even in his state of mind, he was aware enough not to. Instead he closed the phone and sat, the phone still clutched in his fist, knuckles pressed into his mouth.

He was trembling—nervous to know the truth, hoping Nate wouldn't be angry that he'd called his main cell *and* left him a voice mail. He hoped Nate would get the message as soon as he got off the phone—because he had to be on the phone, Nate didn't turn his phone off—and would call him back right away.

But minutes turned into hours, and by that night, he still hadn't heard from him. He went out to see his friends, had dinner at Maxwell and Colin's house. The whole gang was there, the entire group he used to hang out with, and they were so thrilled to see him. He had been looking forward to seeing them as well. Despite being worried about Nate, he made a formidable effort to seem like his usual self and not let his preoccupation show. His friends did comment that he seemed tired. Fortunately he could attribute it to the campaign schedule and the revelry of the previous evening, both very plausible reasons for why he'd be looking less than fresh. He managed to have a good time in spite of his inner turmoil—Colin especially was good at bringing someone out of a funk.

Nevertheless, he went to bed without hearing a word from Nate, without receiving a single acknowledgment of his attempt to contact him. Logically he knew Nate was okay—physically, at least, it wasn't as though he was injured or whatever. But Tom needed to know that Nate was okay emotionally. He couldn't help being worried about the man he loved.

He slept poorly that night, and the next morning, despite his original intention to stay in Atlanta until Monday evening, he managed to swap his ticket and get a flight back to DC that afternoon. He had to explain to Sarah why he was leaving her a day earlier than he'd planned. She wasn't going for it at first, not until he told her why. She knew he was seeing someone, but not who; Tom told her he couldn't get in touch with his boyfriend and was worried about him. As soon as he explained it in those terms, her demeanor changed from disappointment to concern.

"Maybe I should come with you," she told him, a crease appearing in her forehead.

"It's not necessary. I'm sure he's fine. He's got some stuff going on… I can't tell you about it, but I don't want him to spend the weekend holed up in his apartment feeling alone." Tom tried to sound less worried than he felt. He hoped he was right about where Nate might be, but he had no way to be sure.

It seemed he'd sold it to Sarah, though, because she smiled. "You're a sweetie. Go look after your boyfriend. I'm sure he'll be glad to have you there."

Tom managed to return her smile. "Thanks." She gave him a hug and left him to get his packing done and get himself to the airport.

He got into Dulles around seven o'clock and took a cab to his apartment, where he didn't even bother going upstairs to change or leave his bags. He got straight into his car and drove to Nate's building, his hands clutching the steering wheel nervously, hoping desperately that he'd find Nate at his condo. He'd never been there before; he didn't even know Nate's unit number. The building concierge was less than helpful, refusing to even call up to Nate's unit.

"Mr. Harris has had a number of people drop by the building unannounced this weekend," he told Tom coldly, "many of whom claimed to be friends of his. It's not my first day on the job, sir, and if you are a friend of Mr. Harris, he will have provided you with information on how to contact him." Tom tried to object but the man held up his hand. "We're finished here, sir. Now, do I need to call the authorities?"

Tom's shoulders sagged as he acquiesced. In defeat he returned home. His apartment was stale, having been closed up so long. He opened up some windows and let the fresh evening air chase away the stuffiness. He stood at his balcony doors for a few minutes, looking out over the city. It had been an ideal day for a holiday weekend—the whole weekend had been, in fact—but he'd been so preoccupied with his worries about Nate that he'd barely noticed or enjoyed it. He forced himself to take a few moments to calm and center himself. From his window he could see the Washington Monument, usually sparkling, pristine white, now bathed in orange-pink light from the setting sun. He reminded himself of the privilege he had to be here in the capital city of the most powerful nation in the world, something he'd dreamed of since he'd first heard a politician speak. Granted, it had been a Republican candidate who had spoken at his family's church when Tom was still quite young; but the desire it had instilled in him had never waned.

After he'd managed to calm his nerves, he turned and crossed the room to the kitchen, intending to make a cup of tea. He dumped the old stale water out of the kettle and refilled it, and was turning to get a mug when an envelope on his breakfast bar caught his eye. He picked it up and felt his stomach flip to find the single inscription on the front: his first name, in Nate's neat, precise handwriting.

> *Dear T,*
> *Congratulations on your great news. I saw the speech this afternoon and I was in awe. You are amazing—I hope your boss appreciates how much.*
> *I agree with what he said about doing what's best for everyone. It's time to move on. By now you'll have heard that I'm no longer working for my previous employer. With everything that's happened this week, I need a couple of days away. My dad and brother are at the cottage for the long weekend. I'm planning to drive up and surprise them. For the sake of self-preservation, I'm going to keep my phones turned off for the weekend. I really need to unplug from the world, rest, and get some perspective before I deal with the fallout.*
> *We'll talk soon.*
> *Yours,*
> *N*

At last, confirmation in Nate's words of what numerous reputable news organizations had reported, that he had left Erin Michaels. Though Tom wished Nate had called him to let him know, he could understand why Nate might have hesitated to do so. After all, Tom was glad that Nate wasn't by himself, that he had his dad and his brother to support him when Tom couldn't be there himself.

All in all, the letter was written in a way that was quite intentionally vague. He understood that Nate had done this to protect their privacy and security if it were to somehow be found—unlikely at his apartment, but not impossible, he supposed. The letter seemed straightforward enough, and yet....

I agree with what he said about doing what's best for everyone. It's time to move on.

For some reason those sentences seemed to loom ominously before Tom. He read and reread it, each time hoping he'd find some new insight in it; each time failing to do so. Was Nate really talking only about the party when he said it was time to move on? He had already left Erin... what else was he considering moving on from?

Reason told Tom he was overthinking it, but when he considered how Nate had been unreachable for at least a day and a half, something completely out of character for a man who slept with his iPhone no more than eighteen inches away from his head; when Tom couldn't help thinking that Nate could have easily given him a quick phone call to let him know where he was going, instead of leaving a letter at his apartment; all the factors combined to leave Tom feeling very unsettled.

He had tried three more times to call Nate since leaving the message the morning before, twice on the little cell and once on his iPhone, but hadn't left any messages. Nate's letter said he was shutting off his phones (his private phone too) but maybe.... He had to try. He called Nate's iPhone number again, but to no avail. Once more it went directly to voice mail.

"Nate, it's me. I just got home and got your letter. I assume you got to Michigan safely. I'm glad you're with your family, I'm sure they'll take good care of you." Here he paused for a moment before adding, "I've been so worried about you since I heard about you leaving Michaels. I know I wasn't here for you during the week when everything was happening in your life, but... I know you understand that would have been impossible. I'm here now. I came back to DC to see you, to be with you. Please, call me and let me know you're okay. I need to hear your voice. I miss you so much. Please call me." He hesitated another long moment, not knowing what else to say, before he simply ended the call.

In spite of what the letter said, Tom had hoped maybe Nate would at least screen his calls, that he would get Tom's messages and would call him. Eighteen hours later, on Monday afternoon when he'd still heard nothing, Tom called again and left what he promised himself would be the last message. There wasn't really much he could say that he hadn't already said in his previous messages, but he repeated himself anyway, repeating his pleas for Nate to call him.

His phone remained stubbornly silent, with the exception of a text message from Sarah telling him she was home safely, until seven o'clock that evening. He was having a cup of tea and trying to concentrate on a book, without much success, when the silver phone beside him rang loudly. He had turned the volume up as high as possible, not wanting to miss it if it ever rang. He opened the phone and placed it to his ear.

"H-hello?"

BY THE time Nate got home to his condo after his last day of work on the Hill, he had made up his mind.

He spent several hours laboring over writing three pieces of correspondence. Two were in the form of e-mails written to Jason and Erin. In them he thanked them both for the opportunities they had given him, for the experience and education he'd gained working with them and serving the American people alongside them. He apologized to Erin, telling her he wished he had been able to take her into his confidence when they'd spoken a few weeks earlier. He told her he would always support her as a senator, that he would never be convinced that she hadn't been the best candidate, and that he still believed in his heart that she would be the first woman to be President of the United States. He told her he was sorry that his choices had made it impossible for him to continue working toward that day.

To Jason he offered thanks. He told Jason he had the highest respect for him as a boss and a friend, and apologized again for the choices he'd made that had resulted in a betrayal of the trust Jason had placed in him.

As difficult as those were to draft and polish, the final piece of correspondence was far worse. It was a letter to Tom—a real letter, not an e-mail—that he planned to leave at Tom's apartment. He agonized over what to write. He edited repeatedly, taking out as many identifying details as he could in the event that it fell into the wrong hands. He read it a final time, sighed, and signed it. The end result wasn't exactly right, but then he didn't have the talent with words that Tom had.

After he'd sealed it into an envelope, he looked up to check the clock. It was after midnight. He knew if he wanted to get to Michigan at a decent time tomorrow he'd better get to bed now so he could be up and on the road reasonably early.

Early the next morning, Nate packed all the casual clothes he owned into a small suitcase, leaving anything that resembled a suit or a dress shirt hanging in his closet. He put on a pair of running shoes for the first time in two weeks. After giving his condo a quick once over to make sure he hadn't neglected anything, he grabbed the suitcase and the letter for Tom and headed off to Tom's apartment. Once there he let himself in with the key Tom had given him after their trip to North Carolina.

He placed the envelope for Tom on the breakfast bar, propped up against a vase where it was easily visible. He had intended to leave it and go, but now that he was here, it was hard to leave. He looked slowly around at the studio apartment, this one room that had contained so much of his relationship, memories of all the conversations and laughter, of two weeks ago when Tom had drawn him a bath and then given him a massage that put him to sleep, and of course the bed where they'd kissed, made love, held each other all night long, and woken up together. Tom had mentioned a few times that this apartment didn't really feel like his home; but to Nate, this place was Tom, and that felt as much like home to him as anywhere he'd ever lived.

On the bed was a black t-shirt that had been left behind. Nate picked it up and held it to his face, inhaling as he did. It smelled like Tom, sunshine and dark, laughing eyes… and Nate's heart broke.

Half an hour later he was in his car heading north, damp, reddened eyes hidden behind dark sunglasses. It had only been the thought of the long trip that had finally forced him to leave behind that little sanctuary. He had about eleven hours of driving ahead of him, depending on traffic, and he was determined to do it all in one shot, no matter how much coffee he had to drink. At least it was a beautiful day, with a blue, cloudless sky, no humidity, and a temperature that was expected to hit around seventy-five degrees. It was perfect weather for a holiday weekend, and under almost any other circumstances he'd have enjoyed the long road trip with the windows down, music playing and the wind blowing his hair around.

Today he felt like he was being drawn to Michigan, as though someone was calling him home, back to the place where his life had once been so simple. His dad was on vacation this coming week and spending the week at the cottage in Delton, two hours west of Ann Arbor. His brother, Adam, and Adam's partner, Melissa—it felt weird to call her Adam's girlfriend since they'd been together twelve years—were planning to join his dad at the cottage this weekend. They would be surprised to see him, but he felt in his heart and in his soul that this was the right place to be. His family had always been his foundation. They would help him get through the difficult times; they'd support him as he figured out what the next phase of his life would hold.

Making a couple of stops, he got to Delton shortly before eight thirty. The sun was low in the western sky and the dense trees had thrown the road into near darkness when his headlights illuminated the reflective sign at the end of the cottage driveway. He parked the car behind his dad's, and inside the house he could see his father's silhouette as he came to the front door to see who had pulled into his driveway at this late hour.

The porch lights flicked on as Nate got out of the car, and an instant later, the front door was opening. "Nate!" his father called, surprise and happiness both coloring his tone. From inside the house came exclamations of surprise from Adam and Melissa, and by the time Nate reached the porch, they had crowded in behind Ron in the doorway.

"Honey, I'm home," Nate said with a grin as his dad pulled him into a bear hug.

"What a surprise! You didn't say a word about coming home for the weekend!"

"I only decided last night," Nate said truthfully. "Hey, Mel," he greeted, giving her a kiss on the cheek and Adam a hug. "And this morning I got in the car and drove up."

"I wish I'd known you were coming. We'd have saved you some dinner," Ron said.

"Do you have a suitcase, Nate?" Adam asked.

"It's in the trunk." Adam started out the door and Nate added, "Don't worry about it, Adam, I'll get it later," but Adam waved his hand at him.

"No, you go sit, I'll get it. Hit the trunk button."

Nate obliged, then followed Melissa and his dad into the living room where the last rays of sunshine for the day were shining through the picture window that faced the lake. "I've been sitting for hours—I think I'll stand for a while and stretch out my legs."

For the next couple of hours, he chatted with his family, catching up on all the things that had been going on in their lives over the weeks and months since he'd seen them. He didn't tell them about no longer working for Erin. It wasn't a conversation for tonight, and he preferred to have that talk with his dad privately, first, before he told Adam and Mel about it. As it turned out, they had some news of their own to share, and he was very happy to let it overshadow the stuff that had been happening in his life.

"So we didn't think we'd get to tell you this weekend," his brother told him after receiving a meaningful look from Mel, "but since we told Dad earlier today and now you went and surprised us by showing up, I think it's a perfect time."

"Tell me what?"

Adam and Mel exchanged grins before Adam said, "You're going to be an uncle, Nate!"

Nate's jaw dropped and his eyes widened in delight. It was obvious that this was very welcome news for Adam and Mel, as well as his dad. "Oh my God—you guys! Congratulations!" Nate said, jumping up to give them each a hug and a kiss. "When are you due?" he asked Mel, whose smile threatened to split her face.

"December fifteenth. Right before Christmas."

"That's the best news I've heard in weeks," he told them, real happiness and excitement taking the edge off his exhaustion. "And you," he added, turning to his dad, who was grinning broadly. "You're going to be a grandpa!"

Ron, obviously thrilled at the news, nodded and looked back at Adam expectantly. Adam continued, "Something else—we decided to get married before the baby comes. Nothing fancy, just a little ceremony here beside the water—our families, a few friends, totally casual—on June thirtieth. Do you think you can get the weekend off to be here for it?"

"Are you kidding? I wouldn't miss it for anything."

"Well, good," said Adam. "Because I'd like you to be my best man."

"Absolutely. I'd love to." He slung an arm over his brother's shoulders and squeezed tightly, realizing how much he'd missed his family and how good it was to be home. He and Adam had always been close in spite of the six-year age difference between them. When Melissa started dating Adam, she'd quickly become part of the family as well, and they'd been together so long now that Nate pretty well thought of them as married even without the piece of paper. Their respective families had gotten to know each other well over the years. Mel's parents and sisters were wonderful to Adam, and there was much mutual love between them all. The addition of Adam and Mel's baby, though a first for Ron, would be a sixth grandchild for Mel's parents. The only blight on their happiness would be that Nate and Adam's mother wouldn't be at the wedding, would never meet her grandchild.

Mel held up her camera. "Hey, guys, stand together. I want to get a picture of all three of the Harris men." Nate put his other arm around their dad and they all smiled for Mel, who took a couple extra pictures to be safe.

Finally she said, "Well, boys, I'm beat. This baby seems to suck every bit of energy out of me."

"Yeah," Adam said, "I was on the lake most of the day and I'm worn out. I'm going to go too."

After they'd both bid good night, Nate and his dad went out to the screened porch to sit in the now completely dark night, listening to crickets chirp and the bullfrogs bellow down at the edge of the lake. After a few minutes Ron said quietly, "Good news about Adam and Mel."

Nate nodded, tiredly rubbing his eyes as his exhaustion weighed on him. "Yeah, it's about time they made it official, I guess. Especially with the baby coming."

"Good news," Ron repeated. "We've been due for some good news, I think." After a moment he added, "I'm sorry about Erin, son. It's an awful disappointment, her not getting the nomination."

"Thanks. It wasn't easy to accept. She worked so hard."

"You all did. In fact, I'd say you look completely worn out. I hope you get a bit of a rest now that the campaign is over?"

Nate swallowed. He almost told his dad the truth right then, but stopped himself. He wanted to wait until Adam and Melissa had left to go back to Cleveland. He'd tell Adam soon, but not this weekend, not when they were so excited and happy about sharing their good news.

Instead he told his dad, "Yeah. Actually I thought I might spend a few days here with you, if you don't mind the company."

"Of course I don't mind. I see too little of you as it is. This place is as much yours and Adam's as it is mine. You're always welcome here."

The exhaustion and the emotion of the last few days had all taken their toll on Nate's composure. He was glad for the darkness as, for the second time in a day, hot tears stung his eyes. "Thanks," he managed to croak. His father didn't answer, but a moment later a warm, strong hand rested on Nate's. They sat in silence that way for a few minutes more, until Nate couldn't keep his eyes open. He wished his dad good night and made his way to the bedroom that had been his since they built this cottage, when he was seventeen. There he stripped down to his underwear, throwing his clothes carelessly on the floor before he sprawled on the familiar twin bed and fell asleep in seconds.

Nate spent most of the weekend sleeping. Though he felt mildly guilty that he wasn't spending much time with Adam and Melissa, he couldn't help it—he was more tired than he could remember ever being in his life, a bone-deep exhaustion that had been building for months. This place was his sanctuary—coming here was like opening a valve and letting the tension bleed away. Late Sunday afternoon, Adam approached him quietly as he sat watching Melissa float in the water on an inflatable raft, tied to the dock so it didn't drift away with her. Their dad was up in the porch, working on a puzzle, and it was the first time they'd had alone together since Nate's arrival.

"Nate," said Adam seriously, pulling out his iPhone, "I got something in my e-mail this morning that surprised the hell out of me." Nate took the phone, where an e-mail from one of Adam's friends was displayed. It contained a link to an article about Nate leaving Michaels. "Is it true?" Adam whispered.

Nate hesitated a moment before nodding. "It's true."

"Holy shit, what happened?"

"I was going to tell you after I had a chance to tell Dad, and for that I was going to wait until after you guys went home. It's been a weekend of good news. I don't want to put a wet blanket on it."

"I won't tell him."

"Thanks," Nate replied. "Have you said anything to Mel?"

"I showed her the e-mail, but I'll tell her not to mention it to Dad this weekend. Nate...." Adam placed a hand on Nate's arm, concern coloring his face. "Are you okay?"

Nate wanted to tell his younger brother everything—about Tom, about the relationship they had carried on in secret. He might have gone ahead and told him about it now, except for the real possibility that he might become emotional and their dad wouldn't ignore that. For now, he shook his head tightly. "Not really, no."

"Jesus." Adam glanced toward the cottage to make sure their father was still occupied. "I'm sorry, Nate. You know I'm here for you when you're ready to talk."

Nate's throat was tightening. "Thanks."

After a few moments Adam asked, "What are you going to do?"

"First thing I'm going to do is sleep for a week," Nate replied wryly. He made a good start of it, to be sure, going to bed early that night and sleeping in again the next morning. Late on Sunday afternoon, Adam and Mel packed up their car. They hugged Nate and Ron, who stood waving until they could no longer see Mel's SUV through the trees, and then turned back to the cottage.

"Well, just you and me now," Ron said. "Feel like doing some fishing?"

"Actually, Dad, I need to talk to you about something."

The warm expression on Ron's face was immediately replaced by concern. "Of course, son. Let's go sit."

They settled themselves into comfortable chairs on the porch, side by side, looking out over the lake. "So what's going on?" Ron asked, adding, "Something more than being tired and disappointed about the nomination?"

"Yeah," Nate replied, his voice already breaking. "A lot more. I'm no longer working for Erin Michaels. Not in any capacity."

Ron's jaw dropped. "Well, that's a surprise."

"Susan Pollard did a press release Saturday afternoon announcing that I'd left."

Ron was still trying to process the information. "I know you had some disagreements during the campaign about some of the decisions Erin and Jason made, but I didn't think they were things you would resign over."

Now came the hard part. "I didn't resign, Dad," Nate mumbled. "I was fired."

If Ron had been surprised before, he was positively dumbstruck now. "Fired... why?"

Nate had never felt more humbled than he did now. "There were some things that happened that made Jason question my judgment and ultimately my commitment. I can't talk about specifics—" He had already decided that the fewer people who knew the exact reason for his dismissal, the better—even telling his dad the whole truth was a bad idea. "—but to be honest, he was on the right track. I'd been starting to feel... I don't know... *fatigued* with the whole thing."

"The campaigning?"

"Yeah, but even once it started to become clear that Erin wasn't likely to win and that we'd be returning to Washington, the thought of going back to it was...." He paused, looking for the right words to convey how he'd felt. "It used to be the place I loved to be—I couldn't wait to get there every morning. I woke up ready to jump out of bed and get to work. And then, when I thought about going back to that job, I felt so... apathetic. I couldn't fathom it giving me the same satisfaction I used to have, the same desire to *want* to do that job."

His father was obviously trying to draw the logical conclusion as to how this led to his being fired. "So you told Jason how you felt and he let you go, is that it?"

"Not exactly." Nate grimaced. "I had planned to go back to Washington and see if the desire returned once I was back there full-time working in it again. If it didn't I was going to give serious consideration to moving on. But as I mentioned, some things had happened in the meantime—a couple of times where I disappointed Jason and some decisions where I showed poor judgment. I guess it was becoming obvious to him, too, that my focus wasn't as sharp as he needed it to be. He talked to me about it. He gave me a chance to refocus my attention. I couldn't pull it together." It was a vague account, but the essentials were correct. "He and Erin decided together that I wasn't benefiting the team anymore, and on Friday afternoon he let me go."

Nate's father was silent for a few moments as he mulled this over. Eventually he mused, "I know there are some details you're leaving out. No one likes to have to own up to their screwups; I can't blame you there." Nate didn't reply and eventually Ron remarked, "I thought your phone was awfully quiet this weekend."

Nate huffed a short breath, the closest thing he could manage to a laugh. "I've had it turned off since Friday night. Goodness knows what's waiting for me when I turn it back on."

"Have you given any thought to what you might do now?" his dad asked.

"I've thought about it ever since I started considering leaving Washington. But this is all I've done for ten years. I don't know what to do." He sighed. "Maybe I should take some time off—a month or two, perhaps. Rest, decompress… get some perspective. Figure out what comes next."

Ron nodded thoughtfully. "I think that's a wise idea. Your mother was always concerned about you being so committed to your job. Don't misunderstand me, we were incredibly proud of you. I still am, son, even though I can see you're not very proud of yourself right now. But being so focused on work to the exclusion of almost everything else worried us. We always hoped for you to have someone to love, Nate. A partner in life, like Adam has in Mel. It's been such a long time since you've even had a boyfriend."

Nate's heart clenched painfully at the thought of Tom. In a voice barely above a whisper he said, "Actually, the truth is… I was seeing someone for a few months."

"You were? When?"

"This spring," Nate replied, looking out over the lake and willing his eyes to remain dry.

"You *were* seeing him? You're not now?"

Nate's jaw clenched. Not trusting his voice, he shook his head.

"I'm very sorry to hear that," his father replied regretfully. "All things considered, it sounds like you've had a pretty rough spring." His hand covered Nate's where it rested on the arm of the chair, and the tears that had been threatening finally spilled over, making quick tracks down Nate's cheeks before becoming small damp spots on his T-shirt. His father noticed but said nothing, just squeezed his hand a bit tighter. They sat in silence for long moments, listening to the gulls over the lake and the light breeze that was rustling the leaves of the silver birch beside the dock.

Eventually, when Nate had mastered his emotions again, he asked his dad, "Do you mind if I stay here while I figure things out?"

His father withdrew his hand and looked at him squarely. "This is your home as much as it is mine, as much as our house in Ann Arbor is. You never have to ask permission to come home, son." Nate nodded his thanks and Ron continued, "I'm only here for the week, of course, and then you'll have the place to yourself."

"I'm not concerned about having it to myself," Nate said quickly.

"I know you're not. Even so, I'm due back at work next Monday, so I'll be heading home Sunday afternoon," his dad replied. "And now, I have a book waiting for me on the porch, so I think I'm going to go sit with it for a while." He got up to leave, but stopped, resting his hand on Nate's shoulder a moment. "I'm here for you, Nate. If you want to talk some more…."

"I know, Dad," Nate said gratefully. "Thanks."

His father strode off across the lawn then, leaving Nate by himself. His solitude was short-lived, though, as his dad returned a moment later bearing two phones in his hand, Nate's iPhone and the little silver cell he'd bought solely for his calls to Tom. "Those messages aren't going to go away because you ignore them," Ron said sagely. "It's up to you, of course, but maybe you'll find it easier to relax if you get it over with." He deposited the phones on the arm of Nate's chair and left without another word.

Nate picked up both phones, one in each hand. He held them, staring them down, as if in doing so he could intimidate them as they did him. Finally he repeated his dad's advice under his breath. "Get it over with." He stared at them both a moment longer, deciding which to turn on first. He settled on starting with the iPhone, ignoring the twinge of guilt that told him he was being a coward for not starting with the little cell.

With the exception of the days leading up to and following his mother's death, he had never been out of communication with his colleagues for so long, not since he started working for Erin. He expected some missed calls and voice mails from Michaels staffers and some of his friends, and probably some texts and e-mails. He did not expect 143 missed calls, 74 text messages, 157 e-mails, and 37 voice mails. He stared at the display in disbelief, hardly knowing where to start. One place was as good as another, he figured, so he went to the e-mails first.

As the headers loaded, he realized he was only receiving e-mails from his personal account. *Of course*, he thought; the password to his government e-mail address would have been changed immediately once his dismissal was official. He idly wondered who would have the unhappy task of dealing with the many e-mails he normally received at that account.

He scrolled through the list. Many were from former colleagues; from the subject lines it was obvious they'd been blindsided by his departure. The e-mails from his friends were much the same. All of them reinforced the general belief that he'd left of his own accord.

Next he looked at the texts. Almost all were from the same names he'd seen in his e-mails, his friends and former colleagues. The missed calls, too, included all these names plus some reporters he'd spoken to in the past. Several calls stood out, their "Unknown" caller status catching his eye. He had an extensive contact list, and he seldom received calls from anyone outside that list. Out of curiosity he tapped one of them, and when the number displayed on his screen his heart nearly stopped.

It was a number he knew by heart; and no, it was not one he had stored in his contacts list.

With shaking hands he opened the little silver cell and turned it on. The time it took to find a signal seemed interminable, but finally it vibrated, and the display flashed: *14 missed calls.*

He returned to his iPhone and immediately went to his voice mail. When he found the number he was looking for, he tapped it and held his breath to listen.

Nate's heart wrenched to hear the sweet timbre of Tom's voice, worse for the concern that dampened its usual softness. The message had been left Saturday afternoon, and the reports of his "resignation" had reached Tom, who didn't believe they were true. His voice dropped with longing as he told Nate how much he missed him, how it had been too long since they'd spoken or been together.

When the message ended, Nate quickly scrolled to the next unknown number. It was a reporter he'd never spoken to, and he deleted it without listening to anything beyond the caller's name. The next unknown message was Tom again, sounding even more worried than his first message. He'd returned to Washington and received Nate's letter, learning that Nate was in Michigan. He spoke quickly, the worry making his voice far higher-pitched than normal. Nate wondered if anything could be worse than knowing that Tom was almost apologizing for his work, for the obligations that had kept him away from Nate.

He learned what was worse when he listened to Tom's third and final message.

"Nate." Tom sounded sodden with defeat. "Please... I need to hear your voice. I miss you so much. I.... Please don't shut me out." Tom's voice cracked on the final request, and Nate felt hot tears instantly spring to his eyes. Without listening to another message, Nate turned off the iPhone, picked up the little cell again, and dialed Tom's number.

It rang only once before he heard the sweetest voice. "H-hello?"

"Hey, you," said Nate quietly.

"Oh my God, I'm so glad you called. I was dying here." Tom sounded both relieved and reproachful. "You got there safely?"

"I'm at the cottage with my dad. Sorry I wasn't in touch sooner."

"I understand why you turned off your iPhone, if you didn't want to talk to reporters or whatever, but I do sort of wish... I mean, it was a shock to hear that you'd left your job, and I was dying to talk to you and make sure you were okay. I know it's not about me. Except... not being able to reach you or hear your voice was...." Tom was clearly struggling not to chastise Nate too harshly, but obviously his feelings were hurt.

"I'm sorry," Nate answered honestly. "I'm sorry you've been so worried about me. I was being self-absorbed and I just didn't think. I really didn't mean to upset you."

"I know you didn't. It was hard not knowing if you were okay."

"I'm sorry," Nate said again.

"*Are* you okay? I know we've never talked about work, but I didn't know you were thinking about leaving. I mean, everyone knows you didn't want Michaels to drop out. I guess I didn't realize you would leave because of it."

So Tom, too, had drawn the conclusion that Nate had left of his own accord. "It was time for a change," he replied, and though it wasn't technically confirmation, he knew Tom was likely to take it as such. Nate couldn't allow Tom to know that he'd been fired as a result of their relationship—he would never allow Nate to take the fall on his own. Nate was objective enough to know that, as good as he'd been at what he did, Tom was simply brilliant. For him to give it up for Nate's sake was out of the question. It was bad enough that Nate had lost his own career and had to end their relationship. He refused to allow it to damage Tom's career too.

"Wow. So what are you going to do?"

"Take some time off to figure things out," Nate replied. "I'm going to stay at the cottage for a couple of weeks, I think."

"Oh." Tom sounded disappointed. "I… yeah. That sounds like a good idea. Or, you know, you could…."

"What?"

"Well, you could come back to DC and stay with me while you decide what to do," Tom continued hopefully. "I'll be traveling a lot, but at least one of us wouldn't be rushing off somewhere all the time. I'd really love to have you here. I miss you so much, Nate."

The loneliness in his voice tugged at Nate's heartstrings, but there was no way Nate could avoid it any longer. "Tom, we need to talk."

Sounding wary, Tom replied, "Okay."

Nate took a deep breath and began the explanation he'd spent several days formulating. "I don't know for sure what I'm going to end up doing, but I know DC isn't the place for me to be." He paused but there was only silence from the other end, so he went on, "When I return, it'll be to get my condo ready to go on the market and tie up any loose ends I have there."

After a few seconds Tom said flatly, "What… what are you *talking* about? Michaels isn't the only Senator in Washington, Nate. There are fifty-three other Democratic senators, not to mention all the members of Congress who—"

"Tom," Nate interrupted gently. "You don't understand. I don't want to work for another senator or member of congress or any other politician. Not anymore. The whole atmosphere of the city and life on the Hill… I'm exhausted by it all. I'm finished with politics."

"You're leaving the city?"

"Yes."

Again there was a long pause before Tom said in a near whisper, "But… I can't leave Washington."

Nate sighed. "I know," he said resignedly. "I know you can't."

"So what are you saying?"

"I'm saying that… as much as I enjoyed the time we spent together…."

"No. You're not going to do this."

Nate winced. "I'm sorry, Tom…."

"I don't accept."

"Tom—"

"No! We can do it long-distance, Nate. We've been doing okay so far…."

"Have we?" Nate asked. "Are you really happy with the way things have been—sneaking around, spending all our time hidden away so no one sees us? That wouldn't change—it would still be just as important that no one see us together. And then after the election, you'd be working eighteen hour days, seven days a week. Even if I was still in Washington, even if we lived in the same *house*, we'd barely see each other. That's not the way to share a life, Tom."

"But…." It was obvious Tom was crying now, struggling to speak through his tears. "But I love you. I'm *in love* with you. Please, Nate."

Nate, who had been struggling not to cry, could no longer fight his tears when he heard Tom's admission. He wanted so much to return it, to admit to Tom that he was in love too, and had been for weeks; but to do so now would be cruel.

Instead he whispered, "I'm so sorry."

"You said you wouldn't leave," Tom said, quietly accusatory. "That night you showed up at my apartment. I said, 'Don't do this if you're going to leave.' Remember? You said you wouldn't leave." Nate couldn't reply, tears flowing freely down his face now as he stared unseeingly out over the lake in the deepening twilight. They sat in silence, the line still open between them, neither knowing what to say but neither willing to be the one to end the call.

Finally, long moments later, Tom said, "Well, if there's nothing else to say…."

Nate took a deep, shuddering breath, trying to calm the sobs that wracked him. "I never meant to hurt you," he said, knowing it wasn't enough but needing to tell Tom anyway. "Please take care of yourself."

"Good-bye, Nate." And with a click, the line went dead.

Alone at last, Nate dissolved again into grief. Despite the mosquitoes that swarmed him and the damp chill of dew settling over the evening, he remained where he was for over an hour.

When at last he rose and went into the cottage, his father looked up from where he was reading. He looked startled at Nate's appearance, swollen and red as he was from crying.

"My ex-boyfriend…." Nate said helplessly, holding up the phone.

"Oh, son," Ron said, immediately setting aside his book and holding his arms out to Nate. Nate joined him on the couch, letting the comfort of his father's arms warm his body and soothe his soul.

SUMMER

TOM STOOD with the group of mourners who had gathered at the graveside. Despite the Florida sunshine and the heat that was intensifying as the morning approached afternoon, he felt cold and numb. He couldn't remember living through a worse month in his life: not when he finally accepted he was gay and spent weeks in despair; not when he came out to his parents and had to endure the ensuing shit storm; not when his grandfather had passed away. Now, in the space of several weeks, he had lost the two people who mattered to him most: Nate and his grandmother.

The days after his breakup with Nate were horrible. He had actually stayed home for several days afterward, calling in sick to work. Sarah had shown up at his apartment on Wednesday evening with some soup and crackers, hoping to help him feel better. As soon as she saw him, she realized he wasn't suffering from a cold or the flu, but a rather sickness of the heart.

"Oh, Tom," she said unhappily, easing down beside him where he was curled up on the bed. "You were worried about your guy this weekend. What happened?"

There was so much Tom wished he could spill to Sarah, but he couldn't. He found himself simply croaking, "It's over."

Sarah gathered him into her arms then, rocking him gently and holding him as he sobbed out his heartbreak. She patted his back and kissed the top of his head, and while there was nothing she could say to take away the pain, Tom was grateful she was there. She asked a few more questions, but eventually accepted that he wasn't going to talk about it, at least not yet. After crying himself out, he managed to get some sleep that night, and felt he could go back to work Thursday, that he was in less danger of becoming emotional than he'd been for the past few days.

It wasn't easy to go back to work. For the first few days he found it difficult to concentrate on the task at hand. His mind kept wandering back to the last conversation he'd had with Nate, or to happier days they'd spent together, like their trip to Nags Head. By the following Monday, his concentration had improved and by the end of that week he was throwing himself completely into work, being swept up in the pace and the rhythm of the campaign for the general election, letting the constant demand distract him from his personal misery. Mitch appreciated Tom's dedication, even as he warned him to be on guard against exhaustion. Tom was working between fourteen and sixteen hours a day, seven days a week, whether the campaign was traveling or not. When he was working, he was completely focused, and by the time he left work, he was so exhausted that he only had time to eat something and collapse into bed. He tried not to allow himself the time or opportunity to muse over Nate.

It was only a partial success. Tom might be able to force his thoughts away from Nate during his waking hours, but when he slept, it was another matter. He dreamed of Nate almost every night. In some dreams they were together and happy; in others, Nate was breaking up with him and Tom was begging him to stay. The worst were when he knew, could sense in the dream, that Nate was close by and was looking for him, was calling for him, but they couldn't find each other. No matter what the scenario, Tom awoke every morning desperate for Nate, and then he shoved it down, forced it into the back of his mind, where it would remain until the next time it was released in dreams.

By the fourth weekend in June, nearly four weeks after the breakup, Mitch instructed Tom to take three days off, Friday through Sunday, and not do a thing work related during that time. Tom protested, to no avail. He prepared to keep himself as distracted as possible, planning to spend Friday watching that fairy-tale television series. He and Sarah were going to go out Saturday and do some shopping, have lunch and generally enjoy themselves. Sunday he was going to devote to catching up with all his friends in Atlanta—he'd already e-mailed Maxwell and Colin to warn them that they should expect a marathon Skype session—and he was going to call his grandmother when he knew she'd be home from church. He called her almost every Sunday afternoon, but he'd missed the previous week when he'd been traveling with the campaign in Ohio.

Unfortunately, none of the things on Tom's agenda came to be. They were instantly wiped out on Friday morning when Tom received an unexpected phone call from his uncle, the only one on his mother's side. As soon as Tom saw the number on his phone, as soon as he realized it was his aunt and uncle's phone number, he knew. Somehow he knew he wouldn't be speaking to his grandmother that coming Sunday. The emotion in his uncle's voice confirmed it.

His grandmother was gone.

She had gone to sleep Thursday night and not woken the next morning, exactly as his grandfather had passed away. At least she had drifted away peacefully, and though Tom had long ago relinquished his faith in Christian teachings, he still had a vague notion of heaven, where he hoped his grandparents were now together again. For that, and for the fact that they had both lived long, full lives and enjoyed reasonably good health until the end, he could be glad. Objectively, he knew these things.

But on the most fundamental emotional level, he was gutted. His grandmother was the last family member to whom he was truly close. Her death had happened as suddenly and unexpectedly as his grandfather's had. He felt guilty for having missed their usual Sunday afternoon call the week before. He was thrust into the sudden anxiety of having to see his parents again, wondering what their reaction to him would be or whether they'd acknowledge him at all.

And in the midst of it all, he missed Nate. His emotional control was shredded, and the grief he'd been suppressing for several weeks returned in full force. He felt like he was bleeding out through his soul. He longed for Nate's arms around him, to comfort and support him through these moments.

Of course it wasn't Nate who stood beside him on Sunday afternoon when his grandmother was laid to rest. Instead he was surrounded by those he loved in a different way—Sarah, Mitch and Kim, all of whom had given up their weekend to fly down to Miami for the funeral, and five of his friends from Atlanta who'd done the same. His aunt and uncle were very kind to him, insisting he stay with them for the weekend. During that time, his uncle admitted to him during that time that Tom's father had been the reason the two families hadn't spent much time together through the years. Tom knew he bore some responsibility for not making more of an effort to stay in touch with this part of his family after coming out. He promised his aunt and uncle to repair that error, and did the same with his cousin.

There was no change in his parents' and sisters' behavior. They acted as though he wasn't there, as he'd anticipated, and it bothered him less than ever. The day wasn't about them—it was about remembering and saying good-bye to his dear little grandma. He reminded himself again and again to be grateful for the people he did have, the ones who loved him enough to be there and support him. Several of his grandmother's friends from her retirement community were able to attend the funeral and, recognizing him, came to offer their condolences.

The support of his friends didn't stop when he was back in Washington. He received cards, calls, and e-mails from current campaign staff, former colleagues at the City of Atlanta, and friends from all over. Each one warmed him with their kind words, and those who had met his grandmother at one time or another invariably shared a memory of her. It was comforting to know she had touched so many people.

There was one person he didn't expect to hear from, and so it was a shock to Tom when, one day a few weeks after the funeral, he looked through his mail to find a clean white envelope labeled in that neat, confident block printing he'd come to know. The return was N. Harris, at a post office box in Delton, Michigan. Nate was still living at the cottage, then.

The card was much the same as any other sympathy card, vague platitudes about how those we love will always be in our hearts, but beneath the text Nate had written a note:

> Tom,
>   I'm so sorry to hear of the loss of your grandmother.
> I know how special she was to you and how much she
> shaped you into the warm, loving person you are now. You
> are always in my thoughts.
>   Yours,
>   Nate

Tom had tears in his eyes even before he'd finished reading the simple note. He knew Nate could understand how it felt to lose someone so important to him, having lost his mother the previous year. Tom felt sorry for Nate, and sorry for himself, and sad that they weren't together.

Though his friends had been supportive and kind since the funeral, he still felt so alone.

After the funeral Tom had finally begun giving himself the time and the mental space to grieve—not only for his grandmother, but for his failed relationship with Nate too. As days passed and Tom mused on the situation, he couldn't help thinking that Nate, not having gotten what he wanted, had essentially packed up his toys, and gone home, giving no thought or regard to anyone else. Michaels hadn't done things Nate's way, so he quit. He didn't want to stay in DC, so he dumped Tom, whose lifestyle wouldn't suit him any longer. Tom hated to think that Nate could be so self-centered. When they were together, Tom had truly felt as though he knew the real Nate, that he had a sense of his flaws as well as his assets. But now, looking back at everything, he couldn't arrive at another logical conclusion to explain Nate's actions. If it was true, then Tom had badly misjudged who Nate really was.

Tom set the card on the counter. He had a box, a small one designed to store photos, where he'd kept all the cards and letters of sympathy from his friends and colleagues. He would put Nate's card with the others.

Eventually.

He returned to the card several times throughout the evening. The next day was Saturday; he was home, and as he worked around his apartment, cleaning and catching up on laundry, his eyes lit upon it every time he passed it. Whenever he picked it up, he found himself lingering over the words. *Warm, loving. Always in my thoughts.* The sentiments confused Tom. He couldn't believe Nate would say them if he didn't mean them. But if they were true, why had he broken up with Tom?

That night, he and Sarah had plans to go out for dinner. It had been ages since they'd had a Saturday night off, and since their weekend plans several weeks earlier had been lost to the funeral, Sarah was trying to get Tom to go out to a club with her. So far Tom had only agreed to dinner, but he had a feeling she would get her way. He was inclined to indulge her, since she'd been such a good friend to him, especially recently.

They'd planned for her to come over around six, and they would decide then where they wanted to go. Midafternoon, Tom had settled in on his couch with Season 2 of *Breaking Bad*. He made it through one episode and had started into another.... Then the next thing he knew, he was waking up to the sound of someone knocking loudly on his apartment door.

He startled awake. Blinking, he found the clock—6:03. He'd slept over three hours. He jumped up, his heart pounding from the abrupt wakeup, and opened the door for Sarah.

She took in his sleep-rumpled hair, shorts, and old T-shirt before smoothing her hand down the front of a pair of crisp white capris. "You're a little more casual than I'd expected." She grinned.

Tom returned the grin sheepishly. "I fell asleep."

Sarah laughed out loud now. "So I gathered! No worries, honey. We don't have reservations and we can go wherever the wind takes us. There's no rush."

"Make yourself at home," Tom said, gesturing her into the living room that was also his bedroom. "There's wine in the fridge, and you know where the glasses are. I'll go shower." He left her there to make herself comfortable. Forty-five minutes later he was showered, shaved, and dressed in a blue gingham button-down with the sleeves rolled to the elbow and a pair of chinos. As he came back to the living room putting on his watch, Sarah whistled.

"A little more like it?" Tom asked, posing for her.

"God, you're adorable!" She looked him over appreciatively.

Tom grimaced. "Oh, thanks a lot. Just what every guy wants to hear."

"Oh, jeez. Fine. You look *hot*."

"Well, I'm taking out a pretty hot girl."

Sarah tilted her head at him. "Yes, you are. And I've decided where I want to you to take me, so let's go."

Tom gestured to the door. "After you."

Sarah turned to pick up her clutch purse off the counter. As she did, she knocked a small stack of papers off the counter. "Oh, damn it. Sorry, Tom." The papers, mostly bills that had arrived in the past couple of days while they were away with the campaign, fluttered to the floor, but one went skittering off past Sarah.

Tom knelt to pick up the bills as Sarah went for the other item. He was arranging them back on the counter when he heard a small gasp. He turned to look, and found Sarah, her eyes wide as she looked at what she held in her hands: an envelope, with a Delton, Michigan return address.

"Nathan Harris," she said slowly, before returning to the counter and picking up the card Nate had sent. "Yours, Nate," she read. "Tom… 'Yours, Nate' is Nathan Harris? *The* Nathan Harris?"

Tom said nothing. His heart pounded in his chest and his knees felt weak. He could see Sarah mentally connecting the dots. "Oh my God, Tom," she continued, her eyes wide. "The guy you were seeing. The one you couldn't talk about. The guy you couldn't get in touch with the weekend after Michaels pulled out of the campaign. You were so worried about him because he had 'something big' going on in his life. And then a few days later you broke up.... Please tell me this isn't what it looks like."

Tom's face was hot and flushed. "I can't truthfully tell you that."

Sarah looked horrified. She sank slowly into the nearest chair, her mouth open as she struggled to find words. "What... I can't *believe*.... Tom, have you lost your mind? Don't you know what you could have done to the campaign, to your career? If anyone had found out...."

"No one found out," Tom said, but he knew it was only good luck that made it so.

"But you could have sunk the campaign," Sarah said blankly. "Everything Bill worked for, millions of dollars spent, people who gave every waking moment of their lives for months and months. You could have fucked up the whole thing, Tom."

For long moments they were silent, Sarah sitting in the chair and Tom staring at the floor before him, before Sarah took a deep breath and blew it out. "Were you in love with him?"

Tom felt a lump rise in his throat. "Yeah," he murmured.

"He broke up with you?" Sarah asked. Tom hadn't told her exactly how it ended, only that it was over. Now he plopped onto the couch across from her, nodding miserably.

"He quit Michaels and decided he was done with politics, done with Washington and done with me," he summarized bluntly.

"He's leaving Washington completely?" Sarah repeated. "So hasn't he ever heard of a long-distance relationship?"

Tom looked at his hands. "He was pretty clear. He wants a new life, and my schedule doesn't fit in with that."

Sarah digested this information for a moment before she moved to sit beside Tom on the couch. "I barely know what to say," she said. "It could have been a disaster for us all, Tom, but whether it was because you were careful or because you were shit lucky, no one found out. So I guess from that perspective, it's turned out okay, and thank goodness." She put her arm around him and he leaned into her, resting his head on her shoulder. "I'm sorry you got hurt," she murmured. "What a shitty situation."

Tom nodded silently.

"It was nice of him to send you a card, I guess."

"It was a surprise," Tom replied.

"How did he know about your grandmother? Do you guys still talk?"

"No. Haven't talked to him since he broke up with me."

"Hmm." They sat in silence for a few moments before Sarah shrugged her shoulders, displacing Tom. "If we're going to get a table any time before eleven o'clock, I think we'd better get going."

As Tom pocketed his wallet and keys, he thanked his lucky stars that Sarah wasn't going to hold his stupidity against him. If he were to lose her friendship, after losing Nate, he thought he'd be ready to pack it in and go back to Atlanta.

THE MONTH of June hadn't been easy. For the first two weeks after his final conversation with Tom, Nate had done very little except sleep. The first half of the month was rainy and dark, quite conducive to long days spent indoors, and it matched his mood rather well. He had gradually worked his way through the backlog of phone calls and e-mails, eventually getting back to everyone who'd called him—everyone, at least, who was a friend or coworker. He hadn't spoken to a single reporter. The official word from the Michaels camp had described the parting of ways in a manner that was quite a bit more complimentary than he strictly deserved, and he felt it best to let that stand.

His father was there at the cottage for the first week, as he'd promised, and after that Nate had it to himself during weekdays. Once he'd caught up on his sleep, he got into a fairly decent routine. He would sleep till about 7:00 a.m. before getting up to go for a run, though at first he started off by going for a walk, because he hadn't run in months. When he got back and was all hot and sweaty, he would run right across the lawn, kicking off his shoes before he dashed off the end of the dock, diving straight into the water. He would do some "lengths"—an arbitrary distance he had decided went from the end of their dock out to the diving raft and back—and then finish cooling down by floating and paddling around in the water.

He cooked for himself. He cleaned when necessary. There was a week or so that he followed the campaign like an obsession, watching as many YouTube clips of Bill Wagner as he could get his hands on, hoping to hear Tom's words from Bill's mouth. He followed the official blogs kept by Wagner campaign staffers, scanning for a mention of Tom's name. Eventually it dawned on him that being so immersed in campaign coverage wasn't the way to start getting over Tom. There was nothing wrong with being informed on the campaign—he had been a big part of it, after all—but he needed to set some reasonable limits. So he began to limit himself to watching the nightly news and no more than an hour of computer time every day. He knew he might not have an opportunity like this—a summer off, spent doing whatever he pleased at the cottage—again, at least not until he reached retirement age. He needed to use it wisely. He decided to get a membership at the local library. It didn't have a huge selection, but he got lost in some novels, and he picked up nonfiction books on subjects he'd never explored.

Not that he pushed Tom out of his mind completely—not even close. Memories of that sweet smile, the soft blond hair, and unfathomable brown eyes… they were with Nate every moment. He missed Tom so much. He would see or read something, and for an instant, he'd think, *I have to tell Tom about that.* Then he'd remember, and sometimes the realization was so sharp, it took Nate's breath away. At night when he climbed between the smooth, cool sheets of his twin bed, his arms and his heart would both ache, longing to have Tom there with him.

For him it was both a relief and a torment that Tom didn't know the real reason for their breakup. For Tom's sake, for the benefit of his career, Nate could sacrifice his own happiness. Where it was within his power to do so, he would protect Tom's future. It was a torment, though, to imagine Tom thinking of Nate as cold and uncaring, that Nate would end it simply because he wanted a change of city and a change of lifestyle, that a long-distance relationship would be too great an inconvenience. In truth, Nate would have done anything—moved heaven and earth—to be with Tom, if not for the danger of discovery and the subsequent impact on Tom's reputation.

But now, with Tom's future protected, it was time to think about his own, to figure out what the hell to do with the rest of his life. From the time he was fifteen years old, he had never really wanted to do anything *but* work in politics. Weeks ago when he'd first begun to toy with the idea of leaving that world, he'd thought about using his JD to practice law and had almost immediately discarded the idea. Being a lawyer, day in and day out, sounded like his idea of hell. There was a broad range of jobs available to someone with his education, and any of them would have been "good enough." But when would he have this chance again, where he was free to make a brand new start entirely—a new career in any city in the United States where he might decide to go? When would he have the time to really decide without having to consider giving notice and scrambling to move to a new city?

He wanted to give it the thought and consideration it deserved. He spent long days out on the lake, fishing and canoeing, alone with his thoughts. He thought about what aspects of politics he had enjoyed the most. He had always loved helping people, feeling like he'd really made a difference in their lives. He had enjoyed helping them learn, helping them understand how the political system worked so they could make more informed decisions. He had always worked well with new staff members, particularly with young people, interns who were new to the Hill and still learning how things operated there. He remembered what it had been like to be young, new, and inexperienced, and he always found it gratifying to watch the interns find their feet. Out of each crop of interns there would be one or two young men or women who were really sharp, truly motivated to learn as much as they could during their internship, whom he felt certain would have a future in politics, and he found it very rewarding to help guide those people.

Hmmm, there was something there. The common thread, what he had liked most: guiding, instructing, teaching.

He could teach.

With a poli-sci degree and a JD, plus the decade of experience he had in Washington, he could perhaps get a job as an adjunct professor. The pay wouldn't be great, but if he looked for a city where the cost of living wasn't ridiculous, he could get by for a while living frugally on the money he would make when he sold his condo in DC. And if it worked out well, if he enjoyed teaching and wanted to make a career of it, he could pursue his PhD and hope to get on tenure track.

He considered that for a couple of days before acting on it. He talked to his dad when he came for the weekend, and was gratified at the positive response he found there. His dad suggested putting out some e-mails to his old professors. He'd done his own undergrad at NYU and he knew their program well, of course. He'd enjoyed living in New York City when he was in his early twenties... would he feel the same way now? Did he want to live in a huge city—which would claw through his savings pretty quickly—or have an hours-long commute every day should he choose to live outside the city? There was also Cornell, where he'd done his law degree. Cornell had a government program for undergrads and offered specialties on international as well as domestic politics. Ithaca was a much smaller town, right in the Finger Lakes area, with state parks nearby and large open green spaces all around. He could get a dog....

Either way, he'd be in New York State, and though it would take some getting used to longer winters again, particularly if he ended up in Ithaca, he would be a bit closer to his dad, and to Adam and Mel. That would be a welcome change, especially once his niece or nephew made an appearance.

The more he thought about teaching, the more he was convinced that it was the right step for him to take. Even if there weren't any openings available at either of the two schools he'd attended, he had friends from school who had remained in academia, spreading across the country. He would put out some feelers to his friends and see what came back.

Something that came as a surprise in those first weeks was that Jason continued to stay in touch with him. Nate had all but snuck away from Washington with his tail between his legs, not seeing or talking to any colleagues or friends face-to-face after the news broke. He felt sheepish about that, but the friends who really cared about him were very understanding. A week after he was fired, after he'd returned all the e-mails and phone calls and texts from his friends, he got an e-mail from Jason, checking in on him, asking if he was okay and where he was staying. Jason had been his best friend on Erin's staff... well, his best friend in Washington, until Tom. Nate knew he'd betrayed both their professional relationship and their friendship. To know that Jason really did care about him and had forgiven him came as such a relief to Nate that, as he read the e-mail, he teared up a bit.

As weeks went by and they e-mailed back and forth every four or five days, their communication gradually eased, became less stilted, more like the camaraderie they had developed throughout the years. It was a relief to find that their friendship could continue after politics and in spite of Nate's betrayal. They talked on the phone a few times. Jason asked Nate what he'd done about Tom, whether they were still together, and he sounded genuinely sorry to hear that Nate had decided to end it. Jason was, outside of Nate's dad, the best friend Nate had during those weeks when he was trying to figure out what to do with his life.

Adam and Melissa's wedding took place on a sunny, gorgeous day, the last Saturday in June. It was, as they'd said, a small gathering of family and their very closest friends, on the lawn of the cottage overlooking Wall Lake. It was a perfect day. Adam and Mel looked brilliantly happy, with Melissa starting to show a hint of a baby belly under the white cotton sundress she'd chosen for their very casual ceremony. Everywhere Nate looked he saw happiness and love. Even looking at the cottage, he saw what his parents had built together. He saw his mother's touches in the decor of the house.

There was a book on the shelf that she'd been too tired to read; Nate had helped her finish it by reading it aloud to her. How he wished she had been here today, standing by his dad's side as the anchor she'd always been for their family. He wished she'd gotten a chance to meet the grandchild who would be born before the end of the year. He wished she could have met Tom.

Adam and Mel, who were planning to close on a new house in early August, had decided not to go away for a honeymoon. Nate knew that the cottage would have been available had he not been staying there, and so he suggested to them that they take the cottage for the week after their wedding, and he would go to Ann Arbor and stay with his dad for the week. They were thrilled to have it to themselves, and as it turned out, Nate wasn't even in the state of Michigan for much of that week.

The feelers he had put out to his friends asking about possible teaching jobs had returned some results late in June. A fellow NYU grad who was now practicing law in Tucson had a wife who taught at the University of Arizona. There was a possibility of teaching a course or two in their poli-sci program. A law school associate was teaching at Yale and she promised to talk to her head of department about Nate. His name carried some cachet, which helped him stand out from other candidates. Ultimately, it was a recommendation from Jason that found Nate flying to Durham, North Carolina, the first week of July to interview at Duke University with the chair of the Political Science Department and a couple of tenured professors.

The interview went extremely well. Nate found himself warming up to the department chair, a formidable but friendly woman whose own curriculum vitae was impressive. One of the profs was also very friendly; the other, extremely reserved. Overall, he left the interview with an excellent impression of the department and the school in general. He remained in the city a few days, checking out the Raleigh-Durham area, looking into the cost of living and housing locally. Housing prices were almost unthinkably low, at least compared to the costs Nate had become accustomed to in DC. He would probably be able to buy a house outright with the way the market was. Of course, that would constitute a real commitment to living there.

Durham was a small enough city that it wasn't difficult to get to green space pretty quickly; in fact, there was a state park quite close to the residential area north of Duke. It was incredibly hot and humid—a July visit certainly gave him a true taste of what he could expect from the summer weather—but he could handle that. He would be close enough to everything he wanted. The only downside was that he'd actually be farther from his family than he'd ever been before.

It was a lot to decide on fairly quickly, and he'd tried to go into the experience keeping an open mind and not letting himself get too attached to the idea of living there, in case the job didn't come through. He had been far more hopeful about this job, though, than the other possibility he'd had so far in Tucson. He had already spent a lot of time in North Carolina and had loved the state, at least as a visitor. Now he looked at it through the eyes of a potential resident, and over the course of the three days he was there, he saw enough of the area that by the time he was ready to fly back to Michigan, he had made up his mind: if the department offered him a couple of classes, he would accept. He would pack up and sell his condo in DC, and he'd be on his way to North Carolina.

He had an anxious couple of days in Delton, waiting for news of the interview. Jason called Sunday afternoon to tell him he'd heard good things from his friend, the chair of the department who had interviewed Nate. She was impressed, and Jason felt confident that Nate would hear good news soon.

The offer was made: two 100-level classes as an adjunct professor. Nate accepted immediately, setting off a whirlwind of activity that lasted for the next several weeks. Before he even left Delton, he called his real estate agent, making arrangements for the concierge at his condo to let the agent in and get some photos and an appraisal so he could put it on the market. The next day he drove to DC, returning for the first time in six weeks to his condo and the city he'd come to know so well. His agent had been kind enough to open a couple of windows and air out his condo so it wouldn't be stale when he arrived home. The condo was on the market within two days, and by that time, Nate had already packed most of his clothes, most knickknacks and books, kitchen stuff… anything that wouldn't be essential between now and when he could unpack in Durham.

Less than forty-eight hours after it was listed, Nate's condo sold for more than the asking price. There were no fewer than five showings the first day it was on the market, and he ended up accepting the offer that had no financing conditions attached. The sale would close on August 3. Now all Nate had to do was find a place to live.

Despite the flurry of activity, Tom was always at the periphery of his thoughts. Nate constantly battled to keep himself focused on what he needed to accomplish to get through the move, but it was so tempting to imagine how sweet life would be if Tom was joining him in North Carolina. Then, a week after he'd accepted the offer on his condo, Jason called him in Delton to give him some sad news: Tom's grandmother had passed away a couple of weeks earlier.

Though Jason broke the news gently, it still came as a shock. Nate hadn't been expecting any mention of Tom, much less something like this. Though he'd never met the elderly woman, Tom had spoken of her so often and with such affection that he felt as though he knew her. She'd meant so much to Tom, becoming like a mother after his own parents disowned him.

Nate hadn't cried over Tom since the week they broke up, but imagining Tom's grief made Nate feel like his heart was breaking all over again. His arms had never felt so empty as they did now that he couldn't wrap them around the man he loved so much. He longed to kiss the tears from Tom's near-black eyes, brush the soft blonde hair away from his face and hold him as he grieved.

Though a few weeks had passed, he couldn't let the loss go unacknowledged. When his mother passed away, he'd found that the hand-written notes from friends had brought him the greatest comfort. Unable to find a card that didn't already have a verse in it, he added his own carefully worded thoughts, ending with what he now felt would always be true: *yours*.

THE DEMOCRATIC National Convention and the nomination process itself have both changed significantly over the 180 years since the first national convention was held. Many of today's generation of politicos can barely remember a time when the nominees were not already decided weeks or months before the convention. Modern conventions contain few surprises, with much of the focus being placed on the prime-time speakers once the party business has been attended to.

Tom had attended the Convention once before, four years earlier, at the invitation of his then boss, Mayor Isaiah Lee. It was the first time he'd been able to afford it—as a graduate student just scraping by, it had been out of his reach. The experience of being there with the throngs of party supporters was thrilling in itself, in spite of the lackluster field of candidates that year's primaries had produced. It was his first time participating in politics at that level, and the sights, the sounds, the energy of the place was thrilling. The final evening's speech by the nominee, the governor of Oregon, was the pinnacle of the week for everyone, and that night Tom had looked into his own future and thought, "Someone is going to stand up there one day speaking *my* words."

"One day" had come much sooner than he'd bet on.

Not even his exhaustion or the emotional upheaval of the past six months could have dampened the excitement that bubbled up in Tom every time he thought of the week that awaited him in Richmond, Virginia. The Wagner campaign had been steadily gaining momentum despite a minor falter immediately after Erin Michaels pulled out. Bill was now polling a few points behind President Yoder (depending on which poll you read) and little by little, the gap was narrowing.

Tom and Mitch had been developing the convention speeches for weeks with input from Kim and other staff, refining and revising until at last they were as close to finished as they could be. A week before the convention, Bill publicly announced his selection as running mate—none other than the extremely capable Erin Michaels. It came as a surprise to many politicos, and some of the more jaded pundits were inclined to view it as a capitulation to the party members who had favored Erin in the primaries. Tom chose to see it as a hand outstretched in hopes of resolidifying a divided party. He had great respect for Erin and he knew Bill did too. If the vice-presidency was her stepping stone into her own administration, all the better.

With no small regret did it occur to him that if Nate hadn't quit, they might have been working together now. They'd have had an explanation as to how they'd gotten to know each other, and if people realized something had developed between them, it would have been plausible that it hadn't begun until after they began working together.

Instead, Tom's contact with Erin Michaels ended up being Sarah, who was assigned as Kim's liaison with the running mate's staff. Sarah being who she was, she waited no longer than three days before asking Jason Eisenberg if he and Nathan Harris still kept in touch, and what was Nate up to these days?

Jason had a well-deserved reputation for being absolutely discreet, and therefore Tom was shocked that instead of telling Sarah to mind her own business, Jason had apparently shared at least a little information on Nate's new life: Nate had sold his condo in DC and moved to Durham, North Carolina, where he would be teaching at Duke University. He had moved on, and Tom was surprised to realize how much this new information pained him. The only contact they'd had in nearly three months, after all, was the sympathy card. Nate hadn't called or e-mailed— his actions making it abundantly clear to Tom that whatever they'd shared had been a mere transient thing, an interest of the moment that was easily given up at Nate's convenience. Now Tom had to admit that he'd never completely abandoned the hope that Nate would show up at his apartment door again, like he'd done so many times in the past. Knowing that Nate wasn't even in the area anymore, Tom had to give up that fantasy once and for all. That would be easier said than done.

The first two days and nights of the convention passed in a bit of a blur, with actual party business taking surprisingly little time. Tom was introduced to countless individuals, some of whom he knew only by reputation, and others with whom he'd corresponded and could now put a face to the name. On the first evening, one of the prime-time speakers was none other than Mayor Isaiah Lee. Tom had lunch with Isaiah and some of his other former Atlanta coworkers earlier that day. It was an absolute delight to be in the crowd, listening to Mayor Lee deliver a rousing, sometimes humorous, but always heartfelt speech. He focused on how, as a young man, he had come to believe in the principles of the Democratic Party and how it reflected the ideals he strove to uphold as mayor. He was thrilled to support his friend, Bill Wagner, who had garnered his respect when they'd served together in the Georgia senate.

On the second evening, after the keynote address was delivered by the mayor of Los Angeles, Bill's wife, Rebecca, spoke. As someone who had preferred to keep a lower profile throughout the campaign, speaking at the convention was a huge deal for her. Her speech, written by Tom, was short, humorous, and intended to give a sketch of what life with Bill was like. Tom had spent some time with Rebecca before writing her address, getting to know her, observing her speech patterns and the southern colloquialisms she used. A petite blonde woman with a strong southern accent, it would have been easy, at first glance, to write her off as a privileged Junior Leaguer with little to fill her time. As Tom got to know her he learned that she had come from a working-class family in East Atlanta. Her father, a welder, had started saving for her education the day she was born, determined that she would be the first in their family to go to college. Up until Bill had declared his candidacy, Rebecca had been the executive director of an Atlanta chapter of The Boys & Girls Clubs. Tom knew Rebecca Wagner was intelligent and ambitious, sardonically witty, and that she usually surprised those who had written her off as a bored housewife. His task was to produce a speech that illustrated who she really was, and to introduce the nation to Rebecca Wagner, future First Lady.

The result was nothing short of a triumph. Rebecca received a standing ovation from the convention delegates, and the media buzz was that Rebecca Wagner had swept the nation off its feet. That accomplishment sent Tom off to bed on a high. The first two days had gone exactly as they should, and Tom had every expectation that the second half of the convention would only get better.

It didn't quite turn out that way.

Shortly before the call to order on day three, Tom was sitting in his seat in the area cordoned off for campaign staff. As he scribbled some thoughts onto his ever-present notepad, Sarah dropped into the empty seat beside him. She and Mitch had been with the Michaels staff going over the speech Erin would deliver in a few hours, reviewing it for the final time before it would be saved for loading into the teleprompter. Tom looked at Sarah expectantly, ready to ask if the speech was all set, but the moment he saw her face he asked, "Oh no—what's wrong?" She was looking at him with grave concern, and all he could think was that the Michaels staff were raising objections to some phrase or sentence—not that there was any argument to be made about it now, but they seriously didn't need the hassle at this late hour. "What didn't they like about the revisions we made?"

"The speech is fine. The senator loves it. She's all ready for tonight," Sarah replied carefully.

"So what's the matter?" asked Tom, puzzled. "Why do you look like you have horrible news?"

Sarah seemed momentarily lost for words, an unusual phenomenon. "When we were in Michaels's suite…."

"Yeah?" Tom prompted.

"Nathan Harris is here. He was in the suite when I got there, talking to Jason and Erin and a few other people."

Tom was floored. "So—" he stammered. "What does that mean? Is he… is he back?"

"No," Sarah assured him quickly. "From what I could overhear, he's here today and tomorrow to hear Erin and Bill's speeches."

Tom's head was spinning. To give himself a moment without having to speak, he took a drink of water. He almost couldn't swallow it, anxiety constricting his throat.

Peering uneasily at him, Sarah asked, "Are you going to be okay?"

Tom hesitated a moment, hoping his voice would be reasonably steady. "Sure. I mean, it's a big arena. I'm sure we can manage to avoid each other." He knew he'd sounded utterly unconvincing, but if Sarah disagreed, she didn't say it. Her hand rested on his forearm a moment, squeezing it to show her support before she quietly excused herself, leaving Tom to his thoughts. He had been so focused on work that it hadn't occurred to him that Nate might come to the convention. What if they ran into each other—what would they say? Would Nate speak to him?

The more he thought about it, the less likely it seemed that he'd have to deal with it. He doubted Nate had any desire to speak to him, considering how he'd ended it. He would probably avoid Tom and stick with the group of friends he had apparently come to see.

Early evening came and one speaker blurred into the next, with five-minute talks about things like prostate cancer awareness and funding for libraries—important issues, of course, but the thrall of the audience had waned somewhat. Sarah and various other members of their group had wandered off to get something to eat. Tom checked his watch, and, realizing he had thirty minutes before the prime-time speeches, decided to get up and stretch his legs for a while before prime time.

He left the arena and crossed the concourse, going right outside. A cloudburst had struck briefly, lasting long enough only to soak the hot concrete so that steam now rose from it in great curls. Tom strode to one of the circular islands where grass and trees formed a small oasis in the middle of the interlocking brick sidewalk. He listened to the sounds of the city around him and gazed up at the slate gray clouds that still swirled overhead, looking like they could break open again at any moment. He tried to let his brain empty of all the thoughts and concerns that filled it, until he suddenly realized that someone was standing just a few feet away from him. He turned quickly, and looked directly into the warm brown eyes of Nathan Harris.

Nate looked more casual than Tom was used to for this type of event. His shirtsleeves were rolled up to the elbow, exposing forearms that were tanned brown. His face, too, was tanned and covered with a short, soft-looking beard. His hair was shorter, a bit messy. Overall, he looked like all his hard edges had been blunted, softened a bit. He looked healthy.

The look in his eyes, too, was different. He'd always had an intense gaze, but this wasn't the same driven, ambitious look Tom knew. With his hands in his pockets and his eyes earnest, tonight Nate was suppliant.

Tom held Nate's eyes for a long moment, then slowly and deliberately, he tucked his pen into the spiral binding of his notepad and turned to fully face Nate, silently giving permission for Nate to draw near. With a few steps, Nate closed the remaining distance between them.

"Hello, Tom."

"Hello."

"It's good to see you," said Nate.

Tom wasn't convinced he could quite agree with that sentiment. By way of answer, he nodded tightly.

"How are you?" Nate asked softly, his voice full of meaning and concern.

It would have been easy for Tom to reply with something sarcastic or hurtful. Instead he straightened up, lifted his chin a bit and carefully replied. "I'm okay. And you?"

Nate hesitated a few seconds and when he spoke it was without completely answering the question. "I'm living here in North Carolina now—in Durham."

"I know. I heard you're going to be teaching at Duke. Congratulations."

Nate nodded. "I've been catching Wagner's speeches online when I can. You're doing a great job. Brilliant. As always."

"Thanks," Tom answered self-consciously. After a pause he got up the nerve to say, "You look good. You look like you've been outdoors a lot."

Nate gave a wry smile. "I had some free time this summer. I spent a good chunk of it at my family's cottage up in Delton."

"Nice time of year to be off, I guess." A long awkward silence followed, and Tom didn't know what to say. There were so many things hanging in the air between them—to pull at one would have brought the lot raining down. It was probably best to leave those things alone, to let them fade into the past along with the few months of happiness they'd had.

Over Nate's shoulder Tom saw Sarah standing outside the doors into the arena concourse. He knew she wouldn't have interrupted if he wasn't needed, and so he said to Nate, "Well. The prime-time stuff is going to start shortly, and I'm expected indoors."

"Yeah," Nate replied. "Of course."

"So… good-bye, Nate."

"Bye, Tom."

Tom started to move off then, but as he brushed past Nate, he swore he heard a whisper, barely audible: "Miss you." He turned, but Nate strode off, heading toward a hot dog vendor down the sidewalk. Tom almost called after him, but he was gripped by uncertainty as to whether he'd really heard what he thought he had, and soon Nate was too far away to call.

It wasn't easy for Tom to focus on the speakers that evening. Watching Erin Michaels up on the stage certainly did nothing to banish Nate from his mind, so closely did he associate the two. He couldn't stop reliving those brief moments. He was certain he'd heard Nate correctly…

but *why* did he say it? Did he really miss Tom? Was that why he'd sought him out, had actually followed him out of the arena so they could talk? But if so… what was the point of Nate saying it after he'd been the one to end it? Didn't he realize how cruel it was? Did he regret their breakup? Maybe…. Tom went around and around in his thoughts, reasoning out all the evidence in a vain attempt to figure out Nate's thought process, and it wasn't until the audience broke into thunderous applause that he realized Senator Michaels's speech was over and he'd barely heard a word.

Long moments later, when the applause had finally died away after Erin's speech, Sarah turned to Tom. "Let's get a drink," she suggested. He knew she was dying to ask what had happened with Nate. To her credit, she waited until they'd returned to their hotel and ensconced themselves in the bar. When they each had a strong drink in front of them, Tom recounted the short, awkward conversation. Sarah, too, was at a loss, and could only look sympathetic as he repeated the questions that had swirled in his mind all evening. But Tom wasn't looking for an answer, not from Sarah. It helped to be able to talk about it. By their second drink, she had him laughing. He had come to rely on her for that a lot recently.

As they chatted he noticed, several tables away from where they sat, a small group of young men, who looked to be in their late twenties. One of the men kept looking over at Sarah every time she laughed, his eyes lingering a bit longer each time. Eventually the man got up and approached the table, introducing himself as Alex, an aide to one of the House representatives from Colorado. He recognized Tom and Sarah as Wagner staffers and asked if he could buy them a drink. Tom declined, having had enough already, but invited Alex to sit with them. Alex went to the bar to get a drink for himself and Sarah, and Tom took advantage of his absence to lean in to Sarah and whisper, "He's been watching you since we got here."

"Really?" replied Sarah in an excited whisper. "He's adorable!"

Tom grinned. "Want me to take off after he gets back?"

Sarah bit her lip. "I don't know. Hooking up at the convention? Isn't that a cliché?"

With a shrug, Tom said, "Do you care? You never hook up anywhere. If you want to, go for it."

"I don't even know him. I mean, I've seen him on the Hill," she mused as Alex smiled shyly back at her from the bar. "I'm pretty sure he's friends with Jeff Lindsay—you know him, he works for Senator Adams. But…."

"Look," Tom said, speaking quietly as Alex was on his way back. "If you want me to leave, tap your fingernail on the tabletop."

Sarah nodded quickly and leaned back just as Alex returned. He set a cosmo in front of Sarah and a glass of ice water before Tom, saying, "Thought you might want that."

"Thanks," said Tom, pleasantly surprised at Alex's thoughtfulness. Alex sat, and Tom listened quietly as Alex and Sarah carried the conversation. Not that they ignored him, but Alex was so obviously interested in Sarah that he only seemed to remember Tom was with them when Tom actually spoke. Within ten minutes Sarah had tapped the tabletop with her finger. Tom covered up his grin by faking a yawn. "Wow, I'm worn out. I'm sorry, Sarah, but I'm going to have to say good night."

"Of course," said Sarah with a sly smile. "See you in the morning, honey."

Tom grinned and gave her a kiss on the cheek before extending a hand to Alex and wishing them good night. He strolled out of the bar and down the hall to the bank of elevators. He was inside, and the door had begun to close, when a hand reached into the gap, holding the elevator. The door reopened and Nate stepped in, to the very great surprise of both of them.

"Oh!" Nate exclaimed before he could stop himself, then added awkwardly, "Uh… hi."

"Hi," Tom replied. The door slid closed, shutting out Tom's desperate hope that someone else would join them. Nate pushed the button for his floor. Tom expected him to make small talk, but in silence they rode to the ninth floor where Tom's room was. When the door opened Tom muttered, "Bye," and stepped quickly out of the elevator. He was only a few steps down the hall when something made him stop short. During the few seconds in which he stood motionless, he wrestled with his heart and mind, every rationalization and every desire he'd struggled with in the last three months playing on fast-forward as he teetered on the edge of indecision, until suddenly he seized upon a burst of courage.

He whirled back around, ran the few steps back to the elevator, and hit the button as the door was closing. With another ding it slid open again to reveal Nate, slumped against the back wall, his hands in his pockets as he looked glumly at the floor. Tom made no move to enter, and presently Nate looked up, his eyes widening as he realized Tom was the one who'd stopped the elevator.

"Nate" was all Tom said, and suddenly Nate was off the elevator and into Tom's arms, his lips soft after so many months without them. He tasted the same, he smelled so good—warm and spicy—and the beard, new and unfamiliar as it was, added a bit of delicious friction against Tom's face. Tom melted against him, letting the sensations wash over him, his heart pounding in his throat, and all he could think was, *He really did miss me.*

Nate pulled away suddenly, gasping, "Tom, I'm sorry. That was—" But his words were lost as Tom took hold of his shirt and pulled him in again. Nate's hands found their way around to the small of Tom's back, and Tom gasped into Nate's mouth as Nate pulled him tight against him.

"My room," he managed to whisper, pulling Nate down the hall toward his door. The last thing he wanted was for the doors to open and someone to find them here kissing in the hall. They were down the hall and into his hotel room within seconds, and naked on the bed in under a minute. Tom groaned at the feel of Nate's body, warm and strong against him. The dark hair that covered Nate's chest and legs, the lean, muscular arms and tanned shoulders, down to the very last freckle... all were remapped and rememorized. Nate, too, seemed unable to get enough of touching and looking at and kissing Tom everywhere. Physically it was as though no time had passed since the last time they'd been together.

Tom felt all the longing and the loneliness and the heartbreak of the last few months slip away when Nate was finally inside him. Had he ever told himself he was getting over Nate? It had been a lie. Feeling Nate's tongue slide across his own, he knew he was as in love with Nate now as he'd been the day Michaels suspended her campaign. He knew he had never felt this way about anyone in his life and never would again.

He reached up, his hands brushing over Nate's shoulders and down his back, feeling the muscles contract and release with each thrust. Nate's face was flushed, a sheen of sweat across his forehead glistening in the light from the bedside lamp and his warm brown eyes not releasing Tom's gaze for a second. *This is it,* thought Tom. *For the rest of my life— he's the one.* As he started to reach his peak, he gasped, "I love you."

Nate's face creased as though in pain. He buried his face in Tom's neck as he came, crying out Tom's name, just once, like it had been torn from him. He shuddered deeply before all the tension left his body, leaving him panting on top of a likewise-breathless Tom.

Tom kissed Nate's head, the only part he could reach with Nate's face still tucked into his neck. He wrapped his arms around the broad shoulders and felt Nate's breathing slowly return to a normal rate. He never wanted to move, wanted to stay where they were now, tangled in one another.

As the sweat cooled on their skin and he started feeling uncomfortably sticky, he reluctantly nudged Nate. "Hey you," he murmured. "Let me up for a sec." When they had both cleaned up, he lay again beside Nate, each on their sides facing each other. Tom's fingertips traced invisible paths over Nate's skin, across his chest and arms. His stomach contracted, ticklish. Tom chuckled and tried to catch Nate's eye, but it was then he realized that Nate wasn't looking at him.

For long moments they lay, Tom watching Nate's face and Nate keeping his gaze stubbornly directed somewhere around Tom's sternum. The warm contentment Tom had been feeling slowly receded, leaving icy crystals of apprehension prickling uncomfortably in his stomach.

"Nate," he eventually said.

"Mm?"

"Nate," Tom repeated, more insistent.

For a split second, Nate's eyes flickered up, meeting Tom's, but he looked away again just as quickly. The ice that had begun to form in Tom's stomach now spread throughout him, forming into a frozen block around his heart and putting cold fury into his voice when he spoke.

"Oh my God," he said, slow and quiet as he pulled away to sit up. Nate met his gaze then, his eyes widening, but he remained silent, not bothering to pretend he didn't understand the realization to which Tom was now coming.

"Oh my God," Tom repeated, still deadly calm. "Are you kidding me?" Nate sat up, still not speaking. "Tell me I'm reading you wrong," Tom continued, though he felt certain he wasn't. "Tell me you're not going to insist that we can't be together, despite the way we obviously feel about each other." Nate still said nothing. Tom, his voice becoming more dangerous, repeated, "Nate?"

Finally Nate looked him and replied with regret, "I can't... I can't tell you that."

Tom felt like he was reeling. Unsteadily he got to his feet. "I can't believe this. You're doing it again. And I let you. Son of a *bitch*. All I had to do was leave the elevator and go back to my room." No longer comfortable with his nakedness, Tom found his briefs and stepped into them as he spoke. "Three months I've spent getting you out of my mind, trying to forget all the things I let myself believe when we were together." Nate had risen and begun to silently dress as well, looking miserable as Tom became more upset. "What the hell was this, Nate? Are you *trying* to hurt me? Or are you actually so self-absorbed that it didn't occur to you that you'd be *breaking my heart*?" His voice had risen, almost to a shout.

Nate winced at this, closing his eyes against the pain in Tom's voice, but he wouldn't respond. Now dressed, he simply stood in the middle of the room, taking Tom's ire with a sad, silent resignation.

"Aren't you going to even try to defend yourself?"

Nate, his eyes still closed, said quietly, "I have no defense."

Tom shook his head. "You got that right." He walked to the window and stared out at the Richmond night skyline. He was furious, but how could you fight with someone who wouldn't fight back? "You know what? Just go. Go back to your room, go back to your life. And Nathan?" He turned to Nate, whose shoulders were hunched, rounded protectively, belying the proud, confident man Tom had known. "You stay away from me. I don't ever want to see you again."

The embodiment of dejection, Nate turned slowly and walked to the door. His hand on the knob, he paused, seeming to struggle with himself a moment before he looked back. "Tom?" Tom responded with a single raised eyebrow, and Nate said hoarsely, "I love you too." And before Tom could react, he was gone.

Tom stood, speechless, staring at the closed door. Was Nate fucking with him? It seemed impossible that he was; Tom wouldn't—couldn't—believe it. But if it was true, if Nate did love him, then *why* did he insist that they couldn't be together? Why torture them both?

Tom sighed. He felt so confused, so at a loss to explain Nate's behavior, that even with the emotional wringer he'd been through, he couldn't find tears to shed. For that he was glad, because the last thing he wanted was the red, puffy eyes that would have Sarah asking him questions the next morning. He showered before calling the front desk to ask for housekeeping to bring him some fresh bedding. He didn't think he could bear to sleep in the sheets that were permeated with Nate's scent.

At last he crawled into bed, stretching and trying to relax. He focused on his breathing and did every meditation exercise he could think of, trying to quiet his mind. Still, many hours slipped past before sleep found him.

SEPTEMBER

THE MEMORY made Nate want to bang his head against a wall.

When he'd followed Tom outside the arena, catching up with him on the street to speak to him, Nate had managed to marshal every bit of dignity and self-control he had. They'd both conducted themselves with maturity. They'd had a calm, if somewhat awkward, conversation and parted amicably. Nate had been able to speak around the dull ache he felt in his chest when those bottomless brown eyes met his again. Yes, he'd whispered rash words into the air behind Tom—though surely the street noise had disguised that impulsive action—but then it was over, and the worst was behind him. He was proud of how mature they'd both been.

Therefore, he was completely unprepared to step into what he assumed was an empty elevator, to find Tom—of all people. In spite of his desperate attempts to think of something to say, his mind remained stubbornly blank, and as Tom exited, Nate sank back against the wall of the elevator, rubbing his forehead against the headache that was beginning behind his eyes. And then Tom came back…. Nate had never allowed himself to hope that Tom still wanted him, but the look on Tom's face was unmistakable: it was longing. Not only lust, but a soul-deep ache, a *yearning*. And Nate recognized it instantly, because he had been pining for months too.

Memories of the next scant hour would plague him forever: the passion of their reunion; the love he knew would never die flaring hot again in his chest after months of trying to convince himself it would gradually fade; the way his body fell into Tom's, even better than he'd remembered. As they made love, he'd been able to block thoughts of the consequences until Tom choked out those words: *I love you.*

Hearing them tore Nate's soul in pieces. The pain, the loss he'd already lived through, and what awaited him still… it clawed at him, sharpening every sensation into an exquisite point, puncturing his heart even as his body shuddered through climax.

After, as they lay together, Tom's soft fingertips tracing over him, Nate silently berated himself. What the hell had he done? How could he do this to Tom knowing nothing had changed, knowing they still couldn't be together? He'd ended their relationship to protect Tom, goddamn it. He was disgusted with his carelessness for Tom's feelings. He deserved all the anger, all the bitterness Tom spat at him before asking him to leave. He deserved to be banished from Tom's life: obviously it needed to be done if he couldn't rely on his own self-control in the matter. Whatever protected Tom from ever being hurt by him again....

Fleetingly he'd considered packing up and driving back to Durham after that, but decided against it, knowing he was too upset and exhausted to make the two-and-a-half-hour drive safely. He went back to his own room and slept until noon, and by the time he awoke, he knew he'd regret it if he didn't stay to see Wagner speak. He packed his bags and loaded them into his car so he could leave as soon as Wagner's speech had concluded, and then joined the convention in time for the prime-time speakers. He didn't sit with Jason or anyone else from the old team, choosing instead to sit on his own in the crowd. For the first time since being fired, it truly hit him—he wasn't a staffer, wasn't someone in the inner circles anymore. Now he was simply a citizen, someone who sat among the other mindful, concerned individuals and hoped he was listening to the next president.

Logically Nate knew it was Bill Wagner who was speaking, that he was conveying his policies and promises for his hypothetical administration. Despite that, he could almost *hear* Tom saying the words, could picture him speaking—which was slightly ironic considering their rule never to talk about the campaign.

When it was over, he located his friends to say good-bye. Jason walked with him as far as the outside doors before clapping a hand on his shoulder and wishing him a safe drive. Nate arrived home shortly after 1:00 a.m. and collapsed into bed, barely moving for nine hours.

When he awoke the next morning, he decided he could at least be glad that after getting settled into his new house, he'd spent the latter half of August preparing outlines for the semester's lectures, based on the course objectives his department head had provided him, and working on his lectures for the first several weeks' classes. He had done as much ahead of time as possible so he could have the Labor Day weekend mostly free. He was grateful now that he hadn't delayed or left himself anything that really required his focus, because he didn't think he'd be much good for it after what had happened. Instead he was able to spend much of the weekend outdoors—doing yard work, hiking in Eno River State Park fifteen minutes from his house, swimming. He had met several of his nearest neighbors and was invited to a barbecue on Sunday evening, which he enjoyed.

His goal was to keep himself distracted and to be tired out enough to fall asleep easily at night. It was a partial success, but he had to repeatedly force himself to mentally "change the subject" away from Tom and the disastrous convention.

The first few weeks of school distracted him, but not in a way that reduced his stress level. Having been a TA in law school, he'd been in front of a class before. He remembered having led several spirited discussions in a senior class. This was completely different. The students—Nate had a hard time not thinking of them as "kids," they seemed so young—in his freshman American Political System class stared at him blankly as he delivered his lecture. He saw only brief flickers of interest when he made eye contact with them, and that was mainly on day one when he was introducing himself and giving them a bit of his political background. Otherwise he might have been speaking a foreign language, for all the recognition they showed.

Around the third week, he was chatting with Elisabeth, a fellow adjunct who had a couple years' experience on him. Though adjunct professors weren't required to keep office hours, Nate and Elisabeth both chose to be available in the department for a couple of hours on Wednesday afternoons if students wished to seek them out. As it was still early in the term, Nate and Elisabeth found themselves spending those afternoons mostly together. Elisabeth was easy to talk to, and around the third week Nate admitted to her that he wondered if he'd been sorely mistaken to think he could teach. She listened to his frustrations with a sympathetic ear, offering to sit in on his lecture the next week and offer any pointers if she could.

When the class was over and the students had filed out, she made her way down to the front of the lecture hall to where Nate was gathering his notes.

"Okay," Nate said with an expectant look. "Do your worst."

Elisabeth was kind, but she was also pretty blunt. "Nathan, I know it's intimidating to stand in front of a class. Especially freshmen—I mean, they were high schoolers three months ago." Nate nodded. "But if I hadn't already had conversations with you before sitting in on this class, I'd have thought you were possibly the driest person I'd ever met. It was… forgive me, but it was boring. Incredibly so. You remember what it was like in college when you had a professor who stood there and talked at you for three hours a week?"

Nate grimaced. "Ugh. Yeah."

"You don't want to be one of those," Elisabeth continued as they left the Perkins Building, passing the huge Duke Chapel on their way to the Plaza. "I know you're much more interesting than this. I saw you on *Face the Nation* last spring—you were on fire. What you need to do is find a way to engage them. Encourage them to participate, get them talking. Get them interested. Show them why they should major in poli-sci."

"Easier said than done."

"For sure," Elisabeth agreed. "It's not easy. It's one of those things that takes practice. But it does become easier as you do it more."

"I thought I'd be better at this. I've never had a problem speaking in front of people."

"Oh, Nate. Teenagers aren't people."

Nate laughed out loud, dispelling some of the tension from his shoulders and the sickish feeling in his stomach. Elisabeth grinned and said, "Come on, I'll let you buy me lunch. It's the least you can do."

That weekend Nate spent hours on his laptop brainstorming ways to get his students engaged in the topics and stimulate discussion. He had to rewrite the lectures he'd already prepared for the next several weeks, but by Sunday night he had a number of good outlines and was feeling hopeful.

His students seemed thrown at first by the new approach. For the first quarter hour of his Tuesday class, they gave only tentative answers to the questions he had incorporated into his outlines, and he wondered if he'd gone to all that work for nothing. Gradually, however, they started to thaw. Nate had chosen to talk that day about ballot initiatives, and whether they should be used to allow votes on constitutional amendments that would limit the civil rights of some citizens. It was a topic he hoped would be familiar to in-state students because, before the Supreme Court had struck down the ban on same-sex marriage, North Carolinians had voted on "Amendment One," a ballot initiative that had been passed by voters and specified that marriage was a union between one man and one woman.

One student expressed that he supported using ballot initiatives, because in a democracy, activist judges shouldn't be able to overrule what the majority of citizens wanted. After a few seconds' silence, Nate was about to ask another question when a young woman timidly put her hand up. Nate nodded at her to speak, and in a quiet but clear voice she said, "I disagree."

"Would you like to explain why?"

The young woman's cheeks were now flushed from having all eyes upon her, but she held Nate's gaze steadily as she answered. "I understand that people have different values, but sometimes the majority vote in favor of limiting the civil rights of others. Like in *Loving v. Virginia*, where a white man and a black woman were married to each other. That was against the law in Virginia and if the state legislators had made it a ballot question, probably the majority at that time would have said they wanted to continue the ban on interracial marriage. I think it's the responsibility of judges to protect the rights of minorities, especially when it means going against the will of the majority."

Nate turned back to the young man who had spoken first. "Would you like to respond to that?"

From that point until the class was over, Nate had to do very little except moderate or introduce a new suggestion into the discussion. Aside from when he was asked a question—and he was careful to equivocate his replies to include only the law, not his own opinion—the students took the subject and ran with it. Subsequent classes were much the same, with Nate introducing a subject and providing some history and reasoning around that subject, then gradually drawing the students into discussion on it. Sometimes the discussions grew into hot contests, while others didn't provoke strong feelings. No matter what, though, it never resembled those first few awful classes when he'd wondered what the hell he'd gotten himself into.

As the weeks went by and the intense summer humidity lessened into something a bit more tolerable, Nate explored more and more of the area around Durham. He spent long hours hiking through wooded trails at Eno River. He explored the local restaurants, developed acquaintances among colleagues and even visited a gay bar in Raleigh, something he hadn't done in months. He got involved with the Duke Center for LGBT Life.

Despite all the new things he was getting involved in, though, Tom was on his mind all the time. It had become a fact of his life: if he was awake then there was at least a small fragment of his consciousness that was devoted to thoughts of Tom. Nate wondered where Tom was at any given moment, which part of the country he might be in. Was he taking care of himself? Was he completely exhausted by the accelerated pace of the campaign since the National Convention? Did he.... Did he think Nate was utterly contemptible?

Nate couldn't think of what had happened in Richmond without a stab of regret, and he wondered if that feeling would ever diminish. The only way he could assuage his guilt, though, would be to explain it all to Tom, to come clean about being fired and the truth of why he'd broken up with him; and that was out of the question. Tom had a brilliant future ahead of him that Nate wouldn't allow him to sacrifice out of a misplaced sense of liability. He would protect Tom and bear the consequences himself. Tom would be okay. He'd be highly sought-after professionally. Who knew what awaited him, what campaigns he might work on and who he might meet in his career? And eventually he'd find someone to make him happy... someone who wouldn't break his heart or bring a look of cold bitterness to his face.

Perhaps Nate would find someone too. Someday.

OCTOBER

THE CAMPAIGN entered the final month, and political messages were everywhere. From the radio, television, e-mail, websites, and iPhone apps, real-time updates were a constant throughout Nate's day. He was as caught up in the fever of the election as he had ever been. He watched every debate avidly, DVRing them to watch again. The presidential candidates were interesting enough, but for Nate the vice-presidential candidates' debate was a thrill. Not only was it the first VP debate in US history that didn't include a white male—Vice-President John Kim's parents had immigrated from South Korea—but, of course, Erin was a participant. It was wonderful to see her in action again. Over and over Nate found himself nodding along with her as she spoke, exactly as he'd done when he worked for her. Every point was made with grace and aplomb. When she contradicted Vice-President Kim, she was polite but unequivocal. In Nate's opinion, she was perfect.

Only briefly did he allow himself a moment of bitterness that Erin's name was second on the ticket—"Wagner-Michaels" instead of the reverse. Shortly before the Democratic National Convention, he'd had a stern talk with himself about that fact. Wagner *was* the candidate. It was done, and he could change nothing by continuing to be grouchy about it. He'd had to make a decision to view it as a stepping stone for Erin. In eight years she could run again with greater experience to bolster her candidacy.

Because of his previous job, Nate hadn't volunteered for a political campaign at any local level in well over a decade; but now that he was a regular citizen, he had the chance to volunteer in the local efforts for the Wagner-Michaels campaign. He privately enjoyed the look of surprise on the local campaign coordinator's face when he showed up for training prior to his first volunteer shift at the phone bank. She obviously recognized him and stuttered for a moment before telling him how glad they were to have him helping out. He thanked her quietly and slipped into a seat with the other volunteers. He pretended not to hear the whispers around him from those who knew who he was and those who didn't.

His father came to stay with him for nearly a week in mid-October. Nate showed him the neighborhood and the city, taking him around the campus to see the architecture and the large expanses of green space that were starting to turn into orange and yellow and red. His dad asked to sit in on one of his classes. It made Nate self-conscious to have his dad observing, and he avoided his father's eyes throughout the class, but when it was over, it was clear that Ron was as proud of him as could be.

Nate knew his dad worried about him. It didn't matter that Nate was nearly forty years old—Ron had found it very difficult to see him move all the way to North Carolina, so soon after what happened in May. Nate hoped that having Ron visit him here would ease his mind somewhat.

In the evenings they hung out together, watching the news or playing Scrabble, and his dad asked if he often spent his evenings alone. He asked about Nate's relationship with Tom, whether it was irreparable. Although Nate was adamant that their relationship was a thing of the past, he had a feeling that his father saw right through him, that he knew Nate would still be with Tom if he could.

When the visit ended and his dad had returned to Michigan, Nate was somewhat surprised to realize how much he hated the emptiness of his house. He had lived by himself for well over a decade and had never minded it. In fact, he'd greatly valued having a home that was his alone, where he could go after a day on the Hill and not have to see or speak to anyone. But things had changed now. He had the option to spend many of his days alone when he wasn't teaching, and he didn't crave solitude in the evenings as he once had. Now some evenings seemed almost interminable. For the first time, he felt that to be the only living creature in the house was lonely.

A few days after his dad's departure, Nate paid a visit to the SPCA in Raleigh. He had wanted a dog for years, but his old lifestyle had meant he could barely keep a plant alive, let alone a pet. Now he had the space in his life and in his home for a pet, not to mention a fenced back yard. He visited all the dogs in the shelter, not passing over a single one. He narrowed his choices down to a few top contenders, taking each of them out individually to go for a walk and play with him in the yard. He had two favorites, but he kept coming back to one pretty girl, a black Lab-Rottweiler cross. Her smooth, glossy black-and-tan coat had earned her the name Cinnabon. She was around two years old, and Nate learned that she had been carrying a litter of pups when she was brought into the shelter. Those pups had been born, eventually weaned and had now been adopted into their forever homes. Their mama was ready for the same after being spayed.

There was something about her that Nate fell in love with. Maybe it was her black-brown eyes that he couldn't resist. She had obviously been trained by someone—she knew voice commands and obeyed them well. She seemed to enjoy the walk Nate took her on, staying beside him without straining at the leash. She allowed Nate to brush her, and she seemed friendly, her tail slapping the grass when Nate petted her. His decision was made—Cinnabon would come home with him.

It took them a little while to get used to each other. He took her for long walks both on the leash and off, and while she was always game to accompany him, sometimes he wondered if she really liked it there after all. She didn't seem to get too excited about anything—not doggie treats, not walks, not chasing a ball in the dog park. She didn't bark at squirrels or birds in the yard. Even the neighbor's sleek tabby cat, who took a daily perch atop a fencepost in the hopes of taunting Cinnabon, seldom got more than a look from her. At night when he went to bed, she would accompany him to his room, standing beside his bed looking at him with her big doggy eyes, asking to sleep on his bed. Eventually she'd sit with her chin resting politely on his mattress, her eyes never leaving him in the hopes that he'd change his mind. Feeling mildly guilty, Nate would pat her and apologize, telling her that she couldn't sleep on the bed. Her bed was the dog bed on the floor beside him. And when he turned off the light, she would relent, going to the dog bed and curling up.

Nate worried about her. It was true she was always with him when he was home, following him around the house and lying at his feet when he was working, reading, or watching TV. She just seemed... depressed. Was she lonely after having her litter taken from her? Was it possible she missed the companionship of the other dogs at the shelter? And so he went on, fretting about her, trying to get her interested in things, hoping she would start showing some signs of liking him, maybe even loving him.

Nothing changed until the night of Halloween. Nate had spent the evening answering his door, handing out goodies to the neighborhood kids. Each time there was a knock, Cinnabon had gotten up to accompany him on his trip to the front door, then returned with him to the living room where he was watching Bella Lugosi as Dracula on TV. She didn't bark, didn't growl, didn't show the least bit of territorial behavior, even with strangers in odd costumes coming to the door.

Nate ran out of candy around seven thirty. He blew out the candle in his jack-o'-lantern and turned off his front porch light, as everyone else in the neighborhood did. He went to bed shortly before eleven, checking all the locks as he always did before going to bed. He felt like he'd been asleep only a few moments when he was jolted awake by an unfamiliar sound. It took him a moment to place it: Cinnabon, who usually slept on the floor beside his bed, was out in the living room, and she was growling.

The sound was softly menacing, making his blood run like ice in his veins. He sat bolt upright, his heart beating wildly, and threw the covers off. His clock read 12:07 a.m. Silently he slipped out of bed and tiptoed out to the living room. In the near-pitch black of his living room he could make out the outline of Cinnabon, who was standing at the patio doors that went out to the rear deck. Her growls didn't stop, though she must have known he was there; her attention seemed to be fixed unflinchingly on something in the backyard.

His heart still pounding, Nate joined Cinnabon at the window, squinting into the blackness. The trees that surrounded the yard blocked any light from the street, and so Nate slowly reached up to the light switch beside the back door, flipped on the porch light... and jumped at the sudden illumination of a young man standing only five feet from the patio door. For an instant the boy was utterly still, as though frozen in midstep. In one hand he carried a crowbar; the other had begun to reach out as though to the handle of the patio door. In that split second, Nate could see every feature of the young face in sharp relief—pale, shocked, eyes wide in surprise—and then Cinnabon exploded from menacing to terrifying, her growls turned into deep, terrifying barks, jumping repeatedly at the glass. The boy, overcoming his momentary shock, bolted from the deck, dropping the crowbar in his haste as he scrambled up and over the privacy fence and disappeared into the blackness.

The flight of the would-be intruder did nothing to calm Cinnabon. Her barks turned to whines, her blunt nails scraping against the glass as she tried to claw her way through to pursue the boy. Nate stood in shock a moment longer, staring at the spot where the boy had stood, scarcely able to believe all that had transpired in a few seconds. After a few breaths to calm himself, he grabbed the cordless phone beside him and dialed the police.

By the time the police left his home it was nearly 5:00 a.m. They had taken his statement, asking him to repeat several times what had happened. Nate had recognized the young man as Matthew Williams, the son of his neighbor from several doors up the street. Nate had met him once before, at a neighborhood barbecue in late August, shortly before Matthew had headed off to his freshman year of college in Charlotte. He'd even been in Nate's house the afternoon of the barbecue—they'd been talking about a particular brand of laptop, one that Nate happened to own, and Matt had asked to see it, ostensibly to "test drive" it before buying one of his own.

Nate didn't know why Matthew was home, only that he might have succeeded in breaking in, if not for Cinnabon. So when he collapsed into bed at the break of dawn, he had a ninety-pound, black-and-tan companion beside him in bed. Suddenly she really was his dog; or perhaps more accurately, he had become *her* person. Either way, they were inseparable. When she heard his car pull into the garage she was at the kitchen door to meet him, her tail wagging and her big doggy tongue ready to give him a swipe of welcome. She slept beside him every night and was happy to play games of Frisbee for as long as he wanted. When he watched television, she climbed up on the couch beside him and rested her head on his thigh.

And so she was on the night of the first Tuesday in November, her sprawled body taking up much of the length of the couch while Nate stared at the television in disbelief. He was unwilling to accept what was happening. After a long, hard-fought battle, Wagner was going to… concede? Nate felt as breathless as he had when he first realized Erin would not win the nomination. It seemed impossible—he'd never considered any other possibility, nor did he want to start now. But whether he accepted it or not, it was going to happen.

It had been a very close race right up to the end. In spite of how difficult it was to defeat a sitting president, there had been no reason to doubt that Wagner could do it. He had found almost universal acceptance from the party as their nominee once the convention was over and done with. Nate had continued to believe, in spite of everything, that Erin was the better person for the job than Wagner was, but Wagner was the party's candidate. Asking Erin to join him as his running mate had been the right thing to do; between the two of them Nate had thought it was a lock.

Miserable, he listened to Wagner thank his staff, the volunteers, and the voters, everyone who had in their own way contributed toward his campaign. The camera panned along the Wagner staff in the front row, and their dejected faces had tears prickling in Nate's eyes even before the camera reached Tom. When it did, Tom looked haggard and despondent; and Nate went from being numb to being flooded with anguish. He couldn't help the gasp that burst from him at the sight of the man he loved so much, and he put his head in his hands and wept. He wept for Tom's disappointment, loneliness, and sheer longing for Tom.

POST-ELECTION

"THANK YOU. My friends, a short while ago I spoke to President Yoder on the phone, and I extended my congratulations to him, to the First Lady, and their family, on his reelection. I told President Yoder that I wish him well and that he will be in my prayers as he leads the United States of America for another four years.

"My father told me when I was in my teens that if I wanted to succeed in life, to seek the counsel of individuals I respect and admire, and to make sure that my circle of advisors contained several excellent women. I'm proud to say that I have done exactly that. Let me tell you about a few of them.

"When I was in college I met a woman whose excellence far exceeded any other person of my acquaintance, and the day she agreed to marry me was the best day of my life. Rebecca, in everything I've done since then, you have been not just my advisor, but my partner. I could never have come this far without you by my side. Thank you for your support and love. To our beautiful children, thank you for your patience and understanding over these months.

"I've worked with Erin Michaels in the Senate for ten years and have known her to be intelligent and dedicated. It wasn't until these past twelve months, though, that I truly came to appreciate her grace and warmth—not to mention the effect she has on a crowd of people! Every time I hear her speak, I am reminded again that as a citizen and a senator, she is genuinely concerned for her constituents and her country. She has become a friend to me and to Rebecca. Erin, thank you for being my running mate.

"And then there's Kim Harvey. Kim is, quite simply, the finest campaign manager I could have hoped for. She and her staff ran an extraordinary campaign. Thank you to that team and the team across the country, to the volunteers, donors, fundraisers, and to all of you here tonight. Every day, knowing that you were all working so hard and giving so generously, was a boost to our spirits and reminded us of why it was so important to continue in our efforts.

"Henry Ward Beecher said, "Defeat is a school in which truth grows strong." As I stand before you tonight, this is what I know to be the truth: I love this country and I love her people. I am humbled that so many of you considered me worthy to lead our nation. Thank you to everyone who participated in the democratic process, whether by mail, in the early voting, or standing in line today, sometimes for hours, to make sure that your vote was counted. You voted because you love America and because you want her to continue to be the greatest nation in the world.

"Rebecca and I were privileged to meet so many of you as we traveled across the country over the past eighteen months. I was honored by those who shared their stories with me, stories of personal triumph, or of the hardships in their daily lives, and who told me, 'Bill, here's how you can make life better for Americans like me.' I brought every one of those stories with me to this fight, and in spite of the outcome of this election, you can be sure that I will not forget a single person I met in this campaign. Your beliefs are worth fighting for, and Erin and I will continue to fight for you as we resume our roles in the Senate. We will work with our fellow senators to represent the people of this entire vast nation, and we will do everything within our power to get her back onto the right track."

Tom listened to Bill's words as though hearing them through a long, hollow pipe, thin and echoing. He'd written the words himself, a couple of weeks ago, but only for the sake of being prepared. Mitch didn't even want him to write a speech—he said if the campaign considered the possibility of defeat, they shouldn't be running at all—but Tom's pragmatism wouldn't allow him to leave anything until the last minute. So in preparation for writing the acceptance speech, he'd spent an evening at home making an outline of names that would need to be mentioned in any case, and as he wrote the acceptance speech, he made a separate outline noting how he would write it if it was a concession speech. When it was obvious that the concession speech would be necessary, at least he had that much done.

Thank goodness, because he had no doubt it would be impossible to write anything meaningful or important tonight, now that he felt like he wanted to throw up, or curl up and die, or both. He stared at Bill on the stage, scarcely able to believe what was happening, what had been the outcome of the last twelve months of his life and even longer for Mitch and Kim. And for Sarah, who was standing beside him, her head against his shoulder as his arm held her tight to him. She had been fighting tears since Florida had been called for President Yoder, and when it became apparent that Ohio would go to Yoder as well, she was done. Her usually pale skin now sported blotches of red around her eyes and up her neck as she wept unabashedly on Tom's shoulder. Kim Harvey had disappeared into the washroom after the networks had called the election for Yoder, and returned ten minutes later with red-rimmed eyes, though it was the only evidence of her emotions. Even Mitch had become choked up for a moment, his jaw set in determination as he worked to suppress his disappointment.

Tom had no doubt that later on when he was back in his hotel room, in solitude, he would finally allow his emotions to flow. For now, though, he felt numb—completely bowled over. He didn't understand how this could have happened. He'd believed, and polling had borne it out, that Americans in general were shifting to a more liberal social view; that with secularism on the rise, more people would vote based on social issues—marriage equality, social justice, the widening gap between rich and poor. He knew Yoder's strongest points were fiscal, but he also believed that Bill Wagner's plans to continue economic growth were utterly solid. The Democratic Party had retained control of the Senate—of course it wasn't impossible to have different ruling parties in the House and Senate....

His thoughts were a jumble; he couldn't collect them, couldn't make sense of them. The campaign was over and he had no more responsibilities here. He didn't even technically have a job anymore. There would be no transition team to prepare for the inauguration and create a Wagner administration. No speechwriting job awaited him in the West Wing. He had no Capitol Hill job to which to return, as many of the campaign aides did. He had no idea what he would do tomorrow or the day after that, or next week. And tonight, there was nothing whatsoever he could do about it.

So as he stood and listened, he fought to clear his mind, to let it go blank and allow things to unfold around him. He answered those who spoke to him, making an attempt to respond somewhat coherently. He hugged Sarah and kept his arm around her, keeping her close beside him, relying on her strength as much as she was on his. He accepted Bill and Rebecca's thanks and offered his own thanks for the opportunity. He accepted hugs from Mitch and Kim, and other campaign team members who had become not just his coworkers but his friends and family over the past months.

Since the party that was supposed to be a victory party was now the most depressing place in America, no one hung around long after Bill's speech had ended. The staff had planned to be up celebrating all night long; instead they trickled back to their hotel in groups of three or four, most if not all tucked in before 1:00 a.m.—though whether or not they slept was another matter entirely. For Tom, at least, it was almost dawn before he slept; and the next day he got up and took the first flight he could get back to DC, to help with the cleanup at the campaign headquarters and to start figuring out what to do with his life.

Within three days Mitch had spoken to him about his future. Bill wanted Tom to work for him on Capitol Hill. Tom responded with gratitude, telling Mitch how much he appreciated the offer. He was glad for the time to really think it over too. He was exhausted and feeling completely demoralized, almost like he'd been through an engagement that had been called off the day of the wedding. He honestly didn't know what to do. Was this lifestyle really for him in the long term? He'd lived in DC for ten months already, but he'd been busy or out of town so often that he felt as unconnected to the city as when he'd first moved here. He knew being a Hill senior staffer would involve long hours, seven days a week—it was conceivable that years would go by and he still might feel like Washington was a place where he was just staying, instead of a city where he really *lived*. He had to decide if that was his idea of a fulfilling life; if he wanted to come home in the late evening hours every night to a silent, lifeless apartment where no one waited for him, no soft kiss welcomed him home; and no one slept next to him at night.

Because not even the final eight weeks of a presidential campaign could consume him so much that it could push thoughts of Nate from his head. He almost wished it could, those first days after the convention. He'd been so rash, kissing Nate and taking him to his room, blurting out that he loved him.... Tom's color rose in mortification for days afterward when he thought about Nate's refusal to meet his eyes, about how he'd lashed out at Nate and told him never to come see him again—as though

Nate was to blame for what Tom had assumed. Nate had made it plain way back in May that he wasn't interested in a long-term relationship with Tom. He'd been so carefully polite when they spoke outside the arena. Tom had gotten angry when Nate was evasive, but now it seemed obvious that Nate was trying to spare his feelings. And Tom had acted like a teenager.

He'd spent a few weeks being angry at himself and Nate, but eventually the anger had more or less evaporated, and as the intensity of the campaign increased, so did Tom's loneliness. One hotel room after another; sleeping on planes and buses; Mitch and Sarah were his emotional anchors, though neither of them knew to what extent they helped him keep it together. Sarah had no idea he'd slept with Nate that night, and Tom didn't intend to tell her, ever.

Knowing Mitch was coming to visit Tom to discuss the future, Sarah called him shortly afterward to pry from him all the details of their conversation.

"What is there to think over?" she asked with surprise when Tom told her he'd asked for a few days to think it over.

"I don't want to rush into a decision. I know I'm unemployed, but I'm tired, Sarah. I think I should get my head on straight before I decide."

"Well…." Sarah sounded like she was scheming something. "Tell you what: I'm going back to work next Monday, and by then it'll only be a week and a half till Thanksgiving; so it's going to be a quiet few weeks in the office. Why don't you come with me? You can see how things function, get a feel for the senate buildings… it would help you make an informed decision."

To Tom it sounded like a very wise plan, and Mitch gave it his blessing. Tom had been in Wagner's senate office several times during the campaign, but had spent most of his time in DC at the campaign office; so it was actually sort of a thrill to see what was happening in the buildings where the senators' and representatives' office suites were. The newly elected were getting ready to move in; the defeated or resigning were getting ready to move out; and those who didn't have to go anywhere got to watch it all happen.

At lunchtime Tom and Sarah went to the Dirksen cafeteria and enjoyed having the time to eat a meal together, loving that for a change they wouldn't have to bolt down their food and race on to somewhere else.

At one point, as Sarah was giving Tom a tour of the Hart building, they ran into Alex, the aide whom Sarah had hooked up with at the convention. His greeting was polite, if a bit awkward. They spoke briefly before moving on. Once they were out of earshot, Tom asked Sarah, "So what's going on there?"

Sarah glanced over her shoulder before replying. "Nothing, just the one night."

"Aw, that's too bad. He's cute."

"He was really sweet too. But kinda young."

"Compared to what?" Tom estimated Alex was approximately the same age as him, which was older than Sarah by a year.

"I don't know. Just… young." Tom thought Sarah was being deliberately vague, but he didn't push for details. He knew that if she wanted him to know who she had her eye on, he'd have heard it by now.

Tom found that he was beginning to envision himself coming here to work every day, trading in his red ID badge for a green one; and it was plain that Sarah hoped she was talking him into staying.

Each day at 5:00 p.m. Sarah insisted that their workday was over, though she admitted that a nine to five day wasn't usually the case. Friday evening as the day wore down, Tom suggested it was time the two of them went out to do something fun, and Sarah enthusiastically agreed. They each went to their respective homes to change, and a few hours later met at a restaurant Sarah suggested. Dinner was a relaxed affair with lots of wine, and Tom laughed with Sarah as he hadn't done in months. They took several hours over their meal and dessert, and decided to go to a club afterward. Tom wasn't much for noisy, crowded bars, but somehow with Sarah it seemed much easier to handle the crush of people. She made friends wherever she went, with her ability to say anything to anyone, and she drew Tom out of himself. They danced and laughed until two thirty in the morning, and Sarah insisted Tom crash at her apartment overnight. He'd had more to drink that evening than he'd had in many months, and he gratefully accepted the offer of her very comfortable couch.

They both slept late the next day. Tom woke up cotton-mouthed and fuzzy, but felt it was totally worth it. He'd been long overdue to blow off steam, and their evening of pure mindless fun had suited him exactly. He doctored himself up with a couple large glasses of water and some ibuprofen nicked from Sarah's medicine chest. He tiptoed into her bedroom to thank her—she was far worse off than him and probably would spend the day in bed—and then he headed home.

The rest of his weekend he alternated between doing what chores were necessary, and reading, watching TV and otherwise relaxing. It still felt so odd to have time to putter around his apartment. It occurred to him that perhaps, if he was going to stay in the city, he should think about getting a new place, something with a real bedroom, instead of this bachelor apartment that was more like a hotel room. The idea appealed to him, and he wondered if he'd just made a decision to remain in DC after all.

Monday, he returned to work, and when he told Sarah that he planned to accept Senator Wagner's offer of a permanent job in his office, she squealed. "I'm so happy! You're going to love it, I promise. Last week was really low-key, but when it all gets back to normal and everyone's here and things are happening… it's the best."

At home that evening he sat down to open the pile of mail that had accumulated over the past week. He sorted through it, absentmindedly tossing flyers and junk mail into the recycling, setting aside bills, until he came to a long, crisp white envelope that had his name and address hand-printed in block letters, and the return: Nathan Harris, at an address in Durham, North Carolina.

His heart in his throat, Tom slit the envelope and withdrew two folded pages. In that same confident hand was written:

> *Dear Tom,*
> *You told me not to get in touch with you again,*
> *and I had every intention to respect that. But after this*
> *past Tuesday, I just had to write to you. I really am sorry*
> *Senator Wagner didn't win the election. I know you're*
> *heartbroken. I know how much a campaign consumes*
> *your life and how much you have put into this. I don't say*
> *this to sound condescending, Tom: I'm so proud of you.*
> *You're a brilliant speechwriter. You have a gift, and I see*
> *your future career where you are the most sought-after*
> *person in your field.*

Also… I'm so sorry for what happened in Richmond.
The last thing I wanted to do was hurt you again. I love
you, Tom. I always will. Please live well, and be happy.
All my love,
Nate

Tom read and reread Nate's letter numerous times throughout the evening, so many times he lost count. No matter how many times he read it, he couldn't absorb it, couldn't even form an opinion. He was still as speechless when he went to bed several hours later, placing the letter on his night table.

For hours Tom lay awake, feeling only numbness, struggling in vain to understand, trying to decide how to feel about it all. Twice he turned the light back on to read it again. He didn't sleep until 4:00 a.m. and was awake again just after six; but when he awoke it was to a new sense: indignation. How dare Nate do this to him again? How dare he continue to impose upon Tom's heart and his life and his emotions? Several times he was on the verge of tearing up the letter. He stopped himself each time, though barely.

He showered and dressed for work, and by the time he'd arrived at the Hill, he had settled into cold fury. When he burst into Senator Wagner's office suite, Sarah was already at her desk, looking over the day's schedule. It was Thanksgiving week. Most staff were still off and it appeared they were alone in the suite, at least for the moment. Sarah looked up, startled, as he tossed the letter onto the blotter pad in front of her.

"What's the matter? What's this?"

"Bastard! Fucking *bastard*!"

"Who? *What*?" Sarah repeated, unfolding the letter. She read it through quickly before looking up at Tom uncomprehendingly. "What happened in Richmond?"

Tom, who had paced impatiently behind her chair while she read, ran his hands through his hair with annoyance. "I slept with him," he said in an undertone.

"What!" she squeaked. "When? You didn't say a word!"

"Thursday night, after I left you at the bar. We ended up on the same elevator and then I got off at my floor, and I held the door and we kissed, and then it just…." He waved his hand. "Happened."

"Then what?"

"Then he pulled his usual stunt, being all withdrawn and, 'oh, we can't be together,' and blah-blah. And I told him I never wanted to see him again. And then he sends me this! *Bastard*!" Tom collapsed into the chair from the desk next to Sarah's, pounding his hand on the desk as he did.

"I can't believe you never told me about this," Sarah said as she reread the letter, slightly incredulous. "And he... he says he loves you."

"He said it in Richmond too," Tom replied, weariness catching up with him now that he'd started to blow off some of the pressure that had been building up since last night. "On his way out the door."

"Did you ever say you loved him?" Sarah asked.

"Yes. I told him in May. While he was breaking up with me. I said it, hoping that if he knew how important he was to me...." He rested his elbows on his knees and buried his face in his hands.

"Did he say it back?"

Tom huffed a bitter laugh. "No. He said he was sorry. I said, 'I'm in love with you,' and he said, 'I'm so sorry.' Fucker! Why does he keep doing this? He ended it so he could go off and get away from politics. He made it clear he had no interest in staying together, so you think he'd give me a fighting chance to try to get over him." Tom's voice increased in pitch and volume with each word. "Instead he's sending me a sympathy card, and coming to talk to me at the convention, and writing me a letter to tell me how proud he is of me, and telling me he loves me! What the hell?"

"I don't know, honey," Sarah said sympathetically. "Unless...."

"Unless what?" Tom demanded.

She regarded Tom thoughtfully for a moment. "Well... unless he really does want to be with you."

Tom gave her an incredulous look. "He dumped me, Sarah. And then we slept together, and then he pretty much dumped me again. If he really wants *me*, and I mean he wants a relationship, not just sex, why would he keep doing that?"

"If he *doesn't* really want you," Sarah countered, "why does he keep telling you he loves you?"

Tom threw his hands up in frustration. "Hell if I know! Maybe he enjoys fucking with my head." He dropped his head back into his hands and stared at the floor as Sarah continued to peruse the letter. They sat silently for a few moments until she gently cleared her throat. He looked up at her expectantly.

"Have you thought about…. Now, don't bite my head off, okay?" She looked hesitant, and Tom raised an eyebrow. "Well, you have his home address…."

"Yeah?" The eyebrow crept higher as he thought he could anticipate what she was going to suggest.

"Maybe you should… go see him?" Her sentence was more a question than a suggestion, and Tom answered it immediately.

"Absolutely not," he said flatly. "Absolutely not." He snatched the letter back from her and folded it up. "This letter means nothing, and I will respond with nothing." He tucked it into his breast pocket.

"Tom, I'm sorry—" she began, but he cut her off.

"It's okay," he told her, and meant it. "I'm not upset with you, Sarah. I know you're trying to help me, and I value your opinion, but in this case, I think you're wrong. Nathan Harris made his bed and now he's the one who has to lie in it. But I am moving on."

"Okay. Well… you know I'll be here for you, honey."

Tom stood to give her a warm hug. "I know you will," he said gratefully.

They didn't revisit the subject, but for the rest of the day it was present in Tom's thoughts. He was acutely aware of the paper folded in his pocket over his heart; he could feel it through the fabric of his shirt. When he went home that evening, he put it away in his night table drawer, and from that location it continued to hold his consciousness. He meant what he'd said to Sarah—he was going to move on. Somehow he was going to learn how to not love Nate. What was more, he was going to start living an actual life again, whether he remained in Washington or not. He'd had hobbies once, interests outside of work—it was time to take them up again. He would not become someone whose whole life was consumed by their job. Someday someone would tell him again that they loved him, and when that happened, he promised himself, it would be *real* love—not whatever this thing was Nate claimed to have for him.

He slept well that night, and returned to the Hill the next day with a sense of having turned a page. He was the first one at Senator Wagner's offices, and when Sarah arrived with coffee for both of them, he greeted her with a broad smile. The morning went well. Mitch Enns stopped by to get something from his desk before he and his family headed off to the Cleveland suburbs for the holiday weekend. He told Tom he looked right at home there in the senator's office. There were a few other staffers around but it was overall very quiet, and Tom was looking forward to the following week when everyone, including Bill Wagner, would be back and he'd see the office as it typically operated.

As Tom and Sarah returned from the cafeteria after lunch, they found an intern waiting for them in Bill's suite. "I have a delivery from Senator Michaels's office. Is there a Tom McAlindon here?" he said when Sarah asked if she could help him.

"I'm Tom McAlindon," replied Tom. The young man handed over an envelope and excused himself.

Sarah, who was leaning over to look at the envelope, said, "That's Jason's handwriting!"

Tom turned to her with some surprise. "Jason?"

"Jason Eisenberg," she replied. "Michaels's chief of staff?"

"I know who Jason Eisenberg is," said Tom, a trifle witheringly. "I'm a bit surprised you're on a first-name, handwriting-recognition basis with him."

Sarah pulled back and an unmistakable flush crept up her pale cheeks. "Well, I *was* liaison to Michaels's team during the election."

"Uh-huh," Tom replied, skepticism infusing his tone. "Did someone develop a little crush on the devastatingly handsome Jason Eisenberg?"

"I am done being nice to you today," Sarah muttered and turned on her heel. Tom's laughter followed her as she flounced away to her desk. He tore open the envelope and withdrew a note, hand-written on a blank sheet of clean white linen paper.

> *Dear Tom,*
> *I am writing to request a few moments of your time to discuss a matter of some importance. I would be most appreciative if you would stop by Senator Michaels's offices. I will be here all afternoon. The senator's offices are at 407 Hart.*
> *Best regards,*
> *Jason Eisenberg*

Well, this was unexpected. Tom could only imagine one reason why Jason would want to talk to him—for the same reason Mitch had come to see him the week before. Mitch had told him he'd be in demand, but was it really possible that Jason would try to recruit him for Michaels? "Huh," Tom remarked aloud. "Jason Eisenberg wants to see me today."

Sarah, her ire apparently forgotten, popped up from behind her cubicle wall. "Really? Why?"

"'To discuss a matter of some importance.' It doesn't say any more than that." He put the note into Sarah's outstretched hand. "I've never been in Hart. Want to go for a walk?" His gently teasing tone earned him the stink-eye from Sarah, but she agreed to walk him over to the Hart Senate Office building, next to the Dirksen building where Wagner's office was. She refused to accompany him to the door, however, excusing herself once she'd pointed down the hallway to Erin Michaels's office door. Tom took a moment to watch her go, amused to see her flustered for once. Sarah had loads of self-confidence, and he knew she usually had no problem keeping her cool, even around someone she found attractive. This was a new experience.

He opened the door into the senator's offices and found that it, too, appeared to be getting by with a skeleton staff. He spoke to the receptionist, and a moment later he was shaking Jason Eisenberg's hand and being asked to have a seat. Jason closed the door of the office and sat opposite him across a broad, dark mahogany desk. They made small talk for a few minutes, Tom inwardly acknowledging that Jason really was sexy, with the impeccably groomed masculinity and good looks of a star from Hollywood's golden age. They'd been introduced to each other during the campaign, but Tom hadn't ever spoken with him at any length. It felt odd to be sitting in his office now, chatting about what each of them had been up to since election night.

The conversation hit a short pause, and Jason cleared his throat. "So Tom, I'm sure you're wondering why I asked you to meet with me."

Tom was pretty sure he already knew the answer, but he smiled as he said, "You certainly have my attention."

Jason didn't return the smile; instead, a small crease appeared between his eyebrows. "I've made it a policy not to get involved in the private lives of my colleagues, and particularly staff who report to me, which is why I really debated before deciding to talk to you."

Tom felt like he'd missed a step. This didn't sound like the beginning of a job offer.

"I came by Senator Wagner's office yesterday morning, and I overheard you talking to Sarah Lonstein. At first I thought the two of you were having an argument, but then I realized you were talking about a personal matter."

Tom's heart stopped as he remembered the "personal matter" Jason had overheard. Nate's former boss now knew about the affair they'd had when they were employed by different campaigns? Icy shards of anxiety splintered throughout his chest at the implications. Would Jason tell Erin Michaels? What if the news got out—would it affect Nate's new job at Duke? Not to mention that Tom's own career would be in the toilet.

Jason was watching Tom carefully. "I can see you understand what I'm referring to. As I said, I never meddle in peoples' private lives. But in this case, I felt I really couldn't let it be."

"Yes," said Tom slowly. "Nathan Harris and I had a relationship during the primaries, while he worked for Senator Michaels and I worked for Senator Wagner. We could have compromised the two campaigns if anyone found out we were seeing each other. It was a huge risk to both campaigns, and we could have sunk the entire election six months before voting day."

"Ah," said Jason. "Well, yes, that's true. But I already knew that part."

"You knew?" Tom raised his hand to his forehead and felt a cold clamminess.

"I did, and that's not why I asked you to come. When I heard what you said to Sarah, I realized how wrong you are about Nate. It's not your fault, because obviously he misled you. But if you're going to talk about him to others, you need to know the whole story. As it is now, you're dragging my friend's name through the mud."

"I don't...." Tom shook his head. "I don't understand."

"I've known about you and Nate since May. I found out right before Erin Michaels dropped out of the race."

"When Nathan quit."

"Tom, Nathan didn't quit. He was fired," Jason said pointedly.

"He...what?"

"Yes, for all the reasons you said a moment ago. He endangered the campaign. He was deceitful, and showed very poor judgment on an ongoing basis. So in spite of my friendship with him, the right thing for me to do, as his boss, was to fire him."

"Oh my God." Tom was stunned. Everything he'd assumed about Nate over the past six months was wrong. As realization set in, he felt like he was reeling. "He didn't tell me. Why didn't he tell me?"

"If you knew he'd been fired for dating you, would you have allowed him to take the fall on his own?" Jason asked.

Tom thought for a moment, then shook his head. "No. We were equally involved. For him to lose his career while I bore no consequences... I couldn't have lived with myself."

"You'd have resigned," Jason concluded, and Tom nodded. "Nate knew that, Tom. In spite of my advice, he refused to let it affect your career."

Tom looked up at that. "You told him to take me down with him?"

Jason looked reproachful. "I suggested that if he had real feelings for you, as I suspected he did, that he should take the chance at a happy life. It isn't easy to find love, and in this environment—" Jason waved his hand, indicating the political world in general. "—even harder to make it last." After a long pause, Jason added, "I'm violating his privacy like crazy, telling you this. I shouldn't be talking about it at all. And I wouldn't, except...."

"What?"

"Well... he said he loves you, didn't he? In the letter."

"You really did hear everything," Tom said grimly.

Jason had the grace to look abashed. "I didn't intend to eavesdrop," he said, a hint of color rising in his cheeks. "I stayed to make sure Sarah... to make sure everything was okay."

In the midst of the emotions that were churning in Tom, an idea was occurring to him, quite apart from his relationship with Nate. He crooked an eyebrow at Jason as the idea nudged its way into his consciousness. When he spoke, he said briskly, "Well. I have some things to think about, so if you don't mind, I'll excuse myself."

"Of course." Jason stood, gesturing to the door; but as Tom was about to leave, he added, "Tom, one more thing. I've known Nate for ten years. I know him. He's had opportunities for relationships over the years—guys who would have dropped everything to be with him. He was never interested; work was always first for him. When he was seeing you... well, I didn't know at first what was going on, but I knew something had changed. For the first time, his work wasn't all consuming. And we were running a *presidential campaign*—the biggest deal in American politics." He looked intently at Tom to make sure he understood. "You had to be pretty important for him to take his eye off the ball in the middle of that."

Tom nodded thoughtfully. "Thank you, Jason," he said, and let himself out of the office.

He made his way slowly back to the Dirksen building, stopping occasionally, pretending to read plaques on the walls; deep in thought. This morning he'd been so clear and determined. Now he was more confused than he'd been when he first read the letter from Nate. Nate had sacrificed his happiness so Tom would still have a political future. It was unselfish and noble... and *infuriating*. Nate had gone ahead and made this decision on his own, without discussing it with Tom—*he couldn't discuss it with me if he thought I'd automatically resign*, Tom's conscience told him. Nate had lied to him—*Had he, or had he simply declined to correct my assumptions?* Nate had broken Tom's heart— *Though if he loved me, surely his own heart had been broken too.*

Round and round went his thoughts, arguing both sides almost without his input, as though he were watching a debate instead of engaging in it himself. Before he knew it, he was in Senator Wagner's offices, and Sarah looked as though she was about to burst from curiosity. She watched him as he slowly crossed the room to where she sat. He drew up a chair beside her, flopped down in it and looked her squarely in the eyes.

"You're seeing Jason Eisenberg?" he demanded.

Sarah's eyes expanded to almost comical size. "He told you?" she screeched.

"No," Tom replied calmly. "You did."

Sarah spluttered for long seconds before she could be understood. "How did you know?" she managed.

"A few things you said, something he said. I knew if it wasn't true, you'd contradict me." He raised his eyebrow at her. "But you didn't."

"Oh my God," she said imploringly, "*please* don't tell *anyone*. It's only been a few weeks, since election night. I mean, there's nothing wrong with us seeing each other"—a slightly defiant tone emerged here—"and we weren't involved at all during the election. But you know what gossip's like here. We want to keep it private."

"Well, don't worry," Tom assured her. "I only picked up on it because I know you well. I doubt anyone else would realize." They sat silently for a moment or two before he said, "He's Jewish. You can marry in your home synagogue."

"Stop! I know... just, no. I mean, yeah, it would be great... but no! Stop, it's too soon. Please don't jinx it," Sarah blathered, waving her hands as though Tom were a fly she was trying to swat away.

"Your mother's going to have kittens," he added evilly.

"*I know*. I'm not telling her unless it's, like, an absolute certainty, because if it didn't work out, it would *literally* kill her."

After a pause Tom said, "He's hot."

"Seriously." Sarah looked dreamy.

"Definitely not too young!"

"Fuck you!" she exclaimed "He's forty-three. That's only five years older than Nate." The mention of Nate's name slipped out before she thought, and she immediately looked sheepish. "Oh! I mean...."

"Don't worry about it," Tom told her, and meant it. "Really, it's fine. Look—I think since we're the only people in the office, and since tomorrow is Thanksgiving, and you have to fly to Chicago, and I have to get to the market, we should pack up our stuff and get out of here. What do you think?"

She grinned, and he managed to have wished her happy Thanksgiving and said good-bye without her asking why Jason wanted to see him. As he walked to his car he wondered how long it would be before she realized she hadn't asked him, and he was unlocking his car when his phone beeped with a new text.

What did Jason want?

He texted back, *Happy Thanksgiving, Sarah!*

Not ten seconds later it beeped again. *SHIT. HEAD.*

He felt a little guilty that he was relieved to be away from her. His head was swirling with new information—had it been only this morning that he felt like he'd finally taken a step toward putting Nate behind him?—and he wanted nothing more than to go home and sit and think about Jason's revelation. Instead, he had to go grocery shopping to pick up the few things he still needed for the small Thanksgiving dinner he was going to have on his own. Mentally he promised himself the evening to process it all—he had to hang in till then.

Eastern Market was packed, as he knew it would be, but he found everything he wanted, including cornbread for the dressing—he knew he'd be stuck with the leftovers for a week, but it wasn't Thanksgiving without cornbread. He drove home, scowling slightly at the sun that was already near the horizon at four thirty in the afternoon, reminding himself it would only be a month until the days started to get longer again. After all the groceries were put away and he'd had something for dinner, he made himself a cup of tea, turned out the lights in his apartment and got comfortable in the armchair he'd recently moved in front of the sliding glass doors. He propped his feet up on the ledge that went out to the balcony and looked out at the lights of the city, and finally, finally released the brutal hold he'd placed on his mind.

He slid down farther into the chair, gazing out unseeingly. All he could see before him was Nate's face, his pleading eyes that night in Richmond. He heard the words Nate had whispered before closing the door, leaving as Tom had demanded he do. Tom was at once heartbroken for Nate and furious with him. Nate loved him—his own written and spoken words proved that—but had sacrificed himself to save Tom. He'd made the decision for both of them—Tom had been given no say in this, no chance to weigh in on his own future. *You know you wouldn't have let him suffer the consequences on his own, if you'd known.* But Tom wasn't a child who needed to be protected from the consequences of his actions. If what they'd done was wrong, then he was every bit as culpable. He was so angry with Nate, and yet more in love with him now than he'd ever been before. He felt betrayed, fooled by Nate's story. A little part of his brain told him Nate had done it because he loved him. But what was love without trust? Did Nate truly love him if he was unwilling to let Tom make his own decisions based on a real understanding of all the facts?

Mentally and emotionally, it was an odd, confusing place to be. And now, what to do? He'd told Nate to leave him alone. He could leave things as they were—Nate would never know the difference. They wouldn't see each other again. They'd both move on; eventually they'd find love elsewhere, certainly. That was one possibility…

…And, yeah, there was pretty much no way he was going to do that. He'd be doing what Nate had done, making the decision for both of them now that he was the one who had more information. Granted, his information was based on Jason Eisenberg's assessment of the situation. The only way they could both fully understand the situation was to discuss it openly—no more secrets, no misunderstandings, no subjects avoided.

He just had to figure out when and how that was going to happen.

Surprisingly, it wasn't all that difficult for him to fall asleep that night. He supposed he'd missed enough sleep in the last few nights that he was worn out. He woke in the morning feeling refreshed and grateful to have the day off. After he'd put the world's smallest turkey into the oven, he propped up his iPad to Facetime with his friends Maxwell and Colin in Atlanta. They had invited Tom to spend the holiday weekend with them, as he had done every year since he'd started grad school. This year he had declined in advance, assuming that Senator Wagner would win the election and Tom would be inundated with preparations and planning for the transition. Even after Wagner's loss, Tom decided to stay in Washington for the holiday; his heart just wasn't in it this year. But the distance didn't prevent their annual tradition of watching the Macy's Thanksgiving Day Parade, Tom from his armchair and his friends from their sofa in Atlanta. They filled the three-hour broadcast easily, talking as though they were in the same room.

When the parade was over and Tom had said good-bye to his friends, he got to work in the kitchen to make the rest of his Thanksgiving dinner. He had text messages from various friends throughout the day wishing him a happy Thanksgiving. His dinner, though solitary, was delicious, and after he had wrapped up the leftovers and put them in the freezer, he settled into his chair with a novel he'd been wanting to read for months.

It wasn't his greatest Thanksgiving, though he tried hard to make the best of it. Nate was on his mind no matter what he was doing—when he was cooking, when he was watching the parade with his friends, when he was trying to concentrate on his novel. After he'd gone to bed he had nothing to distract him. Where was Nate for Thanksgiving— had he gone home to Michigan? Would he be with his loved ones for Christmas, or was he, like Tom, spending the holiday alone? Tom lay for hours thinking about Nate and missing him so much that his chest ached.

The next morning the ache was gone, but Tom felt restless. He puttered around his apartment for a few hours but couldn't settle into anything and finally decided to get outside and go for a run. It was rainy but mild, and the wet didn't bother him. He ran toward the Capitol, past the Botanic Gardens, and then west past the Smithsonian buildings along the Mall before looping back toward his apartment.

Even after the run and after showering, he didn't know what to do with himself. It was early afternoon, and it felt like the day was crawling by. He was on his own for the rest of the weekend, another three days with no obligations whatsoever. A month ago he'd have given his left arm for a weekend like this. He could settle in with a book or take a nap....

Instead, he pulled on a hoodie. He crossed the room and grabbed an envelope out of his night table drawer before cramming it into his pocket. He grabbed his keys, his wallet and his phone, and he left. Within minutes he was heading southwest on 395, stopping briefly for gas in Springfield. About four hours after he'd left his apartment, his GPS was directing him to leave I-85 and join the steady stream of northbound commuters heading home at the end of their workday. Until now he had been bound by an unwavering determination, without a second thought; but passing suburban homes and knowing he would soon be pulling into the driveway of one of those homes—a home whose occupant wasn't expecting him, and where he had no idea what reception might await him. Tom's palms began to sweat.

Now arriving at your destination on the right, his GPS announced. His heart thudded against his ribs as he pulled into the driveway of a small white bungalow on a corner lot. There were lights on inside as well as on the front porch. Tom turned off the car and sat a few seconds, his eyes closed as he centered himself and gathered his courage. He got out and went slowly up the short front walk, taking the envelope from his pocket as he did. He knocked on the door, then started slightly as a dog barked inside. He was examining the address on the envelope, making sure he had the right house, when the door opened.

And there was Nate. His hair was shorter than Tom was used to; his beard had grown thick. He was looking casual in shorts and flip-flops, and the look on his face was one of utter astonishment. As he stood gaping at Tom, a twenty-dollar bill fluttered from his hand to the floor, landing at the feet of the smooth black-and-tan dog beside him.

Tom had spent his entire drive thinking of what he might say to Nate. Now, standing at Nate's door, he couldn't place his thoughts on even one word. Nate, too, seemed too stunned to speak, and long, silent seconds went by as they stared at each other.

Finally Nate managed a strangled whisper. "Tom?"

To Tom's chagrin, he felt a lump in his throat, moved by Nate's obvious emotion. He had to speak before tears formed in his eyes. He blurted out the first thing that came to mind, and what came out happened to be the question he most wanted answered.

"Did you mean it when you said you loved me?"

Nate blinked before he stammered, "When I... said...."

"In Richmond. You said you loved me."

"Tom...." Nate was too staggered to form complete sentences. "I can't believe... I didn't think you'd...." Again they stared at each other in silence until Nate seemed to realize they were still standing in his doorway. "Will you...." he began haltingly. "Will you come in? Please?"

Tom stepped inside and took off his hoodie, which Nate hung in the closet. He gestured into the living room and Tom followed him in. "Can I get you anything? A glass of water? Beer?"

Tom nodded awkwardly. "A beer." Nate was back in a minute with one for each of them. No sooner had he set them on coasters than the doorbell rang. It was the food delivery Nate had obviously been expecting. Across the breakfast bar Tom saw Nate put the food in the refrigerator before returning to the living room and settling himself on the couch, opposite the armchair where Tom sat.

"You're not going to eat?" Tom asked.

Nate didn't meet Tom's eyes, playing with the label on his beer bottle as he answered. "Suddenly don't have much of an appetite," he said quietly. He took a deep breath as though he was steeling himself. "So...." He looked apprehensive. "You asked about the convention. Tom, what I said to you was...." He stared at a book on the coffee table as the words came out haltingly. "I shouldn't have said it. You asked me to leave you alone. I should have just left. You don't know how sorry I am if I hurt you any more by being so... selfish."

Tom waited, but Nate didn't continue. "But... that's not what I asked. Was it the truth?"

Nate looked up now, his eyes wide and anguished. "Does it matter?"

"Of course it matters!" Tom cried. "Jesus, Nathan, it means *everything*! Either you dumped me in May because you were done with Washington and you blew me off because I didn't fit into your new life, or you took the fall to protect me because your boss found out about us and fired you." If Nate had been surprised before, it was nothing to how he looked now. Tom leaned closer. "Don't you think," he said, his voice softening, "love would make the difference?"

Tom could see Nate processing this, and in a moment he seemed to accept that there was no point in denying it. "I meant it," he murmured.

The tears that had been threatening now welled in Tom's eyes. "And now?" he whispered.

Nate exhaled and his shoulders drooped as he surrendered his secret. "Always." He closed his eyes and, for the first time, told Tom the whole truth, without reservation. "I loved you when we were together. I loved you after I left Washington. I love you still."

Two great tears slipped down Tom's cheeks. *Finally*, the truth. All the months they'd spent apart; all the times he berated himself for misreading Nate so badly; in Richmond when he was certain Nate wanted him just as desperately. So long they'd both been miserable, trying to live without each other.

Tears were dampening the dark fringe of eyelashes that still fanned across Nate's cheeks. Tom got up and knelt on the couch beside Nate. He reached out and, with his thumb, gently brushed away the tears. Nate turned to him. Tom looked into those deep brown eyes, eyes that had once seemed so focused and all-seeing. Now they were reddened and despondent, without hope for a future with real fulfillment or soul happiness.

Nate had confessed the truth to Tom, and still they had many, many things to talk about; for one, Tom wasn't nearly pleased that Nate had made a unilateral decision that affected them both profoundly. But right now, this moment, he needed to bring some faith back to these mahogany eyes, to ease this beautiful, beloved man's distress.

"I told you I loved you in May," he murmured. "And I told you I loved you in August." He moved to straddle Nate's lap and took the softly bearded face gently into his hands. "I love you more than I've loved anyone. I want a life with you. Whatever that looks like, wherever in the world either of us live, I want to be yours and know you're mine." He searched Nate's eyes a moment before adding, "All I need to know is whether you want the same thing. If you do, I need to hear it."

Through red-rimmed eyes, Nate looked steadily back at Tom. "I do. You know I do."

Tom leaned in and felt those warm, soft lips on his for the first time in months. Nate's hands moved across Tom's back, broad and strong, pulling Tom close, threatening never to let go. Nate's scent filled Tom's senses, the warm, clean masculine scent that was inexorably linked with the one his soul loved, the one he desired.

It seemed like hours that they remained on that couch, making out, necking and caressing and feeling, fully dressed, like teens who were exploring for the first time. Finally, when they were too tired, too denim-chafed, too kiss-bruised to go on, they simply lay, tangled up and entwined together in the dark, talking in the hushed tones of lovers. Nate told Tom everything—Jason seeing him talking on a "secret" phone and suspecting him of disloyalty; how he'd gone home to Michigan the weekend he was fired and how much his father regretted that Nate's relationship had ended; that he'd allowed himself to envision having Tom here in Durham with him, sharing a life together. Tom told Nate that, until one o'clock that afternoon, he'd had no idea of coming here today. The idea had occurred, and he'd seized it and gone, before he could think better or talk himself out of it. Nate mightn't even have been home—it was a holiday weekend, after all—but Tom would have dealt with that as it came, he supposed.

Eventually they dozed, occasionally shifting, tightening their embrace, sharing a gentle kiss. When the sky outside the patio doors had changed from black to charcoal to pearl gray, Nate spoke again.

"So… I guess Jason told you," he murmured.

Tom had considered whether he might be able to demur, for Jason's sake, but he decided not to try. "Please don't be angry with him."

"I'm not angry, exactly. More surprised than anything. Jason's, like, the soul of discretion. You don't even know."

"I think I do, actually. He only told me to protect your reputation. He heard me talking to Sarah about your letter—she had already found out about us—and he said if I was going to tell people, I'd better know the truth." Tom sat up, gently disentangling himself from Nate; he needed to use the bathroom and couldn't ignore it any longer. "He's still your friend, even if he had to fire you." He stood up, stretching his arms over his head and groaning softly.

Nate stood too. "Are you hungry? Want some coffee?"

"Maybe a glass of water. After you show me where your bathroom is?"

Nate grinned and kissed Tom on the forehead before releasing him and gesturing toward the bathroom. After Tom had relieved himself and freshened his mouth with a little toothpaste, he rejoined Nate, who was coming out of a powder room off the front hall. Nate got them each a glass of ice water. Tom downed his in a few long swallows, but Nate stood, leaning back against his counter, watching Tom bemusedly.

"I can't believe you're here," he murmured. "If you knew how many times I've pictured you here... the two of us taking the dog for walks, cooking dinner at the end of the day...." He moved toward Tom, but slowly, as though he still wasn't convinced it was allowed. "Living our lives together." He finally reached out and encircled Tom's waist in his arms. The goose bumps that had covered Tom the first time they made love now started to pimple across his bare torso. "I love you."

Nate's whispered declaration made Tom's heart thump wildly, and the searing kiss that followed set his body on fire. Nate's hands stroked across his naked back; Tom reached down to cup and squeeze Nate's ass, pulling their hips closer together. Nate gave a gasp that gave way to a moan. His hands slipped down under Tom's ass, lifting him up. Tom wrapped his legs around Nate's waist and allowed himself to be carried to Nate's room. At the bedroom door, Nate paused, reaching out with his foot to close it. They heard Cinnabon whine slightly as she encountered the closed door.

"She's gonna be pissed," Nate muttered, and they both broke into wild laughter. Tom briefly felt bad for the dog who wasn't used to sharing her human, but he couldn't dwell on it too heavily with Nate placing him on the bed and reaching for his fly. Jeans and underwear came off together in a single tug, and Tom nearly came off the bed as Nate's hot mouth immediately engulfed him. He was very enthusiastic, and it wasn't long before Tom was too close, gasping for Nate to stop. As difficult as it was to hold back, he wanted to go a little slower.

He turned Nate onto his back and removed his shorts and briefs. For a long time, his hands roamed over Nate's body. He stroked those long legs, which seemed more toned now than they had in the spring. He explored the slightly ticklish stomach and softly furred chest, nosed into the armpits, and squeezed muscular shoulders. He lay atop Nate and kissed him for a long time, loving the feel of Nate's hardness against his, occasionally pressing his hips a bit tighter, rubbing a little and loving to hear Nate's pleasured gasps.

Finally, when he couldn't take any more teasing and he didn't think Nate could either, he whispered, "Condoms?"

Nate produced condoms and lube from his night table drawer, saying, "Lie on your back." Tom complied, and Nate spent a long time preparing him, opening him carefully with slick fingers, making Tom's toes curl with the pressure and the sweet burn he'd gone without for so long. When Nate sank slowly inside him, inch by intoxicating inch, it was at once familiar and yet better than it had ever been, since they whispered love and promises and commitment between moans and curses. It was passion as Tom had never experienced in his life, acquainted for the first time with unconditional assurance. It was this realization that at last carried him over the top, wrapping himself around Nate and holding him tight as he rode wave after wave of rapture; and then, a moment later, sensing Nate's pleasure focus into a fine point before shattering.

Afterward they slept, thoroughly spent and exhausted. Even in his sleep, Tom was aware of contentment as he had not known in months, permeating him to his bones. He knew they may not be together every day in body over the months ahead. There were still logistics to figure out, decisions they would have to make. But they would make those decisions together—Tom felt sure that they could handle anything as long as they both committed to full disclosure, real communication of all the facts. The barriers that had separated them for so long didn't exist anymore.

Everything After

Tom did return to Washington, and for almost a year he worked as an aide to Senator Bill Wagner, alongside Mitch Enns and Sarah Lonstein. The pay was less than the campaign, but the pace was far more reasonable. When he wasn't writing speeches and press releases, he worked on a revamp on the materials on Senator Wagner's website.

A few weeks after they got back together, Nate's family welcomed their newest member, Adam and Melissa's daughter, Maya. Nate and Tom met her when they flew to Cleveland for Christmas. It was also the first time Tom met the other members of the Harris family, and they welcomed him as one of their own from the beginning. It was a huge relief for Ron, in particular, to see that Nate was happier and more at peace than he had seemed in months, maybe even years; not to mention that he was thoroughly impressed with the quiet, thoughtful man who made his son so happy. Ron loved Tom for that.

Nate continued to teach at Duke, at the same time doing some political consulting to supplement the meager pay of an adjunct professor. Within a few months, he and his colleague, Elisabeth, who had given him teaching help in his first weeks, had hatched a plan to form a limited partnership. Their combined experience spanned campaigns from local efforts up to high-level politics, with Elisabeth's experience being at the state level, and together they saw an opportunity to change how larger campaigns understood and addressed the concerns and issues faced by local voters. Their first major engagement involved the following year's mayoral election in Charlotte, and they found they made an excellent team.

Tom and Nate weren't entirely public about their relationship, but it wasn't a secret either. Jason Eisenberg knew, of course, as did Sarah; Colin and Maxwell were thrilled when they found out. Soon Tom had told Mitch, and eventually it became common knowledge, at least in the office of Senator Michaels. Throughout that year, though they lived separately they were in almost constant communication, through texts and e-mails, phone calls in the evenings and visits at least every other weekend. In the summer, though he wasn't teaching, Nate was getting busy in the lead-up to the September mayoral election. He managed a week off in the early summer to go away with Tom; the rest of Tom's holidays he simply stayed at Nate's, so at least they had evenings together. By the time the election was over, they'd both had enough of living apart. It was getting more difficult to say good-bye at the end of their visits; Tom in particular was beginning to show ill effects from the stress and from missing Nate.

In late September Nate approached Elisabeth with the idea of adding an expert speechwriter to their team. "I don't suppose you have someone in mind?" she asked with wry humor, and after they worked out what they could afford to pay him, Tom was offered a role in the firm. He left Washington in mid-November; but on his last day in the employ of the United States Government, during his exit interview with Mitch and Senator Wagner, he informed them that he considered them to have the right of first refusal of his services, should Bill choose to run again. Bill and Mitch shared a long look and a smile before Bill said to Tom, "You know how much we value you here, Tom. We know you're one of the best, and that's why we want to talk to you about an idea we have...."

... and that was how Tom came to be standing, three years later, in Madison Square Garden on the first Tuesday in November, watching *Erin Michaels* deliver her first speech as the president-elect of the United States. Beside him, their fingers linked tightly together, was Nate; on the other side of Nate was Jason Eisenberg with his arm was around his wife, Sarah Lonstein-Eisenberg. Tom would not be going on to work for the Michaels administration—it had been a condition of his accepting the job as speechwriter on the campaign. Life in Washington wasn't for him. He was looking forward to returning to the happy, contented life he'd made with Nate in North Carolina.

Tom didn't know that some six months earlier, Ron Harris had given Mary's wedding rings to Nate, suggesting that he might want to have the white gold and diamonds reworked; and he didn't know that a newly created ring had spent two months locked in Nate's safe deposit box and was nestled in a velvet box in Nate's pocket, and that in a few hours, he'd be laughing through tears as he promised to marry the love of his life.

But in spite of not knowing any of those things, Tom was happier than he could have imagined almost five years earlier, on the night when he felt a note pushed into his hand, in the middle of a hurricane.

IN MY life I had known love of many kinds: the constant love of my parents and family, the love and pride I felt for my country, and love for my church and my God. These forms of love were deep, yes, and invaluable. They engendered loyalty, ethics, patriotism… they shaped me as I grew into a man. It was not until adulthood, however, that I discovered the greatest form of love I would ever know. I found it without seeking it, at a time when I was at a great distance from my family and country, and in a place where, I believed, even my God would not accompany me.

I was born in Spain in 1570. My family owned a large quantity of land, some of which was used to raise sheep and some rented to tenants who used it for their own crops and animals. I was named Javier, namesake to my grandfather, who died shortly before I was born. My childhood was spent in a happy and abundant family. My mother and father truly loved each other, and in my early years I thought all marriages were the same. It wasn't until adolescence that I started to understand how many marriages were arrangements of social or business advantage rather than true affection.

As a loyal subject of King Filipe II, I became a soldier in his army when I was not yet fully grown. Though many of my friends dreamed of sailing in the invincible Spanish Armada, and others to join the arquebusiers, my talent lay with the sword. My father, a great, muscular man, had been a swordsman before my birth and had taught me to wield the long blade as soon as I was able to hoist it. The day I donned a white tunic with a red cross, signifying that I belonged to His Majesty's Army, was the proudest day of my parents' lives.

My parents' happiness meant a great deal to me, and I took pride in my abilities. Nevertheless, I was deeply saddened by the knowledge that serving the King would take me away from España, away from the home and countryside I'd known all my life. I was to go to France, with no idea when I would return. It might be years before I would again see my parents, my brothers and sisters, my friends. I would miss the rising sun throwing sparkles across the Mediterranean. I would even miss the Merino sheep my family raised, providing some of the finest wool on the continent.

As the date of my departure drew near, my mother became melancholy as well. She was the person I loved best in my large family. She had always understood me and listened patiently to the things I wanted to talk about. She knew I would rather have remained on our farm, feeding and caring for the flocks, counting new spring lambs and shearing the ewes, than join the army and head off to war. Mami often told me I was her sensitive boy, but she never shamed me for being quiet or shy. I think it was because I was so much like her, more so than any of my brothers or sisters were.

We'd heard stories of the long and arduous journey north on the Spanish Road. The difficulties I would face, both on the trip and once we were engaged in war, were a source of great worry to Mami. Several nights before I left home I woke to her sitting on the edge of my bed, her work-worn fingers trembling as they smoothed over my hair. She was crying quietly, whispering prayers over me, asking the Holy Virgin to bring me home safely. I pretended to sleep on, letting her murmured supplications wash over me. They comforted me; the hard knot that had been growing in my stomach relaxed a bit, at least for a short time. I had never known anyone to refuse my mother anything—somehow I couldn't believe even God would dare tell her no.

I believed, too, that we were fighting a holy battle, a war in His name. My tercio, under the command of the Duke of Parma, would travel north to Brussels. We would continue to Dunkirk, France, meeting the Spanish Armada there. Led by the Duke of Medina Sidonia, the Armada would carry us across the English Channel—la Manche, the French called it. We would invade Queen Elizabeth, who had been excommunicated from the true church, who persecuted those who wished to attend Catholic mass, and in a final disgraceful act, had executed faithful Mary, Queen of Scots. The Spanish Armada couldn't fail, and we, the tercio soldiers, would destroy our Heavenly Father's enemies.

Assuming we arrived in France alive.

The day I left España, I kissed the soil goodbye, wondering if I would ever see my beloved country again. I will not dwell extensively on the journey, except to say that traveling the Spanish Road was quite as awful as expected. The initial journey by ship from Barcelona to Genoa was nothing compared to the subsequent journey overland. With winter approaching we marched twelve miles every day, through the mountains and into the Low Countries, with little food and very poor sleep. Officers were sometimes able to find lodging along the way, but we soldiers were left to sleep along the roadside, under bushes or any makeshift shelter we could construct ourselves. We were accompanied by camp followers, the women who came along, carrying much of our food and supplies on their backs, tending to the sick, and servicing the healthy. As disgusting as many of them were, I sometimes wonder whether I would have survived the trip without their presence. Many soldiers were struck by the black plague, the subsequent deaths greatly reducing our numbers. Those women and the care they provided, such as it was, saved some who would otherwise have fallen.

After many weeks of travel, in early December my tercio finally joined those who had preceded us on the journey, gathering in a large encampment in the French countryside outside Dunkirk. We went from constant movement to almost none, aside from our daily drills, but we were so exhausted from the trip that the period of rest was most welcome. For months we had very little to do but wait—wait for war, wait to see who would live or die. To stave off boredom, we played rentoy and got to know our fellow soldiers throughout the camp. From time to time some of the men would stage wrestling matches and other contests of strength, with the winner's only reward being the right to boast, at least until the next match.

For those who weren't interested in displaying their skills in hand-to-hand combat, the preferred diversion was to travel into Dunkirk, sometimes on a daily basis. The town was busy, always busy, as ships came and went from the port. There were merchants and taverns to serve the citizens, the seamen and soldiers. I often went, accompanied by several friends I'd made in my tercio, Rafael, Antonio, and Cruz. They preferred to visit the taverns. They were a few years older than me and thought of themselves as far more experienced, though they'd never been to war either. When they drank wine or ale, they would become loud and boisterous, and the conversation almost always took a turn toward prurient topics.

On this subject, at least, they certainly seemed to have more experience than I, though I would never confess it to them. Rafael and Cruz, their faces flushed with drink, would try to goad me into admitting it. Antonio, however, always put a stop to their taunts. Antonio and I were in the same tent, and even in the short period of time we'd been in France, we'd become good friends. We talked nearly every night before we fell asleep. He was very kind and seemed to make it his business to ensure I was not ill-treated by some of the older, rougher soldiers. I was often surprised by the power he seemed to have over Rafael and Cruz. They spoke loudly, swaggered, and teased, especially when they'd been drinking, but with one sharp word from Antonio they would become meek and apologetic.

I was grateful to Antonio for diverting their attention from my inexperience. I knew the differences between a man and a woman, of course, the obvious ones and the not as obvious. I had younger brothers and sisters, after all, whom I had occasionally helped care for when they were babies. I knew enough about how young were begotten, at least where sheep were involved. My youthful knowledge of human carnal activities had been gleaned from overhearing loose talk from the coarse men who'd been hired seasonally to help at my family's farm. Those men didn't care that I was considered too young for such talk. As they described the sheer delight of congress, I was intrigued… but at the same time I wondered what deficiency I suffered, because I seemed to have no desire for women, not in the way they spoke of them.

It was a shame, for I had ample opportunities to experiment. The camp followers, the tavern-maids, even some of the seemingly innocent women in the town expressed an interest in me. I knew I wasn't unpleasant to look at. There had been girls in my village in España who hid their faces behind their fans, fluttering their eyelashes at me when I passed. I once overheard one talking to her friend, comparing me to a statue she'd seen of the god Apollo. She claimed the resemblance was striking. After hearing this, I had studied my reflection in the looking glass in my mother's room. I'd shrugged, doubting the validity of the silly girl's memory. Let her think what she would—her giggles and coquetry held no interest for me at all.

I was not completely immune to feelings of desire, however. While driving our sheep through the countryside one day, I had come upon my older brother's friend Armando. He was loading hay onto a wagon, a sheen of sweat glistening as the muscles rippled under his bare, tanned back. That night, when I was sure my brothers were asleep, I closed my eyes and thought of that image. I remembered the summer days when, having spent a hot afternoon watching a flock, I would slip away to a lake with my brothers and a group of their friends to bathe. We would all strip bare without a second thought. I thought of

Armando unclothed, the water streaming down his body as he climbed up a rock to jump into the water…. As the memory played before my eyes, my hands roamed the sensitive area between my legs, feeling my phallus become long and hard under my touch. I didn't understand why touching myself in that way brought me pleasure so intense that my toes curled and my heart beat fast—only that it did happen, each time. And when my pleasure found me, from my throbbing length was released a white fluid—like milk, only thicker.

Once I had admitted to myself the truth—that my carnal desire was for men rather than for women—I made a decision. I would neither live a life that my church told me was an abomination, nor would I agree to a charade of a marriage to a woman. My conscience would never allow me to deceive another human that way, to tie them to a life with one who didn't truly desire them. Despite my family's expectations, therefore, I would simply spend my life in celibacy.

When I was traveling from España to France, I didn't bring myself pleasure for many weeks. Each night when I lay down I fell asleep almost immediately, completely exhausted, and often I had no shelter in which to sleep, so the privacy I needed was not afforded me.

Once we arrived in Dunkirk, however, I had nothing but time in the encampment. Fortunately the winter was not a particularly harsh one, and by the time spring arrived, the weather had warmed enough so as to be quite pleasant for sleeping. Food was decent and reasonably plentiful, and young men had nothing to do but wait for word that the Armada had arrived to carry us across the Channel.

One night in May, I went with Antonio into Dunkirk. Cruz and Rafael stayed behind to play rentoy with some of the other soldiers. It was a mild night, despite the breeze from the cool water that separated France from England. We went to le Chat Gris, a tavern where Antonio had spent several evenings making eyes at the barmaid. He told me that on previous visits, Cruz and Rafael had been so insufferably loud that he was unable to pursue her properly. Tonight, however, since they were not with us, he was free to unleash his charms upon her.

I sat and watched as he complimented her. Despite having no particular attraction to women, I liked Olivie. She was kind to me, and was undeniably pretty, with long red curls and striking brown eyes. She also had all her teeth, a rarity for barmaids in Dunkirk or anywhere else, for that matter. I had had the opportunity to observe their conversations before. Olivie blushed and giggled when Antonio complimented her. She seemed innocent. I did not think she was the kind of girl who would provide extra services to the patrons. Antonio, however, was persistent, and as he'd predicted, without Rafael and Cruz there to impede him, Olivie was soon responding to his advances. Less than an hour after we'd arrived, the two were slipping away to a room upstairs, leaving me alone.

I had no desire to remain in the tavern by myself and was wholly uninterested in waiting for Antonio to return from his activities. This meant, of course, that I must travel back to the encampment on my own. I did not mind. Opportunities to be truly alone happened seldom, if ever. Sometimes I felt as though I could not hear my own thoughts over the voices of the rough men who surrounded me. I got lost in my thoughts as I made my way back through the city. Not paying attention, I took a wrong turn somewhere along the way. By the time I realized my mistake, I was completely lost amid the side streets. Asking for directions was out of the question. The shops were by that time long closed, and knocking at the door of a home late at night would certainly see me staring down an angry Frenchman's musket.

I tried to retrace my steps back in the direction I'd come from, but soon I had to admit that it was pointless. It was far too dark to distinguish one street from another. Unsure of what to do and growing weary, I sat down on the uneven cobblestone in front of a shop, leaning back to rest against the wall under the darkened windows. I hoped that if I stayed here until dawn broke, I would at least be able to use the growing light to tell me in which direction I was headed, and hopefully find my way out of the maze of streets. I also hoped that I wouldn't fall asleep and be woken by a shopkeeper, angry at finding me asleep in front of his store. It had only been thirty years since the Spanish defeated the French in the Battle of Gravelines—not nearly long enough to have softened the bitter memory from the French consciousness. Spanish soldiers were, by most Frenchmen, distrusted at best and despised at worst.

My eyelids grew heavy, despite the sea breeze that had turned the night air chilly. Several times I heard footfalls through the intersection at the end of the street, but no one came near me.

Until he stood before me.

Against my will, I had dozed off. I dreamt that my youngest sister, Maria, was trying to wake me, nudging my feet. Suddenly a sharp voice beside my head startled me into consciousness.

"Monsieur!"

I jumped, reaching automatically for my sword, when a strong hand caught my wrist before I could draw it.

"Arrêtez! Je ne veux pas mourir ce soir," the voice said… a man's voice. My bleary eyes finally opened, and I squinted into the darkness, trying to see the face of the man who had found me, but it was much too dark. I could see only outlines.

He, on the other hand, could apparently see enough to know what I was wearing. "L'espagnol," he said with a hint of disgust. "Parlez-vous français?"

I spoke very little French, having learned the words to ask for ale in a tavern or a bit of mutton at the shops, but could not hope to hold a conversation. I shook my head.

"How about English?" he asked in a heavily accented voice. I nodded slightly. "What are you doing in front of my shop?" he demanded.

"I got lost," I said weakly.

"If I open my door now, are you going to jump me? Have you any friends lying in wait nearby?"

"My friend left me at the tavern," I said honestly, realizing I was at this man's mercy. "I am alone."

He was silent a moment, looking up and down the street. Apparently deciding I wasn't a threat, he unlocked the door to the shop and drew my sword from its sheath before nudging me inside. "Go," he said unceremoniously. I stumbled into the pitch-black shop, bumping into a counter as I did. He closed and bolted the door behind us.

"Wait here," he said, and I obeyed, as there was nothing else I could do. He left the room, returning a moment later with a lit candle. Walking the length of the counter at which I stood, he stopped opposite me and set the candle between us, giving me my first look at his face.

My mother's bedroom at home had a painting of the angel Gabriel when he came to tell Mary that she would be blessed to carry God's son. In the painting, Gabriel had golden hair that fell in ringlets to his shoulders, eyes as blue as the sky, and red lips like the poppies that grew outside our door. I had been fascinated by the painting all my life, but it wasn't until I became a young man that I realized that what truly drew me to the painting was Gabriel himself. I had never seen a man so beautiful.

Until now.

The man who stood before me was Gabriel come to life, and the reality was far superior to the art. His blond hair was pulled back, but numerous unruly curls had escaped the tie and were now falling around his face. Even in the candlelight, his eyes were as blue and sparkling as the Mediterranean Sea, and his mouth, delicate and perfect, was as red as the most brilliant ruby. I gasped at the angelic figure before me at the same time that his eyes widened in surprise.

"Mon Dieu," he swore, "you're a child!"

"I am not!" I replied immediately, indignant at the affront. "I am a soldier of Spain."

"How old are you, soldier of Spain?" he asked.

"I was eighteen last month," I answered gravely.

"And have you a name?"

"I am Javier," I replied with all the importance I could muster.

"Well, Javier," he said, "I am Gaspard, and this is my shop."

"You don't look old enough to own a shop," I countered honestly.

"I see I have wounded your pride," he replied, ignoring my comment. "I couldn't see you very well when we were outside; I didn't realize how young—" He stopped short and then said simply, "Please accept my apology for the affront."

"I accept your apology," I answered stiffly.

"In return for that, I will admit that this is not my shop," he continued. "It belongs to my maman. My papa died two years ago, and she was given the right to continue his business. It will be my shop, though, when I become old enough to own it."

"How old are you?" I asked, because I honestly couldn't tell. Like the angel in the painting, he had both the cherubic face of an infant and the wise look of an ancient.

"I will be twenty-two when the summer has passed," he replied. "How is it that I found you, a soldier of Spain, sleeping on the street outside my door?"

"I told you, my friend left me at the tavern," I answered. "He found a girl, and once he was sure of her, he left me to travel back to the camp myself. I didn't pay close attention to where I was going, and I got lost."

He murmured under his breath, "Thank you, Father, that the soldiers of France have better sense."

I bristled again and muttered an oath at him. I was turning to leave when he reached across the counter to catch my sleeve. "I have offended you again—how clumsy I am. Please, once more, forgive my terrible lack of manners." I remained facing the door, not looking at him. "I still have your sword," he reminded me. I sighed and relented, turning back toward him, but I did not miss the opportunity to cast a glare at him.

"Come," he said, "let us be friends. I know where your camp is. I will take you there." He extended one hand across the counter to me. I looked at it for a moment before finally deciding that I really did want to get back before my commander awoke. This seemed like my best option, or rather the only one. I reached for his hand, intending a quick, business-like shake, but the moment my palm slid into his, a magnetic pull coursed between us. I was frozen, rooted to the floor, my eyes locked on his. I gasped as though I had accidentally grasped a hot pan. At the same moment, Gaspard's eyes widened and his mouth opened as if to speak, but no sound emerged.

I do not know how long we stood, staring across the counter, our hands joined. It was seconds, and it was millennia. Finally he blinked and looked down at our hands. Immediately I released my hold, looking away as I felt my face grow hot. "Your sword," he said quietly, holding it out to me. I took it without meeting his eyes and sheathed it. He stepped to the door and unbolted it, waited for me to step past him, then closed and locked it behind us.

ANNIE KAYE's first "real" job was a career in insurance. After fourteen years, the industry had wrung from her everything it could, leaving her desperate for a change that would allow her to flex her long-dormant creativity. She left her job and took several months off, planning to spend them on the couch in her yoga pants. Not six weeks had elapsed before she'd rediscovered a long-lost love: putting words to paper. Since 2009, Annie has written almost a million words of fiction, each piece bearing a common theme: love and relationships between gay men.

Balancing family, work, creative efforts, and community involvement—and trying to hit the gym once in a while—are all near the top of Annie's to-do list. At her home in the woods of rural Ontario, Canada, she endeavors to carve out her writing space from amid the joyful noise created by her husband, their two children, one dog, one cat, and the woodpeckers who sharpen their beaks on her windowsills.

Facebook: www.facebook.com/anniekayefiction
Twitter: @anniekayefic

www.ingramcontent.com/pod-product-compliance
Lightning Source LLC
Chambersburg PA
CBHW051632260626
47170CB00004B/1145